Through different Eyes

by
Robert Hart

Foreword

This book is a 'midquel' to *Through my Eyes. Again.*

Midquel?

Prequel and sequel are well understood, but there appears to be no term for a book that occurs during another one. The bulk of this book occurs during *Through my Eyes. Again.* and the term *midquel* was suggested by one of my Beta readers.

If you haven't read *Through my Eyes. Again.* a brief introduction will help bring you up to the start of this story. If you are thinking of reading *Through my Eyes. Again.* stop here – go and read it!

• • • •

Spoiler alert for the next couple of pages

A brief recap of Through my Eyes. Again.

It's 1962, the height of the Cold War between the USSR and the western democracies. Colette and her mother defect from communist east Germany to England. MI6 hide them in a house in Herne Bay, on the north Kent coast. Colette is masquerading as a boy known as 'Col' to aid their disguise. Col speaks no English but her mother is fluent in English and other non-German languages, having worked as a translator for the east German government.

Col meets Will – an abused and troubled English boy with suicidal thoughts. Will has a deep secret – the consciousness from his seventy-year-old body in 2020 has somehow appeared in his twelve-year-old body.

Col and Will become friends as they learn each other's language, soon adding a Polish girl, Liliana to their friendship. Col's feeling for Will deepen and she reveals herself as a girl and they become secret boy and girlfriend. In turn, Will reveals his strange nature to Col. At a Christmas party, Lili catches Col and Will kissing and thinks they are gay. To maintain the friendship, Col reveals herself as a girl to Lili.

When US President John F Kennedy is not assassinated, Will knows for certain that the world he is in now differs from the one he previously lived in. Despite the angst an unknown future produces, Will accelerates through school due to the knowledge stored in his 'old' brain. Encouraged by his teacher, he wins a German essay competition – a trip to east Germany. Col and her mother fear that this might expose them as Col's father is a senior officer in the east German secret police (the feared *Stasi*). Due to a complicated set of circumstances, Will cannot pull out of the trip without attracting undue attention that would risk the exposure of his friend.

While in east Germany, Will by chance meets Col's father at a reception, but he returns to England without problems. There, MI6 intercept him. They hid the evidence Col's mother assembled proving her husband was a Nazi war criminal in Will's luggage.

With the danger of the trip behind them, the trio resume their normal life ... until Col is called out of class one day. This is the last Will and Lili know of Col and her mother.

Now read on and discover what happened.

Chapter 1
Late April 1964

"Smith."

I lifted my head from the Maths problem I had been struggling with and stifled a sigh. "Yes, Miss?" She never called me Schmidt, another individual still fighting the Second World War.

She had a note in her hand. "Please go to the headmaster's office."

My stomach flipped: such a call always presaged trouble. I glanced at Lili, who raised an eyebrow in query. I gave her a minimal shrug and weaved my way through the desks and out into the corridor. Every eye followed me, imagining what I had done and with some *Schadenfreude,* what punishment I would receive.

The headmaster's secretary pointed me to a chair and I sat in fidgeting discomfort due to my period and the worry; I couldn't recall doing anything that required the headmaster's involvement.

The worry and my period bloat became intolerable. "Please Miss, may I go to the toilet?"

I received a lingering, disapproving look.

"Please, Miss." My voice reflected my increasing urgency.

She pursed her lips, glancing at the headmaster's closed office door before waving me out. "Be quick."

I slipped into a cubicle, muttering a curse at the continuing need to masquerade as a boy. I wanted to change my tampon, but I'd put them in the bottom of my bag in class. I did my business and folded some sheets of toilet paper inside my panties as insurance against leaks, washed my hands and returned to the office.

The headmaster was talking to his secretary but turned into his office when he saw me. "Come with me please Schmidt." He sat behind his desk, pointing me to a chair. "I've had a message that your mother has been taken ill."

I leant forward, anxiety adding to my physical discomfort. "What's happened, sir?"

"I'm afraid I don't know, but a taxi's coming to pick you up." His patronising tone failed to prevent rising panic.

"Is she in hospital?"

"I'm sorry Schmidt, that's all I know." He stood, guiding me out of his office, his hand pushing on my shoulder. "Come along. The taxi will be here soon." He wanted this interruption to his day gone.

Mutti ... what's happening to you? Are you hurt? Is this about father?

Terrible thoughts battered around inside my skull, each wave reflecting and reinforcing the others.

"Miss Price, please take Schmidt to the front entrance and see him safely into the taxi when it arrives."

"Yes, sir." She gave me a sympathetic look. "I've got your bag here."

I blinked at her – she must have sent for my bag. "Thank you."

"Come with me. I'll see you into the taxi." I'd been mistaken about her disapproval; she was showing only sympathy for me now.

When the taxi arrived, Miss Price handed in my bag. "Thank you."

She smiled and gave me a wave.

I sat, lost in a world of worry. Mutti had been healthy this morning when I left home. What had happened? An accident? Father? I roused as the taxi turned off the main road.

"Where are we going?"

"I have to drop you off up here."

We'd all had the warnings about getting into strange cars ... but this was a taxi. We passed fields and orchards. Why would the taxi drop me off here?

The car swung into a grassy area near the foot of a water tower. Two people got out of a large black car parked there.

Mutti.

I gasped with combined confusion and relief, racing into my mother's arms. "Mutti. Mutti. Are you all right?"

"Shh, Col. Yes, I am perfectly fine."

But I heard anxiety in her voice.

"Please get in the car and I will explain everything to you."

She shooed me towards the car. I scrambled in and Mutti went round to the other side.

"Don't forget this." The taxi driver dropped my abandoned school bag on my lap and closed the door.

The front seat passenger slammed his door and the car accelerated away, pushed hard on the narrow country lanes. Mutti and I grabbed the armrests to steady ourselves against the sways and bounces.

"What's going on, Mutti?"

"Your father is close on our tracks. Something or someone has betrayed us."

My stomach lurched: my English friend Willi had met him ten days ago in Leipzig.

Not Willi? Surely, not Willi...

The swaying of the car made conversation difficult as we hurtled through the lanes of rural Kent. I started to feel nauseous from the car's motion, augmented by my anxiety and period. After an uncomfortable ten minutes, we turned on to a main road. At the intersection were signs for London. We were headed away from Herne Bay. At least the swaying had stopped and my stomach settled.

I turned to Mutti. "What's happened?"

Mutti shook her head. "All I know is Mr Watling left a message at the shop to meet this car off the High Street at ten o'clock. We drove to where we met you and ... well ... that's all I know."

Mr Watling is her MI6 contact. He must know what's happening.

Mutti's eyes held mine, full of worry. "I think your father found us and we need to move."

I slid across to hug her. We stayed huddled in mutual comfort until I sensed something different in the road: signs for the new motorway to London flashed past. But after a while we branched off that to the north and entered the Dartford tunnel under the Thames.

Mutti leant forward, holding the passenger seat in front of her. "Where are we going?"

The man half-turned. "Somewhere safe. It's best you don't know."

We kept on driving as the afternoon passed and I dozed. When I woke up, I was feeling both hungry and uncomfortable, though the nausea had passed. Outside, afternoon shadows were lengthening.

"Mutti, I need to go to the loo."

"Mmm ... I do as well." She leant forward. "How long before we get to wherever we are going?"

The man in the passenger seat nudged the driver, who replied, "Several hours."

"Well, we need to find a toilet and get something to eat."

There was no reply.

Mutti's voice rose. "We need a toilet. Now, please."

The driver glanced at the man in the passenger seat, who shrugged.

"OK – at the next petrol station."

About five minutes later, we stopped. I scrabbled a tampon out of my schoolbag and headed for the toilet. I came out feeling physically better. But as I sat on the toilet, the situation became clear. Our life in Herne Bay was over – and with that realisation came the crashing need to get a message to Willi.

How would he take our sudden and unexplained disappearance?

What he might do terrified me; it might be enough to tip him over the edge.

Mutti and the front seat passenger were waiting for me when I reappeared. I grabbed Mutti's hand. "We must get a message to Willi. He will be frantic at our disappearance and might do something..."

The passenger interrupted me. "In the car. Now."

I tried to hush him. Talking to Mutti about Willi was important.

"Now." He grabbed my hand and firmly moved me towards the car. "We're not safe here. Get in the car." His voice was low, but I could hear the tension. He opened the door and half-gestured, half-pushed me in. I saw Mutti opening her door to join me. As soon as the passenger closed his door, the car moved off at speed, but not spinning its wheels, as that would draw attention.

On the road, the passenger passed us two paper bags containing cheese and tomato sandwiches and packets of potato crisps.

Mutti took them, giving one to me.

"Thank you ... we don't know your names ..."

The passenger grunted without turning round. "No names."

Mutti shrugged and pursed her lips.

"Mutti..." I started, but she shook her head and started eating her sandwich. After a while, she turned to me and asked me, in Polish, what I thought of the sandwiches.

I gave her a puzzled look.

Why would she decide to continue our language lessons at this moment?

She frowned at me, repeating herself in Polish. "Is your sandwich tasty?" Her eyes flicked towards the front of the car, lifting an eyebrow in question.

Oh – of the languages we shared, Polish was the least likely to be understood by our driver and passenger. They might speak German; they'd been sent to pick up two Germans and I supposed they might speak Russian, but Mutti knew my Russian was rusty from lack of recent practice.

We talked about the sandwiches and crisps. Our descriptions become ever more bizarre, testing the understanding of the people in the front seats ... for no reaction. Mutti smiled a wicked smile and in the same conversational tone, called the driver and passenger rude names. They remained oblivious.

She continued in Polish. "They may not understand us. But we must still be careful not to place our friends in difficult situations with the security services." She gave me a serious look. "Now, what did you want to say about ... your friend?" she asked, the pause deliberate.

Ah – no names, no mention of my father ... or Willi.

"We need to get a message to him that my ... that he ... has not found us. Remember how he was when he told us about meeting ... him?"

Mutti pulled me into a cuddle.

"I'm worried if he thinks ... he ... has kidnapped us, he will blame himself."

"At the petrol station, you said that he might do ... something." Mutti's tone was caring but requiring answers. "What did you mean?" Her eyes searched my face.

I took a deep breath.

When did keeping Willi's suicide attempts secret become dangerous to him? Should I ... could I break my promise about this?

Mutti watched me run this through my head and gave me a comforting squeeze. "He has always had an undercurrent of instability, which is understandable given the abuse he suffered." She stroked my hair. "Has he tried to ... harm himself?" Her voice shone with the love she had for both Willi and me.

I swallowed, my mouth dry. Mutti's eyes held mine ... and I managed a fearful nod.

Mutti drew in a deep breath and gave me another squeeze. "We must let him know we have not been kidnapped by ... him." She paused again, thinking. "You will need to phrase the message with care. He must know it is truly from you and not forced from you under duress by ... someone."

I hadn't thought of that complication – and I need to get that message to Willi – and Lili – without delay. I started thinking.

Mutti told me to stretch out and I went to sleep, my head in her lap. At some point we stopped again and I half-roused, drifting back into an uneasy sleep once the car started moving again.

I woke in confusion as the car slammed to a stop. I hit the seat in front of me and ended on the floor with Mutti on top of me. As we struggled to sort ourselves out, I heard loud pairs of bangs.

Gunshots?

Mutti pressed me down as low as possible. "Stay down, Col."

For what felt like a minute but was only seconds, we lay motionless. I heard moaning from the front seat and muffled voices outside. The rear doors both opened. In the glare from the headlights of a vehicle behind us, I saw a man pointing a pistol at us.

"They're here," he called out, in English.

A hand reached in and dragged Mutti out, handing her on to someone else. The hand returned, reaching for me. I decided my father wouldn't win without a fight. I grabbed the hand and bit hard.

The man jerked in surprise and pain. "Shit. The kid bit me!"

I used the distraction to slide across the seat and scramble out the other side. As I turned to run, a set of arms grabbed me, gripping me from behind despite my struggles.

"Settle down, kid. If you bite me, I'll give you a thrashing," a gravelly voice warned. The man gave me a strong squeeze that threatened to crack my ribs and pushed the breath from my body.

"Bring them over here and get them in the car." A woman's voice called out, commanding and cold.

My captor dragged me, gasping, round our car, half-blinded by the glare of headlights from the car behind us. Our driver was slumped forward, unmoving over the steering wheel and another person lay on the road beside the car, a man holding a pistol to his head. I struggled again and my captor lifted me off my feet. I kicked back hard into his shins, the heels of my school shoes making solid contact.

The bearhug tightened. "Bloody hell, kid. I'm warning you ..."

"Get her in the car." That cold, commanding voice again – and she knew I was a girl.

My captor threw me into the back of the car in front of ours, slamming the door as I sprawled across the seat. As I sorted myself out, they pushed in Mutti with my school bag. I tried the handle of my door – it didn't work.

A figure wearing a fedora slipped into the front passenger seat. "Drive."

The car started up with a jerk, throwing us into our seats. Once we were underway, the woman in the passenger seat reached up and switched on the dome light. She turned and gave Mutti a hard look for several seconds.

"You know me as Mrs Henderson and you know I work for British Intelligence."

Mutti stared back. After a moment, she leant forward. "What's going on?"

"Your husband, your father," You-know-me-as-Mrs-Henderson turned to each of us. "... he's lost two agents in England so far. The Eastern Bloc network here and elsewhere is undergoing severe pruning." Her voice glowed with satisfaction.

I switched to Polish before I spat out. "Does she work for British Intelligence?"

You-know-me-as-Mrs-Henderson gave a dry laugh and spoke in Polish. "I heard you were learning Polish." She paused, her eyes lingering on me. "That's quick thinking," she added, in English, but her face was devoid of approval.

Mutti engaged in a staring match with the woman before answering me without turning away. "I met Mrs Henderson when I was being ... interrogated." From Mutti's voice and stare, she did not like the woman.

Mrs Henderson sniffed. "You think your interrogation was hard? How did you expect us to treat someone who could well be a foreign agent trying to slip into our society?"

Their eyes locked before Mrs Henderson turned to me. "What's going on is that we have rescued you from ending up in an East German gaol at the mercy of the *Stasi*."

A shiver ran through me, prickling my skin. "They were working for my father?"

"Not directly, but they were east German agents." She was cold and impersonal.

Mutti leant forward. "Now what?"

Mrs Henderson's face remained expressionless. "Now we take you somewhere safe." I had the distinct impression that our presence was a nuisance to her.

"Go to sleep. We have a long way to go." Mrs Henderson turned off the dome light, dismissing both Mutti and me.

I awoke in the grey light of dawn, cold, cramped and needing to pee. I sat up, trying not to wake Mutti, but she stirred and gave me a grim smile. We were entering a town. Whatever our destination, I would need a toilet soon. After a minute I saw a signpost for "Lancaster city centre".

Mrs Henderson heard us moving and glanced over her shoulder.

I leant forward. "I need a toilet."

She turned to the driver. "How long?"

"Ten minutes."

"Okay."

The car turned off the main road and we entered suburban streets. Some minutes later, we pulled into the driveway of a large house surrounded by tall trees looming against the dawn sky. I tried to open my door, but the handle still wouldn't move.

Mrs Henderson leant across to the driver. "Ring the bell."

The driver stretched as he got out and climbed the steps to the front door. He was about to press the bell when the door opened and a middle-aged woman appeared in the doorway. They exchanged some indistinct words and the woman looked over at Mrs Henderson, who got out and opened my door.

The woman came down the steps and opened Mutti's door. "Come along. I expect you need to freshen up after your journey."

My need for a pee returned with urgency.

"Yes, please." I trotted up the steps, my school bag bumping my legs, with Mutti following.

The woman sensed my problem. "Down the corridor, third door on the left."

I passed an impressive polished wooden staircase and counted doors down the half-lit corridor: number three revealed the haven of a toilet. Despite the sleep in the car, I fell into a doze as I sat there. Giving myself a shake, I finished my business and washed my hands, looking in the mirror. My hands flew to my throat.

Willi's necklace.

As I couldn't wear it to school, I'd left it in its box on my bedside table. I sank down on the toilet seat, tears blurring my vision.

How am I going to find it?

A gusting breath later, I stood and washed my face again.

Not now, Col ...

I heard voices deeper in the house. Following the sound, I ended up in a large kitchen. The talking stopped as I entered. Mutti was sitting at the scrubbed pine table with Mrs Henderson and the woman who had greeted us. I sat in the vacant upright chair opposite Mutti, silenced by their silence.

A kettle started singing on the kitchen range. The woman rose and poured boiling water into a large teapot, warming on the side of the range. She gathered on a tray, cups, saucers, teaspoons, a sugar bowl from a cupboard and milk from a walk-in pantry and brought it to the table. She added the teapot to the table, sitting down. "Would you like milk?"

"Thank you." Mutti answered.

"And you?" She gave me a look laced with curiosity.

"Yes, please."

She poured a black tea and handed it across to Mrs Henderson, who was no stranger here, before adding milk to three cups. She poured the tea, handing cups to Mutti and me. Once that was done, she made a point of looking across at Mrs Henderson, whose face remained impassive.

The woman shrugged and turned to us. "I'm Peg ... that is, Mrs Gittings." She turned to Mutti. "You are Frida Schmidt and..." She frowned. "I was told you were her ... daughter?"

I raised my eyebrows at Mutti. She, too, was confused, and turned to Mrs Henderson. "Would you like to explain what's going on?"

Mrs Henderson's face showed a flicker of exasperation, then she spoke in an uninterested tone. "You have a daughter."

Mutti's eyes narrowed. "And you have decided, without discussing this with me, that my daughter should stop the masquerade that helped us escape and stay safe?"

Mrs Henderson's supercilious gaze held us. "I suppose I could find some other Eastern Bloc agents and hand you over to them, since you felt safe in their care." Mrs Henderson's emotionless tone denied the sarcasm of her words.

Mutti's fatigue and anxiety must have been getting to her. She slapped her hand on the table in frustration, rattling cups and teaspoons in their saucers. "Don't be obtuse. You know that's not what I meant."

Mrs Henderson's expression did not change: the same drawn-out, impassive look. "You will cooperate with what happens if you contribute to the decisions?" The question sounded reluctant.

Mutti gave her a lengthy, probing look. "I'll listen."

Mutti was showing a strength I had not seen in her since our escape from East Germany. The two stared across the table.

Mrs Henderson's "Hmm," sounded equally non-committal.

Mutti turned to me. "Do you want to stay a boy?"

I had not been expecting this, absorbed in the bladed wordplay between Mutti and Mrs Henderson. I blinked, trying to think with a weary brain.

Mutti watched for a moment. "Maybe becoming a girl again would be best. He will be looking for you as a boy now." Mutti gave me an encouraging smile. "Would you like to become a girl again?"

"Yes, please." I burst into tears as emotion engulfed me.

Mutti rushed to my side, hugging me. After a minute, I calmed and Mutti pulled a chair round beside me. "What is it, Col?"

The paradoxical sadness of this situation overwhelmed me. "Willi ..." I gulped a breath. "I longed to be a girl with Willi ... and Lili." Tears rolled down my cheeks. "And now I can be a girl ... but not with them."

Mutti hugged me, knowing there were no words of comfort. After a while, I gave her a tremulous smile. Mrs Henderson's contemptuous gaze swept across me and I winced at her judgement.

Not letting go of my hand, Mutti turned to Mrs Henderson. "Could you please explain what happened to us?"

Mrs Henderson weighed up what she should reveal. "Somehow, your location and your contact's name ... leaked ... and they used it to get you to walk into their arms."

There's a hint of ... something ... in her face. What is it?

"We were watching you following William's trip behind the Iron Curtain. We had concerns. Once we knew they'd picked you up, we got someone on their tail and set up the ambush."

Mutti frowned. "If you were watching me, why didn't you stop me from getting in their car?"

My attention bounced between them, trying to understand.

Mrs Henderson's eyes remained expressionless. "We would not have flushed out a significant part of their organisation here – and beyond."

Mutti gasped. "You gambled our safety to capture eastern Bloc agents?"

Mrs Henderson dismissed Mutti's concerns with a wave. "You're safe and we have two agents – with more about to fall into our laps."

I sat there, astonished. For Mrs Henderson, people like us were pawns, disposable pieces on her board. I suppressed a shudder; I needed her to get a message to Willi and Lili.

"Please, can you get a message to my friend Willi? He will be worried sick that my father has kidnapped me."

Mrs Henderson's face remained impassive. I could almost hear the wheels turning as Mrs Henderson evaluated that request. Her blank stare fed my insecurity and insignificance.

"Give me the message for your boyfriend."

How did she know about Willi and me?

Mrs Henderson scared me, but my concern for Willi pushed me harder than my fear. "No." I surprised myself with how firm my voice sounded. "I need you to promise me you will deliver it."

Mrs Henderson eyed me, unblinking. "In my world, of which you are now a temporary part, there are no promises, there is no certainty." Her tone offered no compromise. "Give me your message and I will see what I can do."

Mrs Henderson scared me – but I needed her. "I have to work out what to say."

"Be quick. I am leaving soon." She picked up her tea and sipped.

I grabbed my school bag off the floor, retrieving an exercise book and a pen. Telling Willi I was safe in such a way that he knew I was not under duress required thought. I sought sideways references to things we alone shared, trying to clear the fatigue, to concentrate. I had a vague idea from thinking about this in the car: the funny discussion about the unintended consequences of my masquerade as a boy. Will had quoted a line from a Scottish poem about spiders and deceit. I experimented a bit before I had something that I thought might work.

I am caught in the web of Scottish spiders in a cedar tree.

We used to spend hours sitting in a cedar tree, reading, while Lili sketched. Willi would understand that it came from me and the deceit mentioned in the poetry was that I was free, not captured. I passed it over to Mutti, who read it and frowned, gazing off into the distance, trying to pierce the message's shroud.

After a few seconds, she smiled. "Ah yes."

I indicated she should give it to Mrs Henderson, who read the note.

"Playing at spies?" Her voice held something beneath the condescension.

"The message needs to be from me and tell him it was not forced by my father and his *Stasi* friends." There was an edge to my voice.

Mutti looked at me. "Col, Mrs Henderson is doing you a favour. Please mind your manners."

I took a deep breath and looked at Mrs Henderson. "I'm sorry, my tiredness is making me cross."

Mrs Henderson remained silent, her gaze lingering on me. Her eyes trapped me as she assessed my worth, her stare sapping all value from me.

"How about a nice hot bath to get the kinks out from sleeping in the car?" Mrs Gittings asked, standing up and ending what had been an awkward silence.

Her voice broke Mrs Henderson's spell and I turned towards her. "That would be lovely, thank you."

"I'll show you your room and get you organised."

Mrs Gittings led me up the wide, polished staircase, along a corridor and into a bedroom larger than mine in Herne Bay – or our Leipzig apartment. She pointed at a door across the room. "You'll share that bathroom with your mother. There're towels in there."

She looked me up and down. "Hmm, I think I can find something to wear that will fit you from amongst my daughter's old stuff. That will have to do for now if you're to be a girl again."

I walked into the bathroom and started the bath. Half an hour later, I'd topped up the hot water twice, but I forced myself to get out of its relaxing depths as I was wrinkling. With a towel wrapped round me, I peeked round the door into my bedroom: no-one there, but a pile of clothes sat on the double bed. I picked over the options and dressed in a skirt and light jumper. I'd washed out my undies and they were drying in the bathroom. No bra – I had only been wearing an elasticised bandage to flatten my almost non-existent breasts. There were knickers I could wear, but no bra. I shrugged – my minimal breasts didn't need a bra. There were no socks or shoes; for the moment I would go barefoot as my boys' school shoes didn't fit this look. Right then, I decided never to wear them again.

The skirt swirled a strange touch round my legs as I walked over to the full-length mirror. I hadn't worn a skirt for about two years apart from those two occasions in Lili's altered dress. I gave myself a head-to-toe inspection in the mirror. Now I was to be a girl again, I'd have to grow out my hair and find a hairstyle. My fingers lingered at my neck.

How am I going to recover Willi's necklace?

I studied my reflection. Scrawny and flabby, I decided. Not overweight, but I hadn't done any sport for a couple of years. My arms and legs had lost the tone they'd had from the regular swimming I'd done at school in east Germany. I would have to do something about that. I had enjoyed swimming and it had been hard sitting on the beach watching Willi and Lili swimming in the sea.

Is there a pool here in Lancaster?

I sighed and headed out to rejoin everyone downstairs. My bare feet were soundless as I padded along the landing carpet to the staircase and started down. I stopped hearing Mrs Henderson's voice. She was on the phone.

"... send the clothes and personal effects here and box up the rest for storage." She paused, listening.

"We can talk about him when I'm in London, but maintain the watch for now; there could be repercussions and we should take advantage of them."

She listened for a second. "I don't know. They can stay here for a while, but we need a long-term solution. We'll discuss this tomorrow."

She hung up the phone and footsteps headed deeper into the house. I returned to my bedroom, not wanting Mrs Henderson to realise I had overheard her.

Staring out of the window at my dressing table, I thought about what I'd heard.

Are they watching Willi? It sounded like it.

I should have included a warning in my message to Willi.

Could I try giving Mrs Henderson a re-worded message? She might realise that I had overheard her.

I was certain she wouldn't like that and might decide not to send my message at all. The rest of the conversation had to be about Mutti and me. Our personal effects being delivered would mean Willi's necklace would be safe. It seemed we were staying here for 'a while', however long that was, but Mrs Henderson intended for us to be set up somewhere else.

Would that allow me to get in touch with Willi – and would it be safe for all of us if I did that?

I had many questions, but sitting there staring into space would not give me any answers. I headed downstairs, and following the voices, ended up in the kitchen. Over cups of tea and coffee, Mutti, our driver, another man and Mrs Gittings were talking about the fruit trees in the extensive garden. I stopped in the doorway, surprised at the banality after all that had happened.

Where is Mrs Henderson? Had she already left?

Mutti smiled and patted the empty chair beside her. "It warms my heart to see you as a girl again, *Liebling*." She turned to Mrs Gittings. "Thank you for the loan of the clothes. Colette and I must go shopping to fit her out properly."

Mrs Gittings looked across at the men. "What do you think, Jack?"

Jack pondered that, looking at Mutti and me. "We need to be careful."

How embarrassing. This voice belonged to the man I had kicked hard in the shins. Should I apologise?

"With the chaos we have caused in their network, Mrs Henderson is certain they don't know you're here and we need to keep it that way." Jack paused again. "It's probably best if Mrs Gittings takes the girl shopping. If anyone asks, she can be ... her niece staying with her." His eyes flicked across to me. "Hmm ... she's recovering from a serious illness, which would explain why she's not in school."

Mrs Gittings gave me a smile. "OK. We'll go shopping after lunch, but we'll need to find you some shoes."

I could see Mutti's disappointment at not being included in the shopping expedition.

Mrs Henderson had left, so I had lost my chance to revise my message to Willi. I hoped Willi would remember the warning Mr Watling gave us a month or two ago. We had been convinced the risk to Willi was over once he returned from the east Germany.

"I want a bath, too." Mutti headed upstairs.

"Please, may I go for a wander in the garden?" I asked Mrs Gittings.

She looked across at Jack, who seemed in charge now that Mrs Henderson had left.

He looked at me. "Stay in the garden. The neighbouring houses can't see through the trees."

Here in northern England, spring was later than down south in Kent. On the far side of the lawn, I spotted a few fruit trees, with the last petals of blossom and fresh leaves emerging from buds.

As I walked past a rhododendron bush, a large ginger cat wandered out and rubbed against my legs. My experience with cats was limited to Lili's Rupert, but this one was friendly: meowing, staring at me with his wide, welcoming eyes and waving his tail. I crouched down and stroked along his back; he responded by butting his head against my hand, his purrs vibrating from nose to tail. I wandered round the garden with the cat always close by. Sometimes he disappeared into the shrubs, but he wove around my legs most of the time, threatening to trip me. After one near upset, I picked him up. He relaxed in my arms, purring his approval.

"I wonder what you name is?"

His green eyes gazed up at me and gave a long blink. He kept purring, rubbing his head against my arm.

I found a kitchen garden set between it and a thick hedge of hazelnut trees marking the rear of the property. By now, the cat was getting heavy and I put him down as we strolled along the rear boundary and the side fence.

As I arrived at the lawn, Mutti appeared waving me in for lunch. The cat accompanied us inside, his tail waving in greeting.

"I see you've met Hawkins," Mrs Gittings remarked as we walked into the kitchen, with the cat following in front, as Rupert did with Lili.

"Yes. He showed me all round the garden."

"That's Hawkins." She glanced down at the cat. "He's gregarious, but he gets under my feet here in the kitchen and I shut him out when I'm cooking." She stooped and gave Hawkins a stroke before smiling at us. "Come along. Lunch is ready."

Mrs Gittings and Mutti carried the chat around the table, with Jack and Charles remaining silent. They both seemed alert to anything beyond the kitchen.

Were they guards?

Once we'd cleaned up, Mrs Gittings hung up her apron and lead me upstairs to try on some shoes. We found a pair that fitted well enough.

Mutti pulled open her purse. "I have enough for a cheap outfit." She held a bunch of notes out towards Mrs Gittings, who pushed the hand away with a smile.

"Mrs Henderson gave me money to cover your expenses. This is on the Firm."

Mutti looked confused. "The firm?"

"Sorry – that's how we refer to MI6. We don't want to bandy that name around in public."

Mutti looked embarrassed.

"You're thinking this is charity?" Mrs Gittings asked.

Mutti frowned.

Mrs Gittings laughed, cutting her off. "The damage we've done to the Eastern Bloc intelligence network has already been huge. We're not finished yet if I've read Mrs Henderson correctly – and it's all down to you. You've both earned this."

Mutti pursed her lips. "Okay." She turned to me, a serious look on her face. "Be careful out there – you're used to being a boy in public. Think about what you are doing." Her face lit up with a smile. "But enjoy the shopping." She looked over at Mrs Gittings. "Don't let her go wild in the shops."

Mrs Gittings smiled. "I'm sure we'll manage." She turned to me with a smile. "Come on. This is going to be fun. I loved shopping with my daughter."

Jack drove us into the town centre and I spent an afternoon trying on and choosing outfits from the skin out under Mrs Gittings' watchful but encouraging eye. The sales assistant became ever more attentive as the pile of clothing on the counter grew. Finally, Mrs Gittings insisted that I have one 'posh' outfit for special occasions. We wandered through the rows of hanging dresses and found a modern design in jagged white and red. Mrs Gittings insisted it looked marvellous, with my dark eyes and hair. We bought shoes for the various outfits. The ones to go with the white and red dress were white with a low heel. They felt awkward when I tried walking in them, but Mrs Gittings assured me I would soon get used to them.

As we were gathering everything up, I realised I didn't have a swimming costume. "Is there somewhere in town I can go swimming?"

Mrs Gittings laughed. "Well, there's the Kingsway baths – but Morecambe beach is an easy day trip by bus or car. We'll have to go there for a picnic when the weather warms up. Come on, let's find you a costume."

I finally selected a dark blue one-piece suit. I wondered what I would look like in a bikini – and what Willi would think of it. That thought bringing a quick flash of goose bumps.

By the time we returned to the house, I was quite tired, but Mutti insisted on going through everything we'd bought before we had tea. I felt strange – almost fraudulent – looking over these female clothes. I had schooled myself to be a boy and now I was a girl again.

Mutti must have sensed something. "What is it, Col?"

I paused, a pair of knickers in my hands. "I don't think I know how to be a girl anymore."

Mutti took the knickers from my hands and put them in my undies draw. "What do you mean?"

"I was a still a child when we fled Leipzig and I became a boy." I looked up at Mutti. "For two years, I was a teenager with Will, but that's all ..." I stopped as I saw Mutti's face cloud slightly and felt mine flush.

"Oh, Mutti, you know we didn't break our promise."

Mutti's face morphed into a smile. "Did you have to prove you were a girl to Willi, like you did with Lili?"

I felt the heat in my face intensify. "Our promise came after that..."

Mutti's smile widened. She now knew I had proved my sex to Willi. I didn't think my blush could deepen, but it did and I turned away in embarrassment.

"Col, *Liebling*." A gentle hand turned me round. Mutti guided me down to sit beside her on the bed, moving a jumper aside to make room. Her arm pulled me closer and we sat in silence for a minute of two.

"My experience of being a girl will not help you. All I knew at your age was surviving Ravensbrück ..." Mutti's voice drifted to a stop. "But I can help you not make the mistake I made."

I looked up at Mutti. "Mistake?"

"Once I returned to Leipzig in 1945, I was ... lost. I did not know who I was – I practically didn't know how to be a person. I had spent ten years being told by the SS guards that I was nothing and treated as nothing." She sighed. "In Leipzig, the Party feted me as I was the daughter of martyred communist heroes. I had survived the death camps, but everything felt ... shallow." She stopped, lost in the miles and years. "All I had were the languages I had learned in the camps and I threw myself into those. And I came to the notice of your father, who was a rising star in the *Stasi...*"

Mutti looked away and I could see sadness in her eyes. I tightened my arm around her waist.

"I married your father because he offered me security in a world that had been insecure and full of death." She gazed off into the distance. "I think he saw me as adding a certain cachet to his career." She was silent for a while, tears forming in her eyes. "But the mistake was not all bad – for you are the light of my life, *Liebling*."

Now the tears were running down her cheeks.

"Oh, Mutti."

We clung as one for a while before Mutti sat up, sorrow on her face. "I can't tell you how to be a teenage girl, Col ... be yourself." Her thumb smoothed a tear from my cheek. "From what I've seen of girls – and boys – in Germany and England, no-one knows how to be a teenager – you learn as you go."

I sighed.

She'd never been a normal teenager in Ravensbrück ...

I headed to bed soon after, exhausted by the stress and excitement of the day. Lying there, my worry about how to be a girl floated through my mind. I would need to watch and try to learn.

• • • •

I SNAPPED AWAKE WITH a vicious jerk, straining my stomach muscles, sucking in a breath. For a moment, I panicked.

Not my bed, not my room.

Even the faint light pattern on the ceiling was unfamiliar. A fading memory of running through an endless building, searching for ... something ... evaporated as I forced myself to relax. Something was scratching at the bedroom door.

I lay still for a half a minute, straining to identify the sound. There it was again, followed by a faint meow: Hawkins.

I relaxed and slipped out of bed, padding across to the door to open it. Hawkins greeted me with a satisfied "*Prrp*" and rubbed round my shins. I walked to my bed, avoiding the purring shadow twining its tail round my calves. As I settled on the bed, Hawkins arrived, curling into and against me, his purrs softening to a faint chuffing as I drifted off to sleep.

Chapter 2
May 1964 – Early September 1964

A gong sounding in the hall announced breakfast – although I had no idea what it meant. I dashed downstairs in a panic.

Fire or some other emergency?

I found Mrs Gittings, her face showing irritation. Mutti arrived seconds later.

"Breakfast's at eight sharp. I won't be banging this gong to remind you again. Lunch is at half-past twelve and tea's at half-past six. Don't be late." She turned and swept down the corridor to the kitchen.

Mutti and I dashed upstairs to finish dressing and joined Mrs Gittings, Jack and Charles. From the warming oven, Mrs Gittings set out plates of bacon, fried bread and tomatoes – along with a thick, round, black slice of ... something. She added scrambled eggs from a saucepan.

I picked up my knife and fork and poked at the strange black thing.

Sitting opposite me, Charles chuckled. "You've not seen black pudding before?"

"No." I viewed the item with some suspicion.

"Go on, give it a taste. It's a delicacy of the north."

Rather gingerly, I cut a tiny portion and tasted it: a rich, dark, spicy flavour spread through my mouth. I took a larger piece, smiling across the table.

Charles smiled. "Told you."

Mutti tried some from her plate and I watched her savour it.

"*Blutwurst*...blood sausage."

"Indeed," Mrs Gittings said. "But we call it black pudding here."

Jack leant towards Mutti. "You must not speak German. You must speak only English." He turned his gravelly voice on me. "That goes for you as well. Only English."

"Is that an instruction from Mrs Henderson?" asked Mutti.

Jack pulled himself up in his chair. "Mrs Henderson placed your security in my hands. No German: it will mark you out."

Mutti put down her cutlery and leant forward. "My daughter is a student, learning English, French, German and Polish. Through a friend, she has a smattering of Latin, and as a student in east Germany, she learned Russian." She stared Jack down. "We will continue to speak and, where we can, read those languages to ensure her education continues." She raised an eyebrow at Jack, who remained silent, avoiding her stare as he chewed a mouthful of breakfast.

Mutti gave a half-smile. "We will only speak English in public, though. If Mrs Henderson has a problem with this, please ask her to speak to me about it." Mutti picked up her knife and fork and went on eating her breakfast.

Jack swallowed, looking across the table. "Fair enough. We'll see what Mrs Henderson says."

Mutti glanced at me and took another mouthful of scrambled egg. Conversation was strained for the rest of breakfast. When Jack finished, he jerked his head at Charles and they both took their dirty dishes through to the scullery, leaving to do whatever it they did.

As we finished our breakfast, Mutti beckoned to me. "Come on, Col. We'll help Mrs Gittings clean up."

We gathered up the plates and carried them through to the scullery, piling them to one side of the big porcelain sink. Mrs Gittings came through and started the sink to fill. The pipes juddered and banged until Mrs Gittings adjusted the cold-water tap.

I'd not seen anything like that before. "What caused that banging?"

"That's water-hammer – the plumbing in this house is ancient and if the flow to some taps is right, it starts up." She stared up at the ceiling, as if scanning through the large house. "One of these days, they'll have to strip out all the plumbing and wiring and replace it."

She swirled the steaming water in the sink with a gloved hand. "I'll wash. You two can dry and put things on the kitchen table for now. When we're done, I'll show you where it all goes." She smiled in gratitude. "I appreciate your help."

She wasn't as hard as the encounter at the foot of the stairs had suggested.

Mutti returned her smile. "Not at all. Thank you for what you're doing for us."

Under Mrs Gittings' guidance, it didn't take long to wash up and put everything away in the copious drawers and cupboards lining one side of the large kitchen.

As we finished, Charles stuck his head round the kitchen door. "Your stuff's arrived. We've put the boxes on the landing outside your rooms."

Mutti and I went upstairs, sorting out the boxes and taking them into our bedrooms. Once that was done, I sat on my bed, staring at the half dozen cardboard boxes of my possessions. With my life in boxes before me, all my worries surged to the surface.

My fear that Will might try to harm himself was roiling my stomach – and it now seemed that my father might target him. We hadn't heard from Mrs Henderson and I didn't know if she'd delivered my message. That uncertainty made things worse and I was jittery. But sitting on my bed wasn't going to fix anything. I made myself get up and open the boxes. I piled my schoolbooks on the dressing table and found Willi's necklace after searching through the boxes. Picking up the necklace in its box sent a shiver of fear and longing through me.

I walked over to the dressing table and sat, placing the box unopened before me. For some time, I stared at my reflection in the mirror in confusion: I had hated taking it off to leave the house and now ... I was hesitating before putting it on. With my hands resting on its box, I closed my eyes, searching for an answer.

Why am I hesitating?

I was a girl again: if I put it on, I would not have any excuse to take it off ... and there it was: putting it on would be my statement of commitment to Willi.

But why am I unwilling to make that commitment – it would only be to myself, wouldn't it?

After a moment, I realised that wearing Will's necklace was a statement to Mutti and beyond her to everyone else. My eyes flicked open.

I love Willi, don't I?

The silent reflection in the mirror returned my gaze.

Why is this difficult? He loves me, doesn't he?

And I was under the cedar tree, arriving in time to stop Willi from slitting his wrist. He had been going to walk away from me in a final way. He still thought I was a boy and I was only a friend. A shiver rushed over me at that searing memory. I had been furious that he would do this because I was making friends with Lili. I told him to get on with it, dropping the knife in front of him, and walked away.

Flushing with shame, I squeezed my eyes closed. But ... but I had returned a minute later when I realised what I had said. We had sat there, tears on our faces, leaning against the cedar tree, talking. He promised to speak to me if he ever felt that way again. That wrenching experience had strengthened our friendship and later that year I found I could not go on deceiving Willi and revealed myself to be a girl.

No – be honest, Col: you had fallen in love with a strange and complex boy called Willi and that trumped any thought of safety – yours and Mutti's.

My eyes flew open as another flush of shame swept over me.

I had placed Willi before my own mother.

My stomach clenched: I had done it again when I told Willi we were from Leipzig, in east Germany. I had longed for his friendship and risked our safety by revealing this. And I let Willi kiss me-as-a-boy at Lili's Christmas party – reckless and unthinking again. We'd had to reveal our secret to Lili. And I'd encouraged Willi to enter the competition that saw him trapped into visiting east Germany, possibly exposing Mutti and me.

I stared into the mirror. I had never put all these incidents side by side before. They were a shameful tally.

Do I have a subconscious desire for the destruction of myself and those around me?

I sucked in a breath.

Is part of my link with Willi a recognition of myself in his self-destructive tendencies?

I squeezed my eyes closed, the thought scraping across my brain.

Why have I repeatedly broken the masquerade that was keeping us safe?

I found a dark knot of ... something ... in that thought, but it resisted my focus. My eyes flew open and I searched for my reflection.

What is lurking there in my eyes?

I would have to keep working on this. With my hand resting on the box, I found another way to ask about the necklace.

What would not putting on Willi's necklace mean?

And I had my answer – at least for now. It would mean I was walking away from Willi and that I could not do. Putting it on was a commitment to Willi, but it was an important commitment to myself.

Once I had the necklace on, I sat there for a while, searching for my real self. Because my life in east Germany had been so constrained, I understood Willi better than myself, with all his inner turmoil and despite the seventy-year-old hiding in his head. Finally, I gave myself a shake.

Somehow, this is going to work out; somehow, I would find myself and find my way to Willi.

I stood up, full of fragile resolve for the future.

There were boxes of useless boys clothing, but amongst them was the one piece of clothing I sought; the blue dress that Lili had given me and Mutti had altered to wear at our Christmas Eve dinner with Willi and Lili. When I found it, my emotions ran away from me. I collapsed on my bed, hugging the dress and its evocation of that golden, candlelit *Heiligabend*. I had worn it one last time: the farewell dinner for Willi before he left for east Germany. My fear for Willi's safety spiralled beyond control and I lay sobbing on my bed..

Mutti must have heard me. The bed moved as she sat, enveloping me in her arms. I leant into her, my sobs softening to tears. She stroked my short hair and I turned to see lines of tears on her face as well.

My recent resolve was smoke in the gale buffeting me. The empty grey expanse of an uncertain future stretched before me, its bleak winds moaning through the rubble of my hopes. "What's going to happen to us, Mutti?"

She inhaled, gusting out a sigh and shaking her head. "I don't know, *Liebling*, but whatever it is, I promise you we will both face it. You are not alone in any of this." Her fierce love powering her hug. "I'm sorry for doing this to you." Self-doubt clouded her voice. "We should have stayed in Leipzig ..."

I pulled away from her, seeking her eyes, but they slid away from mine. "No, Mutti. Don't say that. Don't think that." I gave her hand a squeeze and her eyes returned to mine. "You did what you had to ...and if you hadn't, I would never have met Willi or Lili."

Her face was grim. "And now, because of me, you've lost the only friends you ever had."

I could hear the guilt in her voice and her eyes once again drifted from mine. My guilt at the risks I had taken with our masquerade flared and I hugged Mutti. "What's happened to us is my fault, too. It was me that told Willi we were from Leipzig and revealed myself as a girl. I..."

"Shh, *Liebling*. It's not your fault."

But a part of the fault for what is happening now is mine.

Mutti's arms tightened around me and we sat in silence for a while, each clutching our share of guilt.

After a while, my eyes found hers again. "I've not lost Willi and Lili – I know where they are." I squeezed her hand again. "Once things settle down and it's safe, I'll get in touch with them." My voice carried a certainty that driven by hope.

Mutti's eyes returned to mine and she could not hide the doubt that clouded them. We sat in silence for a while, taking comfort in shared closeness.

Mutti shifted, producing a hanky from her pocket and dabbing the tears off our faces. "Whatever happens, life goes on." She glanced across the room. "I see your schoolbooks have arrived. We must set up school here for you."

I grimaced.

"No, Col." Mutti's serious face reinforced her message. "You need to keep studying. With Willi and Lili, you were doing well at school and you owe it to yourself – and them – to keep working." She winked. "Besides, we paid for them – let's put them to use."

I sighed and Mutti stroked my cheek with her thumb, smiling.

"Wherever we are, you have a future, Col, and you need to have the knowledge to decide what that future is, to take advantage of the opportunities before you."

The sleeve on Mutti's blouse had retreated and I could see the faint blue numbers tattooed on her forearm at Ravensbrück. At my age, she had survived starvation and worse at the whim of the SS in the camp, learning

Polish and Russian from women in her block. She'd started picking up English through the meal hatches in the cell doors of English girls condemned as spies by the Nazis. Through all that horror, Mutti had not stopped learning, though her future might have been measured in hours. I shivered at that thought and leant forward and kissed the tattoo, promising to hold as fast to a better future as she had.

Mutti gave me an understanding smile, sliding her sleeve down to cover the tattoo. She took a deep breath, settling herself. "Let's throw out those boys' clothes and get the books organised." Her eyes travelled round the room. "There's space here for a table you can use as a desk and we can use that bookcase for your books."

The boys' clothes went into the empty boxes. We stacked my schoolbooks on the emptied shelf and I discovered we had three Herne Bay library books.

"We'll have to get these to the library somehow." I opened one. The due date was fast approaching. "They'll be issuing fines soon." I smiled light-heartedly at Mutti. "We don't want a librarian searching for us as well."

"You'd best give them to Jack and ask him to organise it." Mutti suggested, her lips turning up at the corners.

Sorting our things out took the rest of the morning and some of the afternoon. Mrs Gittings found a table and chair, which Charles moved into my room. Later, she took me through the formal drawing room to the library.

"You're welcome to use any of the books here, but please replace them in the correct place."

"Thank you. Can I stay and choose some books now, please?"

"Of course you can. You don't need to ask permission." Mrs Gittings left me to it.

I spent the best part of an hour grazing through the collection with the measured tick of the library clock for company. I glanced through many books before replacing them. Two caught my fancy. *A History of the War of the Roses,* as I was in Lancaster, home of one of the warring houses and a paperback with a picture of a ginger cat on its cover. I marked their places by putting their left-hand neighbour in the wrong way round.

With my selections in hand, I wandered out through the quiet house into the garden. I found a seat in a sunny corner and Hawkins joined me. After purring in response to my strokes, he curled up, leaning against my thigh as I read the cat book: Paul Gallico's *Thomasina*, which suited my sombre mood.

Mutti found me there after an hour. "That cat has taken to you." She smiled, sitting down and giving Hawkins a stroke. "This evening, I want you to get out your school timetable. From tomorrow, we'll be using that to guide your study."

I needed something to keep me occupied and schoolwork would help with that. "The timetable includes sport which I couldn't do because of my 'medical condition'. But now I'm a girl, I want to swim again."

Mutti cocked an eyebrow at me. "Okay...we'll have to ask Mrs Gittings about that. I suppose swimming fits in with your 'recovery from a long illness' story." She shook her head, staring at the trees at the rear of the garden. "I hope we can soon stop having to lie about our lives."

Part of that knot inside me came into focus: I didn't like the continuing deception either.

"Come on, it's teatime and we mustn't be late."

I gave Hawkins a stroke and went inside with Mutti. "I'll be down in a minute." Upstairs, I grabbed the library books and clattered down the staircase, placing them where Jack would sit at the table. Mutti and I set the table, pulling dishes and cutlery from the drawers and cupboards – after of searching for the table mats.

When Jack turned up, he glanced at the books at his place. "What's all this?"

"Amongst my stuff, I found these books that belong to the Herne Bay library." I gave him an uneasy smile. "I need to return them, as the library will expect them soon."

Jack opened the books, checking the due date, I suppose. He made a sour face, shaking his head. "OK. Charles – get these sent off to the Firm and they can sort it from there.

Charles raised a sour eyebrow and took the proffered books from Jack. They were both fed up with this teenage girl that kept making demands of them, this girl who had bitten and kicked them.

It was past time to make amends – though my actions were sort of justified. I caught their eyes across the table. "I'm sorry I bit and kicked when you rescued us." I flushed with embarrassment. "I truly thought you were from my father, coming to kidnap us. Please, can you forgive me … under the circumstances?"

The two men glanced at one another. Jack raised an eyebrow at Charles, who gave him a slight nod. "Fair enough." His tone was dismissive.

Mrs Gittings was standing behind him and gave Jack's chair a kick, causing him to start. "Jack, you ingrate, the lady apologised graciously. You need to accept her apology properly."

Jack swivelled his head, his annoyance at Mrs Gittings showing, but she was not to be cowed, giving his chair another kick.

Jack glanced up at Mrs Gittings, sighing in resignation, before turning to me. "Thank you, Miss."

Mrs Gittings patted him on the shoulder, smiling across at me. "Did you really bite and kick them?"

My blush returned as I glanced at Jack and Charles and Mrs Gittings chuckled. She retrieved a pie from the oven and bowls of mashed potato and brussel sprouts. When she cut the piecrust, a rich aroma spread around the room.

"Steak and kidney pie – fantastic," Charles enthused.

Mrs Gittings served us with pie and we added vegetables to our plates.

"There's more gravy here." Mrs Gittings retrieved a gravy boat from where it had been warming on the range and I sloshed extra gravy over my mashed potatoes.

After we'd all had a mouthful or two and complemented Mrs Gittings' cooking, I accosted Jack. "Do you know when Mrs Henderson is returning?"

Jack assembled a forkful of pie and mashed potato. "Why do you want to know?" He filled his mouth and started chewing.

"I want to know if she's delivered my message."

Jack continued chewing, staring across the table at me. He took his time before swallowing and picked up his glass, taking a sip of water. He placed the glass on the table with exaggerated care. "She doesn't tell me her movements. You'll have to wait." His voice betrayed his complete lack of concern and his eyes fell from mine to his plate.

I clamped down on the frustration that flared inside me. "Okay, thank you."

Jack's eyes flicked over me, trying to work out if there was anything hiding in my words. There was, but I was annoyed at Mrs Henderson, not him.

I turned to Mrs Gittings, "Please, could you tell me how I get to the Kingsway baths? I want to swim again."

"Oh." she smiled. "They're about a twenty-minute walk from here. We'll give them a ring in the morning to find out about times."

"Thank you." I cut another bite of the excellent pie.

After tea, Mutti and I helped clean up before I retrieved my timetable from my school bag.

"Have you got your textbooks for every subject?"

I scanned my timetable. One box had come from my school locker and I had all my texts – but one. "I don't have a Polish grammar text – that's at Lili's house."

Mutti smiled. "Well, I think I can cover that absence for now." She glanced at the timetable again. "School starts at nine."

"Okay."

That night, Hawkins arrived, scratching at my door. He strode across my room to leap on to my bed, knowing with the certainty possessed by all cats that he owned all parts of it. His eyes watched unblinking as I returned to the bed. When I settled, he turned to find the best spot, finally curling up against me, his purrs vibrating my thigh.

• • • •

AFTER BREAKFAST, I set myself up at the table in my room and started working through a chapter of my French text. Because of Willi's work with me, I was past this level – but needed to work on the irregular verbs and their subjunctive forms. I realised I had no-one to practice spoken French with: I'd have to speak to myself. From French I went on to Maths, where I had leant on Willi in the past. I now had to concentrate to understand compound interest. Willi's explanations had always been clearer than the text's. He claimed this was because most teachers wrote texts to impress other teachers, not to help students. I struggled through to the end of the chapter and did some exercises. These seemed to work out when I compared my answers to the ones in the book.

Downstairs at break time, Mrs Gittings produced a glass of milk and some plain biscuits. "I rang the Kingsway baths and they are open for general swimming from two to five every weekday and Saturday from nine to three. Entrance is sixpence per session."

"Thank you." I was itching to get swimming again. "Can I go after school?"

Mutti turned to Mrs Gittings. "I suppose I'd better check with Jack?"

"I've already spoken to him – it's fine for Col to go by herself."

"Will you be OK by yourself, or do you want me to come with you?"

Before I could answer, Mrs Gittings leant over. "Jack doesn't want you going out with Col. He doesn't want you out with your daughter. They are still searching for you for all we know. The two of you together are what they are looking for, not a girl by herself, Jack reckons."

I could see Mutti wasn't pleased with this, but from her face, she understood the problem.

Mrs Gittings gave her a sympathetic glance. "I could take her down, if you like."

I was wary of going by myself, but I sought greater independence. "No, I'll be fine by myself if you write some directions for me."

Mrs Gittings and Mutti glanced at one another.

"Are you sure ..." I could hear the uncertainty in Mutti's voice.

I smiled with more confidence than I felt.

Mutti changed the subject. "What time do you usually finish school?"

"If we allow for the school sport and PE time, can I finish in time to get to the pool at two o'clock three times a week?"

Mutti smiled. "I think we can manage that."

My period had finished overnight and I was keen to get started. "Can I start today, please?"

Mutti's concern for me venturing out alone coloured her reluctant reply. "If you want to."

"Excellent." I finished my milk and headed up to my room to start a history lesson: the Hanoverian monarchy in England. I hadn't realised that the British Royal family had German ancestors.

At half-past one, I had my duffel bag over my shoulder and Mrs Gittings directions in my hand. The walk took me through the centre of Lancaster and past the castle. Inside the Kingsway baths, I paid the sixpence session fee and was told I could change but not start swimming before two, as schools were still using the pool. I wandered into the girls' changing room. Some girls were changing into school uniforms, but I found a vacant spot and put on my swimming costume. I sensed curious glances in my direction: I wasn't in school uniform during school time, but no-one spoke to me. When I was ready, I walked out into the pool area with my towel and found a seat, finding two pools – a twenty-five-meter pool and a diving pool. They had divided the large pool into two sections, with classes running in both. I sat and watched until the teachers blew whistles and the students started getting out.

Someone came in and removed the floating divider, stowed it in a box beside the pool and announced general swimming. I walked over to the pool, lining myself up between a set of lines on the bottom and dived in and swam a couple of meters under water. It felt amazing to be in the water, despite my lack of condition.

That's why I'm here.

I pushed off from the wall and started a slow-paced free style, breathing every three strokes as they had taught me. At the far end, I was gasping. I turned and started a slow length of breaststroke. I swam alternating, slowing lengths until my arms and legs felt like lead. I heaved myself out, found my towel and sat watching the swimmers for about fifteen minutes. My breathing settled and I tried another session of mixed lengths, but after about fifteen minutes, I'd had enough. I felt the walk to the house in the muscles that I hadn't pushed for quite a while.

Mutti was in the kitchen helping Mrs Gittings. "Did you enjoy yourself?"

I flopped on to a chair. "Yes, but I'm out of condition."

Mutti smiled. "Don't overdo it. You'll get there."

A thought that had been hovering pushed its way forward. "Mrs Gittings, when we were finding shoes, there were some gym shoes. Can I try them on and use them if they fit?"

"Of course."

"Thank you."

Mutti frowned in puzzlement.

"I couldn't believe how out of breath I was after a single length. I need to run as well. I thought I'd go for a run before breakfast in the mornings."

"Where are you going to run?" Once again, I could hear the concern in Mutti's voice.

"I saw some playing fields beside the railway line as I walked over the bridge."

"That's right. There's a path this side of the railway line that runs down to them." Mrs Gittings paused, gazing up into the house. "Hmm. I think I can find you a set of my daughter's gym clothes for you to run in."

"Thank you."

After we helped clean up after tea, Mrs Gittings took me up to her daughter's room again. A pair of gym shoes fitted and we found two sets of gym socks, shorts and slips. Mrs Gittings picked up an alarm clock from the bedside table. "You'll probably be wanting this if you're to run and still make it to breakfast."

I smiled, remembering her banging on the gong.

I was eager to be exercising again and was awake before six. The alarm went off as I dressed, waking Hawkins, who yawned and settled down to sleep. I let myself out and set a gentle pace to the sports field to warm up. After pushing hard for four circuits, I was gasping for breath and slowed, heading for home. I had a quick bath and was ready for breakfast at eight. In fact, I was starving, a result of the swimming and running. Mrs Gittings' full English breakfast hit the spot.

That set the tenor for the rest of the school term and by mid-July when the schools broke up, I was in reasonable condition. Mutti had pushed me hard on the schoolwork, insisting that we add Russian to the after-school language program alongside Polish. My Russian had fallen into disuse and I struggled at first, but seven years of Russian at school in east Germany soon resurfaced. Mutti insisted we continue with the language lessons during the school holidays and I found myself teaching her French with the aid of my textbook.

They dropped the restriction on Mutti and me being seen together after a couple of weeks. Mrs Gittings, Mutti and I – always with one man along – visited the sights of Lancaster. I found the mediaeval castle interesting. I'd seen nothing like it before, its thick walls redolent with centuries of history. We picnicked in Williamson Park and wandered through the Ashton Memorial; we swam at Morecambe Beach twice and went down to Blackpool for a day. Mrs Gittings hinted we might head up to the Lake District for a visit, but we never did.

I was sitting outside enjoying the summer weather reading one afternoon in late July, Hawkins sleeping curled against my thigh. Mutti walked out and sat down beside Hawkins, who lifted his head and let her stroke him before settling, eyes closed in adored bliss.

"Mrs Henderson has arrived."

"Oh – I want to ask her if she delivered my message."

"Well, you'll have to wait. She's closeted with Jack and Mrs Gittings in the library." Mutti stroked Hawkins' body and he stretched languorously, inviting me to rub his tummy. I ran my hand up and down through his pale tummy fur and he responded by gripping the edge of the seat with his front paws as he stretched.

"He's such a friendly cat," Mutti murmured.

"He's a softy."

Hawkins stretched again and curled, crossing his front paws over his face, as if shutting out the light to sleep better.

"Carry on reading. I'm going to sit here and enjoy the sun. It's been such a rainy summer."

I returned my attention to my book and we sat in companionable silence for some time before I heard footsteps approach: Mrs Henderson.

We both stood. "Good afternoon, Mrs Henderson."

She inspected us before pulling a garden chair round in front of us.

"I hear Mrs Gittings has been showing you round Lancaster."

I jumped in. "Did you get my message to Willi? How is he?"

Mrs Henderson's glance was full of indifference. She turned to Mutti. "It's important that you learn about Lancaster and the surrounding area.

When we find somewhere for you to go, your background will be from Lancaster." She stared at me. "You need to learn this area as well." She turned to Mutti.

I leant forward, annoyed she'd ignored my question. "What about my message to Willi?"

Mutti put a restraining hand on my arm. "Col, please..."

"No. I need to know what's happened." Frustration and anger coloured my voice.

Mrs Henderson's face, as ever, remained emotionless. Her bleak eyes swivelled towards me. "What you want is of little consequence to my responsibilities."

I glared at her, knowing that I had no way of making her tell me and my fears about Willi boiled over.

"You said you would deliver it." I was bouncing with frustration. Hawkins leapt off the chair beside me, frightened by my agitation.

"I said no such thing, girl."

My voice was now a shout. "Yes, you did. You..."

Mrs Henderson leant across and slapped me. I sat there, shocked into silent stillness. No-one had ever hit me before. My eyes moistened, but I would not give her the satisfaction of tears. Beside me, Mutti leaned forward, still grasping my arm, but Mrs Henderson stopped her with a gesture. Her eyes narrowed, watching me struggle to contain my shock and tears.

"There were no promises. I would see what I could do." To her, it was a simple statement of fact.

Mutti found her voice. "You have no right to slap my daughter." I could hear the anger in her voice.

The slimmest vestige of emotion flashed through Mrs Henderson's expression, the faintest hint of fire simmering behind her eyes. "I won't have some German think she can order me around." She shifted in her chair, icy control in her face as she glanced my way.

"There has not been an appropriate opportunity to pass on your message." Her gaze lingered on me, challenging me to respond. I tried to hold her stare, but cringed, dropping my eyes as her gaze stripped my will.

She turned to Mutti. "Learn everything you can about Lancaster and its surrounds. As soon as we have a solution to the problem of what to do with you, we will move you." She stood and walked into the house.

I slumped, my fears about Willi surging up to replace the anger that had filled me before, my cheek burning where the slap had landed.

"What am I going to do, Mutti?"

Mutti shook her head and reached an arm round me. "I don't think Mrs Henderson likes us at all ... but I don't think she likes any Germans." Her face was bitter. "I wonder what happened to her during the war?" she mused, her eyes drifting across the garden in thought. She turned to me, moving my chin about to examining my face. "I don't think you'll get a black eye. Come up to my room and we'll put some soothing cream on it."

No-one else said anything, though they'd probably heard my raised voice. Mrs Gittings glanced at my face as we helped her get the table ready for tea.

Lying in bed that night, I thought about writing to Willi myself. I could head into town one swimming afternoon, buy envelope and stamps and post a letter. But any message sent would carry a Lancaster postmark – and Willi was being watched by Mrs Henderson and possibly my father's agents. Mrs Henderson's reaction would not be as final as my father's, but I could not risk her withdrawing the Firm's protection out of anger with me.

Willi and I now share getting smacked in the face.

A grim smile crossed my face at the thought and cuddled up to Hawkins, whose whiffling purrs lead me, thoughts meandering around my problems, into sleep.

By mid-August, my swimming was better than it had ever been and my morning run was up to eight laps of the sports field. After a while, Jack was prepared to let Mutti and me out by ourselves. She came to the pool with me one afternoon. I finished a set of lengths and got out to sit with Mutti for a while with my towel round my shoulders.

"Excuse me?" A middle-aged man was standing, looking up at us.

Mutti glanced at me. I shrugged – I didn't know who he was.

"Yes?" I could hear the wariness in Mutti's voice.

"I've been watching your daughter swimming. She shows some promise."

Mutti glanced at me. "And?"

"I was wondering if she would swim some lengths for me...against the clock."

"Why would she do that?" Mutti's voice was laced with suspicion.

"Oh sorry. I should have explained. I'm Fred Hubert. I coach the local swimming team and I thought your daughter might want to try out."

This was a bad idea – anything that drew attention to us was a bad idea. Being on the swim team would draw attention to us. "I don't think I'm fast enough and he'll see that when I swim." I murmured to Mutti, giving her a pointed look.

Mutti relaxed when she realised what I intended. "Very well."

I slipped my towel off my shoulders and followed Mr Hubert down to the pool. I tried to remember if he'd been around about an hour earlier when I had stretched out in the pool.

He showed me an empty lane. "OK, warm up again with a pair of lengths."

I dived in, swimming two lengths at an easy pace, but splashing to appear uncoordinated and then hitched myself onto the side of the pool. Mr Hubert was eyeing me. "OK, now really stretch out and show me what you can do over two lengths."

I turned and pushed off, setting up a faster, splashing pace. After the second length, I was gasping: I had messed up my breathing on purpose.

I hitched myself on to the pool side again, my breath rasping in and out.

"How old are you?"

"Fourteen."

"Hmm." He smiled. "Well, if you suddenly remember how to swim like you were earlier, ask for me at the front desk."

He had seen me stretching out, I realised.

Now what?

He raised a speculative eyebrow. "I'll see you around?"

After a moment, he turned and walked away. This attention made me uncomfortable and I went over to Mutti. "Let's go home."

Mutti understood and she made her way out as I headed into the changing room. I didn't shower, just dried myself and changed, heading out as fast as I could, my hair still damp. Mutti met me outside and we walked off in silence.

After a while, she took my hand. "And?"

I shrugged. "I tried to show him I was useless. But he'd seen me swim earlier." I thought about his reaction. "I don't think he's going to make trouble for us, though. He doesn't want unwilling people on his team."

I was careful at the pool after that, keeping my speed down and swimming fewer lengths. I made up for this by pushing my morning runs harder. Occasionally, Mr Hubert watched me swim from a distance after that, but he did not speak to me.

One afternoon in late in August, when I arrived from the pool, I found Mutti sitting with Mrs Henderson in the kitchen. I stopped in the doorway, anger flaring, but controlled myself. I would not give her another reason to slap me. Mrs Henderson's face turned towards me, her eyes scanning across me. She was assessing my value to her and that made me uneasy every time.

Her eyes returned to my face. "You've hardened up over the summer."

A subtle shiver coursed over me. As always, Mrs Henderson remained unreadable. Somehow, she made me feel I owed her – and I feared one day she would arrive demanding payment I would not want to provide.

"We'll go to the library. Come with me." Mrs Henderson stood, gathering a battered leather briefcase from beside her chair.

Mutti's face was closed. After our previous encounter, she lacked any trust in Mrs Henderson. Mutti stood, beckoning with her eyes and we followed Mrs Henderson in silence through the house into the drawing room. She waited until we were inside before she turned and locked the door.

What is Mrs Henderson worried about?

She walked across the room and I saw her check the windows were closed. She opened the library door and walked across to the single tall window, slamming it shut. I followed Mutti into the room and turned to close the door.

"Leave the door open." Another command.

"Sit." Mrs Henderson took a large, buttoned-backed leather chair. It gave her a view of the window and through the open door to the drawing room.

"Sit." She waved at the chairs and pulled two large envelopes from the briefcase, holding them on her lap.

"We have been trying to find somewhere safe for you and have a solution. For this to work, these arrangements must remain completely secret."

That explained the cloak and dagger way she set up this meeting. Her tone made me feel like superfluous furniture about to be stuffed into a dark, dank basement or dusty, spider-infested attic.

Mutti glanced over at me. "Understood."

"Keeping you in this country is not possible. There is a high probability they would find you again — unless we split you up."

I saw Mutti stiffen.

Mrs Henderson silenced her incipient disagreement with a glare. "We considered Canada, but that's close to our American ... friends. They do not always see things as we do." She paused, her eyes moving between the two of us. "There was only one place that offered the anonymity and security required: Australia." Mrs Henderson sat motionless in her chair, watching us.

I froze in place. She was sending me halfway round the world, as far as possible from Willi and Lili. The enormity of it crushed and paralysed me before I half rose. "No. You can't send us there." It burst from me as soon as I could think, move.

Mrs Henderson's face remained impassive.

"Mutti, tell her we won't go."

Mutti reached across, taking my hand. "Shh, Liebling. Let Mrs Henderson finish." She pulled me down into my chair. I settled, realising I was risking another slap.

Mrs Henderson's calculating eyes skewered me, reinforcing how worthless I was to her, how much she desired to be rid of me. Her eyes moved between us. "You will be different people. Still German, as that's difficult to change, your linguistic expertise notwithstanding." She looked at Mutti. "We have found you housing and work. For your daughter, there will be a place at an appropriate school."

"And?" Mutti raised an eyebrow.

The silence drew out as Mrs Henderson sat, impassive.

I could see Mutti wanted Mrs Henderson to answer her.

Finally, Mutti sighed. "What about our safety? What if he finds us again? We'll be alone in a far country with no-one to help us."

Mrs Henderson blinked: she had not expected this request. She gathered her thoughts. "I will make arrangements to provide you with an emergency contact in Australia."

Mutti sat upright. "And if we turn down this offer? What are our options?"

Mrs Henderson sat motionless, only her cold eyes moving between us. I again felt how little we mattered to her.

"I cannot permit you to stay here. You have caused significant damage to the KGB and its various client operations in the Eastern Bloc – and they are searching for you." She let that sink in for a second or two. "It is dangerous for people near you if you stay here. They no longer want to arrest and imprison you; they want to make an example." Another longer pause as her eyes assessed us. "They want you dead."

My stomach hollowed out and my mouth dried in an instant. My father wanted me dead – and he had command of the resources to make that happen.

Mutti surged forward in her chair. "That was you – you used us and placed us in this situation."

Mrs Henderson shrugged, brushing Mutti's outburst aside. "You think that defecting to the west is cost free? There is always a price to pay ... for everything ... and this is yours." Her eyes flicked across me before returning to lock gazes with Mutti. "Think of your daughter – she deserves a life, not to have it end – horribly – at the hands of an agent sent by her father."

Mutti's face blanched at Mrs Henderson's impersonal brutality. She swivelled towards me, guilt distorting her face. "I'm sorry, *Liebling*. So sorry."

I was numb, detached. The burst of emotion had, for the moment, burned out my ability to feel, to think.

"You need to learn your identities." Mrs Henderson's unconcerned voice strode through our silence. "All the information you need is in these packages. Learn them well, for once you leave this house you must be these people – and the packages will be taken from you. These identities are your only chance of having a life. Learn them."

From her lap, she pushed an envelope across the table towards each of us. "Study them well. You leave in two days." She produced a key from her briefcase, laying it on the table between the envelopes. "Keep the material locked in that drawer." She pointed at the writing desk in the corner. "Do not take it out of this room, where I suggest you spend these two days studying."

Mrs Henderson stood. "Learn your identities until ... they ... are ... you." She let the emphasis sink in. "Read both packages – and test one another. A single slip and you will leave a trail your husband and father will follow."

I squirmed – I knew all about such slips.

Mrs Henderson's icy gaze settled on Mutti. "You have seen the consequences of a slip in Ravensbrück. Make your daughter understand." She stood silent for a moment before she turned and walked out, closing the door behind her. In the strange way that tiny details can become huge, I noticed she had a slight limp.

We sat in silence, the envelopes heavy on the table. I did not want to pick mine up: it sounded the death knell for my previous life, the end of my hopes of returning to Willi and Lili.

Mutti's voice cracking with emotion pulled me out of my spiralling thoughts. "I'm sorry, *Liebling*." Tears dribbled down Mutti's cheeks. I knelt by her chair.

"No, Mutti. Please, don't feel guilty. You had no choice but to leave Leipzig." I reached up, hugging her.

We stayed that way for a while until Mutti took a deep breath and pushed me away, sniffing.

"I wish she had been less brutal about this, but we have no choice, Col. We must do as she says." Mutti reached past me for her envelope and opened it.

She tilted her head towards mine. "Go on, sit down and read through it all."

I picked myself up and sat down, watching Mutti pull about twenty typed sheets out of her envelope and then tip out a set of black and white photos onto the table.

"Open yours and read through it." She watched as I opened my envelope and pulled out about half a dozen sheets with a single photo – a man in British army uniform. Writing on the reverse declared him to be "Sgt Ryan Miller, Royal Engineers."

I started reading. I was to be Karlota, known in the family as Kal, not Lottie, which would make things easier. My birthday was still my birthday, but my father was Sgt Ryan Miller, the man in the photo. My mother had married him in February1948 while he was stationed in Frankfurt. He had died in an accident at work in February this year. None of my grandparents had survived the war, victims of Luftwaffe and RAF bombs. My parents were both only children. I had no family but Mutti.

I read through the rest of my pages, but finished well before Mutti finished hers. I picked up her pictures and started leafing through them. The writing told me they were pictures of places in Frankfurt that I suppose we needed to know.

After a while, Mutti finished reading through hers. "Come on, let's swap." She glanced up at the ticking library clock. "There's time before tea." We exchanged envelopes and started reading, with Mutti examining the Frankfurt photos whilst I finished reading her longer set of papers.

I sighed when I finished. "How are we going to learn all this in two days?"

Mutti stretched, reaching out to pick up her envelope, adding the photos to it. "We'll learn it because we have to. We're going to practice it, every day." She stared across at me. "We have no choice, Col... err ... Kal. We must be perfect if we're going to stay safe." She paused and gave me a tiny smile. "No, whilst we're here, you're still Col."

Mutti locked the envelopes in the drawer, slipping the key into her cardigan pocket. "Come on, it's teatime. Let's see if Mrs Gittings needs a hand." After tea, we went to the library, accompanied by Hawkins, who sat on my lap as I went through my papers again. I was glad that Willi had trained me well – his fierce concentration had rubbed off: I was mastering my part.

But in spite of the work we were doing, I was worried that we would forget important details; in bed, I recorded in an exercise book what I could remember from both my and Mutti's information packs — in Polish.

In the morning, two trunks arrived. Mrs Henderson told us we were to pack the things we didn't need for the thirty-five-day voyage to Australia in these, ready to be picked up that evening. A single large suitcase would suffice for the voyage. I would have my duffel bag for personal items. Apart from an hour packing, helped by Hawkins who kept jumping into my trunk, we spent every minute that day in the library. We'd left Frankfurt when I was two. No-one would expect me to describe the scenes in those photos, but I learned about them from Mutti. She regaled me with her life in Frankfurt, her parents and meeting my father, Sgt Miller.

In bed, I added to, checked and corrected the information I had recorded the previous night. Hawkins had noticed the change in our routine and was clingy, pushing at my hand as I wrote and demanding strokes. We had been told to be up and ready to leave at seven o'clock in the morning. I set the alarm for six.

I was up at five, checking everything into my duffel bag. Mutti must have heard me in the bathroom as she came through to my room and gave me a hug.

"Ready?"

How could you ever be ready for something like this?

But we had no choice. "There's these things for the suitcase." I pointed to my running gear that had been drying on the radiator.

Mutti picked them up. "I'll pack them and see you downstairs." I picked up my duffel bag. Hawkins followed me as I walked downstairs.

Mrs Gittings was in the kitchen. "Breakfast?"

My stomach was fluttering. "No, thanks."

"Nonsense. Sit down." She smiled and put the usual breakfast in front of me, adding scrambled egg from the stove and poured me a cup of tea.

I sat staring at the plate, sipping my tea. Mutti received the same treatment when she arrived.

She saw my untouched food. "Eat something, Col. I don't know how far we're going today or when we'll eat again." She picked up her knife and fork and started eating.

The tea had settled my stomach and once I started, my appetite arrived and I polished off my plate.

Jack came in. "The car's here. I've brought the suitcase down."

A new man followed him. He stood in silence, watching us finish breakfast. He must be our driver or guard.

Mrs Gittings produced a pack of cheese and tomato sandwiches wrapped in greaseproof paper and wished us both a safe journey before they hustled us out.

At the front door stood Mrs Henderson. "Your information packages?"

Mutti pulled the key out of her pocket and we followed her into the library. She opened the desk and pulled out the envelopes. Mrs Henderson pocketed the key. She took the envelopes to the table and tipped them out, checking the pages and photos were all there. She replaced everything except the photograph of Sgt Miller, which she handed to Mutti. "Your dead husband."

Mutti winced at Mrs Henderson's callousness.

Our packages went into her briefcase and she pulled out another bulky envelope.

"Passports, travel and various papers. Go through them in the car."

Mutti put it in her shoulder bag.

"Go." Mrs Henderson's voice was emotionless, as always.

I took a deep breath and locked eyes with Mrs Henderson. "You haven't passed on my message to Willi, have you?"

Mrs Henderson's face remained expressionless.

Mutti took my hand. "Leave it, Col."

Hawkins twined around my ankles as we came down the steps. Jack was heaving our suitcase into the boot and the strange man from earlier was standing by the car with another in the front passenger seat. I crouched down to give Hawkins a cuddle. His eyes reproached me for abandoning him.

"Come on, Col. Get in." Mutti pushed me towards the nearest door and went round to the far side. I settled with my duffel bag on the floor between my feet, my unease stirring my full stomach from breakfast.

Doors slammed, the engine started and we swept down the drive towards a different life.

Chapter 3
Sept – Oct 1964

O nce the car left the house, Mutti opened the bulky envelope and shook its contents into her lap. She passed over my British passport. I was now Karlota Miller. I didn't like my photo. My hair looked awful and I decided that once it had grown, I would ask Mutti if I could have it styled. Mutti was reading through a folder with a colourful picture of a ship on the front.

"We are travelling by ship from Southampton to Sydney. It will take about thirty-five days, it seems. But we're not stopping there; we're going by plane to Brisbane wherever that is."

I recalled my geography lessons. "I think that's north of Sydney, on the east coast of Australia."

Mutti examined the papers again. "The ship leaves tomorrow. I wonder where we'll spend the night?" Mutti returned to the package, pulling out a booklet called *Information for Immigrants*. She passed to me as she continued working her way through the contents of the envelope.

"Hmmm."

"What?"

"It seems you have a scholarship to the Brisbane Girls Grammar School for the four remaining years of your schooling, starting in January."

"Why would I need a scholarship for a grammar school? The one here was free, wasn't it?"

Mutti shrugged and passed the letter across to me. "It must be different in Australia."

The scholarship was from the Royal Engineers Benevolent Fund – my supposed father's regiment. The scholarship covered everything except uniforms. A letter from the school asked us to visit as soon as we had settled in Brisbane to 'ascertain an appropriate educational curriculum' for the 1965 academic year, starting in late January.

As we drove south, I continued browsing through the *Information for Immigrants* booklet. It sang the praises of Australia as the place to start a new life. I pulled a wry face when I read that – it applied to us in ways the writer did not intend. It had a map of Australia and I showed Mutti where Brisbane was, about 1,000 km north of Sydney, but not even halfway up Australia's east coast.

Studying the map made me realise how huge Australia was. Vast areas of the continent were empty – or at least there were no cities marked. In geography, we had studied New South Wales and Sydney, the state capital, but that was a small part of Australia. From the map, Western Australia was about a third of Australia and only the state capital, Perth, was marked on the map. The booklet's claim that immigrants like us would 'create modern Australia' had some truth, it seemed. We would be pioneers. After a while, I ran out of things to read and wedged myself in the corner and dozed.

I came half awake and jerked upright, startling Mutti.

"Col ... Kal. What's the matter?"

My head swivelled round and ... I realised I wasn't in the car, with my father's agents kidnapping us. I let out an explosive breath and my heart slowed from its frantic beating.

"What's wrong, *Liebling*?" Mutti leant across the backseat to stroke my cheek.

"Sorry, Mutti. I thought I was in the car when we were kidnapped. I panicked." I took several deep breaths. "I'm OK now."

Mutti gathered me into her arms. "Oh, *Liebling*."

I could hear the guilt in her voice beneath the concern.

We arrived in Southampton in the early evening. The streets were slick with rain, reflecting the streetlights into the car. They deposited two of us, our hand luggage and our big case in front of a hotel outside the docks and drove off. We struggled the large case into the hotel through the drizzle. Mutti produced our reservation paperwork from the package in her shoulder bag.

The hotel was used to people waiting for a ship. They told us that breakfast would start at half-past six and to be in the foyer at half-past eight. A bus would take us to the *SS Oriana* in Southampton docks. We ate dinner in the hotel and Mutti suggested we get an early night.

I lay in bed for a while, trying to stretch out the kinks from sitting in a car all day. I wondered what Lili and Willi were doing – and if they were thinking of me. School would have restarted for the autumn term.

Were they still meeting after school and practicing their languages?

Choking sadness welled up inside me at the loss of my close friends, of our tight little community with its shared secrets. I was travelling half a world away and reconnecting with them some time in a distant future would be difficult. I could feel moisture gathering in my eyes, but I remembered what Willi told me about his previous life: he had emigrated to Australia. If he emigrated in this life, we might meet up – a rather forlorn hope but some comfort. Threatening dreams invaded my sleep that night, but they faded before I could grasp their evanescent fragments. I woke uneasy at what lay ahead.

We arrived at the docks in wind and rain, the cream-painted steel cliff of the ship towering above us. We walked across the dock and up the gangway with our hand luggage. Stewards directed us through the ship to our cabin on D deck towards the rear of the ship. Mutti unlocked the door to reveal a room about half the size of my room in Herne Bay. It had a pair of bunk beds, a desk, a handbasin and a window. I'd seen a sign to the bathrooms down a side corridor.

The steward directed us inside. "We will deliver your luggage soon." He pointed at the desk. "There's a map of the ship there. I suggest you take that with you if you want to explore as it's easy to get lost. We're sailing at two o'clock and once we're at sea, there'll be a lifeboat drill before dinner."

Mutti frowned at him. "What?"

He smiled. "In the unlikely event of something happening, everyone must know where to go and what to do. It's a great opportunity to meet people."

I could tell from his confident smile he'd had this conversation lots of times with nervous passengers.

"Your lifejackets are stowed in the cupboard." He opened the door and pointed them out. "You need to put those on for the lifeboat drill." He gave another reassuring smile. "Now, I'll let you get settled in." He left, closing the door behind him.

I examined the map of the ship, working out what it offered.

Mutti turned slowly and shivered. "Thirty-five days in this small space..."

I'd not seen Mutti react like this before and it added to my angst.

Was the limited size throwing up memories of her time in Ravensbrück?

I smiled, trying to reassure her. "We have a marvellous view out of our window and we don't have to be in here except to sleep. There'll be lots to do on the ship." I examined the map, wanting to give Mutti something else to think about. "There's three swimming pools – but they look short." I was itching to get into the water and to run again after two days in the library and a day sitting in a car.

Mutti peered over my shoulder. "Is there a library?"

"I don't see one ... Oh yes, there it is." I pointed to the map.

"Come on, let's find it."

I sensed Mutti's unease when we set off with the map as our guide. After some wrong turns and directions from the crew, we arrived at the library to find it closed until the following day. We wandered up to an outside deck and stood watching people arriving. The rain stopped and we wandered across the ship to look out across Southampton docks.

England was grey – drab sea and sky echoing with the ugly screech of the gulls. They slid beneath ragged clouds to mob any bird lucky enough to find a morsel of food. There had been gulls in Herne Bay, wheeling elegantly about the cliffs, but here they seemed rough and uncouth.

My tummy rumbled, but Mutti was lost in a distant stare across the water. I touched her hand. "Do you know when and where we get lunch?"

Mutti pulled herself into the present from wherever she had wandered. "Mm?"

Her face was full of sorrow. "What's wrong Mutti?"

She turned to me, taking my hands. "I can't apologise enough for doing this to you, *Liebling*."

I reached across to hug her. "Please don't." I could see moisture in her eyes. "We talked about this before."

Mutti shook her head. "I've torn you from your friends, dragging you across the world..."

"Mutti, we had no choice in all of this – we, us, had no choice." I gave her a gentle shake. "We could not stay with a murderous war criminal."

Mutti closed her eyes. "I know..."

"Come on. Let's find lunch." I pulled Mutti's reluctant hand and she followed me inside in my quest for food.

Lunch was a buffet of cold meats and salads to suit the continuous arrival of passengers, I suppose. Our suitcase had arrived in our cabin after lunch and we spent some time packing everything away in the drawers and cupboard. The rain and wind returned by the time we sailed. We watched from our window as we manoeuvred away from the quay and started down the Solent. About half an hour after we sailed, they called the lifeboat drill. We donned our lifejackets and, with the aid of the map and directions from the crew, made our way to our lifeboat, sheltering as best we could from the rain. Around us was considerable chaos. It took a while for the crew to sort everyone out and get them to their lifeboat station. Finally, they released us to warm up and dry off in our cabins.

Life on the ship settled into a routine. I swam every day although the pool started off quite cold. At least that meant my swimming was uninterrupted by other people. Once we were through the Suez Canal, the pool warmed and this forced me to swim earlier in the morning. There was nowhere I could run, so I depended on the repetitive exercise of three strokes, breath, three strokes, breath to soothe me.

During the long days, I spent many hours sitting in a deckchair, fingering Willi's necklace. The distant horizon held my gaze as I tried to come to terms with the loss of my friends, of my life. We would all change with time and those changes might create gulfs of separation. If we were to meet again, Willi and I might look at one another and see...nothing.

I was fortunate the deck was quite empty that day and no-one saw the tears I added to the ocean.

Another day I explored the clouded knot of emotion and impulse associated with revealing our secrets to Willi and Lili. Behind those impulses was a dislike of deceit. When I examined that idea, I found it stronger than dislike: deceiving people close to me made me feel ... nauseous. Wishing for the comfort of Hawkins on my lap, I realised the deception was in both directions. Willi had hidden who and what he was from me, as I had hidden my truth from him. But our deceptions extorted a high price and we had both risked much in revealing them. Willi had been startled and confused when I revealed I was a girl, not a boy. But I flushed with shame as I recalled the harshness of my reaction to Willi's secret. I had pushed him away, accusing him of being a pervert because he had the memories of a seventy-year-old in a thirteen-year-old's brain. This had hurt him deeply, even though I knew from the events beneath the cedar tree how dangerous to him that could be. I'd risked his life that day as I'd risked ours by revealing our secrets.

I could not sit. The urge to run or swim the shame and darkness out pulled me to the pool – but all I could do was swim interrupted lengths, which didn't help. In our cabin, I threw myself on the bed. Mutti sensed my dark mood when she arrived, pulling the unread book from my hands and hugging me.

"What is it, *Liebling*?"

I cringed in my pit of shame; I could not make myself tell Mutti my anger had me urge Willi to kill himself. "Why did I risk revealing us by telling Willi we were from Leipzig, that I was a girl? I let Willi kiss me at Lili's party – risking everything again." I stared at Mutti in anguish. "We pushed Willi into a corner about visiting the east Germany – where he met my father." Anguish twisted my face. "Why did I do those things? I'm the reason we're here ..." My voice sputtered out, overcome by the consequences of my thoughtless actions.

"Shh." Mutti hugged me tightly. "We don't know those things had anything to do with your father finding us."

I searched Mutti's face for reproach, but all I could see was love.

Mutti smoothed a lock of hair from my face. "Things happen, *Liebling*; we all make mistakes, particularly when we are growing up." She paused, understanding my anguish. "You told me I bore no guilt for dragging you away from Leipzig and now England, however hard it is for me to accept. Now I must tell you not to be guilty about your mistakes."

She stroked my cheek. "Don't let guilt cloud the love you and Willi share. You can only have one first love and it should be a cherished memory. Whatever happens in the future, don't let it be soured guilt."

Her eyes spoke of the love she had for me – and for Willi.

"I worry about him."

"I know, *Liebling*. I know." She engulfed me in another hug and we stayed that way in silence for a while. Her hand stroke my neck and she chuckled. "We need to get you to a hairdresser and find you a hairstyle."

I scowled at my reflection in the mirror on the wall. My hair had grown since May.

"Do you want to grow your hair longer or do you want a shorter style?"

What do I want? Does it matter?

I gave myself a shake.

Snap out of it, Col.

I tried to generate some enthusiasm: Lili's hair had been quite long, below her shoulders when not plaited. I had envied her that as my hair had to be boy short.

"A shorter style would suit me best. Long hair takes a while to dry after swimming."

"That's practical – let's see what they can come up with."

We made an appointment for the following morning.

"Do you want me to come with you?" Mutti asked.

She caught my thoughtful face and smiled. "You're growing up, Kal. It's your hair – I want you to choose how you look."

I realised Mutti had been encouraging my independence. Sending me out running in the mornings and allowing me to walk alone through the city — and now choosing my hairstyle.

"Okay, Mutti."

I arrived at the salon on time to be assigned to Kylie. She wrinkled her nose at the strange grown-out boy's cut sulking on my head and asked what style I wanted. The photos on the walls showed elegant, styled heads of hair, but they weren't me.

"I don't know." I admitted, unsure of myself.

"Well – what do you like doing? How are you staying amused on this voyage?"

"I read books from the library and I have my schoolbooks..."

Kylie tossed her head. "No – what do you do for fun?"

"Well ... I enjoy swimming and running."

"Hmm –you're active. I think you need a style that's easy to look after." Kylie grabbed a magazine from the waiting area and flipped through the pages. "What do you think of this?"

The picture showed a blond with a hairstyle that looked like a helmet. "It's called a pageboy. Your hair's quite short. I think that general style will suit you, particularly if we thin your hair down a bit." She used a finger to indicate shorter fringe and sides. "What do you think?"

I couldn't picture myself in any hairstyle; I shrugged. "Why not?"

Kylie huffed at my lack of enthusiasm. "Let's get you shampooed and get to work."

Forty minutes later, I sat staring at myself in the mirror, amazed by what Kylie had achieved. My hair wasn't a glistening helmet like the picture in the magazine, but textured. The style was simple, but the head staring at me looked elegant, sophisticated.

Kylie was standing behind me. "Okay Kal, now I want you to shake your head like a dog shaking off water."

I hesitated, unwilling to destroy the image before me. I caught her smiling eyes in the mirror.

"Go on, shake like a dog – you'll be surprised."

I took a last look at my elegant self in the mirror and shook vigorously. My hair flared out from my head, destroying its careful lay ... and settled it settled back with just a few stray strands. Kylie swept her hands through and it was perfect.

"That's amazing." I said, smiling at Kylie in the mirror.

"Do it again and this time you sort it out."

I did – and with gentle guidance, I achieved the same result.

"You've got lovely hair and it falls naturally into this style. After you swim or shower, if you let it dry naturally, you won't have a problem. Be careful of hair dryers as they will fluff it up – particularly in dry weather."

I shook again, running my hands through to settle my hair in place.

"Perfect." Kylie laughed. "Off you go and stun the boys."

My stomach clenched, but I kept my face neutral. I wanted to stun only one boy ... and each second, the subliminal thrum of the engines took me ever further from him. I wandered out on deck and stood, letting the wind of our passage riffle through my new hairstyle. Willi had been central to my life: everything in this new life highlighted the hole created by his absence. Losing myself in exercise and trying my hairstyle in the pool was an immediate priority. The pool was short and people swimming made it difficult, but I managed enough lengths to calm myself – somewhat.

Mutti was in our cabin after my swim. "Give me a twirl. Let me see your hair." It wasn't quite dry, but I rotated slowly. "Oh, *Liebling*." Mutti sighed. "You're growing up."

I glanced in the mirror and flicked some wayward strands into line.

Mutti patted the bed beside her. "Come on, Kal. We need to practice our identities again."

It was easy for me – she was still Mutti, but she had to remember to call me Kal. She went through meeting and marrying Sgt Miller in Frankfurt, but something felt wrong. I pulled out my notes in Polish to check.

Mutti gave me a surprised look. "What's that?"

"I made notes in the evenings in bed to help us remember." I explained.

Mutti laughed and took the exercise book from me, leafing through it. "Mrs Henderson would have your hide if she knew you'd done this."

I shrugged. "Did she expect us to remember all that information in two days? Anyway, there's nothing she can do about it now."

Mutti gave me a wary look. "We should burn this once we settle in Australia. We don't want someone finding it."

"Well, we'd better have things sorted out by the time we arrive." I frowned. "You got your wedding date wrong."

Mutti gave my book a hard look. "Hmm ...You wrote the correct date?"

"I think so."

She pulled our papers from a desk drawer. Flipping though she found her marriage certificate. "Well done. Your date is correct." Mutti paused. "We need to be careful about this. I don't think people would normally be letter perfect on everything the way we are trying to be. It might look suspicious."

I frowned. "Do you think so?"

"Yes, I do think so." Mutti returned my frown. "Once we've learnt everything and burn the book, our memories will start to slip and confuse things. After all, can you remember everything about Leipzig?"

I thought for a moment. "Probably not."

Mutti smiled. "Come on, let's take a walk round the deck before lunch and blow some cobwebs away."

· · · ·

WE ARRIVED IN FREMANTLE, Western Australia in late October and in warm sunshine, the start of the southern summer. From Fremantle, we skirted round the south coast of Australia to Adelaide, Melbourne and finally Sydney in early in November. From there, the ship was heading to New Zealand, which is why we had to fly to Brisbane.

Our trunks were unloaded and would travel up to Brisbane by train. We disembarked with our suitcase and hand luggage and went by bus to Sydney airport for the flight to Brisbane. I was nervous about flying and hoped I would manage better than Willi's friend Ginnie, who was air sick on their flight to Berlin. As we waited for our flight, I saw Mutti looked pale.

"Are you OK, Mutti?"

She looked at me, wetting her lips. "Are you nervous about flying?"

I gave her a wan smile. "I was thinking about Willi's friend, who was sick on the flight to Berlin, hoping I would fare better."

Mutti's half laugh sounded hollow. "I had forgotten about that."

"Willi always told me that flying is safer than going by car. We'll be fine."

Mutti pursed her lips in disbelief, which I shared; after all, we always heard about terrible air crashes.

After a brief wait, we boarded the plane and the flight was almost a disappointment. The acceleration on take-off startled us, but the view of the ground falling away from us was amazing. We lost that fascinating sight when we flew into cloud. The aircraft climbed and we burst into sunshine, the sudden glare from the cloud-tops blinding us. The brilliant white carpet obscured the earth and looked solid enough to walk on. We flew above this strange landscape most of the way to Brisbane.

The cloud broke up as we neared Brisbane. We could see the city with a river snaking through it as we descended: this was to be our home. A shiver of ... excitement? ... fear? ... slithered through me, accompanied by sadness;

I could not share these experiences with Willi and Lili – and we had shared everything.

Fortunately for our nerves, the landing was smooth. Once off the plane, we collected our big bag and joined the other two families from the ship on a bus to the Yungaba Immigration Centre. They gave us a room with two beds on the first floor, looking towards the river. Tea would be served soon and we went downstairs, sitting on the veranda to wait in the balmy air.

"Mrs Miller?"

"Yes?"

"I'm Margaret Rivers, a member of staff here." She smiled at me. "And you are..." she glanced down at a paper in her hand, "Karlota."

"Yes."

"Your house won't be ready for about a week, I'm afraid." She looked down at the paper again. "I see you have a position at McDonell & East, Mrs Miller. Do you know when they expect you to start?"

"Their letter said to go in once I arrived."

"Well, you can probably get there tomorrow or the day after." Mrs Rivers looked down at the paper and looked up at me, a surprised look on her face. "Karlota, it says here that you will go to Brisbane Girls Grammar School." She frowned at Mutti. "Is that correct?"

"That's right. We were wondering why there are school fees. In England grammar school is free..."

Mrs Rivers sat up in her chair. "Girls Grammar is the best girls' school in Queensland. It is a private school, not a state school. I don't know what the fees will be, but I can find out for you." She gave Mutti an appraising look. "It will be expensive ..."

Mutti smiled. "The fees are paid. My daughter has a scholarship from her late father's regiment."

Mrs Rivers looked askance. "I hope you are sufficiently prepared to take advantage of such an education."

Did I detect a hint of envy in her tone – or was it disbelief that a 'new Australian' would benefit from attending the school?

Mutti gave Mrs Rivers a gentle smile. "My daughter is doing well in all her subjects. She is quite capable of taking advantage of the education offered at this school – or any other."

The two women eyed one another.

"The school has requested that Kal and I visit them as soon as possible to determine where to place her. Is the school far from here?"

"It's north of the city. I'll get you a map of the tram and trolly bus system and show you where to go for the school and McDonell & East."

"Thank you. That would be most helpful."

A gong sounded, reminding me of Mrs Gittings in Lancaster.

"That's tea." Mrs Rivers pursed her lips. "It is expected that you will help clean up after tea."

Again, I heard something in her voice that I couldn't quite work out. Was she a touch supercilious?

Mutti smiled. "Of course."

As we sat eating lamb chops, beans and mashed potatoes, a woman leant over Mutti's shoulder, placing a tram and trolley bus map on the table. "I'm Janet. Mrs Rivers told me to give you this. I've marked McDonell & East and Girls Grammar on the map." She pointed to each one.

Mutti looked up. "Thank you, Janet." Mutti put the map in her handbag. "Can I use English money here in Australia?"

"Oh, I don't think so, though we use the same names for our money as in the old country. The main office can exchange some money for you in the morning, but after that, you'll need to visit a bank." Janet saw Mrs Rivers waving at her from across the room and hurried off.

Mutti and I looked at the map. Yungaba was in a suburb called Kangaroo Point, which made me smile. We could catch a trolley bus across the river into the city and trams to both McDonell & East and the school.

"Would you like to come with me tomorrow into the city to see where I'm going to work?"

"Yes, please." I wanted to explore my new home.

"I'll change some money at the office in the morning and see if we can phone your school to make an appointment to visit them."

After the meal, we helped with the clean-up, listening to the people and accents around us. They made friendly inquiries about where we were from as our accents were not yet English. Mutti explained we were from Lancaster and before that, Frankfurt. When she explained her English husband being killed in an accident, everyone expressed their sympathy and the questions immediately stopped, to my relief. I was feeling quite uncomfortable during this initial run of our fake lives.

When we were upstairs in our room, I wanted to talk about this with Mutti, but she quieted me with a shake of her head and pointed to her ears and the walls. This might not be a safe place to talk.

I lay in bed, uneasy about the concocted story of our lives. Something bothered me ... but I couldn't pin it down.

• • • •

AFTER BREAKFAST, MUTTI checked she had the documents we needed and changed some English pounds into Australian pounds; they looked similar – they had the English Queen on them. After she phoned the school, making an appointment to see the headmistress at two o'clock, we headed to the trolleybus stop. We crossed the river on a huge iron bridge that towered above us and changed to a tram to take us down to George Street and McDonell & East. The city basked in the sunshine, but the city lacked the older buildings I was used to seeing in Germany or England. Everything seemed recent without war damage. Lots of people were about, dressed for an English summer's day. It felt at least that warm and it was still spring.

We got off the tram at George Street and, after working out which way the numbers went, walked down until we came to the impressive McDonell & East building. Mutti pulled the letter from McDonnell & East from amongst the papers in her bag and we walked into the store and stood looking around.

"I suppose we'll need to ask someone how to find ..." she looked down at the letter, "Mr Chapman."

Mutti walked up to a make-up counter with a saleswoman behind it. "Excuse me, please could you tell me how I might find Mr Chapman?"

The saleswoman gave Mutti a quizzical look and Mutti proffered the letter.

The saleswoman scanned it and smiled. "Oh, wait a moment. I'll take you to his office."

She caught the eye of another saleswoman. "Janice, watch my counter for a minute, please. I'm taking this lady to see Mr Chapman." She turned to Mutti. "I'm Angelique. Please come with me."

I thought I heard a hint of a French accent before and she pronounced her name with a definite French accent. I thanked her in French.

Angelique turned, a surprised look on her face. She stared at me for a moment before asking me – in French – where I learned to speak French. After a brief conversation, she returned to English.

Angelique smiled. "You speak French well." She looked at Mutti. "She is your daughter?"

"Yes." I could hear the pride in her voice.

"I hope her school here will allow her to keep learning. I do not think there are many schools that teach French." Her voice sounded sad. "Come with me, please."

Angelique led us to the rear of the ground floor and through a door marked *Staff only*, up three floors in a lift and along a passage with office doors opening from it. She stopped at one and knocked on the open door.

"Mr Chapman? There's a Mrs Miller to see you."

A man behind a desk looked up. "Come in."

Angelique smiled and waved us into the office.

Mr Chapman stood as we entered. He was a middle-aged man, going bald on top but with an upright, military bearing.

"Please, have a seat." He pointed at two chairs and sat down once Mutti had seated herself. "How can I help you?"

Mutti offered him the letter on McDonell & East notepaper.

"Ah, yes. Mrs Miller." He stood up and pulled open a drawer in a filing cabinet, searching through for a moment. "Here we are." He pulled out a file.

He sat down again, opening the file in front of him.

"The immigration department sent me your details and we wrote to you about a possible job."

I saw Mutti stiffen at that. There had been no hint of the job being 'possible' in the letter.

Mr Chapman looked down at the file, turning pages to remind himself of its contents. "Hmm ... You certainly have experience suited for the women's clothing department." He looked up at me. "And this is your daughter..." he looked down at the file, "Karlota?"

"That's right."

"Hmm." He glanced down at the file again. "When did you arrive in Brisbane?"

"Yesterday."

Mr Chapman raised an eyebrow at that and turned a page in the file. He picked up another file from his desk, checking something.

"Well, we can offer you a position in the women's clothing department. Three month's trial and the starting salary is one hundred and seventy-six pounds a year, payable monthly, plus 2% commission on sales."

His speech was clipped, but he smiled at Mutti.

"Thank you."

"Can you start tomorrow? We're short staffed. Two of our ladies left last Friday to have babies."

"I could start tomorrow, I suppose. We're still in the migrant hostel at Yungaba for a week and we have to organise our house when we get one."

"We can give you a day or two's leave, unpaid of course, to get settled in your house when the time comes. Come and see me when you have a date."

He was about to reach for the phone when he stopped and looked at me. "When do you start school, Karlota?"

I was impressed. He remembered my name. "Not until January, sir."

"Hmm – would you be interested in working here until Christmas on our candy counter?"

I blinked and looked at Mutti.

She raised her eyebrows. "Would you like that, Kal?"

"It would be three days a week. We have strict rules about child labour." Mr Chapman smiled at Mutti before looking at me. "The pay is a ninepence an hour on weekdays and a shilling an hour on Saturdays."

"I'd like that, sir. Thank you."

"Excellent. We'll get you both organised to start tomorrow." He dialled a number, watching us with the phone to his ear. "Mary? I've two staff for you to organise ... yes, now ... Please come and collect them from my office."

He replaced the phone and smiled at us. "Miss Winterbotham will get you organised."

A minute later, a lady appeared in the doorway. Mr Chapman explained who we were and the positions we were to take. Miss Winterbotham whisked us around various offices, filling in forms, showing us the female staffroom, organising us a locker to share and two uniforms for me and three for Mutti. Finally, she took us to the clock-in station, putting our timecards in the appropriate alphabetical place.

"You both need to be here by eight o'clock tomorrow morning. Come to this rear entrance in Tank Street – the door is unlocked at half past seven every morning." She opened the door. "I'll be down to the ladies' staffroom shortly after eight to get you settled in." She waved us out and closed the door.

Mutti and I looked at one another, dazed at the speed with which things had happened. We walked down Tank Street to George Street and Mutti pulled out the tram map.

"We've time to call into the Commonwealth Bank and get that organised before we find somewhere to have lunch and head to your school."

The bank turned out to be a short walk, but it took Mutti half an hour to get things sorted out. I sat in the foyer, wishing I had brought a book. When Mutti reappeared from a side office, she presented me with a booklet.

"This is your passbook. You can deposit your wages in this now you have a job."

I opened it up to find she had deposited five shillings in it for me. "Thank you, Mutti," I smiled.

We found a café and had corned beef and pickle sandwiches for lunch. Then caught a tram to Gregory Terrace and walked down to Brisbane Girls Grammar School.

As we approached, we could see girls in navy blue skirts and white blouses in the grounds. When we walked through the gates, we stood looking around, lost as to where to go. A girl saw us standing there and came over.

"Can I help you?"

Mutti took out the letter from the school. "Yes please. We have an appointment with Mrs McDonald, the headmistress, at two o'clock."

"I can take you to her office. Please come with me."

She led us into the main building, past classrooms and into an office area.

"Please Miss, this lady has an appointment."

"Thank you, Denise."

The girl bobbed her head and left.

"You must be Mrs Miller and..." she looked down at the diary on her desk. "Karlota."

"Yes. We have an appointment with Mrs McDonald at two o'clock.

"Please have a seat. Mrs McDonald will be with you momentarily." She pointed at a leather couch.

Before we could sit, a short, dark-haired lady strode into the office, her eyes flicking towards us. "Mrs Miller and Karlota?"

"That's us."

"I'm the headmistress, Mrs McDonald." She held out her hand and Mutti shook it.

"Please come in and sit down."

Mrs McDonald swept behind her desk and sat down. She was an imposing lady, diminishing my confidence as she focused her gaze on me.

"Come, come. Sit down."

We sat on the chairs in front of the desk whilst Mrs McDonald opened a file.

She fixed me with her gaze. "I have your report from Lancaster Grammar School, Karlota. Your teachers speak highly of your language skills."

I swallowed. Mrs Henderson had been busy, it would seem. I had learned my supposed teacher's names from my package.

"Hmm...what 'O' levels would you have taken, do you know?"

"Ummm, in a year's time ... I suppose English language and literature, French, Maths, History, Geography and general Science." I tried to summon some saliva into my dry mouth.

"Do remember any of your German?"

I blinked, surprised to be asked this. "Of course."

Mrs McDonald looked over her glasses. "Unfortunately, we do not offer that language here."

Mrs McDonald looked at Mutti. "Our third form will do their end-of-year tests in two weeks. It would help us place Karlota if she could sit the English and Maths exams with them. Would that be acceptable?"

Mutti looked at me, raising her eyebrows in question.

I shrank into my chair, thanking Mutti in my head for not letting me slack off my schoolwork whilst we were in Lancaster and on the boat. I looked up at Mrs McDonald.

"Would you mind doing that, Karlota? Just the English language and Maths exams?"

I glanced at Mutti, who leant forward.

"Karlota has a job on the candy counter at McDonell & East, starting tomorrow morning." Mutti glanced at me. "Sitting the tests may need to work around that."

Mrs McDonald stood up. "A moment, please." She walked to the door and spoke to her secretary and returned to her desk.

"That's forward of you to find yourself some work, Karlota. Well done." She looked down at the file again. "What sports do you like?"

"I swim ... and run, but I couldn't do them properly on the boat."

"We don't have our own swimming pool. We use the Boy's Grammar pool by arrangement. I'm sure our PE staff will soon sort you out."

Mrs McDonald looked up at a tap at the door and her secretary gave her a sheet of paper.

"Hmm. Third form English is on Thursday 26th in the afternoon and Maths the day after in the morning. Do you think you can manage those dates?"

I looked at Mutti.

"We'll talk to her employer, but I expect that will be acceptable."

Mrs McDonald scribbled the information on a sheet of notepaper, handing it to Mutti. "I see the fees are to be billed to your late husband's regiment, Mrs Miller. But you will need to buy uniforms." She stood up. "Please let my secretary know about the English and Maths exams. We can always have Karlota sit them out of class if there's a problem."

She ushered us out and her secretary waylaid a passing student to guide us back to the gate.

On Gregory Terrace, we caught a tram into the city and walked to Yungaba. The city was clean and neat, but young compared to cities in east Germany and England. By the time we reached the immigration centre we were hot and sweaty: it wasn't the temperature, although it was hotter than England, but the humidity. It made me wonder about swimming. Was there a pool I could get to? The thought of running in this heat and humidity wasn't attractive.

As we walked into Yungaba, Mrs Rivers appeared from the office. "You look hot, Mrs Miller – you'll both want to get wide-brimmed hats to keep the sun off." She seemed friendlier today.

Mutti pulled off her English hat and fanned her face with it. "I saw some ladies wearing gloves in the city. I don't know how they could."

Mrs Rivers chuckled. "You'll get used to the heat – and most women in Brisbane have given up on gloves now." She looked through the open door at the bright sunshine splashing on the front steps. "It doesn't get much hotter than this, but the humidity can be high in the afternoons later in summer. Then we get a thunderstorm which cools things down, at least for a while."

She turned to walk away.

"Please Mrs Rivers, is there a swimming pool I can use in Brisbane?" I asked.

"Of course. There's the Valley Pool in Wickham Street. I'll see if I can find out when it's open for general swimming."

"Thank you."

We headed upstairs to our room, which felt like an oven when we walked inside.

"We need to remember to leave the window open." Mutti gasped, pushing it open. She sat on her bed and pulled out the information from the school; after a moment, she chuckled. "The place to get your uniform is ... McDonell & East."

I smiled. "That will make it easy."

Mutti fanned herself with the papers. "Let's have a cooling bath and sit out on the veranda until teatime."

Chapter 4

October – early December 1964

We were up and left the immigration centre early in the morning, arriving at McDonnell & East in plenty of time. Once we'd changed into our uniforms, we waited in the women's staff room for Mary Winterbotham. A bustle of people arrived and some realised we were new and introduced themselves. Most gave us a quick glance and went about their business, not unfriendly, but busy. Mary arrived a few minutes before eight o'clock with an older teenager in tow.

"Karlota, Victoria here will show you the ropes on the Candy Counter." She turned to Victoria. "Take Karlota to clock-in, Victoria."

"Come along." Victoria turned and walked out. I gave Mutti a quick wave as I left. Victoria walked fast and I scurried to keep up.

We clocked-in and she led me through the ground floor of the shop to the Candy Counter. Once there, I helped her restock the shelves and fill the glass jars with the correct boiled sweets. Victoria pointed out the prices and register category as we went. Near the end of that task, a loud bell rang.

I raised an eyebrow in question as I replaced the lid on the jar of Lemon Drops.

"That's the ten-minute warning – doors open in ten minutes." Victoria told me.

A minute later, a lady appeared at our counter and placed a tray on it, calling out to Victoria. "Cash drawer."

"Thank you, Miss Jones." Victoria signed the sheet and slid the drawer into the cash register. "This has our float in it. They'll come round and collect the drawer and register roll at the end of the day." She pointed to the paper roll on which the register recorded every transaction.

As it was a weekday, trade at the Candy Counter was slow. This gave Victoria time to show me the subtleties of the cash register, which sweets went against which category on the register. As we worked, she thawed and we exchanged stories. My fake background slid from my tongue and caused no comment, despite my unease.

Would that fade with time?

Victoria had left school at sixteen the previous December and had worked at the Candy Counter since then. She wanted to move to Ladies Fashion; I didn't tell her that Mutti was working there.

Mary Winterbotham came round about halfway through the morning. "Here's your roster, Karlota. You're working Tuesday afternoons along with Thursday mornings and Saturday mornings." She handed me a printed form with my shifts written in. "Mornings you clock in by half-past eight and for the afternoons by a quarter past twelve."

"Thank you, Miss Winterbotham."

"Everything going OK, Victoria?"

"Yes. Kal's catching on well." Victoria gave me an encouraging look. I smothered my relief – she'd been guarded until now.

Miss Winterbotham headed off.

We had no customers and Victoria leant against the counter, checking her lipstick in a compact mirror from her handbag. "Why aren't you starting school until next year?"

I shrugged. "The school year in England finished in July and started in September as we were about to come here. Your school year is about to finish and starts again in January. I have to wait for it."

Victoria was no longer concerned with school, but I added, "Anyway, I'm taking an English and a Maths test soon, to put me in the right class."

"Oh." Disinterest washed through her voice.

Victoria pursed her lips to spread the lipstick and checked in the mirror again. "Have you started wearing makeup yet?"

"No ..." I corrected myself. "Well, last Christmas Eve, Mutti helped me with a little lipstick and blush when my boyfriend came for a special meal."

"Ooh. You have a boyfriend?" Victoria's interest perked up.

"Had ... he's in England and I'm here." I heard my voice crack.

Victoria didn't seem to notice and snapped her compact shut. "Never mind, there's lots of nice boys here. I can fix you up with someone."

Her off-hand comment slammed into me and I turned away, trying to prevent a collapse into tears. After a moment, her hand squeezed my shoulder. "I'm sorry Kal."

I leant on the counter before turning, blinking to control incipient tears.

Victoria searched my face. "It was serious?" I heard the empathy.

Had her heart been broken, too?

My shoulders slumped as tears started down my cheeks. "It still is."

"Oh, dear." The hand squeezed my shoulder.

"I'm sorry." I sniffed. "I thought I had control of it … b … but I don't."

Victoria made an apologetic face. "Here," she produced a hanky from her handbag. "I'll be okay by myself for five minutes. Go to the toilet and sort yourself out."

I sniffed and slipped out through the staff door. In the toilet, I washed my face and stared into my mirrored reflection, stifling the churning inside me. I leant on the handbasin and closed my eyes.

This is hard.

My anguished reaction to Victoria's statement had surprised me – had all but overwhelmed me. I couldn't keep falling apart like this.

The outer door banged: someone else was coming in. I ran my hand through my hair, blew my nose, straightened my uniform and headed to the Candy Counter.

Victoria gave me a caring smile. "Better?"

"Yes, thank you."

Victoria turned away to serve a customer. Once she'd finished, she turned to me. "Want to talk about it?"

Do I want to share something precious and deep with someone I barely know?

I shook my head, but realised I was being hard. She'd reached out to me. "Not right now."

Victoria's lips thinned. We were subdued for the rest of my shift.

My relief arrived before my shift ended and Victoria introduced me to Carol before shooing me off to clock out. Once I had done that and changed, I headed into the store to find Mutti in Ladies Fashion.

She was busy with a customer helping her choose a blouse, but I caught her eye. After about five minutes, she wrapped one up, placing it in a McDonnell & East bag. She rang up the sale and the lady walked off, swinging the bag.

"Finished for the day?" Mutti asked.

"Yes. Can I go to the Valley Baths and find the times I can swim there?"

"OK. You'd better have some money for trams. My purse is in our locker. Take two shillings. I'll see you at Yungaba for tea."

"Thanks, Mutti." At our locker, I raided Mutti's purse and checked the tram map. If I walked down George Street to Adelaide Street, I could catch a 60, 70 or 71 that would go past the Valley Baths.

When I got to the pool, I stood and gaped: an Olympic 50-meter pool – I could do proper lengths. That hadn't been possible since Leipzig. I checked the times with a smile on my face. General swimming happened from 5 to 8 in the morning and 3 to 6 in the afternoon on weekdays; entry was thruppence for each session. I'd have a talk with Mutti this evening about going three times a week – or maybe more. I didn't think I could run in this heat. Whilst I was earning, I could afford that, but once school started, it would be difficult. I sighed; in Leipzig entry to the pool had been free. Could I work some hours on the Candy Counter once I started school?

Walking between the pool and the school would happen often. I decided to see how long it would take, as I couldn't afford to be paying for trams all the time. The person in the pool kiosk directed me to Gregory Terrace and I set off. It turned out to be a reasonable walk. From a student at the school gate, I got directions to McDonnell & East, but got lost. I confused myself thinking the sun would be south of me in the sky, but of course it's north in the southern hemisphere. I had to ask for directions again. Once outside McDonnell & East, I walked to Yungaba.

The reaction I'd had to Victoria's off-hand remark had been muttering at me from deep in my thoughts as I walked through the city. Cooling down in the bath, I tried to make sense of my feelings about Willi now we were far apart – and likely to remain apart for quite some time.

Not forever ... don't even think that.

My attachment to Willi was an unfamiliar experience. Before I met Willi, I had no friends: my father was *Stasi*, a secret policeman. That threat kept people distant in east Germany. Then Mutti discovered my father was a Nazi war criminal and we defected from east Germany to escape from him. When I met Willi, he was troubled to the point of attempted suicide because of his abusive father. Somehow, sharing our fear of our fathers and a deep, mutual craving for companionship pushed us together. This energised our language lessons into friendship. From there, our shared curiosity propelled our learning and drew in Lili.

Willi's suicidal tendencies scared me to the core – and my shame at goading him to get on with it under the cedar tree still burned. But that scare had driven us closer and we had revealed our dangerous secrets. For him, I sloughed off the deception of being a boy and our relationship changed and deepened.

Then Willi revealed his unbelievable story and his composite nature ... a seventy-year-old mind from some other future in a twelve-year-old body.

That afternoon, I had branded him a pervert and chased him away.

I sank down into the bath, letting the water surge over my face, trying to cool the blaze of shame. After about half a minute, I sat up and leant forward on my knees, gasping for breath. Somehow, he forgave me and we drew closer. I took another deep breath and blew it out, scattering mingled drops of water and tears. Our separation was an open wound, scoured by my tears.

Controlling my emotions had been difficult in Lancaster, but there I had hoped we could reunite. Now our separation measured half a world and shrouding our future in uncertainty. We had shared everything and now I had much to share – and I couldn't even write to him.

How do I live with this constant ache? How do you forget someone who is as integral to you as ... as your hands? How to un-love someone?

I sat bathed in the cool water and yet scalding in frustration at what had happened to us.

"Hey. You gonna be in there all day?"

It jerked me out of my fugue of misery. I was sitting on the veranda when Mutti walked up, perspiration almost dripping from her. She paused beside my chair, fanning herself with her hat.

"How did you go to the swimming pool?"

I roused myself, trying to smile. "It's an outdoor Olympic pool. They have public sessions every morning and afternoon for thruppence."

"And?" She gave me a sympathetic smile, sensing my downbeat mood.

I tried to put my despondency over Willi to one side. "Well, I was thinking of going three times a week, like in Lancaster. I walked from the pool to the school and to here. We can't afford trams and trolley buses all the time and besides, the walking is exercise: hot, but exercise."

"Well, we'll have to see where we are living, but for now, that seems OK."

I summoned a morsel of enthusiasm. "I'll go tomorrow afternoon?"

"Okay." Mutti wiped some sweat from her brow.

"Why don't you have a cool bath? There's time before tea."

"Good idea." And Mutti headed inside.

I sat on the veranda, surveying the different trees along the riverbank. Australian trees – eucalypts – seemed disorganised and scruffy compared to European trees. Bark hung off some and others had new leaves growing and falling off without respect for the season. Amongst them were other trees, lacking leaves but covered with profuse purple blossom. Every day, I was seeing things I wanted to share with Willi, things I wanted to talk over with him. He had lived somewhere in Australia for decades during his old life, but we'd never talked about Australia. After the cedar tree incident, when we had come close to disaster, he hadn't blinked when I suggested 'Gundagai' as our 'stop everything and talk about it' word. I sighed at the memory. Gundagai is a town in New South Wales, mentioned in a song my geography teacher played to us.

I could feel my mood spiralling down, but the gong went for tea. I stood up as Mutti came downstairs and we went into the dining room. As we sat there, Mutti produced a note from Mrs Rivers someone had slipped under our door.

"It seems like our house will be ready this weekend, after all. Would you like to come and inspect it with me tomorrow evening?"

"Yes, please. Shall I meet you at McDonnell & East?"

"I'll ring the agent tomorrow morning and confirm the time. If you come up to Ladies Fashion by five o'clock, we can both go. I'll let Mrs Rivers know we may be out for tea tomorrow."

"Okay."

When Mutti arrived in our room after speaking with Mrs Rivers, she had a flyer about the German Club in her hand, which she handed to me.

I read through it. "Are we going to join?"

Mutti shook her head. "I'd like to, for your sake, to keep up your connection with our culture, but don't think we can. There will be people there who know Frankfurt and I don't, though I'm supposed to be from there. Our story would be uncovered as a lie and we can't risk that."

We'd have to keep our German going between the two of us as we worked on all our languages – but I ached to be sharing them with Willi and Lili.

The following morning, carrying my duffel bag with lunch and swimming things, I walked down to the German Club in Vulture Street and stood opposite. A surge of longing, of wanting to be part of something, to belong somewhere, ran through me. But belonging to anything was going to be difficult.

Walking towards the city, I found a German butcher and a bakery. It had *Schwarzbrot*, Mutti's favourite dark rye bread – something to remember when we got our own house. I walked into the city and wandered around. For my sanity, I needed this place to be my home – but my heart was telling me something different with each beat. For all its sunshine and welcoming, open nature, I hated Australia.

No, Col. Not hatred ...

Mutti had taught me the dangers of hatred. I gusted out a deep breath. I resented Australia even though I was here to be safe from the killers my father would send after us.

But I longed to walk round to Willi's house in the morning and meet up with Lili on the bus to school and chat in our various languages and do that again on the way home; to sit in Mrs Wisniewski's kitchen, the three of us working on our homework in the day's language. I ached to sit with Willi, wrapped in blankets against the winter as we read and read and read. I yearned to snuggle and explore our feelings, as we had on those few delicious, dangerous occasions after Willi returned from east Germany.

And all these were barred to me.

A clock tower striking one roused me; I'd been walking on autopilot and I found myself outside the City Hall. I sat for a while, watching people flow around me. Their joys and sorrows carried past without touching me.

After a while, I pulled out the sandwiches I had made in the Yungaba kitchen after breakfast. As I finished, I saw a sign advertising the City Library on the noticeboard. I went over to read it: the main library was in William Street, towards the Botanic Gardens.

Make the effort to like this place, Col.

I put the library and Gardens on my mental exploration list. But today was for swimming.

I was at the pool before three o'clock and changed in time to swim as soon as the school students were chased from the pool. The water soothed and I lost myself in the extended rhythm of 50-meter lengths, which hadn't been possible since we fled from Leipzig. I did two sessions of about thirty minutes with a break between them, pushing myself for the last couple of lengths each time. I left the pool tired but less anxious. The rhythmic exercise helped me deal with the separation from Willi. And I wondered how he was coping. He still had Lili – and a spike of jealousy pinned me to the hot pavement.

Would Lili try to move in on Willi now I am not there?

I could see frowns as people sidestepped around me. I dropped my head and started walking again, thinking about Willi and Lili. Lili was a beautiful, talented girl.

How would Willi react if Lili makes a move on him?

She had wanted me as a boyfriend when she thought I was a boy and she had joked about me stealing Willi, the second-best boyfriend (after me) when I revealed I was a girl. But not once had I thought that she could envy me with Willi. I had asked Lili to watch Willi's moods and let me know if they darkened. I had skirted the issue of suicide, but Lili could have realised what I was not saying. My disappearance would have hit Willi hard, throwing them together; he would need support that caring, generous Lili would provide.

They are my close friends. How would I feel if they become a couple?

A confusion of emotions propelled me to Yungaba. Willi would need Lili's support, but ...

• • • •

THE PREVIOUS DAY'S emotional confusion was still with me when we met the agent to inspect our potential house, a modern version of a style referred to as a Queenslander. This meant a single storey, weatherboard house on concrete stilts with shaded verandas. To a European, it seemed an odd design, but all the houses around were the same. The agent explained it allowed the air to flow above, below, around and through during the hot summer months. I wondered what weather was to come if we were still awaiting the hot weather.

The sight of the concrete stilts caused a memory to bubble up from Russian children's tales I'd heard in Leipzig. "It's Baba Yaga's house on chicken legs, Mutti."

Mutti laughed. "Which Baba Yaga am I – the good Baba Yaga or the wicked one?"

"Oh, Mutti." I summoned a smile. "You're the friendly one, rescuing people and animals lost in the forest."

The agent stood there, bemused by the strange culture of these new Australians. She shrugged and turned us towards the house. We climbed the stairs to the front door, which greeted us with a blast of hot air on opening. The agent opened windows and doors and the evening breeze blew through the house, demonstrating the reason for this strange design as it cooled.

According to the agent, this was a standard Housing Commission house – three bedrooms, lounge room, bathroom, toilet, kitchen. We were lucky as this area already had sewerage, which was not the case yet for all the suburbs.

"What do you mean?" I could hear the surprise in Mutti's voice.

"Not all the suburbs are on the sewer system – at least not yet. They have dunnies – outdoor toilets," she added as she saw our puzzled looks.

In the capital city of Queensland, there are houses without indoor toilets?

We walked round the house, opening cupboards and drawers. Everything seemed clean and in good order, although the house was not new.

"What do you think, Kal?"

I shrugged. "It's fine." I didn't care where we lived in Australia, as I didn't want to be here. This house was bigger than the one we had in Herne

Bay and both differed from the Leipzig apartment. But the Herne Bay house was home; though we'd lived there for less than two years: it held all my dearest memories.

Mutti held my eyes for a second – she must have sensed my mood. I looked away and Mutti turned to the agent to fill out the paperwork. I wandered down the back steps into the garden as the light in the sky faded. The land sloped: the rear of the house was a meter off the ground, but most of the house was high enough to walk under. Beneath the house was a dim forest of concrete stumps, screened from the road by bushes in front of the house. As I walked amongst the bare concrete trunks towards the front of the house, the bushes growled, chittered and shook with violence. I dashed out and round to the veranda.

"Mutti, Mutti. There's a wild animal in the bushes in front of the house."

The agent listened for a moment. "Oh, that's possums having a domestic."

Mutti and I exchanged a glance. "Possums?"

The agent chuckled. "Umm ...like large squirrels? They won't hurt you – unless you corner them. They'll try to climb you like a tree – and their claws are sharp." She listened as the growling and chittering died down. "Out here you'll get wildlife – mostly possums, but there's koalas around in the trees and wallabies some mornings on the playing fields. Koalas mostly sleep, though."

They finished up the paperwork and Mutti wrote a cheque for the month's rent. We walked round, closing the house. Out on the veranda, the agent paused, glancing around.

"You'll need to watch out for redbacks under the house and there could be snakes around as well."

"What's a redback?" Mutti asked, a nervous tone in her voice.

"They're black spiders with a splash of red on their back. They won't kill you – well, they haven't killed anyone yet, not like the Sydney funnel webs. But a bite can make a kid quite sick."

Spiders I thought I could handle. "Snakes?"

"Well – around here you'll get carpet pythons – they're big, six feet or more. They can bite if you scare them – but they're not venomous. Mind you, they'll eat a small dog – or a child."

I swallowed at that thought.

"It's the red bellied blacks and the browns that are dangerous." The agent gave me a comforting smile. "But not to worry – we've got anti-venom for all the snakes now. Get to the hospital fast enough and you'll be fine." From her face, she wasn't joking about that.

Mutti's eyes were as wide as mine. I was getting the feeling that this was a different sort of country from Europe.

The agent chuckled at our reaction. "Most snakes run from you if you're noisy. Anyway, don't wander down by the creek unless you're wearing boots and long daks – er ... long pants ... as that's where the snakes like to go when it's hot."

As we walked down the front steps behind the agent, I found my eyes scanning the ground below.

At the foot of the stairs, the agent turned to Mutti. "You need a lift into the city?"

"Thank you, that would be most kind."

We climbed into her Holden station wagon and she dropped us off outside Yungaba. We were in time for tea, after all. After the clean-up, Mutti and I sat and talked about what we'd need to organise for the house. By the time we'd made a list, I was getting worried.

"Can we afford all this, Mutti?"

Mutti reassured me with a smile. "When your father was killed, we received a payout from the army; we have enough to equip a house." She winked. "And I think I can get a staff discount at McDonnell & East."

Mrs Henderson, or someone in MI6, had been more generous than I expected.

"Okay."

"I'll start getting this organised tomorrow during my lunch break and see if we can move in over the weekend.

Mutti went through McDonnell & East on a whirlwind buying mission. Once Mr Chapman heard she was setting up a house from scratch, he took her down into the damaged furniture storeroom. Mutti acquired our beds, a chest of drawers each, a sofa, fridge, kitchen table and chairs at a substantial discount. The store truck would deliver these on Saturday morning. Mutti also organised enough sheets, towels, crockery, saucepans and such to get us started and they would come out with the furniture as well.

We arranged to be off shift for Saturday. We packed up at Yungaba, said our goodbyes to Mrs Rivers and headed up to our house in Kedron by tram early in the morning, hauling our suitcase and three bags with us. By the end of the day, we had a house. A bit basic, but that evening we showered in our own bathroom before cooking our tea. Mutti had bought lamb chops from the line of shops round the corner in Leckie Road. Tonight, we would sleep in our own beds in our own house for the first time since April.

Lying in bed that night, I realised that, in spite of my misery at separation from Willi and the threat of spiders and snakes, Brisbane felt safe. In Herne Bay, I always felt that father's eyes were out there, seeking us. Underneath Willi's — and later Lili's — friendship existed a thread of fear in my life. Sometimes that thread was imperceptible in the warp and weft of my life. Yet it could also be a coarse, dark line threatening to wreck the careful weave we were making. Somewhere on the oceans we crossed to reach Australia, that thread had thinned to gossamer. But I yearned to be in Herne Bay despite its tinnitus of fear.

I was safer because Europe and its troubles were half a world away. But the care with which MI6 had constructed our lives engendered a part of my feeling. I did not like Mrs Henderson and her cold-hearted, abusive attitude, but her organisation had done well for us, and been generous too. The money Mutti was using for the house and my scholarship were evidence of that. I drifted off to sleep, with images of Will and Lili flickering through my dreams.

On the following Tuesday, our trunks arrived, and we spent an evening unpacking them. We needed a bookcase — I still had my schoolbooks from Canterbury — and a wardrobe in each bedroom for clothes. After another visit to the damaged furniture storeroom, two wardrobes, a bookcase and a desk arrived on Friday morning before I left for the pool.

With my schoolbooks here, Mutti insisted we restart school – hence the desk which we set up in the third bedroom. Mutti declared that each day would be a different language at our house and we rotated through English, German, Polish, French and Russian. I had used Willi's books for Latin and it had to drop by the wayside. Now we had a home address, we could join the library with its foreign language collection. We didn't want to advertise that we spoke Russian, but I asked about Polish books. The librarian told me that the Polish club in Milton had a library: another place for an excursion.

We established a rhythm to our lives, with both of us working at McDonnell & East and me swimming as often as I could. The exercise worked to soothe my pining and those occasional pangs of jealousy threatening my thoughts.

I went into the school and took the Maths and English exams, getting some curious glances from the third form girls. These would be the girls I would be with for the rest of my education and I offered them a wary smile.

The house on one side of us was empty, but on the other there lived an Italian family with two small children. The mother's English was almost non-existent and when the father discovered we were German and not English, the atmosphere chilled. I wished I could explain that Mutti had been a prisoner of the Nazis, not a supporter, but that was impossible. A low wire mesh strung on star pickets marked the border between our properties. The backyard next door was half grass and half cultivated, with a riot of things growing in neat rows. I recognised tomatoes but nothing else. I had seen the man of the house working in the vegetable patch – studiously avoiding us if we went outside.

As I took a bag of rubbish out to the bin one morning, the two children were playing in the grass alone.

The girl, about five years old, looked up at me. "Hello."

I replaced the dustbin lid and walked over to the fence, smiling. "Hello."

"I'm Calista and this is my little brother, Giorgio. What's your name?" By this time, she had walked up to the low fence between us – quite self-assured. Her English was surprising, as I had only ever heard the family speak Italian.

"I'm Karlota. But you can call me Kal."

The girl gave the fence a shake, frowning. "No, that's my name."

I crouched down to put us at the same height. "Well, can we share a name?"

Calista paused, thinking about this. "All right," she conceded. By now, her brother was taking an interest and wandered over to hide behind his big sister, his nappy drooping.

Calista's face took on a serious mien. "Our father says you are nasty Germans."

I rocked on my heels. Had he meant a Nazi German? "Well, I'm half-English." How easily the lie slipped from my tongue, although accompanied by a stab of discomfort.

"You're not a nasty German?"

"No." That was the truth.

Their mother walked onto their veranda, calling out in Italian to the children. Calista smiled and turned towards her mother, calling out something in Italian and pointing to me.

I saw the mother blush beneath her dark hair. She walked across, flustered by what her daughter had said. She seemed young to have a child as old as Calista.

"*Scusi* ... I ... sorry." She frowned down at her daughter. "You not ... *tedesca* ...German?" Her accent was strong and her English limited.

I smiled. "I'm half-English."

She cocked her head, as if to understand more.

"My mother is German, but my father was English." I spoke slowly.

"*Inglese?*"

I scratched around for words. "Father...umm ... *padre?*"

"*Si, padre...*" She smiled in encouragement.

"*Padre inglese.*"

"Ah." She smiled in understanding. "*E tua madre?*"

Context is a wonderful teacher. What was it she had said before ... *tedesca*, that was it.

"*Madre tedesca*...German."

Calista was watching our stumbling conversation with some frustration. She pulled at her mother's skirt. "*Anche lei si chiama Cal.*"

The mother frowned, puzzled. "You Cal?"

I pointed to myself. "Karlota...Kal."

"Ahh." She pointed to herself, her daughter and son. "*Signora Greco... Ginevra Greco, Calista e Giorgio.*" She pointed at her house. "*Mio marito si chiama Carlo ... Carlo Greco.*"

Hmm, *maritus* was Latin for husband. "*Marito ... mari ...* husband?"

"*Si, marito ...* 'usband?"

"Husband." I emphasised the 'h'.

She shrugged. "*E tua madre?*"

Hmmm. I wondered how many mistakes were in this attempt as I assembled it. "*Mia madre ... chiamo ... Frida Miller.*"

Mrs Greco laughed, correcting me. "*Mia madre si chiama Frida...,*" her eyes became thoughtful. "*Stai imparando l'italiano ...* you ... learn ... *l'italiano ...* er...?"

Learn another language?

I smiled and shrugged.

Cal tugged at Mrs Greco's skirt. "*Mamma, Giorgio puzza.*"

Mrs Greco leant down, inspecting her son's droopy nappy. She laughed, wrinkling her nose at the smell. "*Si, Cal. Giorgio puzza.*" She smiled at me. "I go ..." She shook her head, lacking the words and gestured at her son.

"To change your son's nappy." I smiled, trying to mime actions to my words. I'd changed nappies as a *Thälmannpioneer*, helping in an orphanage in Leipzig as part of my service to society.

Mrs Greco smiled, nodding her head again. "I go...*addio.*" She picked up Giorgio and took Cal's hand, walking into the house.

I wondered if relations might thaw between us now. We Germans had a terrible reputation amongst the European nations. Mussolini's fascist Italy had been an ally of the Nazis until the people tossed him out. But then the Nazis took over and were brutal.

I had tea ready for Mutti when she arrived. We sat down to eat once she'd had a wash and freshened up and I told her about the Greco family. We were finishing when we heard a car pull up and a door slam, followed by the sound of footsteps on our front stairs and a rap on the screen door.

Mutti raised a querying eyebrow. I shrugged and went to the door, turning on the outside light. A youngish man in a shirt and tie was standing there, about to rap on the screen door again.

He studied me for a second. "Umm ... Karlota Miller? Is your mother home?"

My stomach flipped as I realised that he somehow knew my name. I turned to find Mutti arriving beside me and a reassuring hand landed on my shoulder.

She studied the man for a second. "I'm Karlota's mother."

The man looked past me. "Mrs Miller. A mutual friend asked me to call on you."

I could see Mutti tensing – what mutual friend?

"Who would that be?" Mutti's voice sounded suspicious.

"Mrs Henderson, from England, asked me to get in touch when you'd settled in."

Mutti and I stood in silence before I remembered. "Mutti, you asked Mrs Henderson about this."

The man's eyes travelled between us. "Can I come in? Discussing things here on the veranda is difficult."

Mutti leant past me and opened the door, allowing the man to walk in. With the increased light inside, I realised he wasn't as young as I thought, with blond hair above a face that showed some lines about his eyes.

I went to the table and gathered up the dishes, stacking them beside the sink. Mutti turned up the radio and gestured to the man. We all sat at the table.

The man frowned at Mutti. "Please send your daughter to her room."

Mutti snorted but kept her voice low. "Mrs Henderson didn't brief you well if you think that's going to happen. Kal is involved in all of this."

His eyes flicked over me and he gave Mutti a long stare. "Very well. I'm ... Mr Carlson."

I heard the faint pause before he gave his name. Was it false, as we suspected was the case with Mr Watling, Mutti's MI6 contact in England?

"Good evening, Mr Carlson. What can we do for you?" Mutti's voice was cold. Our encounters with Mrs Henderson had not been pleasant and those emotions were feeding into this meeting.

Mr Carlson cleared his throat. "Well ... er ... I work for ASIO, the Australian government department equivalent to MI6 in England. We've been asked by our friends in England to get in touch and provide you with a contact if you feel threatened." He produced a piece of card from his pocket and wrote his name and a phone number on it.

"This is how you can get in touch with me." He passed the card to Mutti.

She examined the card. "That's not going to help as we don't have a phone yet. I have asked for it to be installed, but they told us it will be two months, at least."

"Is there a phone box around here?"

"The closest is about ten minutes' walk."

"Oh."

Mutti stared at him, pointedly. "MI6 could make things happen faster in England."

Mr Carlson looked at her for a second or two. "Oh ... hmmm." He lapsed into silence.

Mutti and I sat there staring at him and he shifted in his chair.

"Ummm ... well, that's all." He stood up. "Get in touch if you need to."

Mutti and I escorted him to the door.

At the door, he stopped and turned. "Oh, if anyone asks who I was, tell them I'm from the Immigration department, talking about English Language classes." He reached into his pocket and pulled out a crumpled leaflet, which he handed to Mutti.

Mutti opened the door and watched Mr Carlson down the steps to his car. Once she'd closed and locked the front door, she turned to me. "He did not inspire me with a great sense of confidence."

"No. He almost forgot his cover story."

Mutti pulled a face. "I suppose I could ring this number and ask to speak to his superior ... but I think it's wiser to ring him and test the system."

If we complained about him and he got into trouble, that might work against us if we needed assistance. Mr Carlson's visit had left me feel more vulnerable.

Through November into December, the weather continued to warm up. Once or twice a week, there would be an afternoon thunderstorm with accompanying lightning and occasional hail. The storms cooled things down, but the temperature and humidity would build up over the following days until another thunderstorm happened. Neither Mutti nor

I were used to this and took to wearing light clothes in the evening once we got home. I would have liked to sit outside on the veranda, but the mosquitos were savage. Most of Queensland was Malaria-free and Australia had an eradication program. Being feasted on by mossies (Australians seemed to shorten every word they can) was unpleasant at the time and itchy afterwards – as Mutti and I discovered. Thank goodness the fly screens stopped the mossies entering the house.

Mutti talked with a colleague at McDonnell & East, who told her to buy some mosquito coils; these smouldered for over an hour, discouraging the mosquitoes. We picked some at the local shop and they worked well if there wasn't a breeze.

As the woman had spent some time in Malaya, she described the Malayan sarongs she wore at home in the hot weather. Mutti made us two each from lengths of light cotton fabric. Sarongs are fabric tubes held up by rolling them above the breasts like a towel, coming down to below the knees. They were cooler when you didn't wear anything underneath. I sighed with longing: Willi and I would both enjoy exploring this mode of dress. I did some research in the library one afternoon after swimming and Malayan men wore these as well, but wrapped at the waist, which was food for dreams. With Willi half a world away, dreams of being close to him were all I had.

We received a letter from the school placing me into form 4A to start on Wednesday, 27th January. With it came a list of the uniform and supplies they expected me to have. Mutti asked the women in Ladies Fashion about buying the uniforms. She was told to wait until after Christmas as that's when the uniform stock would arrive, but to get in early as popular sizes frequently ran out.

As we moved into December, McDonnell & East put on its Christmas finery, which felt odd. For me, Christmas was associated with wintry weather and snow – not heat, humidity and thunderstorms. Trade on the Candy Counter picked up and our displays all switched to Christmas fare – candy canes, Turkish Delight, net bags of chocolate coins in gold foil, special Christmas boxes, tins of chocolates and shortbread. Saturday mornings were a particular rush and needed three of us on the counter at a time to cope. This meant some extra shifts for me and I was there for three afternoons. Whilst this meant a pay increase and I could travel home with Mutti, it cut into my swimming time. I wondered about going to the pool for the early morning sessions, but never got round to it.

One evening, as we walked down to the tram stop after leaving the store, Mr Carlson walked up to us. From the frown he gave me, he was not expecting me.

"Please come with me." His voice was curt.

Mutti gave me a questioning look and I shrugged. We followed Mr Carlson up Tank Street, where a large car pulled up beside us.

"Get in, please."

I looked at Mutti and she gave me a fractional shake in return. "I think not, Mr Carlson. Our experience of entering cars with people we don't know has been poor."

Both Mutti and I stepped away from the curb and Mr Carlson stood there, looking rather lost. The front passenger door of the car swung open and another, older man got out.

"Get them in the car." The voice sounded frustrated rather than commanding.

Mutti and I stood with our backs to the building behind us. My stomach was clenching and it felt like it would soon churn. I was ready to scream for help.

"They won't get in, sir."

The man looked at us and realised we were close to running, yelling for help, or both – which would call attention to the two of them.

"Hmmm." He took a breath and let it out, slowly. "I'm sorry. Can we start again? I'm Mr Franks, Mr Carlson's superior officer."

Mutti looked at him for a moment. "We are not getting in the car."

The man looked at us, frustration across his face. "All right." His tone was quite sharp, but he pulled himself up and continued from beneath a veneer of geniality. "But I need to speak to you." He thought for a moment. "How about I take you both to dinner at a restaurant? We can walk there from here."

Mutti glanced at me. "That would be acceptable," she said.

Mr Franks – if that was his real name – gestured for Mr Carlson to get in the car. "Go to Gambaro's and get us a table in a corner. Bring the car there at eight o'clock." He turned to us. "It's about a fifteen-minute walk. The car's here ..."

Mutti gave him a bleak smile. "A fifteen-minute walk will be fine, thank you."

Once we were away from the crowds on George Street, Mr Franks broke the uneasy silence. "If anyone asks, I'm a friend who served with your late husband in Europe. He let me know you were coming out to Brisbane. It disturbed me to hear of his untimely death."

Mutti looked sideways at him and we continued in silence. Mrs Henderson had shared our 'history' it seemed.

"How are you finding the work at McDonnell & East?"

Mr Franks wanted to chat, but Mutti remained silent, her lips a thin line.

Three people walking in company and not talking might be suspicious and I spoke up. "I'm working there too, on the Candy Counter. It's busy with Christmas approaching."

"I suppose it is." He glanced down at me, searching for something to keep the conversation going. "What do you like doing for fun?"

Since the day I'd got into the taxi in Canterbury, there'd been no fun in my life. "I go to the Valley pool three times a week – or I did until they asked me to do extra shifts on the Candy Counter."

"Made any friends yet?"

"No." I wanted to snap at him. But it wasn't his fault that I'd been torn away from Willi and Lili.

He must have seen the sour look on my face and we walked the rest of the way in silence. At the restaurant, they showed us to a table towards the rear.

Mr Franks opened the menu passed to him by a waiter. "Have you tried any of the seafood here in Brisbane yet?"

We shook our heads.

"Well, you are in for a treat. Let me order for you."

I limited my experience with seafood, only the cockles we had dug up in the mud on Herne Bay beach at low tide and cooked at home.

"I think you'll like it, Kal." Mutti gave me an encouraging smile.

Mr Franks and the waiter entered a discussion – which involved bugs. I had visions of a plate of beetles or some such appearing on the table.

"I don't eat bugs." I said with some vehemence.

Mr Franks raised his eyebrows and gave me a condescending look. "Ah – these are a different sort of bugs. They're like a lobster and are a local delicacy."

The waiter gave me an encouraging smile as he left with the order.

Mr Franks' gaze traversed the restaurant. He smiled at us, leaning forward in his chair, hands crossed on the crisp, white tablecloth in front of him. "I have the impression from your phone call that Mr Carlson's visit was not entirely positive."

He raised his eyebrows at Mutti, who remained impassive, face closed.

"Hmmm ..." Mr Franks paused before continuing. "It is important that you believe we can help you." He smiled at each of us. "As an example, the phone you need will be installed promptly."

His smiles felt increasingly insincere.

"Thank you." Mutti's face remained closed, cautious.

Mr Franks gathered his thoughts, engaging Mutti's attention. "I realise it takes time to establish trust in a relationship, but I hope we are doing that."

He paused as a waiter approached with a jug of water tinkling with ice cubes. He filled our glasses and placed the jug in the centre of the table and retreated.

"Another thing that helps build a relationship is working together." Mr Franks looked at Mutti, his face smiling, but his eyes hinted at something else on his mind.

Mutti blinked, puzzled. "What do you mean?"

Mr Franks waved an airy hand. "In any government organisation, there is always pressure from above. Politicians don't enjoy spending money on things they can't see an immediate benefit from – such as parts of the security services. Ensuring your safety has a cost – a cost that would be easier to justify if you were helping us."

Mr Franks stopped as a waiter approached with a bottle of white wine and a wine cooler. He tasted the wine and then gestured for the waiter to fill Mutti's glass. "Ah – I think you will like this, Mrs Miller." He sipped appreciatively. "Go ahead – try it."

Mutti tasted her wine, keeping her face blank.

Mr Franks leant forward. "I realise Europe produces many excellent white wines – with many from Germany. But Australia produces excellent wines."

At that moment, our seafood platters arrived and talk was suspended as we ate. I'd never seen a lobster except in pictures, but the bugs looked like them. I did not know how to eat them until Mr Franks demonstrated, removing the fleshy tail and dipping it into the butter sauce. They were delicious – as were the prawns, which again required a peeling demonstration from Mr Franks. I allowed myself to be talked into trying a raw oyster, but I found the texture and taste unpleasant, as did Mutti. Mr Franks ate all the oysters with relish.

Once they removed the platters and we'd dabbled our fingers in lemon scented water to clean them, Mutti looked at Mr Franks. "You were explaining about us helping you."

Mr Franks' eyes flicked round the restaurant before returning to Mutti. "If you could help us, you would be an asset to the department and protecting you a requirement, not a cost."

Mutti glanced at me. "Help you how?"

"Well now, Mrs Miller, I understand you are an accomplished linguist – a trained translator of English, German, Polish and Russian." Mr Franks gave Mutti a questioning look.

"Yes." Mutti's voice was guarded, grudging.

"Here in Australia, we are a migrant society, with people from all over Europe. Inevitably, these people want to find people like themselves. They form clubs where they congregate and talk. My department needs to know what they talk about."

Mutti gave Mr Franks a hard look. "You want me to join some of these clubs?"

"Exactly." He smiled at Mutti. "We live in a divided world at a threatening time. You could pass on to my department any interesting snippets of information you heard, information that might help the security of the country you are now living in."

Mutti shook her head. "I cannot join the German club as I would be certain to meet someone from Frankfurt – where we are supposed to come from. They would rapidly see through the superficial information I have about the place."

"Hmmm – I see. What about the Polish and Russian clubs?"

"What reason could I have for joining the Polish club? We're not Polish. Why would they let me join? They would suspect a German – of all people – wanting to join and suspicion is dangerous." Mutti's voice was low but intense. "And you have not thought things through if you want me to join the Russian Club. It would be tantamount to me carrying a label round my neck saying 'Defector from east Germany'. West Germans don't learn Russian, but all east Germans must." I could hear the anger in Mutti's voice. "I thought Mrs Henderson put you in touch to protect us if we needed help. What you are asking me to do would expose us immediately."

Mr Franks sat there looking dazed at Mutti's vehemence. This was not the reaction he had expected. He pulled himself together. "Well, if you can't help us ..." His voice trailed off, replete with unspoken meaning.

No. He is going to abandon us – or expose us out of revenge.

I saw his anger at Mutti's refusal. I had the terrifying realisation it was down to me. It closed my throat, but it was all we had. I swallowed my fear. "I could do it ..."

Mutti swivelled in her seat. "No, Kal." The fear in her voice increased. "No."

Mr Franks ignored her. "What can you do?" The disdain almost dripped from his words.

Summoning my courage, I looked him in the eye. "I speak the same languages as Mutti – not quite as well for Russian and Polish, but I am learning. I was going to visit the Polish club this week to see if I could find a textbook to help me."

"Why were you learning Polish?" Mr Franks' puzzled face peered at me.

"I have ..." I corrected myself, "... had – a friend in England from a Polish family. There were three of us that used to do our homework together — in multiple languages. I'm learning French and can read Latin too."

Mr Franks gave me a calculating look. "This could work for both Polish and Russian clubs – and maybe for the German." I could see wheels turning in his head.

"What sort of person are you, using a child to do your dangerous work?" Mutti was almost spitting with controlled anger.

Mr Franks' head turned to look at Mutti. "You, of all people, should know that age has nothing to do with such things."

What had Mrs Henderson shared with the Australians? Not everything or he would have known about my language skills, but it seemed he knew Mutti had been in Ravensbrück as a child.

Mutti glared at Mr Franks. "And you do not know the personal cost of such things. Why should my daughter do this?"

Mr Franks locked his hands over his belly. "Well, of course, she doesn't have to." His eyes held Mutti's. "But we don't have to protect you."

It was no longer a veiled hint. The threat lay on the table as real as the remains of the bug tails.

Mutti drew in a breath, her eyes flicking to me. I swallowed. We needed to know that someone was watching out for Eastern Bloc's attempts to find us. Mrs Henderson had made it clear my father wanted us dead in retribution for the damage done to their network. I pleaded with my eyes. Mutti couldn't do this, but I could.

Mutti's eyes held mine and before switching to Mr Franks, who had sat watching our silent exchange. "Kal and I need to talk about this."

"Very well." He paused, considering. "I'll give you two days." His voice was threatening, but he was no Mrs Henderson. "You have our phone number."

He stood up and his voice returned to that genial veneer. "It's been a pleasure to meet you both. Have a safe trip home and don't forget to ring me." His voice might have been friendly, but his eyes were hard.

Mutti said nothing and we walked out to catch the tram home.

Chapter 5
Early – mid December 1964

W e could not talk about Mr Franks on the tram; instead, we sat in strained silence as the tram rattled up Lutwyche Road towards Kedron. Mutti's frown told me she was angry with me for suggesting to Mr Franks that I could do his bidding. But my fear that Mr Franks would abandon us, or worse, trumped Mutti's anger. If we didn't help, he'd leave us exposed. Mutti couldn't do it. That left me. The idea frightened me, but my father's agents arriving to kill us scared me more.

Leaving the tram, we walked home in a silence that deepened with Mutti's frown. Her footsteps on the pavement sounded heavier, harsher, pushing her anger towards me. She unlocked the front door and the day's heat poured out.

"Don't open the windows on that side of the house, Kal." Mutti gestured towards the Greco's' house.

"Why?"

"Just don't, Kal." She snapped and relented with a sigh. "We don't want to be overheard." She was almost whispering, but I could hear the tension in her voice.

I unlatched and opened the windows on the other side.

Mutti turned on the radio, retrieved a jug of cold water from the fridge and put two glasses on the table. I sat, watching Mutti pour us a cold drink. As she sat down, her conflicting emotions ran across her face.

"Co...." She almost used my real name. "Kal, what were you thinking, making that suggestion to ... him?"

Mutti was being careful – in England we had been circumspect in our conversations, trying to hide behind careful allusion. We'd need to do that if I got involved with Mr Franks. Who knows what ears might be listening.

I tried to stay calm by taking a sip of water. Thinking about Mr Franks' threat pushed my fear towards panic. I took a deep breath and gripped the table to help steady myself.

"If we don't help him, he's going to ..." I paused, swallowing at what the withdrawal of protection could mean, "... make life difficult for us." I screwed my face up at how ridiculous that sounded given the reality of the danger.

Mutti's voice softened and she reached across to hold my hand. "He could be bluffing." She didn't sound convincing.

I snatched my hand away. "Why would he bluff? We can't risk him making good on the threat." I could hear the tension in my throat.

"Kal, I know it's difficult, but we must stay calm or we can't think." She reached her hand across the table, trying to reassure me. When I took it, she gave me a comforting squeeze. I took a steadying breath, willing myself to relax.

Mutti's face was thoughtful. "What if we tried to get in contact with ... the lady that slapped you?"

Contact Mrs Henderson?

"How?"

Mutti raised an eyebrow. "Well, I still have ... the number they gave me."

Oh yes – the number for Mr Watling, her contact. "Can we dial that from here?"

Mutti shook her head. "I don't know ... but someone at McDonnell & East must know how to do it as they buy stock from England."

"Won't that sound odd, asking about that?"

"No, I don't think so. After all, we're from England and it's perfectly reasonable that we might need to contact someone in England." Mutti thought for a moment or two. "I'll ask Mr Chapman about it tomorrow."

"Okay – but we don't have much time."

Mutti had a determined expression on her face. "It's going to be okay, Kal. If that doesn't work, I've different cards to play." She gave me a confident smile. "Have a shower...I'd make you a hot chocolate if we were in England."

After my shower, I lay in bed, thinking about Mr Franks. I yearned to talk with Willi about this, to feel his reassuring arms around me and hear ideas from his unique perspective. Finally, I turned on my side, hugging my pillow instead.

• • • •

MR FRANKS AND THE THREAT he posed was top of my thoughts on waking, a choppy swell on the dark sea of gloom about Willi. I ate breakfast with Mutti in a restless silence.

She gave me a fierce hug as she left. "It's going to work out, Kal."

Mutti seemed confident this morning, but her lift in mood left me flat. To keep myself occupied, I resumed my study habits based on my Canterbury timetable, a time and place that now seemed almost fantasy.

Studying had been enjoyable shared with Willi and Lili; alone, it took my mind off our troubles – French irregular verbs and Cartesian geometry require concentration. After a morning's working with my schoolbooks, I set off for a swim in the early afternoon.

I wanted to do something for Mutti to thank her for ... well, being Mutti. I pondered this on the tram into the city: the German bakery in Woolloongabba. I detoured there to pick up some of Mutti's favourite *Schwarzbrot* as a treat. It would go well with tonight's cold meat, cheese and salad. The bakery was out of the way and I couldn't afford to go there often as the tram fares were as much as the bread, but this was a treat for Mutti. With the bread wrapped and in my duffel bag, I set off to the Valley pool. I stepped off the tram, anticipating a cooling swim. The day was building towards a thunderstorm, but my mind needed the rhythm of exercise to soothe my troubles. I changed and went to sit and wait for the schools to leave.

As soon as they announced general swimming, I was into a lane and pushed down the first length, full of nervous energy. I schooled myself to slow down over the second length and swam for another fifteen minutes before pulling myself out for a break. As always, the discipline and rhythm of swimming lengths had settled my emotions, but sitting watching people swim allowed my mind to wander to Mr Franks.

Mutti might reach Mrs Henderson – but there was no guarantee that she would – or could – tell Mr Franks to stop. She might well think that Mr Franks was correct to use the tools to hand to further the needs of national security. Mrs Henderson had no compunction about using us for her purposes, which is why we ended up here.

"Hello."

My rising agitation was such I hadn't noticed a girl sit beside me and I jumped. Turning, I saw a girl with blond hair tied up in plaits on her head. She was about my age, still wet from the pool with a towel draped over her shoulders.

"Sorry – I'm Elizabeth – Lizzie. I didn't mean to startle you."

"Oh..." I wondered what she wanted. "I'm Kal – Karlota."

"Pleased to meet you, Kal." She smiled, holding out her hand.

Somewhat bemused, I shook it.

"I've watched you swimming here. You swim well."

"Thank you." I gave her a half-smile.

"Would you be interested in a race? My mum says I'm lazy and don't push myself if I'm not competing."

My mind was still half on Mr Franks; I blinked, replaying what she'd said. "Well, I don't know that I'm competitive; I swim for exercise."

I could see questions in her eyes, but she suppressed them. "Come on, it'll be fun."

It was about time for me to go in for another set of lengths, anyway. "Okay."

Lizzie's face almost glowed with the smile she gave me.

I stood up and she grabbed my hand, pulling me along the row of seats. "Come on."

We walked down to the pool from where I had been sitting in the stands.

Lizzie shrugged the towel from her shoulders, draping it over the railing behind which two middle-aged women sat, chatting. "You can leave your towel with my mother."

I pulled the towel from my shoulders and left it beside Lizzie's. One of the well-dressed women peered up at me through impenetrable sun glasses from beneath her wide-brimmed hat.

I smiled and shrugged as Lizzie grabbed my hand again and pulled me away. She dragged me to the end of the pool, where we found two adjacent empty lanes.

"One length or two?" Lizzie was almost fizzing with energy.

I thought for a moment. "I think two."

We took our positions at the pool's edge. "On the count of three?"

"OK."

"One ... two ... three...Go."

I started with my usual dive and, as I surfaced into my stroke, I could see Lizzie was already ahead of me. I pushed harder, but Lizzie drew away from me, tumble turning as I arrived at the far wall. By the time I turned, I could see the splash of her feet ahead of me. I dug deeper to stay with her.

Lizzie clung to the wall, pulling in deep breaths, as was I. After regaining our breath, she smiled across at me. "Oh, that was great, Kal. You pushed me on the second length."

We pulled ourselves out and walked round to where we left our towels.

The lady beneath the straw hat captured Lizzie's eyes. "Elizabeth, please introduce us to your friend."

The cool tone didn't seem to touch Lizzie. She gave me a quick glance, flashing raised eyebrows at me. "Yes mummy. This is Karlota – Kal."

Her mother's gaze swept over me. "I'm pleased to meet you, Karlota. I'm Mrs Robinson." She indicated the lady beside her. "This is my friend, Mrs Kaufman."

"Good afternoon, Mrs Robinson, Mrs Kaufman."

"Can we get an ice cream, please Mummy?" Lizzie became a younger girl as she wheedled her mother.

"Yes, dear." Mrs Robinson's voice sounded exasperated. "But you and your friend will need to swim afterwards. You must be careful of your figure if you are to attract a suitable man."

She produced a pair of shilling bits from a leather purse, handing them to her daughter.

"Thanks, mummy." Lizzie rolled her eyes at me once we had turned away. "Come on, Kal." And she was off at a trot to the kiosk. Lizzie was in almost continuous motion.

"D'you like Eskimo pies?"

"What's an Eskimo Pie?"

"Don't you know what an Eskimo Pie is?" Her face showed amazement at my lack of knowledge.

I gave her a blank look and Lizzie pointed to a picture on the side of the kiosk.

"Oh – that's a Choc Ice." I laughed.

Lizzie raised an eyebrow. "Okay – but it's an Eskimo Pie here in Australia." She turned to the man in the kiosk. "Two Eskimo Pies, please."

"Right you are. Lizzie, coming up."

My friend was well known here, it seemed.

"That'll be one and sixpence, please."

"Thanks, Jack." Lizzie paid and handed an ice cream to me and we peeled off their cover.

"Come and sit in the shade." Lizzie led me to a low wall shaded by the building behind it.

We sat for a while, licking our ice creams and trying to catch the chocolate covering as it cracked off. This was the least motion I had seen in Lizzie.

"Where are you from, Kal?"

"I'm from England."

"Well, your English is excellent, but I can hear ... something in your voice – and you didn't know what an Eskimo Pie was ..." She regarded me speculatively. "You're a New Australian, but not Greek or Italian ...?" Her voice trailed off in a question.

I smiled at her and repeated. "I'm English."

Lizzie's eyes assessed me, not believing me what I had said. "But there's something else." She insisted.

I laughed. "I'm half German. My mother's German but my father's English. Or was." I let my face and voice drop a touch, something I'd practiced in front of my mirror.

Lizzie's face fell. "Oh, Kal. I'm sorry. What happened?" Then she realised she was being impolite. "Sorry, Kal, I didn't mean to pry."

I put my hand on her arm. "It's okay, Lizzie." I took a deep breath. "My dad was in the Army and met Mutti in Germany. He took us to England when I was two." I paused for a moment. "He died in an accident at work earlier this year."

Lizzie gave me a compassionate smile. "Mummy says I'm impulsive and need to stop and think before I blurt things out."

"It's okay, Lizzie," I smiled. "Your mother's friend – Mrs Kaufman – that's a German name." I was worried about meeting any Germans and having our deception revealed.

"Is it? Her family's been here practically since the First Fleet. Her husband owns a vineyard on the Granite Belt. It's been in his family since before the first war." I saw a flicker of anxiety in her eyes at the mention of the war. "We have visited. One winter there was snow there. Can you believe it?" Her voice showed a tinge of awe at snow in tropical Queensland.

Willi had always been careful to avoid talk of the wars and it seemed people here were careful about mentioning Germany's defeats to me as well. From the sound of it, meeting Mrs Kaufman would not present a problem, as the connection with Germany was distant. Anyway, I couldn't be expected to remember anything about Frankfurt; we'd left it when I was tiny, I reminded myself. I heard an echo of Willi's recital of those lines from the Scottish poem – this dissembling made me uneasy.

"Where d'you go to school, Kal?"

I blinked – I'd got lost in my thoughts for a moment.

"Ummm ... at the moment, I don't." I explained about the difference in school years.

"Oh ... you lucky thing."

I pulled a face. "Mutti insists I study from my English textbooks. I was studying all morning."

With our ice creams finished in companionable silence, Lizzie jumped off the wall. "Come on, let's have another race."

"Okay – but let's make this one four lengths." I might overhaul her in a longer race.

Lizzie gave me a speculative glance. "Four lengths?"

"But let's warm up first."

Lizzie cocked an eyebrow at me. "Hmmm ... are you trying to wear me out?"

I awarded her an enigmatic smile.

We couldn't find two adjacent lanes free, so we sat and waited.

"Where do you live, Kal?"

"In Kedron – north of the city. What about you?"

"We live in Hamilton." Something about her tone of voice suggested that she thought this was special.

I laughed. "I've no idea where that is."

Lizzie scrutinised my face as if she didn't believe me. "How long have you been in Brisbane?"

"About six weeks."

Lizzie's face relaxed. "Well, no wonder you don't know your way around yet. Hamilton's on a hill north of the river. It gets lovely sea breezes in the afternoons." Lizzie scanned the sky at a distant rumble. "It sounds as if this afternoon's storm is arriving. We'd better delay the next race. Mummy will want to get home before it breaks."

"Okay."

"Will you be coming here tomorrow?" Lizzie asked.

"I can't until Monday afternoon, I'm afraid."

"Oh." I heard the disappointment in her voice. "Well – I'll have to come then too." She gave me a smile. "Date?"

I smiled in return. "Date."

We went and grabbed our towels and headed for the changing room. When we came out, Lizzie's mother and her friend were waiting for us.

"See you on Monday, Kal."

"Bye, Lizzie. Bye Mrs Robinson, Mrs Kaufman." I waved as I set off for the tram.

As it rattled north, I watched the storm approach, its dark clouds tinged with green. It arrived with a tram-shuddering blast of wind. The gusts filled with sheets of billowing rain and I dashed from the tram into the open shelter at my stop, chased by the blowing rain. Our house was a ten-minute walk: I'd have to run for it. I was close to home, splashing through the pouring rain when the hail began.

"Ow."

A cherry-sized stone hit the top of my head. I lifted my duffel bag and rested it on my head as I ran. Now, some stones reached the size of ping-pong balls, smacking into the pavement and shattering. I slipped into the limited shelter of a tree. Hail was ripping leaves and twigs off and I sheltered as best I could against the trunk, the duffel bag over my head. The hail and rain were intense, the noise incredible, punctuated by lightning and crackling thunder. The wind slapped my soaked dress around my legs and I was feeling cold.

I thought I heard someone shouting and peered around the trunk to see Mrs Greco on her front veranda, waving me towards her house. The hail was not as big or frequent. I ran along a pavement that had become a rushing stream pebbled with shattered hail stones, up the front steps and into the shelter of the Greco's' veranda.

Rain and hail hammered on the corrugated iron roof, making it difficult to talk. Mrs Greco disappeared into her house and reappeared with some towels. She draped one round my shoulders as I was shivering. I used the other to dry my hair and neck. Mrs Greco saw my shivers and started rubbing my shoulders with the towel to warm and dry them.

The thunder and hammering of rain on the roof lessened as the wind gusts lost some of their fury. I saw two sets of eyes peering at us through the screen door.

Now the noise was less scary, Cal crept out on to the veranda with Giorgio in tow. "You're wet."

I smiled down at her, shivering. "Yes, I am." I was standing in a puddle where water was dripping off me.

Mrs Greco rubbed my shoulders and arms, trying to warm me up. "You cold...*Stai tremando. Vieni dentro per un caffè.*"

I smiled – I had no idea what she was saying.

Mrs Greco put her hand on Cal's shoulder. "Cal, *dille quello che ho detto.*"

Cal's voice was serious. "Mamma says you are shivering and to come inside for coffee."

I glanced across to my house – the hail had almost stopped and the rain was hard but no longer torrential. I wanted to get out of my drenched clothes and into a hot bath. If I ran home, I wasn't going to get any wetter than I already was.

I smiled at Mrs Greco and crouched down beside Cal. "Please tell your mother thank you, but I will run home and have a hot bath."

Cal's wide eyes stared at me. I smiled, gesturing to her mother.

Cal turned to her mother. "*Mamma, dice grazie ma torna a casa per un bagno.*"

Mrs Greco smiled at me. "Ah ... hot ..." She hugged her arms around herself.

"Yes." I said, handing her the towels. "Thank you for your help, Cal."

I smiled at Mrs Greco. "Thank you ... er ... *grazie?*"

Mrs Greco waved. "*Arrivederci.*"

"Bye – and thank you again."

I trotted down the steps and sprinted across to my house through the rain. Our floors were lino, which didn't mind me dripping on it. I dripped my way into the kitchen.

The bread ...

I rather gingerly opened the duffel bag, expecting to find a soggy mess of rye bread, but it was barely damp at one end. It seemed my swimming towel had soaked up any rain that got in. I put the bread on the side in the kitchen and went along to the bathroom and started a hot bath. Pulling off my wet clothes was difficult as they clung to my clammy skin.

Even though the bath was far from full, I got in, splashing myself in the shallow hot water as it deepened around me. I stayed in, my worried thoughts cycling between Mr Franks and Willi, until the cooling water pushed me out. Once I was dry, I padded into my bedroom and dressed in a sarong, listening to the storm grumble away into the distance.

I hung my wet clothes and swimming things up on the veranda and suspended my duffel bag upside down to dry from a convenient hook. By the time Mutti arrived home I had tea ready – but I had hidden the *Schwarzbrot* in the bread crock.

I met her on the veranda and she spied the things on the line. "Did you get caught in the storm?"

"Yes – but how did you get on phoning England?"

Mutti's eyes narrowed. "Let's go inside, shall we?"

I frowned in frustration.

Be more careful about what you say and where you say it, Col.

Mutti turned on the radio, pulled the jug of cold water from the fridge and poured us both glasses. "Wait a moment." She stood up and opened her bag, retrieving two lemon-sized fruits – but they were a rich green. "These are limes." She cut one into quarters and passed a quarter to me. Sitting down, she squeezed the juice into her water and slid the squashed segment into her glass.

"Try it, Kal."

I followed her lead and took a sip. The lime juice made the cold water much more refreshing. "Mm ... that's better than plain water."

Mutti took an appreciative sip, her eyes holding mine over the rim of her glass. "Mr Chapman was most kind and helped me book a call to England. I must ring the international operator from the phone box at seven o'clock. I've shilling bits to pay for the call.

"And if we don't get through to her – or if she refuses to help?

"We'll see. But let's leave that for now and have tea."

I retrieved the salad, meats and cheese from the fridge, trying to quell my unease.

Mutti surveyed the table. "No bread?"

"I'll get it." I pulled the breadboard out and retrieved the *Schwarzbrot* from the crock, shielding everything with my body.

"Ta da."

Mutti's eyes widened. "Is that *Schwarzbrot*?"

I handed her the bread knife and she cut a slice, inspecting the texture and savouring the aroma. She broke off a piece and popped it into her mouth – and her head lifted and her eyelids drooped.

"Mm ..." She smiled across at me. "Where did you get this?"

"It's from a German bakery in Woolloongabba. I found it when we were still at Yungaba." Mutti cut two slices and handed one to me.

"I found a German butcher too. They have a wide selection of *Würste*."

Mutti smiled. The *Schwarzbrot* made the meal almost a traditional *Abendbrot*. The familiarity helped me forget about Mr Franks for a while as we chatted about her day at work. After we cleaned up, we sat down at the table. Mutti got me to tell her about the storm – and I told her about Lizzie. At a quarter to seven, we headed off to the phone box in Leckie Road.

Mutti told me to stand beside her to hear what was being said and dialled the operator. After a brief discussion, Mutti fed five shillings into the phone.

We heard a series of clicks and burrs followed by beeping.

"I'm sorry, caller, but that number is unobtainable."

Mutti's eyes flicked sideways to me. "What does that mean?" She asked the operator.

"It means that the number is no longer connected. You have the correct number?"

"Oh ... yes ... er ... thank you."

"Can I try another number for you, caller?"

"Um ... No thank you." Mutti hung up and the phone clunked, returning her shilling bits.

We were on our own and my stomach sank. We walked back to our house in silence.

Once we'd opened the windows and Mutti had the radio on, I asked. "Now what?"

She leant forward, resting her elbows on the table and cupping her chin on her hands. "I don't want you doing that man's bidding."

"I can't see what else we can do. If you try to do something, we'll be exposed and if we do nothing, we'll be exposed."

"And what would you do?" I could hear the frustration in her voice.

"I thought I'd use my interest in languages to get into the Polish Club."

"What do you mean?"

"Well, I don't have a Polish textbook – we were using one that Lili's mother found us. The library told me that the Polish club had its own library. I was going to visit there and see if I could find something to help."

Mutti raised her eyebrows. "And?"

"Well, I thought that might get me accepted and I could work from there."

"And what about the German and Russian Clubs?" Mutti asked.

"Well, neither of us can admit to speaking Russian. I won't be trying there." I paused – because this was touchy. "I thought of a way that I might approach the German Club without involving you."

"Go on."

Mutti was coming round to my ideas. "I thought I could tell them my mother insisted we integrate into Australia and would not let me speak or read German at home. But I want to maintain my heritage ..." I was watching Mutti's face and saw her wince. She loved the German language and culture; she would never do something like that.

Mutti sat for a while. I started feeling uncomfortable and shifted in my chair.

Mutti nodded. "That's quite clever. I suspect that there are many Germans in Australia who are trying to put our disastrous past behind them by walking away from their heritage."

"Will you let me try?"

Mutti's chest rose as she took a deep breath. "Because of my experiences in the prisons and camps, I know how to conduct myself and be someone else, the person I need to be for that man." Her eyes wandered into her memories for a moment. "Staying safe from the SS guards and manipulating them when I could taught me useful skills." She sighed. "But I can't do what we need." She gave me a speculative look. "But ... you can do it by being you — a curious girl." She paused again. "Of course, I'll help."

"We'll tell him I'm going to do it?"

Mutti's face held a grim half-smile with a hint of guile in her eyes. "Of course not."

I blinked in confusion. "What?"

"We ... negotiate." Mutti's smile was almost predatory, something I had never seen on her face before.

I took a startled breath. "What do you mean?"

"In circumstances like these, you never agree to the initial offer; Ravensbrück was a masterclass in this." Mutti pondered for a moment. "That man needs us and we still have the English organisation that we can hint at. I don't think his superiors would like it if ... that woman ... got involved."

"We have to give him an answer tomorrow." I heard the fear in my voice.

"Oh, but we don't." She gave me a conspiratorial smile. "We are going to speak with him tomorrow and we might give him an answer – if we reach a mutually satisfactory agreement."

Mutti's eyes stared at me as if assessing my sale value; for a moment she reminded me of Mrs Henderson.

"We need to decide what we are going to ask of him in return for our help."

This was a new, self-assured side of Mutti. She relished vying with and besting Mr Franks.

"I'll ring him tomorrow and set up a meeting." She pondered for a moment. "We need somewhere safe, though." Her focus shifted into the distance. "I doubt that man has approval from his bosses for his threat to disown or expose us." She smiled at me. "And that gives us a bargaining advantage."

I sat, wondering how she was going to make this work, watching a glimmer of that predatory smile flicker across Mutti's face as she pondered tomorrow's meeting.

After a minute, she stood up. "Come on, Kal, let's head to bed. We've both got to be up and at McDonnell & East by eight o'clock. That means catching the ten past seven tram."

I lay in bed for a while, thinking about what I was about to do. As I drifted off to sleep, I constructed an elaborate fantasy as a beautiful and dangerous spy, using my wiles to ferret out information that would save the world.

• • • •

I WOKE IN THE GREY pre-dawn to hear the raucous laughing of kookaburras. A family had decided our veranda railing was the perfect place for their morning chorus. I got up, wrapped a sarong around me and peeked round the blanket we were using as curtains until Mutti had time to make some. A complete kookaburra family sat there – mum, dad and three growing children: cute, but not winning friends by waking me early.

I padded out to the kitchen. The wall clock told me it was barely a quarter to five, wretched birds. Out on the veranda, the kookaburras fluffed their feathers at me and shuffled along the railing before diving off to wake some other poor unfortunate. I stood, enjoying the cool as the sky brightened, but with the Mr Franks issue menacing my calm. At least that immediate problem suppressed the darkness around my separation from Willi.

I breathed deep breaths, trying to create a calmness within me until faint, plaintive ... meows? ... from somewhere nearby caught my attention.

I tiptoed down the steps, keeping a wary eye out for wildlife. The sounds seemed to come from below the front of the house, towards the bushes.

There amongst the still wet detritus under the wattles was a bedraggled ginger kitten. It retreated, back arched, when I tried to pick it up. Reaching past, I captured the mite without a struggle. The poor thing was drenched and shivering. Clasping him to my body to give him some warmth, I ran upstairs and wrapped him in a towel, massaging his fur to dry it and give him some warmth. With the kitten tucked in the towel in the crook of my arm, I poured a little milk into a cup and sat down. A finger dipped in milk held in front of his nose resulted in a tiny pink tongue appearing to rasp the liquid from my fingertip. We sat there like that for a while until the kitten yawned, padded at the towel and drifted off to sleep.

I woke to find Mutti's hand on my shoulder. "Where did you find the kitten, Kal?" she asked.

"In the bushes at the front of the house after I was rudely woken by a family of kookaburras."

Mutti saw the milk in a cup. "I don't think cats are supposed to have cow's milk. I wonder where the mother is?"

"She probably got separated from this little one in the storm."

"He?"

"Yes – Lili knows about cats and she said that most ginger cats are male."

"Oh ... well, we need to find somewhere to keep him safe whilst we are out – and somewhere for him to do his business."

Two blue eyes surrounded by ginger fluff stared wide-eyed up at us. "He's certainly cute enough." Mutti remarked, ruffling his now dry fur with a finger. "We can cut down a cardboard box and put some earth in it. He can go in your study room for the day – but we'll need to open the window a crack to give him some air."

I took him down to the study and put him on the floor, unwrapping the towel to free him. He got up on his unsteady paws — his nose probing my fingers for a drink. Mutti came in with a shallow bowl of water, which she put on the floor. The kitten investigated and started lapping it up, his tiny pink tongue spreading ripples across the surface.

Satisfied that he would be safe for the moment, I went and arranged his dirt box. Mr Greco had been digging right on the fence line and I lifted handfuls of damp soil into a cut-down cardboard box. I carried this indoors and put it in the study, with layers of the local newspaper underneath. I placed the kitten on the dirt tray and he nosed around, did his business and clambered out.

Mutti stuck her head round the door. "Come on Kal, get moving. We need to leave in fifteen minutes."

"OK."

I washed, dressed and arrived in the kitchen in under ten minutes, where Mutti presented me with a ham sandwich she'd made and my lunch box.

"Get your things, Kal. You can eat the sandwich on the way to the tram."

I checked on the kitten. Mutti had chopped a slice of ham into tiny pieces and he was eating; he'd be fine for the day.

As we walked to the tram stop, Mutti told me she would make the phone call to that man at lunch time. I was to meet her in the women's staff room once we'd both finished for the day. I was doing a double shift, with a forty-five-minute break at midday.

With Christmas less than two weeks away, the Candy Counter was hectic, keeping all three of us girls on our toes throughout the morning. As well as sales, we had to keep the stock up, which kept one of us going to and from the stockroom. My feet were grateful for the break when it came. I sat down in the women's staff room, pulled my shoes off and rested my feet on another chair, my toes wiggling in delight at their escape from shoe prison. Mutti would phone Mr Franks soon; my throat constricted. She had been confident that she could negotiate a satisfactory deal for us with Mr Franks, but in the cold light of day that seemed as real as the fantasy I'd enjoyed as I drifted off to sleep.

Tension rose in my stomach and throat. I closed the lid of my lunch box over the uneaten sandwich and banana. If I wasn't careful, I would be as taut as a violin string by the time I met up with Mutti. I cast around in my mind for a distraction: the kitten.

Would Mutti let me keep him?

I had enjoyed befriending Hawkins, Mrs Gittings' ginger cat in Lancaster, and this morning the kitten had relaxed in the warmth of my arms. My mind wandered, summoning up names for the rest of my break.

Doreen was in charge for the afternoon shift and we were busy again, which helped keep my mind off Mr Franks. But at one point, Doreen raised an eyebrow at me when she had to ask me twice to get another couple of boxes of Scottish Shortbread tins. I gave her an apologetic smile and dashed off to the get the boxes. I fought to concentrate on the job in hand and not let my mind wander, getting through the rest of my shift without another lapse.

But by the time I returned to the women's staff room, my uncertainty was mounting.

Should I tell Mutti to go along with what Mr Franks wants me to do?

If we annoyed him, he might go through with his threat and ASIO would stop protecting us. He might leak information about us to the *Stasi*. As I sat there waiting, I marvelled Mutti had survived the constant tension inside Ravensbrück. I closed my eyes trying to find the centre of calm from this morning, going over the names for the kitten I had thought of at lunch time.

"Come on, Kal, get changed."

I jerked my eyes open. "Sorry Mutti." I rushed out of my uniform into street clothes.

"Ready?"

"Okay."

"Let's go."

We walked towards the tram stop on George Street.

"The meeting is at a café on Alice Street, opposite the Botanic Garden — a public place to prevent any tricks."

A tram down Queen Street pulled up as we reached the stop. It took us half-way to the Botanic Garden.

"We'll need to walk fast, to be there first." Mutti set a rapid pace. I was thankful for the previous day's thunderstorm; it had cooled things down today and we didn't arrive dripping with sweat.

Mr Franks wasn't there. Mutti picked a table at the front by the window and ordered us each a glass of lemonade with ice. Sitting there, my anxiety continued to mount.

Mutti leant across the table. "If you're going to do this, you'll need some skills, Kal. This is your first lesson." She kept her voice low. "Sitting here, we can be seen from outside and that gives us some protection during the meeting."

Mutti could see the tension running through me. "It'll be fine, Kal." Mutti leant across and patted my hand. "You don't have to say anything. It's probably best that you don't speak – and don't react to what is said. Any reaction weakens us and strengthens them."

I sipped my lemonade, concentrating on Mutti's guidance. We chatted about our workday until I saw Mr Franks walking towards the café with Mr Carlson.

I kept the same quiet tone of voice. "Here they come, Mutti."

Mutti smiled at me, stood and came round to my side of the table, but she remained upright. I blinked in realisation: she'd sat opposite me to let us watch in both directions. Another thing to learn.

The café door jingled and Mr Franks walked over to us, followed by Mr Carlson.

"Good evening, Mrs Miller, Kal." Mr Franks' tone was cordial.

"Mr Franks, Mr Carlson." Mutti gestured them to the seats opposite us and sat down beside me. Her hand dropped to my thigh and gave me an encouraging squeeze.

Mr Franks surveyed the café. "I think our meeting would go better over there, don't you?" He pointed to a table in the far corner, which would be hard to see from outside.

"Here is fine, thank you," Mutti responded.

Mr Franks shook his head and started towards the corner. Mutti cleared her throat, causing Mr Franks to turn.

"If this meeting does not reach a satisfactory conclusion, your superiors and their English friends will be quite upset." Mutti's voice sounded quite normal.

She's threatening them?

My anxiety spiked and I struggled to keep my face blank. Mr Franks walked to our table, a mixture of irritation and confusion on his face. He was about to remonstrate with Mutti.

"Please sit down, Mr Franks, Mr Carlson." She kept her voice low and inviting, but with a hint of steel. "We all want a satisfactory outcome." Mutti again gestured at the chairs opposite us.

Mr Franks knuckles whitened on the chair opposite Mutti and a long silence dragged out. Then he leant across the table with an unpleasant smile. "I don't know what you think you are doing, but it's not going to work." He gestured to Mr Carlson and sat down.

Mutti smiled at them. "A fresh lemonade? We can recommend it, can't we, Kal?"

"Yes." I sipped of mine. The anxiety was still there, but I hid it beneath my astonishment at Mutti. This was a side of her I did not know.

Mutti did not wait for a reply but smiled at Mr Carlson. "Please arrange refills for us as well. It was warm walking up from McDonnell & East."

I watched from the corner of my eye as Mr Carlson stood and went to order the lemonades, but my attention was on Mutti and Mr Franks. Their eyes locked.

"Are you married, Mr Franks?" Mutti's voice was still conversational.

He frowned at this unexpected question. "What?"

"Hmmm." Mutti's face showed some disapproval at the brusque retort. "Are you married? Do you have children?"

I could see the puzzlement on Mr Franks' face. "Yes."

"I expect that you and your wife would do anything to protect your children."

"Of course." Mr Franks' voice was curt, mirroring his frown.

"Then you understand my position regarding my daughter."

Mr Franks' eyes flicked over me before returning to Mutti. He frowned at Mutti as Mr Carlson slid into his seat.

"We all want this meeting to go well." Mutti smiled across the table. "Why don't you tell us what you want?"

Mr Franks huffed, arrogance writ large on his face. "Very simple. You do as I say about the foreign clubs or ... I withdraw our protection." He paused, leaning forward in his chair, staring at Mutti.

My knee shook up and down as fear coursed through me. I pushed my foot flat to the floor as I fought to hide this, sipping my lemonade to cover my feelings.

Mutti's voice showed puzzlement. "Why would you want that? It could severely limit, possibly end, your careers. Can we not find a conclusion that will enhance your careers?" She paused, eyeing the men opposite us. "I'm certain you'd prefer that outcome."

The waiter distributed the lemonades and returned to the depths of the café. Mr Franks stared at Mutti with narrowed eyes. "Do you think that some insignificant refugee from the Soviet Bloc can do anything that would harm my career?" I could hear the dismissive tone in his voice.

Mutti acknowledged that truth. "No, you're correct, there's nothing I could do to harm your careers…"

I saw Mr Franks lean forward in victory, ready to claim his prize. My shaking leg started up again. I clamped my hand on my knee, trying to stifle it.

"…because I have already done it."

Mr Franks blinked. "What do you mean?"

"The actions that will end your careers and cause an international incident between Australia, Britain are already underway. Yesterday, I had an interesting phone call to the UK." Mutti paused, allowing that to sink in.

I waited for Mr Franks to laugh at this bluff, but his reaction was a miniscule flicker of his eyes towards Mr Carlson.

Mutti continued. "But I, with Kal at my side, can stop that happening."

"You're threatening me?" Mr Franks growled.

"I think it's called mutually assured destruction." Mutti's smile was icy. "Why don't we start again?" Her face had a hint of the predatory to it. "This time I will tell you the conclusion that will benefit us both."

I glanced at Mr Carlson. His face showed a mixture of disbelief and fear at what was happening. If Mr Franks' career ended, so would his. Mutti waited for Mr Franks. His face was impassive, but I suspected his thoughts were galloping. His Adam's apple bobbled as he swallowed, giving a grudging nod.

"Under my direction," Mutti emphasised the words, "Kal will visit the Polish club and sound things out. We will tell you what transpires from this." Her eyes were locked with Mr Franks'. "As we already have a tactic that will give Kal a reason for entry, I see no problems in her becoming a regular visitor there."

Mutti looked across the table. Mr Franks gave a miniscule nod of agreement.

"Excellent." Mutt's acknowledging smile was mirthless, her eyes hard. "We will use another prepared tactic to move Kal into the German club and we see no problems there." Again, she paused, until Mr Franks responded.

His "Okay." was grudging.

"By the end of February, you will have lines into two of the clubs you are interested in and we will begin work on placing Kal into the Russian Club." Her eyes held Mr Franks'. "This will be difficult, dangerous and likely take some time and careful planning."

Mr Franks was puzzled. "But that's exactly what I asked you to do..."

"Not quite, Mr Franks." Mutti's voice became harder, but stayed low. "It will be done under my direction." Her gaze across the table was almost contemptuous. "No more of these amateur meetings or people coming to our house. We will use dead drops to pass information." She paused. "I presume you know what a dead drop is?" Her voice held a touch of disdain.

Mr Franks' face darkened. "Of course."

Mutti Frida's eyes held Mr Franks' before she sighed, picked up her lemonade and sipped it. Placing the glass on the coaster, she smiled across at Mr Franks. "Now there's the matter of our fee."

Mr Franks' head jerked up. "Fee?" His head swivelled, looking around the cafe as he'd almost shouted in astonishment.

"Yes, our fee." Mutti's gaze was full of steel. "If we are providing you with a service, payment is required. Our fee is thirty pounds per month, payable in cash, in advance, with an upfront fifty pounds to cover initial expenses."

Mr Franks almost choked. "Impossible." He looked across at Mutti.

"Not so, Mr Franks." Mutti's smile, terrifying in its ownership of the moment, was one I hoped she never turned on me. "Think what we are giving you." She paused. "And we must still stop those actions I mentioned."

Mutti and Mr Franks locked eyes again.

"Think of the career advancement a successful operation will bring."

Mr Franks pursed his lips, thinking. "Twenty pounds a month."

I clamped down on my astonishment.

He was bargaining. Mutti had him.

Mutti's eyes lidded. "Twenty-five."

Mr Franks huffed out a breath. "Twenty-five."

"Agreed, for now." Mutti raised an eyebrow. "When we successfully penetrate the Russian Club, that fee will double to compensate us for the increased danger."

Mr Franks tried to maintain an impassive face, but I could see his internal conflict. Penetrating the Russian Club was important to him, but fifty pounds a month was a large amount of money.

"If you penetrate the Russian Club, we will talk about that."

"Very well." Mutti raised her lemonade glass. "To a profitable mutual arrangement."

Mr Franks' hand crawled across the table to his glass and hesitated before he lifted it to clink it against hers.

Mutti pulled her purse out of her handbag, extracted a folded ten-shilling note and passed it to Mr Franks. "You paid for the dinner the other night. It's fair that I pay for the drinks this evening." She smiled. "Keep the change."

Mutti replaced her purse, picked up her handbag and stood. "Come along, Kal." She glanced down at Mr Franks. "Get in touch without delay. Those actions I mentioned still must be paused and there is a limit to how long we can wait before they go into automatic action."

We left to catch a tram home. As I opened my mouth, her look silenced me. "When are you going swimming?"

Of course – ordinary chat in public. My brain was in a whirl after Mutti's incredible performance.

"I'm meeting Lizzie on Monday afternoon."

And we chatted about work, the kitten and anything except what had happened with Mr Franks. My side of things sounded stilted to me, but Mutti, buoyed by the success of the meeting, kept things going.

Once we got home, I rushed in to check on the kitten. His fur had fluffed up now it had dried. He stretched, yawned and squeaked a meow when I picked him up. Mutti opened some windows, turned on the radio and pulled the jug of water and cut a lime from the fridge. We sat, the kitten purring in my arms.

I was both confused and elated. "What happened at the meeting?"

"Kal, we need to be careful when we speak." Mutti cautioned me. "That's why I turn the radio on; it will make it harder for anyone to make out what we're saying."

Another thing to store away.

She lowered her voice further. "As for the meeting? Well, Ravensbrück was a hard school, with daily practical tests. Failure carried ... consequences." Mutti sighed. "I thought that was all behind me after using those skills to get us across the border and into England." I could see sadness in her eyes, but there was steel there as well. "Mr Franks was expecting to deal with a beaten down refugee – and a woman. He thought he held all the cards and was completely unprepared. Because of that, he had lost before he started."

If I was to play this game, I had a lot to learn. "What's a dead drop, Mutti?"

"I learned to use them in Ravensbrück. It's a way of exchanging information and small items without having to meet. When I gave him the folded ten-shillings note, inside was a slip of paper setting up a dead drop – a location for us to exchange information. I'll put instructions for a new drop location there tomorrow and they'll drop our fee there when they pick it up."

The dead drop made sense. "Why did you need that in Ravensbrück?"

"Sometimes we worked with a greedy guard, although they were rare. Occasionally we could steal things from the forced labour factories or a prisoner smuggled a possession into the camp. We'd exchanged them for food and medicine. If the guards were caught, they would probably be shot along with us; meetings were dangerous and negotiations were held through dead drops."

Mutti stared off into the distance for a while before her eyes returned to me. "I think you should visit the Polish club this week and ask about a

Polish language textbook." Mutti thought for a minute. "Find out if there is a Polish language newspaper that you can read. If there is, try to get some old copies ... we'll need to work out who's who in the Polish community in Australia."

"I could go on Monday morning. School's finished and I'm meeting Lizzie at the pool about two o'clock. That gives me plenty of time."

Mutti took my hand. "You need to be you, nothing more, when you go." Her voice became stern. "Don't improvise." Her hand shook mine in emphasis. "You're establishing yourself as an innocent schoolgirl trying to keep her language skills current. You can tell them you had a Polish friend in Lancaster and you were trading languages. We'll need to think of a name..."

"Okay."

"Now let's eat."

The kitten had slept through our discussion but woke when I put him on the sofa as we prepared *Abendbrot*. Afterwards, I sat with him and he curled under my chin, falling asleep with a purr that vibrated my throat.

Mutti sat down. "Do you want to keep the kitten?"

"Yes, please."

This disturbed the kitten, who stretched, gazed at me with his blue eyes and yawned before nestling back under my chin.

"Well, he's your responsibility." Mutti ruffled the fur on his head with a finger. "He'll need a name."

"I've been thinking of names all day. I'm going to call him *Imbir*. He's the most ginger cat I've ever seen."

Mutti chuckled. "In Polish, a ginger cat is *rudy kot*. *Imbir* is the spice."

I blinked. "Oh." I thought for a moment and smiled at Mutti. "I'm still going to call him *Imbir*, as that will remind me to be careful in my translations."

"Okay." She stretched. "I'm going to have a shower and head to bed."

"I'll follow you."

"Sleep well, Kal, *Imbir*."

"Good night, Mutti."

I put *Imbir* down beside his water bowl and dirt box whilst I showered. When I got to my room, he had somehow clambered up and was lying on my pillow, having sought my scent. I was worried I might roll over and squash him, but he snuggled beside me on the pillow and we slept.

Chapter 6

Mid December – late January 1965

After breakfast on Sunday, we sat around in our sarongs with the radio playing to mask our conversation.

"How are you going to approach the Polish Club tomorrow, Kal?"

"It might not open. I'll have to see."

"We still need to have a story ready for you to tell the Polish and German Clubs – you never know, there may be some membership crossover, though that seems unlikely."

"Would it be better if we told everyone you stopped allowing German in the house after my father died?"

Mutti thought for a moment. "That sounds reasonable – for something completely unreasonable." Her face betrayed distaste at this subterfuge. "What about your Polish friend – what is to be her name?"

"I don't know. What do you think?"

Mutti's eyes became distant for a moment before refocusing on mine. "Nina Kamiński." She sighed. "Nina was a friend of mine at Ravensbrück." Mutti recognised the question in my eyes. "She died there." Mutti's voice carried a weight of sadness on its shoulders. "Using her name honours her memory."

Over the weekend, *Imbir's* name shortened to *Imbi* in 'Aussie' fashion. He proved to be a curious kitten, exploring the house and getting into and onto everything his miniscule size would permit. I discovered him, rear end swaying as he measured the jump from the chair onto the windowsill in his room, although I don't think he would have made it. But when we left on Monday morning, we removed the chair, foiling any escape plan as we had to leave the window open a crack to give him some fresh air.

Muttu and I travelled into the city together before I changed trams at George Street for the Polish Club in Milton. Walking along Marie Street, the purple Jacaranda blossom littered the pavement and coloured the trees. If it was closed, I hoped to find out when it opened. This was my inaugural mission as a spy and my stomach was fluttering. I was doing what I had intended to do before the agreement with Mr Franks, but the butterflies took no notice.

The club was in a large, attractive Queenslander – and it was closed on Mondays. I pulled an exercise book out of my duffel bag and jotted down the opening times and the phone number from a sign attached to the fence. As I finished, a car pulled up. The car doors open and I turned to see a woman standing on the pavement whilst a man walked round the front of the car.

"You are interested in the Polish Club?" The woman's accent reminded me of Mrs Wisniewski.

"Yes."

The man stopped in front of me. "You are Polish?"

"No."

The man frowned.

"I had a Polish friend in England and I started learning the language with her."

The frown deepened. "You speak Polish?" The Polish snapped out of him, suspicion in his voice.

Licking my lips in concentration, I assembled my reply in careful Polish. "I speak and write Polish a little, but I want to keep learning." I fumbled the delivery because of nerves and not wanting to sound too proficient.

The frown morphed into a smile. "Well done. Your accent is not bad, but you are still thinking about what you are saying. Yes?"

I was glad to be speaking English again; my jangling nerves made concentrating difficult.

"So, how can we help you?"

"The city library told me you had a library here. I don't have a Polish textbook anymore as it was my friend's. Perhaps I could find one here – and a Polish/English dictionary?"

"Hmmm."

As we were talking, the woman opened the front gate and walked up to the door.

"I am Mr Jaworski," he gestured towards the woman. "And that is my wife. You are?"

"I am Kal ... um ... Karlota Miller."

"I see." He paused, his eyes narrowing. "Come, let us see what we can find."

The building was heating up and Mrs Jaworski went around opening windows. Mr Jaworski led me into a room labelled *Biblioteka*.

"I think we have a suitable Polish grammar text here..." Mr Jaworski searched along a shelf. "Ah yes, here we are." He pulled a slim volume from the shelf and turned to me.

"But there is a problem. You are not a member of the Polish club."

That was a problem: I had assumed it would be like a normal library.

"Umm ... can I join?"

Mr Jaworski raised his eyebrows. "Well, now. Children have free membership – if their parents are members. I don't think we have a way for young people to join by themselves."

He stood there, thinking for a moment. "Here." he handed me the book. "Sit down over there and look through that for a minute whilst I talk to Mrs Jaworska."

I started leafing through the book and found a chapter on conjugating verbs. After about ten minutes, both Mr and Mrs Jaworski came into the library.

Mr Jaworski looked at me. "Where are you from?"

"I'm English."

He looked at me. "Karlota is not an English name – and I can hear something else."

We'd not thought about this. All I had was Mrs Henderson's story. "My mother is German and my father is ... was English."

Mrs Jaworski moved closer. "Was?"

"He died in an accident at work." I could see warring emotions of dislike and sympathy on Mrs Jaworski's face. Poland had suffered but endured under the Nazis.

Would losing my father awake her maternal instincts?

"I am sorry about your father."

"Hmmm." Mr Jaworski peered intensely down at me. "And does your mother speak Polish?"

"No ... umm..." I let my voice peter out.

Mr Jaworski noticed my hesitation. He leant forward. "You were going to say?"

I hesitated, playing the nervous schoolgirl. "She doesn't know I'm here. My mother even insists we stop speaking German. She wants us to become Australian." I pulled a rebellious face. "But I will be learning French at school,"

Mr and Mrs Jaworski shared an understanding glance; this was something they had come across before.

"But you want to continue learning Polish. Why is that?" Mr Jaworski's voice was kindly, but held a trace of ... suspicion?

"I like languages." I shrugged. "It would be a shame to waste the effort I had made to get this far."

Mr Jaworski rubbed his chin. "Perhaps there is something we could do for you. Can you come here tomorrow morning?"

"I'm working tomorrow morning. Would after lunch be Okay? About three o'clock?"

"That will be fine ... but remember, I'm not making any promises."

"I understand."

Mr Jaworski smiled. "We will see you tomorrow afternoon and ... maybe ... have something for you."

Standing up, I picked up my duffel bag. "Thank you."

Mr Jaworski held out his hand. "Our book?"

I flushed.

Did he think I am going to steal it?

I pressed the book into his hand.

"I'll see you out, Karlota." Mrs Jaworska led me to the front door, turning before she opened it. "You don't want your mother to know you are continuing with your languages, do you?"

"No, I don't."

"And do you still speak German well?"

I turned, blinking in surprise at her fluent German. "Of course."

"And do you wish to keep speaking German?"

"Yes. It's since ... since my father died that my mother has refused to speak German with me."

Lying again ...

Mrs Jaworski's eyes narrowed. "I see."

What is she was seeing?

I walked out to Milton Road and caught a tram back to the city. All this tram travel was expensive; I was glad Mutti had insisted on Mr Franks paying us. In the city I wandered down to the Botanical Garden where I ate my lunch sitting in the spreading shade of a Poinciana. According to the information notice, the tree produced brilliant red flowers from November to January. This one was late, but I could see buds opening amongst the fern-like leaves.

I had plenty of time before I met with Lizzie at the pool. I saved the tram fare and walked there. Sweat trickled under my clothes on arrival and I relished the thought of plunging into the cool water.

Lizzie found me sitting in the stands as general swimming started. "Ready to swim, Kal?"

"Of course."

Mrs Robinson was alone today. I waved to her as we draped our towels over the railing where she sat. We claimed a pair of vacant lanes.

"Race?" asked Lizzie.

"Okay – but four lengths this time." I stipulated. "And we'd better do a warmup couple of lengths."

Lizzie made a face. "I suppose ..."

"Lizzie," I chided her. "You'll end up hurting yourself if you go all out without a warmup."

Lizzie sighed. "I know ..." I could see her bouncing on her feet, aching to swim all out. "But I can't wait to race."

We both dived in and I swam a leisurely pace for a length as Lizzie fizzed ahead. I stretched out on the return. We clambered out and stood smiling at one another.

"Ready?" I asked.

"After three?" Lizzie asked and turned to her lane – "Three." And she was off, the cheat.

I dived after her. As we turned for the third length, she was still up on me, but when we turned again, I was ahead. I pulled further away from her on the last leg, winning by a body length.

"You cheat – you said after three." I smiled. After all, I had still beaten her.

Lizzie smiled. "I did not cheat – I said after three and that's when I started." She gave me a slap on the arm. "But you still beat me."

"I did." I laughed as we recovered our breath. "Anyway, I want to do some more lengths."

We paced off four more lengths, staying shoulder to shoulder. But when I turned for the fifth, I was by myself. I settled in and concentrated on my rhythm and breathing for about another 15 minutes. The exercise soothed the residual nerves from the Polish Club. I pushed myself for the final two lengths, arriving at the wall to stand and suck in deep breaths.

I heard Lizzie's voice above me. "That's impressive."

I squinted up at her in the bright sunlight, my chest still heaving. After a minute, I pulled myself out onto the side and we walked across to our towels. I grabbed mine and draped it over my shoulders, after giving my hair a shake.

"Karlota, you should join the swimming club." Mrs Robinson peered over the top of her impenetrable sunglasses.

I turned, hesitating.

"Oh, yes." Lizzie jumped on her mother's words. "Please do, Kal. It would be such fun to have you there."

"I'd need to speak with my mother first."

Lizzie grabbed my hand. "They'll have a leaflet at the kiosk. Come on." She grabbed my hand and pulled me after her.

The junior team met on Wednesday at five in the afternoon and on Saturday mornings at seven. A closer read of the leaflet mentioned that juniors wishing to join could go to one meeting to try out.

"What does that mean?" I asked Lizzie.

"Oh, don't worry about it. You are fast enough to make the squad ... and the team." She thought for a moment. "We don't have many long-distance swimmers like you."

I waved the leaflet. "Okay. I'll put this in my bag and speak with Mutti about it tonight."

Lizzie was sitting with her mother when I returned. She waved me over and I sat down beside her.

Mrs Robinson cocked her head sideways. "My daughter tells me you've recently arrived in Australia from England ... but you're half German." I caught a faint whiff of disapproval in her voice.

"That's right." I answered, catching a surreptitious roll of the eyes from Lizzie.

"Where are you going to school?"

"Brisbane Grammar School, I think it's called, but I'm not going until after Christmas."

Mrs Robinson leant forward. "Do you mean Brisbane Girls Grammar School?"

"Yes, that's it."

Lizzie gave me a broad smile. "That's wonderful. That's where I go."

Mrs Robinson's gazed at me, reassessing my value as a friend for Lizzie. "And where do you live, Karlota?"

"North of the city, in Kedron."

"Hmm – a newer suburb." Mrs Robinson's tone hinted that was a point against me.

Lizzie was fidgeting in her seat, uncomfortable at her mother's interrogation. "Come on, Kal. Let's swim." She grabbed my hand and pulled me down to the far end of the pool. "I'm sorry about that, Kal. She's a real snob sometimes."

I shrugged. "Let's swim."

"Okay. How about you show me what you can do over a length?"

I smiled. Lizzie was a sprinter, not a distance swimmer. "Fair enough, but this time I'll do the count."

"Okay."

We lined up at two adjacent lanes.

"One ... two ..." I realised Lizzie had over-reached her stance and was going to overbalance.

She splashed into the pool and lifted herself out again, laughing at me. "Not fair, delaying like that."

I laughed. "Let's try again...one...two...three."

My earlier swim had stretched me out and I powered into the length, digging deep with my arms. Lili still pulled away from me, beating me by most of a body length. We clung to the wall, gasping for breath.

"You swim well, Kal." She studied me. "Have you had any training?"

"I only swim for the exercise."

"Hmm. We'll see what coach can do for you."

The incident at the pool in Lancaster jumped into my brain, leaving me uneasy.

Would I draw attention to us by competing here in Australia?

I tried to damp down Lizzie's expectations. "I need to speak with Mutti about the cost and there's the time it takes once school starts."

Lizzie frowned at me. I don't think money was something she had to worry about.

"Let's swim some more lengths."

Once again, Lizzie stopped after four lengths. I settled into my rhythm and swam for about another fifteen minutes. When I pulled myself out, Lizzie was sitting with her mother.

"What's your phone number, Kal?"

"We don't have a phone yet ... I don't think we'll get one until after Christmas."

"Oh bother. Well, I'll give you mine. You can ring from a phone box and tell me about the swimming club once you've spoken to your mother." She reached across to her mother's handbag and pulled out a posh card done in flowing italic script. "This is my phone number and address."

"Thanks, Lizzie. Can I phone tomorrow evening?"

Lizzie nodded.

I checked the clock. "I have to get home and start tea for when Mutti gets home from work."

"Where does your mum work?"

I smiled. "We both work at McDonnell & East. I'm part time on the Candy counter and Mutti works in Ladies Fashion."

I heard a sniff from Mrs Robinson and I caught Lizzie's frown. She smiled with a subtle roll of her eyes.

"Give me a ring about six o'clock tomorrow, Kal."

"Okay."

Lizzie returned to the pool. I headed off to shower, change and catch a tram home.

Imbi was pleased to see me when I opened his door, squeaking his welcome with his fluffy little tail pointing straight up. I picked him up and perched him on my shoulder as I went round opening windows to cool the house. When I changed into a sarong, *Imbi* wanted to resume his shoulder perch, but kept digging in his tiny, sharp claws to keep his balance. When I put him down, his piteous meows of abandonment were too much. Sighing, I put on a thin shirt, placing a sock under it to save my shoulder and lifted *Imbi* to perch there, parrot-like.

With tea underway, I sat down with my French Grammar text. *Imbi* curled up against my neck and went to sleep.

When Mutti arrived home, she had a card in her hand. She leant down to give me a kiss with a stroke for *Imbi* and dropped the card in my lap before turning on the radio.

I looked at the card – Mr Franks had been at work. Our phone was to arrive tomorrow afternoon if someone was home.

"I can't be here tomorrow afternoon. I have to visit the Polish Club again."

"Ah." She took the card from me. "There's a number I can ring tomorrow morning and tell them to come on Wednesday morning. Okay?"

"That's fine. I won't be going out until later."

Mutti sat at the table. "Now come here and tell me how things went this morning."

I told her about my encounter with Mr and Mrs Jaworski.

"Why do they want you there tomorrow?"

"I don't know, but I think they are going to see if they can bend the rules to allow me to join."

Mutti mused for a moment. "Did you see any Polish newspapers at the club?"

"Oh, sorry. I forgot to look."

Mutti's eyes showed her disappointment. "I know it's difficult, but we must use every opportunity to gather information. We must prove our value to that man." She smiled to soften her words and changed the subject. "Did you enjoy your swim?"

"Yes ... Lizzie wants me to join the swimming club there." I dug the leaflet out of my duffel bag.

Mutti glanced through it. "Do you want to join?"

"I don't know. I've not swum competitively ... but I'm worried that this might draw attention to us. Remember that man at the Lancaster pool?"

"Hmmm ... I don't think there's the same danger here – if we keep that man happy." She smiled. "Would you like to join?"

"We don't have to decide straight away. I can go along once to see if I like it." I gave a small shrug. "But they might decide I wasn't fast enough."

"Do you think that's going to happen after Lancaster?" Mutti smiled. "Does Lizzie think you are fast enough?"

I let those thoughts sink in for a second and frowned. "You're sure it's safe for me to compete?"

Mutti shook her head. "Kal, we can never know for certain, but it's important for us to have a normal life ... if we can."

On Tuesday, I was out of my work uniform and raced to the tram. I was both nervous and curious walking up the steps of the Polish Club. I rang the bell and waited.

The door swung open, revealing Mrs Jaworski. "Ah, Karlota. Welcome, come in."

She ushered me into the library, where Mr Jaworski was sitting with two men, talking in Polish. When Mrs Jaworski led me in, they stopped talking.

Three pairs of eyes inspected me, disapproval in their gaze.

"Please sit down, Karlota." Mr Jaworski paused and looked at the older man. "This is Mr Taciak. He is the president of the Polish Association here in Brisbane and Mr Franc, our treasurer."

I had the distinct impression from the tone of voice that this meeting was most unusual and I was privileged to be sitting with these august gentlemen.

Mr Taciak was a short, neat man with white hair and a pointed beard. "So, Karlota. Mr Jaworski says you are learning Polish and came here looking for a textbook?"

"I heard you had a library and I wanted to borrow one."

"How does a half-English, half-German girl come to be learning Polish?"

His voice held a note of suspicion. I shrank into the chair. My eyes flicked to Mr Jaworski, who gave me an encouraging nod. I licked my lips. "I had a friend who was Polish..." My voice withered under Mr Taciak's stare.

Mr Taciak's eyes bored into mine. "And?" He couldn't believe a Polish girl would befriend a German girl.

"Well ... we had a homework club and swapped languages. I learned Polish and Nina learned German."

"Hmph." Mr Taciak grunted.

Mr Franc leant forward, giving Mr Taciak a sideways glance, speaking Polish. "Mr Jaworski tells me you speak Polish."

I glanced at Mr Jaworski. "Yes, a little." The Polish limped from my dry mouth.

Mr Taciak leant forward, waving a hand as if to brush aside this irrelevance, launching into Polish. "Some suggest we permit you to join the class we run for the children of Poles." He paused, almost glaring at me. "Why should we do this for a Hun?"

I heard sharp intakes of breath at Mr Taciak's rudeness. Without thinking, I replied. "I know what that means."

Silence engulfed the room before Mr Taciak coughed. "I apologise." His eyes dropped from mine before returning. "I do not hold Germans in high regard." His faced softened and he continued with a sigh. "But you are a child. What happened is not your fault."

Had he survived a death camp?

I wanted to tell him I understood, to share Mutti's story, but controlled myself.

Mr Taciak glanced at Mr Franc. "Let her join the class. Our children need to see that German children are not the monsters we encountered in Poland. We must all be Australian now."

I stood up and dipped my head in respect. "Thank you, sir".

Mr Jaworski led me out. "Come with me and we'll fill out a membership form..." He smiled at me. "...as best we can."

Once that was done, he pursed his lips. "The class has closed for Christmas and starts again once school returns. You will get a letter giving you the details, but it meets here on Thursday afternoons from half-past three to six o'clock."

"Thank you ... but please don't send me a letter. My mother might see it."

"Ah yes, I forgot about that." He turned to a calendar. "Hmmm...the first class will be here on Thursday, the twenty-eighth of January." He wrote this on a piece of paper and handed it to me. "There is a fee to pay the teacher for their time. It's two shillings and sixpence a term." His eyes queried mine. "Can you afford that?"

I swallowed. That was a lot of money. "I have a part-time job, but that might stop after Christmas."

Mr Jaworski's face softened. "Well, come along anyway and see me before it starts. I'm sure we can work something out." He pursed his lips. "You will need to buy the textbook and a dictionary." He picked up a slip of paper from a folder. "Here, you can buy them at this shop."

"Thank you."

As we walked out, I saw a pile of *Wiadomości Polskie*, the Polish newspaper. "Please Mr Jaworski, may I take a newspaper to give me something to read in Polish?"

He stopped and thought for a moment. "You'd have to pay for one of those, but I think we can find you some old copies. Wait here a moment." He disappeared into the depths of the building, reappearing after a minute with a small bundle of newspapers. "Here you go. This should keep you going for a while."

I folded the half-dozen newspapers and stuffed them into my duffel bag.

"Thank you, Mr Jaworski."

"We'll see you again at the end of January."

I headed to Milton Road and a tram home. Away from the club, I let a glow of achievement spread through me: I had accomplished my first mission.

That evening, I walked down to the phone box and called Lizzie to tell her I would try out at the swimming club on Wednesday. Mutti and I spent some time leafing through the Polish newspapers, learning about the Polish community.

On Wednesday morning, the PMG arrived to install the phone. *Imbi* chased cables as they were being dragged around. I saw the frown he received from a technician and scooped him up, sequestering him in the study until they finished. After, I sat for a while, worrying about trying out for the club, despite what Mutti had said. To distract myself, I made some sandwiches. I checked Imbi was safe in his room with water, food and the window open a crack before I left.

Walking through the city, my worries about Willi and Lili returned with a vengeance. I had buried them beneath the stress associated with Mr Franks and getting into the Polish Club. My hand strayed to Willi's necklace. I knew Mrs Henderson hadn't delivered my message; it didn't benefit her.

Willi's survival hung by two threads – his promise to me and my request that Lili tell me if his actions seemed strange. I hadn't expected to disappear, but I thought having Lili watching his moods would help. I contemplated Willi's suicidal tendencies, hoping those two threads were enough, though their frailty made me shiver in fear.

By the time I arrived at the pool, I could feel panic flickering at the edge of my mind. I was in the pool as soon as they announced general swimming. Three lengths of pounding rhythm calmed me. I continued for some better controlled lengths before hauling myself out to sit for a while. For my sanity, I could not let my fears about Willi overwhelm me.

Should I talk about this with Mutti? Is there a way I could get a message to Willi?

I sat there, lost in thought.

"Kal? Are you all right?"

I took a sharp breath and opened my eyes, blinking in the bright sunlight. "Lizzie."

A gentle hand rested on my shoulder, turning me. "You were miles away."

I tried to chase away the dark thoughts. "Sorry, Lizzie. I've a lot on my mind."

Her caring eyes stared into mine. "Oh Kal, I'm sorry." Her hand squeezed my shoulder. "Pushing you about the swimming club hasn't helped, has it?"

"That's not true, Lizzie. The rhythm of swimming helps a lot. It helps me calm down and sort things out."

"Can I help with anything?" She asked, almost timid.

I sensed Lizzie was unaccustomed to confronting problems and covered her hand with mine. "Thank you. You're helping by being my friend."

Lizzie cocked her head to one side, sharing a quirky expression. "I can keep secrets, you know." She gave a half-embarrassed laugh. "With my snoopy mother, I have to."

But can she keep them all?

I smiled. "Okay."

Lizzie raised her eyebrows in expectation, looking away when I didn't continue, pulling her hand down into her lap.

I put a hand on her shoulder. "I'm sorry, Lizzie. It's difficult ..." I could see some hurt in her eyes as my voice petered out.

We sat in awkward silence until Lizzie roused herself. "Come on, Kal. Let's swim."

We swam for a while and ate our sandwiches. When the swimming club started, Lizzie introduced me to the junior swimming coach. As I hadn't swum in competitions before, he had me warm up and swim a length against the clock. Lizzie must have been speaking to him as he then had me swim a 400m race against another girl, Olivia. I didn't know how to pace myself and concentrated on staying with Olivia for 200 meters. As we turned onto the penultimate length, I stretched out. After the final tumble turn, she was ahead and I went all out, touching a second behind her. We stared at one another over the lane markers, regaining our breath.

Olivia leant across to shake my hand. "Nice swim."

"Thank you. I don't know – I've only been swimming for about six months."

Olivia's eyes widened in surprise. "Well, damn." She glanced round. "Oops – I shouldn't have said that." No-one else seemed to have heard. She shrugged and smiled. "Once coach gets you trained, I can return to the 100m where I'm best."

I could see the coach was talking to some people and he waved me over.

"Kal Miller, isn't it?"

"Yes."

"Your swim was quite impressive. I understand you haven't had any training or swum competitively before?"

I was feeling more and more uneasy, as I could feel several eyes on me.

Coach sensed my reserve and smiled. "Don't worry. We can train you if you decide to join – which we'd like you to do."

"I'll need to speak to my mother."

The coach smiled again. "Of course. This is the final training session until the end of January. Come along then and we'll sort you out."

In the changing room, Lizzie was bubbling with delight. "It's great to have you in the club. We'll have such fun."

"I do still have to speak to my mother." I said, trying to keep her enthusiasm contained.

"Okay." Lizzie bubbled on. "Can you come swimming again before Christmas?"

"I don't know. I'll ring you."

"Okay." Lizzie sounded disappointed. I gave her an encouraging smile as we walked out to catch our respective trams.

At home, Mutti served me *Abendbrot* and sat at the table as I ate, the radio playing the classical music station to mask our conversation.

"How did it go?"

I finished my mouthful. "They want me to join. Can we afford all this – the membership, tram fares and the fees for the Polish Club?"

"The work for that man will earn us my salary over again." Mutti gave me a warning look. "But we need to be careful that we do not overspend. That would draw suspicion down on us."

"We can afford it ... but shouldn't? Is that what you are saying?"

"Yes – but there's the matter of your time."

I could hear the concern in her voice. "What do you mean?"

"Well, you'll be going to school at the end of January and you'll need time to study." Mutti gave me an appraising look. "You'll be at swimming one evening and Saturday mornings and at the Polish club one afternoon. Can you do all this and keep up with your schoolwork?"

I shrugged. "Until I see the work, I won't know. But I found the school Maths and English tests quite easy."

Mutti thought for a moment. "I don't think you can continue working part time on the Candy Counter after Christmas. Your Saturday mornings will be taken up with swimming."

"I wonder if I can work there in the holidays?"

Mutti raised an eyebrow. "Would you like me to speak to Mr Chapman to see if this is possible?"

"Yes please. If I'm earning something, it would make it easier to be spending money."

"I'll see what I can do."

I gathered up our dirty dishes and took them to the sink.

"Wash them and put them in the drying rack."

As I did that, I thought over my near panic earlier in the day. I went and sat beside Mutti on the sofa. "Mutti, can I talk to you about Willi?"

"Of course, *Liebling*."

"I don't think Mrs ..." I stopped myself in time. "... that woman sent my message and I'm worried about him."

Mutti stroked my arm. "And ...?"

"Do you think if I sent that same message to him on a postcard, it would be safe?"

Mutti's eyes gazed into the distance as she thought this through. After a minute, her eyes returned to mine.

"I don't think that would work. He is possibly being watched ... by both sides."

I'd been expecting this. "What if I wrote to Lili instead? She would realise it's a message for Willi and pass it on."

Mutti sighed. "I don't think that would be safe either. Her mother's actions over Willi's trip to east Germany will have drawn attention to her family as well."

"But if I can't tell him we're safe, he might ..." I squeezed my eyes closed, trying to hold in the tears. "... kill himself ..." My voice collapsed and tears rolled down my face.

Mutti gathered me into her arms, holding me. After a while, she lifted my chin. "You two spoke about this?"

"Mmm."

"And?"

Worry fluttered at the edge of my brain. "I made him promise to talk to me if he was heading ... there ... again." My face screwed up in distress. "But I'm not there and he can't talk to me..." I dissolved into tears again, drawn into Mutti's enfolding embrace.

The comfort of Mutti's arms was seductive, but as my tears subsided, I realised I was using them as an escape. Once I left Mutti's supportive embrace, my problems would remain. I pulled away. Mutti sensed something was different and raised an eyebrow.

"I have to sort this out."

Mutti's thumbs brushed the tears from my cheeks. "Yes, *Liebling,* it is your problem and you have to work it out." Her smile bathed me in love. "But you can talk with me about anything, anything. You know that, don't you?"

I returned her smile, though teary and thin. I had no idea how to live with my fear for Willi's life, unable to do anything about it. Willi told me that in his world, the Eastern Bloc collapsed in 1988, which gave me a date on the calendar when I might again become Colette Schmidt and go looking for him. I hoped somehow to bring that date forward – a long, long way forward.

Like tomorrow.

I took a searching breath and pulled away from Mutti's caring embrace. Life went on – and there we had the Polish newspapers to read. I brought them out and we sat reading for a while. Mutti looked up, catching my eye. "We need to track the important people in Polish Australia."

"Yes, but how do we know who's important?"

"We don't." Mutti's smile was enigmatic.

I frowned in confusion. In return, Mutti queried me with her eyes. I shrugged, at a complete loss.

"We keep records of events and people to track what's going on. That way, we'll see who is important." Mutti thought for a minute. "We need a card index system. We'll need one for German Australia as well once you visit the German Club and find out about German-language newspapers. I'll look in the stationery section at work tomorrow."

"I can do that before I start my afternoon shift on the Candy Counter."

"I have my lunch break at twelve o'clock tomorrow. You can meet me in the staff room and tell me what you've found. If they don't have anything we might need to visit a business supplies shop."

Lying in bed with *Imbi* curled under my chin, my worries about Willi surged to the fore, threatening to consume me. I longed to contact him, to share my life with him, to keep him from the precipice.

If I can't send him my letters, I can still write to him...

That thought drifted around for a while. It seemed pointless to write letters I could not send, but they would tell me who I was ...

And how I am changing.

Peril limned the scary cloud around my love for Willi. He was associated with a past me: by changing, I would leave Willi behind. My heart thudded at this and I fought to breathe deep, calming breaths.

I knew I would change ... but it also meant as Willi changed, he was leaving me behind. I stiffened.

We would become different people.

If ... no, when we met, showing Willi how I grew from the Col he had loved would help rebuild our connection. If I wrote him letters, I would place them in his hand; he could trace from the me he had known through to the person I had become. When we met, I would have to search for the thread linking to the Willi I had known in Herne Bay.

My rigidity eased in that acceptance: we would both change. Lying there, understanding came that those changes could well change our feelings for each other and tears of loss dribbled onto my pillow.

Imbi stirred, staring into my eyes. With a finger, I ruffled the fur on his forehead and under his chin. After several long blinks, he sensed I had calmed and settled against me. Tomorrow I would buy something I could use as a journal for my letters to Willi. It wasn't a solution to my pain, but it would have to do.

• • • •

AFTER MUTTI LEFT IN the morning, I rang Lizzie to give her our phone number and to set up a swim date on Friday afternoon. I played with *Imbi* for a while; he's an adorable scamp, chasing string with total commitment. He has such fluffy paws that he can't stop on the lino. Instead, he rolls head over heels as he slides, trying to grab the string as he passes and lies on his back waving his paws to catch the end while I tease him with it. After about twenty minutes, he stopped where he was and dropped into sleep. I picked him up, settled him in his cardboard box bed, checking his water and window. Picking up my duffel bag, I locked up and headed into the city.

The McDonnell & East books and stationery section had cardboard bound journals, bigger than my exercise books. They would do for my letters to Willi and I bought one. I spied some card index boxes with cards as well. Mutti arrived soon after twelve.

"They have card index boxes in stationery." I told her.

"Thanks Kal, I'll pick up a couple."

"I'd better get moving." After changing into my uniform, I headed off to the Candy Counter.

Mutti met me in the staffroom after work. She had a heavy McDonnell & East bag and a large box labelled "Singer" beside our locker.

Mutti saw the question on my face and smiled. "I picked up two index boxes and enough curtain material for our bedrooms in the sale." She gestured to the box labelled Singer. "I've borrowed a sewing machine."

With the two of us alternating carrying the sewing machine and heavy bag of fabric, we had a slow walk to the tram and then to our house. We were both hot and sweaty and I blessed the designer of this style of house: once opened, it cooled as the sea breeze flowed through. When I opened the study, *Imbi* stretched and his yawn would have done credit to a lion.

After tea, we measured up the windows in our bedrooms and laid the fabric on the floor to cut it. *Imbi* decided this was a wonderful game. After he leapt onto the material for the umpteenth time, Mutti looked at me with a pained expression on her face. I shared a rueful smile and shut him in the study.

"Where did you learn to sew, Mutti?"

She sat on her haunches. "Like many things, forced labour in Ravensbrück." Her eyes were distant as my question stirred bitter memories.

I pulled a face. "Sorry Mutti, I wasn't thinking."

Mutti leant across the fabric to take my hand. "Oh, *Liebling.* You don't have to apologise for what happened to me." She took a deep breath. "I kept it hidden from you when you were little, but now I don't have to – and that night with Willi, I let slip more than I should have." Her eyes locked with mine and her voice became hard-edged. "I don't hate, but I have not forgiven. There are still many people out there who deserve judgment ... like your father."

We returned to measuring, cutting and pinning the curtains.

Chapter 7
Late December 1964 – late January 1965

"What's wrong, Lizzie?" Her face wore an unusual frown as she walked up to me beside the pool.

"My mother. She's such a bi ..." Lizzie stopped herself, grinding her teeth at the effort. "She's such a snob ..." Her voice had started with a snarl but drifted away to a sigh.

I stifled a smile at her almost swear word and raised an eyebrow.

"Oh – I asked her if I could invite you to our Christmas party tomorrow." Lizzie looked at me apologetically. "She refused – because she doesn't think you're from the 'right sort of family'."

I smiled. "Oh, Lizzie. I'm friends with you, not your mother."

"She's ridiculous." Lizzie threw her hands in the air in frustration.

She was winding herself up again; I took her hand, pulling towards the pool. "Let's swim – use all that energy to beat me over four lengths."

We tossed our towels over our chairs and found a pair of lanes.

"We should do a couple of warm up laps." I cautioned.

Lizzie gave me a fierce look and dived in, pounding down the lane. I dived in and swam the two lengths at a gentle, warm up pace, stretching the muscles in my arms, shoulders and legs. Lizzie was already out, offering me a glower for being a slowcoach. I pulled myself out and we lined up.

"One ... Two ... Three ... Go."

From our previous races, I was learning about pacing myself. Lizzie almost sprinted down the first length, more than a body length ahead of me by the turn. I pushed a little harder on the second length, holding my position as Lizzie realised she couldn't sprint for four lengths. During the third length, I pushed harder and we turned for home with me in front. I pulled away from Lizzie, finishing well in front of her.

We clung to the wall, breathing. Lizzie reached across and play-punched my arm.

"You're learning, Kal." She was smiling, shamefaced. "I should have controlled myself ... but I was furious."

She had burned out her mad in the swim.

"Come on, it's my turn to buy the ice creams."

We ate our Eskimo Pies and swam again. Lizzie insisted I swim a length or two of back and breaststroke, neither of which I do well.

"I can't swim again until after Christmas." I told Lizzie as we changed.

"Okay." Lizzie nodded. "Shall I ring you after Christmas?"

"Excellent."

And we set off on different trams.

When Mutti arrived home, she gave me a sheet of paper announcing the McDonnell & East New Year BBQ in New Farm Park on Sunday 3rd of January. "As the store is busy before Christmas, they have their end-of-year celebration after New Year."

I looked over the flyer. "What's a BBQ?"

"It's a barbeque – meat cooked over hot coals." Mutti smiled. "The invitation says we can bring a guest."

I could see hesitation in Mutti's eyes. "Do you want to ask Lizzie?"

"If you think that's okay? Isn't there anyone you'd like to ask?"

Mutti smiled, shaking her head. "Not this year. Anyway, you're working there – you're allowed to bring a guest."

"Have you spoken to Mr Chapman about me?"

"Everyone's busy with the Christmas rush and I thought it best to wait until January. Are you working after Christmas?"

I shrugged. "I'll find out when they bring round the week's shifts."

After tea, we retrieved the Polish newspapers and started filling the card index. We worked hard for an hour, entering names on cards and adding story titles and dates. Most of the names seemed to be from Melbourne and Sydney, but we found a few Queensland stories. *Imbi* wanted to sit on the newspapers, but I restricted him to my shoulder or lap most of the time.

After a while, Mutti looked up. "I think the Polish community here in Australia is conservative in its outlook. If I'm correct, we won't be sending in many reports — unless there are Eastern Bloc agents trying to stir things up."

I remembered Willi's characterisation of the Stasi files as 'full of boring detail' when people examined them after the Wall came down in his world.

Were our reports going to mimic them?

Maybe the German community would be different.

When we pushed the drained newspapers away from us, Mutti stretched her shoulders. "Would you like to ask Lizzie to join us for Christmas Eve ... *Heiligabend*?"

For a second, I stared with widening eyes at Mutti. My throat constricted, tears dribbled down my cheek and I sank forward onto the table. Memories of the previous two Christmases played a mocking loop across my eyelids, taunting me with their magic. Those Christmases, delicate flowers of intense joy, were now ... splintered shards ... dust and ashes. Sobs racked my body as I floundered in a gyre of misery.

Some unknown time later, a tiny tongue rasped my hand and I felt a gentle movement on my hair. *Imbi* was licking my fingers and Mutti was stroking my head, each providing solace. I turned my head. *Imbi's* blue eyes gazed into mine, as if he understood my grief, my loss. He had lost his mother and littermates ...

"Oh, *Liebling*." Mutti gathered me in her arms. "I'm sorry, so sorry."

Tears slid down her face and I heard them in her voice. With a string of breaths, calming knots on a rope, I reeled myself into the world and pushed myself upright. "I'm sorry, Mutti. This is ... foolish."

Mutti shook her head, sighing. "No, *Liebling*. It's me that should apologise for stirring up hard memories."

Shaking my head, I scattered a tear or two from my face, startling *Imbi*. "No, Mutti." I breathed again, struggling to hold a slippery thought before it wriggled free. "No, Mutti. They are beautiful memories and I'm tarnishing them with sadness and tears."

Mutti's face showed her confusion.

Despite my words, tears still ran down my cheeks as I struggled to explain. "They are beautiful memories of special times with my closest friends – and with you. They are a beacon for what I want to find again." Things came into focus. "I must cherish all my memories of Willi and Lili. I can't cloud them with sadness. If I do that, we might never rediscover it."

Mutti's eyes searched mine for understanding. After a painful silence, she asked, "No Lizzie?"

I smiled, sniffing. "Wanting to keep the memories of my dearest friends untrammelled doesn't mean I shouldn't have friends here." I pulled a wry face, remembering what Lizzie had told me. "Lizzie wanted to invite me to her Christmas party, but her mother wouldn't let her. I'll ring her tomorrow morning and see if she'd like to come, but I don't think her mother will allow that either."

Mutti leant forward, planting a gentle kiss on my forehead.

"Thank you for suggesting Lizzie come for *Heiligabend*, Mutti." I gave her a kiss in return, sagging from emotional exhaustion.

"Are you all right, *Liebling*?" Her hand reached out, lacing her fingers through mine.

I gave her a sad, tear-stained look. "No, Mutti, I'm not." I closed my eyes for a moment, summoning another infusion of calm with a breath. "...not yet." I saw the tide of anxiety rise in her eyes and squeezed her hand in reassurance. "But I'm working on it."

Mutti's gaze held mine as she grappled with what I had admitted. "All right, *Liebling*," she said, with soft encouragement. "You can always talk to me."

"I know, Mutti. Thank you."

• • • •

I STARTED WRITING TO Willi once Mutti had left for work and rang Lizzie after nine o'clock, inviting her to spend Christmas Eve, *Heiligabend*, with us. She told me she had to speak to her mother, who was out. She rang about an hour later.

"Hello, Kal...." I could tell from her downbeat voice the answer was no. "Yes?"

"I'm sorry. I'd love to come and share a German Christmas Eve with you, but my mother says we're too busy."

"That's all-right Lizzie, thank you for ringing. I'll give you a ring after Christmas about meeting up for a swim."

"Okay. Happy Christmas." Lizzie's voice hinted at her frustration with her mother.

"Happy Christmas." I had the impression that Lizzie had wanted to say more but couldn't – her mother was probably listening.

Would she accept me once I started at the same school as Lizzie?

With a sigh, I returned to my journal to re-read what I had written.

Monday 21ˢᵗ December 1964

Dearest Willi

I have wanted to write to you since that last morning. I tried to get a message to you and Lili, but despite writing the message, the only messenger available didn't deliver it. When we meet, I'll tell you all about what happened.

I wanted to explain, but I couldn't leave any written clues that might give people a loose thread into our previous lives. This was difficult...

I can't send you the letters I write here, but I am writing anyway. This way you can link the me that exists when we meet again with the me that you knew. We will both change, I know, but I want the connection, the love we had to grow again when we meet. It will be difficult because of those changes, but with these letters, you will see them as they happen to me. I hope this will help you reconnect with me and, through that, help me connect with you.

I picked up my pen, but stopped, making a firm decision: no edits. Whatever I wrote would be immutable to keep my writing truthful — and complete. But there were things I couldn't say – particularly everything associated with Mrs Henderson in England and Mr Franks here. Somehow, I must put in reminders to myself to tell Willi about the things that were dangerous to write about. During the rest of the day, I added to my letter in fits and starts.

Mutti and I have ended up in Australia – in Brisbane, the capital of Queensland.

I almost wrote how Willi had lived here for decades – but stopped myself in time. Keeping his secrets secure was just as critical as protecting my own.

This is such a strange country –like England and yet so different. Instead of squirrels, we have possums and koala bears in the surrounding trees; instead of thrushes, we have carolling magpies; kookaburras sit on our veranda railing in the grey pre-dawn and wake us with their raucous laughter. And there's all the dangerous spiders and snakes. I've come across redback spiders under the house, but I've not seen any snakes yet. I suppose I will sometime – a thought that makes me nervous. We've been here two months and I keep seeing things I want to tell you about ... and that sharpens your absence. I am fighting to keep those beautiful times with you and Lili as happy memories, but it is hard.

I miss you.

Mutti has a job in Ladies Fashion at a department store. I've been working there too, on the Candy counter in the run up to Christmas as I can't start school until January. I've started swimming again. Ha - I bet that surprises you, after my refusal to go into the sea in England – but you know why that was. I've joined a swimming club and made a friend, Lizzie Robinson. Unfortunately, her mother is rather a snob. She doesn't seem to think I – a new Australian and a 'nasty German' as the Italian family next door thinks of us – am a suitable friend for her daughter. Lizzie wanted me to go to their Christmas party, but her mother refused. I asked her to join us for Heiligabend, as you and Lili did, and she wasn't allowed to do that either. But it turns out that we will be at the same school when I start in January; we'll see what happens.

We retrieved all our things from the house in Herne Bay and I have your gold chain, which I now wear all the time.

I almost talked about not wearing his necklace when I masquerading as a boy. So much had to remain unspoken in these letters ...

As I sit writing this, my left hand is fingering it.

All my textbooks arrived with everything else and Mutti insisted I keep on studying. I think the Latin I learned with you will get lost as I can't find a way to study that here, but the other languages seem possible. I don't have a Polish textbook, but I will join classes the Polish Club runs for the children of members and I'll be studying French at school. Not having you around to help me with Maths has been a problem – but I was using you as a crutch. I've found that if I stick to it, I can understand enough to answer the exercises in the textbook – most of the time.

I hope you are still working with Lili; when I sit down to study, I picture you and Lili in her kitchen as we all used to do. I wish I'd asked Lili for a drawing of you – but I'll have to make do with these letters and your necklace.

We've acquired a kitten. I found him sheltering under our house after a furious thunderstorm. He's a tiny fluffy ginger ball of fur and we've called him Imbir (Imbi for short in the Australian way). He likes to sit on my shoulder, but he clings on using his sharp claws. I put padding under my top to keep him from drawing blood. With the summer weather, we both get hot, though.

I had been thinking for most of the day about how to add a reminder for me to talk with Willi about Mr Franks. As the afternoon drew on towards evening, I added the following.

About a week ago, we went to a seafood restaurant. I was uneasy when I was told we were going to be eating bugs – but they turned out to be like small lobsters and delicious. I didn't like the oysters, though – or the people we ate with.

That's all for now, Willi. Please stay safe.

I love you,

Kal

I was about to sign off as Col, but remembered in time. I hoped that me saying I did not like the people at the restaurant would act as a reminder to talk to Willi about Mr Franks and what we were doing. After I put down my pen, I chided myself for not telling Willi about my fear that he and Lili would end up together. Thinking about it was hard; writing about it for Willi to read some distant time in the future was scary.

What would he think of me?

Confronting my fear about Willi and Lili is about me.

Giving imagined jealousy room to grow would poison all possibility of a future with Willi. Thinking about that now was difficult – tomorrow would suffice. I closed the journal and picked up *Imbi*, who had been sleeping on my lap, and went to get tea ready.

When Mutti arrived home that evening, she turned on the radio and beckoned me to sit down with her at the table. Once I sat beside her, she pulled an envelope from her bag containing seventy ponds in used ten-pound notes.

"Mr Franks has agreed to our suggestion."

My stomach clenched. We were now undercover agents for the Australian government.

"So, Kal." Mutti's face was serious. "You're being yourself at the Polish Club and soon the German Club, but you'll need to be alert and observant. You'll have to see, hear and remember everything that goes on around you." Her eyes locked with mine. "Also, you must keep track of anything that might threaten you."

I blinked. I hadn't thought I would be in danger.

Mutti's face remained serious. "Being alert and observant is part of gathering information. After each visit to the Polish Club, we'll sit down and you'll go over your entire visit from start to finish. We'll look at every detail, every person you see and every snippet of conversation you hear."

I swallowed.

Mutti's face softened. "Don't worry. You'll soon find that you can recall a great deal." She leant across and took my hand. "You've a well-trained mind already, thanks to all that study with Willi and Lili."

I don't feel confident about this.

Mutti opened her purse and gave me five one-pound notes. "We need to be careful about how we spend this money. You'll have expenses – trams, your Polish books and such – and this is to cover those." Her eyes held mine. "Don't use it for anything else."

I put the money in my purse and Mutti gave my hand an encouraging squeeze. "Come on, let's eat."

· · · ·

MUTTI AND I SPENT A muted *Heiligabend* preparing the traditional feast. As our duck roasted, the strangeness of the situation overwhelmed me. Sitting on the shaded veranda looking at the brilliant evening sunshine in Brisbane's heat and humidity didn't feel like Christmas Eve at all. As dusk fell, we heard a knock at the door and Mr Greco stood there with Cal. In his arms, he held a box of vegetables – from his burgeoning garden, I suspected.

"Mrs Miller, Kal." He greeted us with a smile that hinted at embarrassment. "I want to apologise. I 'ave not been a good neighbour." Despite his English, I now understood where his daughter's English came from.

Mutti held the door open and Mr Greco walked through to the kitchen and put the box on the bench. Cal awarded me a secretive smile, which I returned. We had talked across the fence, her excitement building as Christmas approached.

This was unexpected. It flustered Mutti, as we had nothing to give in return.

Mr Greco must have sensed her embarrassment. "Enjoy. *Buon Natale* – 'appy Christmas." And he swept out, with Cal in his wake, giving Mutti no opportunity to talk.

We inspected the box. It contained two plump, purple aubergines, some tomatoes and courgettes, red capsicum, carrots, a lettuce and a bunch of Italian parsley. Mutti stood looking at the box, shaking her head in bemusement.

After a moment, she roused herself. "We must find something to take to them, Kal."

We shared a questioning glance as we tried to work out what we had available.

On the counter, I spied the *Dresdner Stollen* we had made. "Why don't we cut slices of *Stollen*? We can't eat all of it today."

"Excellent – and I have a box with a Christmas scene on it we can put them in."

Ten minutes later, we knocked at the Greco's front door. Mr Greco opened it, with Mrs Greco hovering behind him.

Mutti offered him the box. "Happy Christmas, Mr Greco."

The entire Greco family spilled onto the veranda. Mrs Greco opened the box, with Cal peering into it as she held Giorgio's hand.

"*Un momento, per favore.*" Mr Greco lapsed into Italian and disappeared into the house.

Mrs Greco inspected the contents and looked up, eyebrows raised in query.

"It's *Stollen* – a traditional rich German fruit loaf for Christmas Eve." Mutti explained as Mr Greco reappeared with a bottle and three glasses. Mrs Greco looked bemused until Cal translated for her.

"A Christmas toast," Mr Greco exclaimed, pouring a pale-yellow liquid into the glasses. He handed one to his wife and another to Mutti. "It's *Limoncello* – a lemon drink we make in *Italia* – and now 'ere."

Mutti smiled. "Thank you."

Mr Greco raised his glass, clinking it against Mutti's and his wife's. "To friendship ... *Allacia.*"

Mrs Greco shared a shy smile, but raised her glass. "*All' amicizia.*"

"To friendship ... Cheers." Mutti sipped her drink, pulling her glass from her lips as the alcohol hit her tongue. "Goodness, it's quite strong ... but nice."

Mr Greco translated for Mrs Greco, who smiled.

Mutti took another sip. "We cannot stay. Our dinner is in the oven."

Mr Greco raised his in understanding. "Also ours. *Buon Natale* – 'appy Christmas."

Mutti finished her drink. "Happy Christmas to you all – and thank you for coming to our house."

Mr Greco smiled, waving as we went down the steps to our Christmas celebration.

• • • •

AFTER CHRISTMAS, I sat down and wrote to Willi. I told him how I had been scared that he and Lili would become a couple and forget me. But I now realised that was about me, not them. As I wrote, I saw the years stretching ahead of us. Would my fierce love for Willi fade? Would I meet someone else and end up removing Willi's necklace? I sat for a while, fearful that I would meet someone and betray Willi. Sitting pen in hand, I almost vowed myself to celibacy ...

How am I going to live my life until I can escape to England and find Willi? How is he going to live his, unable to trace me?

The second question wasn't mine to answer – and I suppressed a shudder as memories of Willi's suicidal tendencies ambushed me. He had promised to talk to me, but Lili was watching him now.

It has to be enough ...

I fluffed the soft fur on *Imbi's* neck and inhaled his scent. These letters to Willi would record my faltering journey towards an answer to that first question each time I wrote.

I hope Willi's there to read them ...

I tried to flick these dark thoughts away, startling *Imbi* with my sudden movement. His brilliant blue eyes reproached me and I cuddled him. Which of us most needed the reassurance of touch and warmth was unclear.

On the Sunday after Christmas, Lizzie rang. We agreed to meet at the pool the following day at ten o'clock. As Mutti was working, we made a day of it, swimming, chatting and lazing about. Lizzie worked with me on sprints and helped me with pacing my longer swims. I swam a 400m under her guidance and she suggested I might think about 800m as well when the club restarted at the end of January.

As we sat on the wall, eating our Eskimo Pies, I asked Lizzie if she would like to come with me to the McDonnell & East Christmas party on January 3rd.

"I'd love to," smiled Lizzie. "But will my mother let me?"

I shrugged. "Well, all you can do is ask her."

Lizzie's mouth opened, but she thought better of what I suspected was a disparaging remark about her mother. She gave me a bleak smile. "I know my mother means well, but she's trying to run my life." She huffed out a breath of exasperation. "All she sees in my future is marriage to some up-and-coming doctor or lawyer and providing him with a home and a bundle of kids." She stopped, her eyes sweeping round the pool as if seeking an alternate future. "But that's not enough." Her hand slapped the wall and her shoulders slumped. "I mean, I'm not against marriage – or against having children, but I want the freedom to choose my life."

Mutti differed from Lizzie's mother; Mutti wanted me to have a rounded education that gave me options.

Lizzie looked sideways at me and her voice dropped. "Making kids sounds like it's fun, scary fun, though."

She had a slight blush on her face as I raised my eyebrows and gave her a wicked smile in return. I leant closer, almost whispering. "I don't know – we never got that far."

Lizzie's eyes widened. "You had a boyfriend and ..." her voice dropped, "... did things?"

I blushed, holding Lizzie's eyes. "Mostly kissing..."

Lizzie's eyes were almost bulging and I could see she had a thousand questions. She turned away, her face flushing. "I'm not allowed to date and I've never been properly kissed." Her voice a blend of fear and yearning.

I patted her hand, keeping my voice low. "We can talk about this ... somewhere less public?"

Lizzie's head swivelled round, taking in the people nearby, a guilty look on her face. She turned to me. "Please."

"You'll have to visit my house one day and meet my kitten."

Lizzie smiled in understanding. "Come on, let's swim or my mother will go nuts about me putting on weight again."

As we swam, it became apparent that I was a long-distance swimmer, not a sprinter. But Lizzie had listened to the long-distance coaches and helped me work to improve. Once the swimming club restarted, I would have a few useful skills.

Lizzie's tram was the first to arrive. "I'll give you a ring about the McDonnell & East party – and coming to meet your kitten."

"OK."

That evening, Lizzie rang and I heard the excitement in her voice. "My mother said 'yes', Kal. I can join you at the BBQ."

I blinked in surprise – Mrs Robinson wasn't as down on me as I thought. "That's fantastic, Lizzie. It starts at 12 noon; why don't you come to my house in the morning and meet my kitten, *Imbi*? We can all catch the tram to New Farm Park."

"Hang on a minute." I heard a muffled conversation; Lizzie must have covered the mouthpiece. "That's OK. What time should I arrive?"

"How about nine?"

"Right ho. Should I bring anything?"

"Umm – I don't think so. The store is providing food and drink."

"Okay. See you."

"Bye."

I clattered the phone on to its base and hugged myself in excitement. Having Lizzie come with me to the party would be fun. I was still an outsider with the older Candy counter crew and they were the only people around my age I knew, apart from Lizzie.

Mutti and I spent New Year's Eve together and were in bed before midnight. *Imbi* woke, startled by some nearby midnight fireworks. I gave him calming strokes along the side of his face as he stared into my eyes, his ears flicking in agitation. The fireworks died down and we both slipped into sleep.

I was waiting on the veranda for Lizzie when a gleaming white Mercedes pulled up in front of our house. Lizzie climbed out, a shoulder bag in her hand and a wide hat shading her face. The dazzling sunshine made me squint as I ran down the steps, fizzing with excitement. "Hi, Lizzie." My face almost split in two with my wide smile.

I looked through the open car door and managed a restrained tone. "Good morning, Mrs Robinson."

Mrs Robinson slipped from her car, a silk scarf round her neck. "Hello, Karlota." I could see her looking around, assessing the area through her impenetrable sunglasses. She turned towards me. "What time does the party finish, Karlota?"

"I think it goes until six o'clock."

She swivelled to Lizzie. "Ring me when you get back here."

"Yes, mother."

I heard footsteps behind me and a hand rested on my shoulder. "Good morning. I'm Mrs Miller, Kal's mother."

Mrs Robinson walked round the front of the car, her hand reaching out in a languid, elegant gesture to shake Mutti's. "Mrs Robinson, Elizabeth's mother."

I saw Lizzie squirm; she hated being called 'Elizabeth' – and her mother's superior air.

Mutti smiled. "I'm pleased to meet you. It seems our daughters are becoming friends."

Mrs Robinson's smile was reserved, almost tight lipped. She looked across at Lizzie. "Ring me when you get back."

I saw Lizzie's eyes roll. "Yes, mother."

We waved as Mrs Robinson pulled away.

"That's a beautiful car your mother has," remarked Mutti.

"Yes." Her face showing embarrassment at her mother's attitude.

"Come and meet *Imbi*." I grabbed her hand and we ran up the steps into the house. "How did you persuade your mother to let you come today?"

Lizzie gave me a mischievous smile. "Easy. I didn't ask her. I got my father alone and asked him." Lizzie giggled. "My mother wasn't pleased he'd said yes. I think they had words about it later."

Imbi was dozing on my bed, quite happy to be picked up and cuddled by Lizzie. After a while, he meowed. When Lizzie put him down, he headed into the study for a drink. Lizzie watched him, entranced at the delicate laps of his tiny pink tongue. When *Imbi* finished and climbed onto his blanket for a snooze, she glanced around the room, noting the textbooks and desk.

"Are those your textbooks from England?"

"Yes." I wasn't sure where this was heading.

She glanced between me and the books. "And you've been studying them, though you're not at school?"

I shrugged. "Studying is a habit I picked up in England. I used to study with my boyfriend and another girl at her house every afternoon after school." I didn't know what I could – or should – tell Lizzie.

She pulled a face. "You studied every afternoon after school?"

"Yes."

Lizzie's eyes narrowed as her internal picture of me shifted. She stepped across to the bookshelf, cocking her head sideways to scan the titles.

"You're a swot?"

What am I hearing in her voice? She isn't being dismissive, but I can hear ... something.

"I like most subjects – except Maths. I enjoy languages the most."

"Languages?" She scanned the bookshelf, seeing only my French text. She turned to me with a puzzled frown on her face.

Oops. I need to talk with Mutti about what I can tell her.

"Well, I speak German and English too. Our neighbours are Italian and I've picked up some of that."

"How did you have time for study and swimming? Mother makes me go to ballroom dancing classes twice a week and with swimming twice a week, I don't have much study time."

I smiled. "It's mostly about being organised. My friends helped me a lot with that."

It was on the tip of my tongue to suggest we study together, but I stopped myself until I spoke to Mutti.

How close can I let myself get to Lizzie?

We spent the morning chatting on the veranda or playing with *Imbi* under the house when he scampered down there. I was half expecting Lizzie to quiz me about Willi, but I think she wanted us to be alone; we could hear Mutti above us putting the finishing touches to the lounge room curtains.

The party in New Farm Park was fun. Lizzie and I entered some races, but we didn't win anything; most of the time we were laughing so much at the fun we were having. I introduced her to the rest of the Candy counter crew, but they were older than us and we spent most of the time with Mutti, sitting under a Jacaranda. I could see Lizzie relaxing as she saw Mutti was not like her mother. The three of us sat chatting in the half-shade, batting away the flies trying to share our BBQ.

Lizzie rang her mother as soon as we got home and we sat on the veranda waiting for her, mossie coil smoke wafting around us to keep the wretched things away. Mrs Robinson stayed in the car when she arrived, sounding her horn to announce her arrival. I went down with Lizzie.

She gave me an enormous hug and a whispered "Thank you for today" before climbing into the car beside her mother.

I waved as the car pulled away and saw Lizzie's arm wave in return.

• • • •

I WENT INTO MCDONNELL & East with Mutti one morning the week after the party to get fitted out with my school uniform, coming away with three bags. I left another filled with shoes for Mutti to bring home in the evening.

When she arrived, she turned on the radio and beckoned me to the table. From her bag, she pulled out an envelope I recognised as the same as the one the money had arrived in: Mr Franks. Mutti let me read the decoded note, dated 29th December.

What is happening? Results?

My shoulders tensed and shot a worried look at Mutti.

"Relax, *Liebling*. He knows that you've been to the Polish Club and can't go to the German Club yet. He's flexing his muscles, trying to assert control."

I had hoped his fear of us loosing Mrs Henderson on him would keep his impatience in check, but that seemed not to be the case, which didn't help my level anxiety.

Lizzie and I met up at the pool two or three times a week as January drifted towards a hot and lazy close. My distance swimming was improving. Lizzie pushed me to try an 800m, with her walking alongside, calling out times and encouragement. By the end, I was a breathless, limp string. Soon after that, I called it a day and we showered and set off home.

Thinking about my breathlessness on the tram home, I realised that I would have to start running again, despite the humid heat. I hung up my swimming gear to dry and walked round the local area. I found a track alongside a stream leading to a playing field. This would do.

In the cool of early morning, I donned my running gear from Lancaster and set off. Nearing the playing field, I ran past an upright, white-haired man walking his ancient dog.

When I reached the open area, I stopped in surprise. "Kangaroos."

A voice came from behind me. "Not kangaroos, lass. They's wallabies."

I turned. "What's a wallaby?"

The man laughed, pointing. "They's wallabies."

It was a stupid question and we shared a smile at his quick response. "I mean, what makes these wallabies, not kangaroos? They look like kangaroos."

"Aye, I'll warrant ye that, lass," he smiled. "But kangaroos are bigger – tall as ye and taller."

His dog snuffled round my feet and he saw me glance down.

"Donna fash yesel' about Dodger there. 'E canna see n'needs t' smell ye to know ye when next we meet."

The dog looked up at me – his pupils were white. "What's wrong with Dodger's eyes?"

"Cataracts." The man sighed. "Dodger and me, we're both gettin' on in yairs. E's past sixteen 'n that's good for a collie." He gave me a smile. "If ye's goin' to run here regular, I 'spect we'll meet again." He waved and the pair of them started up the path.

I watched them amble away, Dodger staying close to the man's feet. I looked across the playing field, comparing it to the one in Lancaster ... four circuits seemed about right. The cool shower at home was welcome.

As I lay in bed a few nights later, *Imbi* nestled against my shoulder, I realised that in less than a week I would start school, the swimming club and Polish classes. I would have to head to the German Club and try to find a way to visit there regularly. My ordinary and my secret life were piling up around me. In the warm, humid Brisbane darkness, I shivered at what lay ahead.

Oh Willi. How I wish you were here to share all this with me.

Chapter 8
Late January 1965

"**A**re you ready, Kal?" Mutti's voice floated into the study where I was trying to steady my new-school nerves by checking all was well with *Imbi*.

I took a deep breath. "Coming." I ruffled *Imbi's* soft fur, checked the window, closing the door with care. School bag over my shoulder, I joined Mutti in the kitchen.

"Here's your lunch." Mutti handed me the lunch box I had used at McDonnell & East. It joined my pencil case and some blank workbooks in my otherwise empty school bag.

Mutti held me by the shoulders, looking me up and down in my school uniform. "You look smart, Kal." She knew I was nervous and gave me a fierce hug. They had bullied me about my German accent when I started school in Herne Bay. After a moment, she kissed my forehead. "Say hello to Lizzie for me." Her eyes shone with love and care.

I swallowed, grateful that I was not stepping into completely unknown territory. We locked up, heading for the tram. Two girls wearing the school uniform joined the tram in Lutwyche. They sent curious glances my way as they sat down, identifying me as someone new. At Gregory Terrace, they left the tram and walked ahead of me towards the school. As I walked, I watched posh cars dropping off girls at the gates – and one chauffeur got out of a Rolls Royce to open the door for a girl. I stopped outside the gates, nerves jangling, hoping that Lizzie would be there to make things easier; I procrastinated, thinking about what problems crossing this threshold might bring me while girls brushed past.

"Kal, Kal." Lizzie startled me out of my shoulder-hunching worry, running towards me. She skidded to a stop.

"Don't run, Miss Robinson," a prim voice rang out over the hubbub.

Lizzie rolled her eyes at me and turned towards the teacher. "Sorry, Miss Feathers." She almost turned away, but pulled me over to the teacher.

"Miss Feathers, this is Karlota Miller. She's new this year. I met her at swimming during the summer."

Miss Feathers dragged her attention from the girls streaming through the gates. "I see." Her eyes gave me a quick uniform inspection. "Welcome, Karlota." Her eyes flicked to Lizzie. "Please show her around and see she finds her classes."

"Yes, Miss Feathers."

"Off you go." Miss Feather's eyes returned to the arriving girls.

"Yes, Miss Feathers."

Still holding my hand, a smiling Lizzie pulled me into the main building. "It's great having you here."

She took me to the office where I was told I would be in form 4A, which was Lizzie's class. The day passed in a whirl as we collected textbooks for our various subjects. It turned out Miss Feathers was our Maths teacher and we started out with algebra – simultaneous equations, which I'd done in England, with Willi's help.

"Well done, Karlota." Miss Feathers murmured quietly as she passed round the class, checking our progress on the exercise she had set.

By the end of the day, I realised I was ahead in every subject and that eased my nerves.

Lizzie was a popular girl and she ensured they welcomed me into her coterie for lunch on the grass under a tree. The girls had a lot of catching up to do from the holidays and that spared me an interrogation – at least for the moment. I caught some sideways glances, perhaps a result of my less than perfect English accent.

At the end of the day, Lizzie and I walked down Gregory Terrace towards the trams.

"Bring your swimming things with you tomorrow. We should have a practice before the club meets on Wednesday."

"That should be okay. I'll check with Mutti tonight and ring you."

We separated to our different tram stops; Lizzie had to head into the city and change for Hamilton. The sun was beating down when I stepped off the tram; I was looking forward to stripping off the school uniform and having a shower. Walking towards our house, I could hear squeals of glee from the Greco's garden. Cal and a naked Grigorio were dancing in the water from a sprinkler as Mrs Greco watched on. The walk home had me dripping with sweat and I envied the children their cool shower.

I gave them a heat-fatigued wave as I trudged up the front steps and headed in to open the house and cool off in the shower. Later, wrapped in a sarong, I sat on the veranda thinking about going to the German Club. Mr Franks' impatience pressed on me. Mutti insistence it was nothing to worry about hadn't helped.

My life was filling up. Tomorrow I was swimming with Lizzie and Wednesday was Swimming Club. My Polish classes started on Thursday and Swimming Club met again on Saturday morning. Could I get to the German Club after school on Friday? I'd have to talk with Mutti about this when she arrived home.

Imbi was winding round my legs, demanding his tea of diced sheep's hearts and purred at full volume when I placed his bowl on the floor. That allowed me to organise our tea and I had things ready when Mutti arrived home.

As always, she turned on the radio when she arrived to mask our conversation and gave me a serious look. "Let's eat – we need to do some work before you go to the Polish Club."

What sort of work?

I pulled the cold meat and salad from the fridge, setting the table whilst Mutti showered and changed into her sarong. When we sat down, *Imbi* must have smelled the ham as he jumped up on to my lap and started plaintive meows, importuning for food.

Mutti gave me a half-smile across the table. "Put *Imbi* down, Kal. You must train him not to importune for food."

"Yes, Mutti." I lowered him to the floor "Down you get, *Imbi.*", He made to jump up on to my lap but I stopped him with my hand. His ears flicked in disapproval and, giving me a hurt look, wandered off to inspect his food bowl in the study for any unnoticed morsel.

"Can I go swimming with Lizzie tomorrow after school? We need to practice for the club meeting on Wednesday."

"Do you have any homework?"

"Not yet – and if I do, I can do it when I get home."

"That's true. But we need to be careful that your schoolwork doesn't suffer with all that's going on."

I gave Mutti a reassuring smile.

Once we'd eaten and cleaned up, I rang Lizzie and confirmed tomorrow's swimming. Mutti sat me down at the table. "Let's work on your observation and memory. I want you to talk me through your day."

I wasn't expecting this.

"Well, when I arrived at school, Lizzie was waiting for me and she took me to the office ..."

"No, *Liebling*." Mutti interrupted. "Not like that. I want you to remember everything, every detail."

I raised my eyebrows and Mutti sighed. "Close your eyes and start again. Recall what you saw and tell me."

I closed my eyes. "I walked in through the school gates and there were some girls standing around..."

Mutti's soft voice interrupted. "No Kal. Start from getting off the tram when you left me."

I throttled a sigh. "The two girls on our tram walked ahead of me ..." I thought for a moment. "... a blond and a dark-haired girl, taller than the blond. There were cars dropping off girls – and one chauffeur driven Rolls Royce. The chauffeur got out and opened the door for the girl."

"What did she look like? What was the number plate?"

I opened my eyes and stared at Mutti.

How was I supposed to remember all this detail?

"She is from a wealthy or important family; we need to find out who she is." Mutti smiled. "Carry on."

"The girl and the Rolls were too far away. I'll watch out for them from now on." I closed my eyes, encouraging my mind's eye to replay this morning. "When I reached the gate, there were ... three groups of girls standing about, chatting, about ... five girls in each group inside the gate. Lizzie was with one group. She ran over to me and a teacher – Miss Feathers – told her not to run. Lizzie took me over to Mrs Feathers and introduced me ..."

Mutti's voice pulled me up. "Describe Mrs Feathers and what she was wearing?"

My eyes flicked open.

Mutti smiled again. "Every little detail, *Liebling*. Every time you go to the Polish or German Clubs, I want you to tell me all you can remember. As we don't know what might be significant – everything is."

I pulled a face and Mutti gave me a wry smile.

"Come on, *Liebling*. Practice makes perfect."

And we went on through my day. Prodded by Mutti's questions, the detail I could recall surprised me. But I found it exhausting and fell into bed. *Imbi* had forgiven me and curled up on the pillow beside me as we drifted into sleep.

• • • •

DURING MY MORNING RUN, I scanned my surroundings, wondering if Mutti would quiz me about what I saw. The wallabies were absent; I grinned to myself, ready to report no communist wallaby agents on the oval, but the *Cark* of the crows sounded suspicious. At school, I remained more aware of my surroundings. Mutti's training was having an effect ... we would see how much this evening.

After school, Lizzie and I walked down to the pool and we swam two lengths to warm up. Lizzie had me swim a 400-meter race against the clock. My morning runs were helping as I had better breath control. I timed Lizzie on a 50-meter swim against the big clock on the side of the building, with its constantly sweeping second hand; Lizzie was fast.

Lizzie turned to me as we were taking a break in the stands. "We can do this again tomorrow before swimming club – and on Thursday too."

"Sorry – I can't on Thursday."

Lizzie gave me a questioning look, but I couldn't respond. Lizzie pulled a face and turned away.

Damn ...

I hadn't spoken with Mutti about what I could — or should — tell Lizzie. We sat and my silence built distance between us. I'd have to tell her about learning Polish. But I was nervous, conscious of the mistakes I'd made with Willi and Lili.

"I'm sorry, Lizzie. It's nothing terrible ..." I realised I could use her 'swot' comment to explain things. "I'm ... cautious about appearing to be a swot."

Liar ...

Lizzie's closed face turned towards me. "What do you mean?" Her voice had an edge to it before she blushed, remembering her comment. "Oh ... I didn't mean it like it was ... bad," she stammered, her eyes dropping.

"Well, you remarked about the languages I was learning ..."

Lizzie flinched. "Oh, Kal. I'm sorry. I didn't mean it like that." She grabbed my right hand in both of hers. "Sometimes my mouth is way ahead of my brain and I say things I don't mean." Her face twisted in anguish.

I put my left hand over hers. "It's okay, Lizzie." She relaxed as a picture of Willi, Lili and I sitting round Mrs Wisniewski's kitchen table flickered through my brain. "I suppose I am a swot." I added, "You see, I'm learning Polish."

I'll keep the Russian a secret, though.

"Polish?" Lizzie's face reflected her astonishment. "Why Polish?"

"I made friends with Nina, a Polish girl at school in England. She'd been born in England, but her parents insisted she learn her language and culture. She learned Polish from birth, I suppose."

"You learned to speak Polish by being around her?"

"No." I laughed. "My boyfriend and I studied every afternoon after school, sharing our languages as well."

Careful, Kal...

"Nina joined us. We learned Polish and she learned German. We were all learning French at school and my boyfriend was learning Latin. I started picking up that as well."

Lizzie's eyes narrowed as her understanding of me shifted. "You studied every afternoon after school?"

"Yes." I relished the memory. "We had an official language every day – English, French, German or Polish. We had to do everything in that language."

Lizzie blinked. "When did you find time to swim? What about other friends?"

"Well, they were my friends – and I didn't start swimming regularly until last summer in England."

Lizzie's brows furrowed. "And you're this good already?"

I smiled. "You're way better than me, Lizzie."

"But I've been swimming since I was eight – and you're fit."

I shrugged again. "I run every morning, too."

"What?" Lizzie looked at me as if I were an alien, stepping out of a UFO.

I'd been trying to downplay things, but it hadn't worked. "One day, I looked in the mirror after a bath and realised I was … flabby." I explained.

Lizzie's eyes flicked over my body and she raised a questioning eyebrow.

"I wasn't fat … but … flabby and decided to do something about it." I stared out across the pool, remembering my time in Lancaster and its cocktail of emotions. After a second, I took a deep breath and continued. "There were playing fields close by where I lived in Lancaster and a twenty-five-meter pool in the city – I ran and swam."

Lizzie shook her head, her drying braids flicking diamonds of water from their tips. "You're different, Kal … you've a … a focus … that my other friends don't have."

I shared a secretive smile.

The differences were more than she suspected.

"I'm nothing special."

Lizzie winced. "I didn't mean it like that, Kal."

"Oh, Lizzie. I know you didn't. We're friends."

Lizzie's eyes held mine before dropping. "Thanks, Kal, I know we are."

Was Lizzie's bubbly exterior a mask? Underneath, was she a lonely, insecure teenager like Willi, Lili – and me?

"Anyway, Thursday afternoon I'm going to Polish classes at the Polish club. That's why I can't swim." I smiled. "Come on, there's time for another swim before I go home and get tea ready." We raced and Lizzie was her usual self when we left.

That evening, Mutti again ran me through my day and she laughed at my description of the communist wallabies and suspicious crows. I reported on my school day, but I couldn't do as well in terms of the walk to the pool and the time there.

Mutti looked at me, her voice a gentle scold. "It doesn't matter what you are doing, Kal. You need to pay attention to what's going on around you."

"But I can't when I'm swimming."

Mutti smiled. "Of course not. But you sat and talked with Lizzie and couldn't remember anything happening around you."

I sighed. "We were sorting out a problem. I had no room for that."

"Oh, *Liebling*. Anything I can help with?" Mutti became full of care for me.

"I need to work out how close I can let Lizzie come – what I can tell her."

I saw Mutti's lips purse but carried on. "And I think Lizzie is another one of us."

"What do you mean, one of us?" Mutti's voice echoed the confusion on her face.

"Oh, sorry. I meant like Willi, Lili and me – lonely teens in need of friends."

Mutti stared past my shoulder for a second or two. "Perhaps..." Her body shifted and she looked me in the eye. "Be careful. You can't tell her anything about our real life."

"I know." I gusted out an exasperated breath. "She wanted to go swimming on Thursday, but I've got Polish class and I didn't want to explain, because I was uncertain if I should." I gave Mutti a pained look as I tried to make her understand the problem. "Lizzie took offence at my silence." I stopped for a moment, wondering how Mutti would react. "I told her where I was going and about Nina ..."

Mutti was silent for long seconds. I could almost hear her thinking.

Finally, her gaze returned to me. "I understand, *Liebling*, but we must be careful. You will need to be careful you tell her – and anyone else – the version of our lives given to us in Lancaster."

"I know." My voice was subdued by the lies I would be telling.

"I think it best to tell people as little as possible." Her head cocked to one side and she stared hard at me. "Your father will kill us if he finds us." She stopped again, a shadow passing through her eyes. "And I think ...

that man ... would sell us out if we are of no further use. I don't know that threatening him with ... that woman ... would stop him."

This was not the confident Mutti I had seen negotiate with Mr Franks. A shiver ran down my spine, despite Brisbane's tropical warmth. Here in sunny Australia, distant from the tortuous politics in Europe, it was easy to forget the threat hanging over us. My confidence ebbed and I turned a forlorn face towards Mutti. "Will we ever be free of this?"

Mutti took my hand. "I don't know, *Liebling*." She stopped, staring through the window into the darkness of our future. "If there's a change in the Eastern Bloc ..."

Willi's tangled timeline had told me that in his original world, the Eastern Bloc collapsed in 1988 – twenty-three years away. But I knew this world was different; President Kennedy survived the assassination attempt in this world, but not in Willi's. There was no guarantee that what happened in Willi's world would happen here. The division of Europe could continue for grim decades beyond 1988.

That evening before bed, I added to my current letter to Willi, sharing my time with Lizzie. And I poured out my fear that the two of us would remain separated for many long years yet.

After a while, fatigue overcame my angst. *Imbi's* unconditional love, curled up, purring against me, helped me find sleep.

• • • •

I DIDN'T SEE THE CHAUFFEUR-driven car, but Lizzie was waiting for me at the school gate. Again, her coterie, which met up at lunch, welcomed me. As we ate, I noticed a girl – Susan, I think, but I was still learning names – giving me curious glances. After a while she leant towards me.

"Karlota. That's an unusual name ... where are you from?"

She asked with simple curiosity, but I flinched, remembering the bullying when I started school in England.

"I'm from Lancaster, in the north of England." In her eyes, I could see that hadn't dampened the interest. "I'm half English. My mother is German."

"Oh." She paused. "Do you speak German?"

I held a smile on my face, trying not to think about the school in Herne Bay. "Yes, of course."

Lizzie looked between us and I sensed she was about to say something. I gave her a subtle stare and pushed ahead of her. "But since my father died a year ago, my mother thinks we should speak English and won't speak German with me."

Lizzie frowned at me. I could see questions in the eyes of some girls, but they felt awkward now I'd told them my father had died. Slowly, the conversation restarted in safer territory.

After school, Lizzie and I headed down to the pool for a swim before the club meeting. The afternoon was, as usual, warm and humid and we were looking forward to getting into the pool. Once we were away from the school and not surrounded by students, Lizzie turned to me as we walked. "What was that look about at lunchtime, Kal?"

I walked on a few paces. "You were going to tell everyone I was learning Polish, weren't you?"

Lizzie flinched. "But you are."

We were under the shade of a tree; I grabbed Lizzie's hand and pulled her to a stop. "Yes, I am." Our eyes locked, almost glaring across the intervening space. "But I don't want to be marked out as a swot."

Lizzie stood in awkward silence, searching my face.

She needed an explanation. "It's difficult, Lizzie, being a new Australian and a new girl at school – and it's worse if I'm different." The dark phantoms of the school bullies in Herne Bay swirled round me. "When I started school in England, I had a strong German accent ..." I floundered to a stop. I didn't want to whine.

"Why would that matter?"

I sighed. "England suffered badly at the hands of Germany in the war. I was called awful names and no-one would talk to me."

"Oh." Lizzie thought for a moment. "I don't think it's like that here. If you were Japanese ..."

"Japanese?"

"Australia fought mostly against the Japanese – and they treated our prisoners of war badly. They put them in terrible camps and worked many of them to death."

"Oh. Umm ..."

The Japanese had death camps too?

I paused, recollecting my thoughts. "I want to get to know and become known to people gently."

Lizzie's look was uncertain, not understanding someone who wanted to stay in the background. "Okay."

I gave Lizzie an encouraging smile. "Come on, let's get to the pool. I need a swim."

Lizzie's eyes brightened and she turned, pulling me along. Not wanting to overdo things before the club, we swam well within ourselves for a while, practicing technique and not racing. We ate our sandwiches and had an Eskimo Pie for dessert. Once the club assembled, Lizzie and I were in the junior section and after some questioning, they handed me to the distance coach, who put me through my paces. I joined a group that was learning the Dolphin kick to use after a tumble turn. I struggled – but I realised Lizzie couldn't do it either and that was something for us both to practice.

Later, Lizzie and I traipsed out to our tram stops, tired from the exercise.

"See you in the morning, Kal."

"Bye, Lizzie. We'll have to practice that Dolphin kick next time we swim." My fatigue made it difficult to keep my eyes and ears open during the trip home.

Mutti could see I was tired. "I know it's warm, but would you like a hot chocolate?"

I thought for a moment. "No thanks. Iced water, please."

Mutti poured us each a glass and placed mine in front of me before sitting down. "Should you run in the morning on club swimming days, *Liebling*?"

I shrugged, indecisive.

Mutti smiled. "Go to bed. We won't rehearse your observation skills tonight."

I pulled the exercise book I had used for Polish with Willi and Lili off the shelf in the study. It's precious memories brought moisture to my eyes. It held much happiness, hidden between its scruffy covers.

Would using it tomorrow distract me?

It had sat on Mrs Wisniewski's kitchen table as we worked, the three of us smiling despite the underlying threat to Mutti and me. Taking it would share the experience with Willi and Lili. I thought for a moment about not setting the alarm for my run, but decided that was laziness. As always, *Imbi's* whiffling purrs lulled me to sleep.

• • • •

I WAS UP AND RUNNING at half-past five, showered and ready for school by half-past seven. Mutti and I walked to the tram.

"Keep your wits about you this afternoon, Kal." Her smile contained a promise of a deep interrogation this evening after my time at the Polish Club.

Thoughts and cares distracted me during the day.

Lizzie noticed. "Worried about the class this afternoon?" She whispered as we walked to class from lunch.

"Yes." I had no idea what standard they were expecting. I supposed that everyone else would be from a Polish speaking family ... and beneath everything lingered the secret reason for my attendance.

"You'll be fine." Lizzie smiled.

As I walked up to the Polish Club from the tram, my stomach churned. Had it not been for Mr Franks, I would have turned away. The Polish Club front door was open, but I stood on the steps and rang the bell, unsure about entering. After a moment, I saw Mrs Jaworski coming down the hall towards me, wiping her hands on her apron.

"Karlota, welcome. Come in."

I took a nervous step into the house. "Good afternoon, Mrs Jaworski."

She smiled. "You're early, Karlota. Come into the kitchen with me and have a cold drink."

She sat me down at a table and placed a glass of lemonade in front of me and returned to buttering bread and making sandwiches.

I watched her for a while, sipping my drink. "Mrs Jaworski, would you like some help?"

She turned with an appraising look on her face.

"That is most kind of you, Karlota." She reached another apron from behind the door. "Here, we can't have you getting your school uniform dirty."

Mrs Jaworski set me buttering the bread while she filled the sandwiches. We chatted about my school.

After a while, my curiosity got the better of me. "Have you been in Australia long, Mrs Jaworski?"

She tensed, slices of tomato in her hand and gave me a suspicious look. "Why would you want to know that, Karlota?"

Had she seen through me?

I swallowed and gave her my most innocent face. "You seem at home here and I'm wondering how long it will take me."

Mrs Jaworski's shoulders relaxed and she gave me an ambiguous smile. "I have been here for over ten years and I do feel at home; it's a friendly country." She sighed. "But my proper home is Luban, in southern Poland." She paused, pursing her lips. "Though I don't think I will see it again in this lifetime." She returned to her work and started assembling a cheese and tomato sandwich. "The German bombs ..." she pulled herself up, remembering who she was talking to. "The Nazi bombs destroyed our house in 1939 and we spent the war on my cousin's farm. We fled south to Austria when the Soviet's approached; we had heard about the Soviet massacre of Poles in the Katyn forest..."

Her eyes revealed her hurt and we returned to making sandwiches in silence until Mr Jaworski walked in. "Are the sandwiches ready?"

Mrs Jaworski finished halving the stack in front of her and arranged the cut sandwiches on a large platter. "Yes – I think these are enough."

Mr Jaworski noticed me. "What is ..." He couldn't summon my name.

Mrs Jaworski laid a hand across my shoulder, emphasising my name. "Karlota has been helping me."

Mr Jaworski turned a suspicious gaze on me. He was having trouble acknowledging a German might want to help a Pole.

"Hmph," he grunted. He reached for a sandwich and his wife smacked his hand.

"These are for the meeting later." She gave me a secret smile, one woman to another. "Why don't you show Karlota to the classroom? It's about time for the class."

Mr Jaworski gave her a brief nod and turned to me. "Come with me Karlota."

I pulled off the apron and handed it to Mrs Jaworski.

She smiled. "Thank you for your help, Karlota."

I returned her smile and thought for a moment, assembling the Polish in my head. "Thank you for letting me help."

Mrs Jaworski dipped her head, repeating her thanks in Polish.

Mr. Jaworski took me to a room with four trestle tables arranged with chairs behind them and a blackboard in front. A twenty-something woman, glancing through a book, stood beside the blackboard.

"Here is your first student, Mrs Kowalczyk." Mr Jaworski turned and walked out.

Mrs Kowalczyk gave him a surprised look before she turned to me, speaking Polish. "Hello. I'm Mrs Kowalczyk, the Polish teacher. Would you tell me your name?" She picked up a clipboard and poised a pencil over it.

"I'm Karlota Miller."

"Ah yes – the German girl who wants to learn Polish." She checked my name off the list.

I was uncertain how to respond to this and thought for a moment. "I'm half German." Before adding, "My father was English."

Mrs Kowalczyk blinked in surprise as she realised what I'd said. "I'm sorry to hear about your father." She looked sideways at me. "You already speak Polish well..." Her voice trailed off, almost in a question. "Ah yes. I was told about you learning Polish with a friend in England."

"But if I don't keep practicing it, I will forget it, won't I?"

"Don't you have anyone to practice with?"

"Not since I left England." I could hear the sadness in my voice. "I speak to myself in Polish, French, German and Latin, trying to keep them fresh, but I don't think that works well."

Mrs Kowalczyk gave me a puzzled frown. "But your mother is German. Why don't you practice German with her?"

I looked down at my feet. "She says we must become Australians and speak English."

"Oh." Mrs Kowalczyk's lips pursed. "There are Polish parents like that as well."

Children started trickling in until the room was full, ranging from primary school children to a few older than me. I pulled my Polish exercise book from my bag and Mrs Kowalczyk distributed a thin Polish grammar text.

"Now children, turn to page 35 of your grammar ..."

The class held a range of Polish language skills. While I was not fluent, I was better than most. The class helped me brush up on formal grammar that chatting with Mutti in Polish didn't cover. Towards the end of the class, Mrs Kowalczyk produced half a dozen copies of the Polish newspaper, *Wiadomości Polskie*. The advanced students read articles in pairs, questioning one another. At the end of the class, I asked Mrs Kowalczyk if I could take some newspapers home to practice with.

She awarded me an approving smile. "I expect that will be acceptable, but I will need to check. Wait here a minute."

I leafed through the copies, selecting out the half dozen most recent ones.

Mr Jaworski walked in with Mrs Kowalczyk in tow. "Karlota, I thought it might be you that was asking for newspapers." He almost gave me a smile.

"It's such a help to my vocabulary, reading through an entire newspaper. Would it be alright if I take these?"

He saw the papers I had assembled. "You think you'll read all that before next week's class?"

"Yes."

He shrugged. "They'll end up in the rubbish if you don't take them. Go ahead." He turned to Mrs Kowalczyk and they left, talking about the class.

I repacked my school bag, fitting in the newspapers. About a minute later, I walked out into the hall. As I did, an angry Polish voice rang out through another doorway.

"There are many excellent things the communists are doing."

"What? The communists are wrecking our country."

Was that Mr Taciak's voice?

I stopped and listened, but for a moment the conversation was indistinct. I edged closer. The first voice returned, louder and angrier.

"It's not worth talking to you. You have a closed mind."

A man strode out and almost barrelled into me. I jumped out of his way, crashing into the wall and ending in a heap on the floor. Mrs Jaworski must have heard me as she came rushing out to see the man stomp out.

"Karlota. Are you hurt?" She reached down and helped me to my feet.

Mr Taciak, the president of the club, appeared beside her. "What's going on?"

Mrs Jaworski frowned at him and turned back to me. "Are you all right, Karlota?"

I rubbed my left elbow that had hit the wall quite hard. "I think so."

Mrs Jaworski turned to Mr Taciak. "I heard that Drozd character arguing with you in the bar." She sniffed in disapproval. "I presume he stormed out and bowled Karlota over."

Mr Taciak pursed his lips. "Soon, Jan Drozd will annoy enough people and we'll expel him from the club." He turned to me. "I must apologise on behalf of the club for his behaviour."

I summoned my best Polish accent. "Thank you, sir."

Mr Taciak awarded me an indulgent smile.

Mrs Jaworski gave me an approving look. "Thank you again, Karlota, for your help." She walked me to the door and was still standing there when I turned at the gate. We shared a smiling wave.

I wanted to read the Polish newspapers during the tram ride home, but I couldn't do that in public. Mutti had made clear we must not draw attention to ourselves. I made do by pulling out *The Lord of the Flies*, which we were reading in English. As I read, anxiety dragged me from the pages: the boys in the story were from the sort of school Willi went to.

Were Willi's peers at school like these boys?

I hoped – no, trusted – that Willi would cope with everything; he had Lili's strength to support him, but he was fragile.

Please, take care of yourself, Willi.

At home, I put the newspapers on the kitchen table. I still felt anxious about Willi, but my foray into the Polish Club had gone well and looked forward to telling Mutti all about it when she arrived home. Tomorrow I would visit the German Club ... my self-admiration evaporated back to anxiety.

When I told Mutti about Jan Drozd, she stopped me to get the index cards out, checked through and made one out for him. Mutti made me give her a detailed description and had me recall what he had said. I went through the whole incident twice, prodded by Mutti's questions.

"He sounds like a communist sympathiser. I think you earned us our pay today, Kal." She smiled in encouragement and handed me a newspaper. "Now we must trawl through these to see what we can find."

We settled down at the table and spent an hour working through the newspapers. We didn't find anything for Mr Franks, but we added information on who's who in the Polish community to our card index.

As we packed up, Mutti leant across the table, her eyes thoughtful. "See if you can get some information about Jan Drozd, *Liebling*. Keep an eye out for people he talks to if he's there ... and an address would be useful."

I raised my eyebrows at her. "I have no idea how I might do that, Mutti."

She laughed. "I know, but you never know what opportunity might turn up. Be ready to grasp opportunity when it appears. But be careful, remember you're a schoolgirl trying to keep her language skills alive ..." A wicked smile curled her lips. "... in defiance of your mother."

We both chuckled at that, but mine had a brittle edge.

"I'm thinking of visiting the ... the other club tomorrow after school."

Mutti stopped, her eyes resting on mine, before she gave a slow, acknowledging nod. "Hmmm ... Could you visit the German baker and butcher in Woolloongabba for me?" She winked: she was giving me a cover story to use with my school friends.

"Right." I smiled.

She reached into her purse. "Here's a pound. Pick up a loaf of *Schwarzbrot* and see if you can get some *Blutwurst*."

"Okay." I stashed the bills in my purse.

"And keep the receipt – it's evidence to support our fees ... and a justifiable expense." Mutti kissed me goodnight.

I scooped up *Imbi* from the sofa and we headed to bed.

· · · ·

I WAVED AS I PASSED the old man and Dodger, his collie, on my morning run to the playing fields, trying to still the anxiety about what lay ahead. As I completed my third circuit, he was standing where the track emerged onto the field. I realised I knew his dog's name, but not his.

I slowed my pace and stopped in front of him, taking deep breaths. His eyes travelled over me – but it wasn't creepy like I'd felt with some men at the swimming pool. In return, I studied him. He was thin – wiry and upright – an athlete's build, for all his age – and I realised he'd been assessing me the same way.

"Ye run well, lass, and ye've got fine shoulders." He ran his eyes over me again. "D'ye swim?"

"Yes." I smiled, hoping my words would not seem impertinent. "And you ... are a runner?"

"Oh, aye, but many a yair ago." He smiled and extended his hand. "Euan MacDonald at your service, lassie."

I shook his hand. "Karlota Miller."

"Karlota ...now, that'd be a German name." His voice lacked judgement.

I worried where this was leading.

His gaze lifted over my shoulder. "Aye, I thought I haird it in ye voice." His eyes, imbued with dark memories, returned to mine. "Ye lot and mine, we's had troublin' times, troublin' times indeed." His gaze moved off into the distant past.

He was of an age to have been involved in both wars. Dodger was snuffling around my feet, reacquainting himself with my smell. I ignored him and searched Mr MacDonald's eyes as they wandered over the far horizon, feeling my anxiety rise at what he might say.

He blinked and smiled. "Hmph. S'all right, lassie. Dinna fash yesel' about an old man an' his memories." He sighed. "T'weren't ye fault."

We were in awkward territory and I returned to our shared interest. "What sort of runner were you, Mr MacDonald?"

He grunted with annoyance, "The name's Euan, lassie," smiling to remove the sting. "I was a distance runner in me time. I was thinkin' of tryin' for the Olympics. They were in Berlin, ye know?"

I must have frowned – he looked too old to have been competing in the 1936 Olympics.

He laughed. "Nay, lass, not Adolf's games. My Berlin Olympics never happened. They were t'be in 1916." He snorted and I could see the pain return to his eyes. "But we did compete that year." His voice darkened, spitting out the syllables. "Oh, aye. Quite a tussle."

We were again in uncomfortable territory and he sensed my nervousness.

"Lassie." He sighed. "Ye folks' and grandies' mistakes are no' ye fault." Memories stilled him for a moment. "Stand tall and be proud o' yesel'." He drew himself erect, his demeanour pulling me along, his staring eyes glistening from hard memories.

After a moment, he looked down at his dog. "Come, Dodger. We'll let this lassie be off about her business." He gave me a nod and walked past me, trailing memories I could almost feel.

I turned, watching him. "Goodbye, Euan."

Without stopping, he raised his hand in acknowledgement, his slow walk easy for Dodger's stiff gait and blind eyes. After a moment, I ran home, uneasy that Europe's dark history had found me here.

What would Euan say to Mutti's stories of Ravensbrück?

Showering lifted my mood, but thoughts of Euan's life lingered. I chatted about the day ahead with Mutti on the tram. Once again, the two girls cast their eyes over me when they boarded in Lutwyche.

Should I speak to them – or would that break some social taboo? I should try to find out who they are.

Lizzie might know.

As I walked behind them up to the school, I spotted the Rolls Royce coming towards me and checked its number, fixing it in my memory.

School was settling into a rhythm it knew well, pulling me into its routine. Lizzie's group had its shady spot under a tree where we gathered for breaks and lunch. I was still an unknown to most of Lizzie's friends, but they had accepted me. During lunch, the pair of girls from the tram walk passed and I asked Lizzie about them.

"Oh – they're sixth formers. They wouldn't notice us." Lizzie pulled a face. "Why do you ask?"

"Being curious, I suppose. They catch the same tram as me."

"You'll be at swimming in the morning?"

"Of course," I smiled. "Do you know when the first competition is?"

"Not yet." Lizzie shrugged. "They'll probably let us know tomorrow."

The bell reeled us into class from the various shady spots around the grounds. As we left school, I walked across the road with Lizzie to catch a tram into the city.

Lizzie raised a questioning eyebrow at me. "Where are you off to this afternoon?"

"Mutti wants me to go to the German baker and butcher in Woolloongabba to do some shopping – *Schwarzbrot und Blutwurst* ... umm ...dark rye bread and blood sausage."

"Eww – that sounds gross." A shiver of disgust shook Lizzie's pigtails.

"They're delicious. In Lancaster they have something like it called black pudding."

"Ugh – well, I wouldn't eat it."

"You're missing out. They're delicious." I smiled, repeating myself.

She shuddered again and we chatted as the tram bumped and lurched towards the city.

Lizzie waved as she got off. "See you in the morning."

By myself, my anxiety built as the tram rattled through the city. A trolleybus carried me across the river and stopped at Vulture Street almost outside the German Club. I hoped the club was open on a Friday afternoon. I already knew where the German butcher and baker were, but asking at the club was an easy entry. People were walking inside and I followed. At the entry was a desk, attended by a woman who gave my school uniform a questioning look.

I smiled, speaking German. "Please, can you help me? I'm looking for a German butcher and baker here in Woolloongabba."

The woman frowned in confusion and held up a finger, indicating I should wait before whisking off deeper into the building. She returned a minute later, preceded by a portly, middle-aged man.

"Guten Tag. Meine Tochter sagte, du batest um Hilfe bei etwas." He gave his daughter a frown. "Leider, spricht sie kein Deutsch."

How come she doesn't speak German? Everyone at the Polish club speaks Polish.

"Oh," I switched to English and gave her an apologetic look. "I'm sorry. I thought everyone here would speak German."

The man smiled at me. "Not so. We Germans have been here in Brisbane almost a hundred years and we have many members who speak no German at all."

This differed from the Polish Club, where I heard more Polish than English.

I stayed with English as the woman didn't speak German. "Umm ... my mother heard about a German butcher and baker near here and wanted me to buy some *Schwarzbrot* and *Blutwurst*."

The man continued speaking German. "You and your mother are both German?"

"My mother is German, but I had an English father."

I could see the woman becoming frustrated with her father. He caught her disapproving look and switched to English.

"Your mother is going to join the German Club?"

I wanted to appear nervous – which was easy as I was. I shifted from foot to foot and looked down. "Ummm ... probably not."

"Why not?"

I raised my eyes to his face, but they slid away as I spoke. "Ummm ... since my father died and we came to Australia, she insists we speak English."

He was nodding in understanding, lips pursed.

"She says we must be proper Australians ..." My voice trailed away.

The man was now smiling. "Yet she wants *Schwarzbrot* and *Blutwurst*?"

I remained silent as his eyes held mine.

"But you don't want to stop being German? Hmm? You still speak excellent German."

"It seems a waste to ... let it go."

He turned to his daughter. "Karin, find one of our leaflets about German food and drink here in Brisbane." His eyes flicked over me and he returned to speaking German. "I see you are at an excellent school. Where in Germany are you from?"

"I was born in Frankfurt – but we left when I was two." I shrugged. "I don't remember it.

"And your mother, she was born in Frankfurt?"

"I don't know. All her family were killed in the bombing, except her."

Is that suspicion I can see in his eyes? Or am I reading my lies reflected there?

"How are you going to keep speaking German if your mother won't let you?"

"I don't know ..." I frowned and made myself stop. "If I can find German books to read, that may be enough."

"You enjoy reading?"

"Yes."

"Hmmm. We have a book club here that reads German literature – in German – and discusses it, mostly in German."

Karin reappeared, handing a leaflet to her father.

He smiled as he took it. "Did they make any leaflets for the Book Club?"

"I don't think so. There's something on the noticeboard, though." Karin gave me a speculative look. German bread and sausages she could understand, but a girl interested in a dry-as-dust book club?

"Hmmm – would you be interested in joining the book club...err." He stopped, realising he didn't know my name. "Please, accept my apologies. I didn't introduce myself. I am Herr Steiner, the club secretary; Karin is my daughter." He smiled in apology. "And you are?"

"I'm Karlota Miller."

"Well, Karlota. Let's see if we can find that information about the Book Club."

He led me across the foyer, where we scanned the noticeboard. "Hmmm ... here it is. It meets on Saturdays at 2pm and it seems they are starting Günter Grass' *Die Blechtrommel* – the Tin Drum." He gave me a querying look. "Have you read it?"

"I've never heard of the author."

"Well, I have. Though I've yet to get round to him," he laughed. "Anyway, here's the information about German food shops." He handed me the leaflet. "We'll see you tomorrow?"

"Yes." I looked up from the leaflet that listed the nearby baker and butcher. "Thanks for the information."

I walked along Stanley Street to pick up the *Schwarzbrot und Blutwurst* and headed home.

We started the *Schwarzbrot* at *Abendbrot,* but left the *Blutwurst* for breakfast. Once we sat down after we'd cleaned up, Mutti quizzed me about my day. She had me run through yesterday and today, tracking back and forth to tease out all the details, including the Rolls' number plate.

"Well done for remembering that. Now we must find out who that car belongs to," she mused. "Can you ask Lizzie?"

"Perhaps. I don't want to seem too curious. I asked her today about the girls on our tram."

"And?"

"They're sixth form girls who would have nothing to do with us lowly fourth formers."

After we'd gone through my time at the German Club, Mutti gave me an index card.

"Start an index card for Herr Steiner and his daughter. Did you see any German-language newspapers there?"

"No." I started a card each for the Steiners.

"I think there is one. You need to watch out for it. You're going to the Book Club, aren't you?"

I sat there for a moment. "They're reading a book called *Die Blechtrommel.* Have you heard of it?"

"No, I don't think so."

I shrugged. "I have to join the book club. That's the only way of spending time there."

"True – at least for the moment." Mutti smiled in agreement.

"I'll stay in town after the swimming club meeting and go to the Book Club."

"Okay, *Liebling.*" Mutti smiled. "You've a busy day ahead of you tomorrow. I'll make some sandwiches for you to take. You head to bed."

"Thanks, Mutti." I gave her a hug. *Imbi* was already curled up on my pillow.

Chapter 9
Late January – early February 1965

*I*mbi complained when my alarm roused us at half-past five: no run this morning though as I was off to the swimming club. I dressed in shorts and a t-shirt but, along with my swimming things, I packed a skirt and top in my duffel bag; I needed something conservative for the book club – at least that's what my anxious brain told me.

Mutti was up and making coffee as I finished a quick breakfast of Wheaties. "Enjoy yourself, *Liebling.*" She hugged me and I grabbed my sandwiches from the fridge, along with a pair of bananas from the fruit bowl.

At the pool, Lizzie bounced up to me, excitement flinging her blond plaits loose from the hairpins. "The competition schedule is out. There's a competition here in two weeks." She pulled me over to where she had left her towel.

I dropped my towel on the chair next to Lizzie's. "Well, I don't expect I'll be swimming in a competition yet."

"You don't know that," Lizzie quipped.

I smiled and helped her re-pin her hair.

A coach blew his whistle and the ever-enthusiastic Lizzie led me to where the junior team coach was organising today's training. We started off with more Dolphin kick practice – I was getting the hang of this – and more drills: tumble turns, breathing rhythms, starts and such. I watched Lizzie fly through a 50m and a 100m swim: she was fast, beating some older girls. I was sure she'd be in the team.

They called the distance swimmers for a 400m race. As we assembled, I could see the other girls were all older than me. Lizzie must have seen my anxious face as she sidled up to me as we moved to our lanes.

"Don't worry about it, Kal. Concentrate on what we practiced."

I gave her a nervous smile and mounted my block at the end of lane of eight. After about half a length, all I could see of the girl next to me was the splash of her feet as she pulled away from me. I settled into the swim, pacing myself. I lost sight of the girl in the lane next to me until we crossed. Coming into the last turn, I felt good and pushed hard down the final length. Looking round after finishing, I thought I had come last, but as I pulled myself out, Lizzie ran up.

"Awesome, Kal. You beat a junior."

"Oh, I thought I'd come last." I looked across at the girl in the lane next to me who was still in the water, listening to a coach leaning over her. "Who's that?" I asked.

"That's Jacinta." I heard the respect in Lizzie's voice. "She's our best distance swimmer – I think she'll make the state team this year. She missed out last year because she was sick."

"Oh, right. I don't feel bad that she blitzed me in a single length, then."

I was unsurprised I didn't make the team for the upcoming competition, something that left me conflicted; I didn't want to draw attention to myself, but I was enjoying the competitive swims at the club.

Lizzie and I walked out and she sensed my darkening mood. "Never mind, Kal. I know you'll improve with training. You already are."

"I suppose." I sounded unconvincing to myself.

Lizzie rounded on me. "Don't do that, Kal."

I stopped, lowering my eyes. "Do what?"

"Put yourself down." She grabbed my shoulder, pulling me to a stop. Her gentle shake turned me towards her. "You're new at competitive swimming and you're already good. Not making the team doesn't mean you're useless." Fierce conviction blazed in her voice.

Our eyes locked and I could see a slight flush on Lizzie's cheeks and then her voice softened.

"I've watched you at school. You stay in the background and you shouldn't. You are the most interesting of my friends, curious about everything ..." she stopped, searching for the right words. "Be yourself, not a ... a shadow person."

We stood, looking at each other and Lizzie's eyes dropped with embarrassment at her impassioned outburst.

I reached across and took her hand, giving it a gentle squeeze. "My experience of being noticed has not been good. I told you about the bullying at school in England." Lurking behind that was my isolation in east Germany.

"Oh, Kal." She took a deep breath and I saw determination fill her eyes. "But I won't let that happen to you. I won't."

Her tram rolled up the street.

"Gotta go. See you at school." She dashed across the road and we waved as she boarded her tram.

I watched her leave and wandered into the city. Several hours stretched ahead before the book club. I spent some time looking through shop windows at the fashions on display and found a bookshop to browse in. It had a small foreign language section – more French than any other language. No Polish books and I found nothing of interest in the scant German section.

As I glanced sour faced at the sparse shelf, a supercilious voice came from behind me.

"Are you looking for anything in particular?"

I turned, startled, to find a tall, spare, redheaded woman peering down at me through glasses with heavy black frames.

"Umm ... well, I'm looking for *Die Blechtrommel* ... umm ... *The Tin Drum* by Günter Grass."

"We have it in English, but not in German." She peered at me over the rim of her glasses. "That's a ... difficult book in English. Are you sure you can handle it ... in German?" Her voice suggested its unsuitability for a young girl.

I was trying not to shrivel under her gaze. "I expect so."

She sniffed her disapproval and her eyes narrowed, trying to intimidate this girl in front of her who wanted to read a book beyond her years. I flushed under her frowning gaze but returned the stare, unwilling to submit, thinking about what Lizzie had said.

After some seconds, she sniffed again. "Well, you might find it at the foreign language bookshop, near the corner of Elizabeth and George Street."

"Thank you." I moved to walk past her.

"We have a children's section. You might find something more ... suitable ... there."

I walked past her. Lizzie would have been proud of me – I think.

I looked around at Brisbane's unfamiliar cityscape as I walked. I still half-expected to see an older cityscape scarred by war. That had been true of Leipzig and Canterbury and to a lesser extent of Lancaster. Here in Brisbane, almost everything was less than a century old and most buildings much younger. Many of the buildings pretended to be older through their architectural style. It felt strange – almost hypocritical – as the buildings reached for more ancient roots to cloak themselves in the respectability of age. And they were unscarred, with no wounds familiar from the catastrophe that had engulfed Europe. The people in the streets differed from England, let alone east Germany; They exuded a more relaxed, more casual attitude in their movements and dress, the young people in particular.

After walking through this disconcerting environment for twenty minutes, I arrived on the corner of Elizabeth and George streets and spotted the bookshop's narrow frontage.

Entering was like being loosed in Aladdin's Cave; the shop was stacked with new and second-hand books in ramparts of bookshelves separated by narrow valleys full of shadow. A musty, delicious, bookish smell pervaded the air. After searching past several languages, including what I took to be Chinese, I found the German shelves. These held several books, new and second-hand, by Grass, including *Die Blechtrommel*. I pulled a battered second-hand copy of that off the shelves, hoping it would be cheap. As I wandered to the front of the shop, I noted the Polish shelves; I'd have to ask Mrs Kowalczyk for recommendations. The large Russian section stopped me.

Were there a lot of Russians in Brisbane?

I smiled at two books side by side – *Война и мир* and *Анна Каренина* – Tolstoy's classic novels *War and Peace* and *Anna Karenina*. Mutti had often mentioned these. I reached up and started pulling Anna Karenina from the shelf.

A voice arrived beside me. "You speak Russian?"

Lost in myself, I jerked in surprise, losing hold of the book. We juggled it between us on the way to the floor before the white-haired owner of the voice dropped it. We both ended up kneeling, eyeing each other, the book lying between us.

The man rescued the Tolstoy novel, brushing its cover with a gentleness speaking of love and respect. "I'm sorry, young lady. I didn't mean to startle you. Are you all right?"

I gathered up my Grass and gave the old man an embarrassed smile. "I think so." A knee had hit the floor rather hard and I stood up, rubbing it. "I'm sorry – I shouldn't have jumped like that."

"Please come and sit down and I'll get you something to drink." He glanced at my knee with concern.

I followed him through the shop to a chair beside the counter, limping a little.

Handing me the Tolstoy, his eyes again flicked to my knee. "I think we could both use a cup of tea." Before I could reply, he pulled aside a curtain and disappeared through a door behind the counter.

I checked my knee. I could see bruising, but no other visible damage. Sitting waiting, I opened *Die Blechtrommel*: I should have some idea of the book before I walked into the book club. I heard a kettle whistle and soon after, the man appeared with a tray carrying a beautiful teapot, with matching cups, saucers, sugar bowl and milk jug.

"Here we go." He put the tray on the counter. "Shall I be mother?"

"Thank you."

"Milk – or would you prefer it black?"

I noticed slices of lemon on a saucer and remembered the tea that Willi's mother had served us. "Is it black Chinese tea?"

"Why, yes. You've had it before?"

"Mmm ..."

"Black with a slice of lemon, then?"

"Yes, please."

He poured two cups, adding a slice of lemon to each, and passed one to me. "How is your knee?"

I looked down and gave it a rub. "Sore – I think it's bruised."

"Ah, I have something that may help." He disappeared through the door behind the counter to reappear after a minute with a small bottle, which he passed to me.

"Put a few drops on your knee and rub it into the bruise."

I looked at the bottle with suspicion. "What is it?"

"It's witch hazel, good for bruises."

I opened the bottle and dripped a little onto my knee. As it hit the warmth of my skin, a faint, earthy smell drifted up. I rubbed the drops into my knee. "Thank you." I handed him the bottle.

"Young lady, we should introduce ourselves." He smiled genially. "I am Lukas Caune, the owner of this little shop." He spread his arms wide as if to envelop his kingdom, eyes twinkling at his grandiosity.

"Pleased to meet you, Mr ... Caune ...?" I looked up, checking my pronunciation.

"That's right – it's Lithuanian."

"I'm Karlota Miller."

Mr Caune looked at the books in my lap. "And you speak German and Russian?"

I thought fast. "As I'm half German, of course I speak German. I don't speak Russian – but I had a Russian friend for a while that taught me their alphabet. I was curious about the book. I like languages ..." I dribbled to a stop, the lies fragile on my tongue.

"Hmm. You like languages. You speak English, and I presume, German well. Do you speak any other languages?"

I examined Mr Caune's face. *What could or should I tell him?*

"Well, I'm learning French at school and I swapped languages with a friend from a Polish family in England. I'm going to Polish classes at the Polish Club."

Mr Caune raised an eyebrow. "And you want to learn Russian?"

I shrugged. "I like languages and I'm good at them."

As we talked, an assistant dealt with the purchases of a few customers and disappeared again into the shelves before returning. "Excuse me, could you help me with a customer?"

Mr Caune smiled at me, placing his teacup on the saucer with a musical clink. "Wait a minute – I may be able to help you." He disappeared into the bookshop with his assistant, to reappear with a customer. He rang up the sale, thanked the customer and returned to me.

"I have an old friend – a Russian lady – who is mostly housebound and starved of conversation. Could you spend a little time with her each week, talking and learning Russian?"

I thought about how full my life was. "I don't know ..."

"Well, I'll talk with her. Can you come here next Saturday?"

"I suppose." I felt trapped.

"Excellent. How's that knee of yours?"

I flexed it in front of me – it was still sore. "I'm sure it will be fine, thank you." I stood up. "How much for my book?" I indicated the Grass.

Mr Caune picked it up, glancing inside. "You don't want the Tolstoy?"

"No, thank you."

"Perhaps in a few weeks." He smiled, eyes twinkling. "Shall we say one and sixpence for the Grass?"

I pulled my purse from my duffel bag and paid him, putting the book on top of my lunch box to keep it away from my damp swimming things at the bottom of the bag.

"I'll see you next Saturday?" He raised an eyebrow.

"Okay. Thank you for the tea – and the witch hazel."

I slowed my walk because of my knee, but it loosened up as I made my way down to the Botanical Garden. Sitting in the shade of a flame tree, I retrieved my lunch box and *Die Blechtrommel* from my duffel bag. With a sandwich in hand, I soon realised that this was a strange book – and why the bookshop lady had thought it unsuitable for a young girl. I was a little surprised that Mr Caune hadn't said something.

After lunch, I walked through the botanic gardens to the ferry, catching one across the river to Christie Street. As I walked down Vulture Street towards the German Club, my anxiety rose. The butterflies in my stomach churning up my lunch. I stopped in front of a shop window for a minute to calm myself with some soft, deep breaths. I was resentful of Mr Franks and his machinations that had forced us into being his tools. Despite the warmth of the Brisbane summer, a shiver of revulsion ran through me. After a few more breaths, I peered at my reflection in the shop window.

Come on Kal – you can do this.

I did not mirror my reflection's confidence, but resumed walking all the same.

Karin greeted me in the club foyer.

"You're here for the book club?"

"Yes."

"It's upstairs, the first room on the left. You're early, but I think there are some people there already."

"Thank you."

Upstairs, I could hear voices coming through the open door of the first room on the left. I stopped in the doorway. A middle-aged man and a younger woman were talking, but the conversation ceased when they noticed me.

"Excuse me ... is this the book club?"

The woman glanced at the man and walked over to me. "Yes, it is. Can I help you?"

I swallowed. "Herr Steiner told me about it. I'd like to join, please."

The woman lifted an eyebrow in surprise. "We're reading a book – in German."

"I know. I've got a copy of the book." I swung my duffel bag off my shoulder and fumbled out *Die Blechtrommel*.

The woman glanced across at the man. "You speak German?"

I could see doubt on her face. "I was born in Frankfurt. My mother is German, but my father was English."

The man walked across to us. "I don't think the book club is suitable for someone as young as you."

I dropped my eyes. "But Herr Steiner told me about it and suggested I come ..."

A glance passed between the two people and the man turned to me. "I think I'll have a word with Mr Steiner. Wait here, please." He walked out and I heard him start down the stairs.

The woman looked at the book in my hand. "You've been reading it?"

"It's ... strange..."

She smiled and raised an eyebrow. "It certainly is." She cocked her head to one side. "How old are you?"

"I'm fifteen."

"And does your mother know you are reading that book?"

I paused, summoning a sheepish face. "My mother doesn't know I'm here ... and I can't show her this book." I dropped my eyes. "She says we must become Australian now. She doesn't let me speak German at home anymore, not since my father died and we came here."

The woman lifted my chin with a finger. "I'm sorry to hear that ..." Her eyes scanned my face. "I'm Miss Bauer, a German teacher. What is your name?"

"I'm Karlota – Kal – Miller."

"Well, Kal. I'm not sure that you should read this book at your age. It has some ... adult ideas in it."

"I know. I've read the first thirty pages." Searching Miss Bauer's face for some sign of support, I paused, seeking a way to influence Miss Bauer. "I understand the words, but I'm not sure I understand what the author is saying all the time." The fear they might refuse my entry was rising.

Miss Bauer laughed. "Well, Kal, you wouldn't be alone in that. It is a book that has many twisted threads and levels. That's why we're reading and discussing it in the book club." She gave me a lengthy, appraising look. Footsteps approached the door and the man returned with two new people who walked past us further into the room.

Before the man could speak, Miss Bauer turned to him. "John, we should let this young lady, Kal Miller, stay. I think it would enhance our reading and discussion to have a youthful perspective."

The man stopped. "Well, Mr Steiner is supportive of her staying. Although I have reservations about such a young person reading this book."

Miss Bauer turned to me. "Well, Miss Miller, if you weren't allowed to stay, would you still read this book?"

I blinked in surprise at this question. "Yes, of course. From what I've read, it's complex but interesting – and I need to keep practicing my German."

Other people were arriving. They glanced at our little knot of tension and went further into the room, sitting in the circle of chairs.

After sharing a look with Miss Bauer, the man turned to me. "Miss Miller, I'm Mr Fraser, the organiser of this group. Please come and sit down."

I stifled a sigh of relief. I'd found my way into the German Club as we had promised to Mr Franks.

Several questioning glances came my way as Mr Fraser called us to order, but no-one objected to me being there. I pulled out a pencil and started marking the sections in chapter two that people talked about in German but sometimes in English. This allowed me to write names as I learned them, trying to memorise a description for Mutti and the index cards. The discussion – with some reading of sections of the text – went on for over an hour and was interesting. I had some reading to do, as the book club had now finished with chapter two and we were to read chapter three for the following Saturday. When the discussion broke up, we lingered over tea and biscuits after contributing sixpence.

I watched as people poured their tea.

Miss Bauer walked up to me. "You didn't say anything today – but you were writing in your copy ..." I heard the question in her voice. Miss Bauer was in teacher mode.

"When I have something useful to say, I'll speak. But I'll wait until we get deeper into the book and I understand more." I gave her a diffident smile. "I was writing things to help me with the book's themes, things to watch for as we read further into the book."

Miss Bauer paused, inspecting me. "Where do you go to school?"

"I started at Girl's Grammar this term."

She nodded. "That's a school with an excellent reputation. And you want to study languages?"

I shrugged. "Perhaps. I'm better at languages than I am at Maths ..."

"Don't neglect your Maths," Miss Bauer smiled. "Are you studying any languages other than German?"

"I'm not studying German at school. They don't teach German and anyway, my mother won't let me. I'm studying French..." after a moment's thought, I added, "And Polish at the Polish Club."

"Polish?" I could see the surprise on her face. "Why Polish?"

I smiled in return. "In England, I swapped languages with a Polish friend as we did our homework. It seemed a shame to let it slide." I glanced up at her. "My mother doesn't know about the Polish Club, either."

Miss Bauer's conflicting feelings about this deception ran across her face. "Let's get a cup of tea," she said.

I noticed a small stack of newspapers on a side table, *Die Woche in Australien*, the Week in Australia. I put my tea down and picked up the top copy from last week.

"Ah – you've found the German newspaper, I see." Mr Fraser came up beside me.

"Are these old copies? Can I take some to read to get a German perspective on Australia?"

"Hmm ... I don't think you can take these. They're here for members to read. You can buy copies downstairs."

I gave him my best doe eyes. "I don't have enough money to buy copies ... aren't there old copies that would get thrown away?"

Mr Fraser pursed his lips. "Umm ... yes. Let me see what can be done." He walked across the room. He talked to Miss Bauer, who glanced across at me and slipped out. I folded the newspaper and put it on the stack and finished my tea, glancing round the room, putting names to faces and rehearsing their description.

A few minutes later, Miss Bauer returned, several newspapers clasped under her left arm. "These are for you, Kal. I'll see if I can get a copy of the paper for you each week."

"Thank you."

Miss Bauer paused, her face serious. "I am feeling rather conflicted about this. After all, you are deceiving your mother about continuing with your German – and Polish."

She stopped, expecting me to respond, but I did not know what to say. I hadn't thought of how it would look to others because Mutti knew all about it.

Miss Bauer seemed to mistake my silence for embarrassment. "Well – I think your mother is ..." She came to a stop, searching for the right way to talk about my mother, before continuing in a gentle voice. "... is ... misled about making you stop your languages. I am prepared to support what you are doing." She gave me a hard look and her voice tightened. "Are you certain your mother would stop you if you told her what you are doing?"

I stared down at my shoes, trying to think what to say. After a few seconds, I looked up. "She's a wonderful mother," I paused, grimacing. "But she's been through a lot recently, losing my father and moving to a new country. I hope I can tell her what I'm doing sometime ... when we've settled in." Our eyes engaged and I let my anxiety show. "We've only been here about four months."

Miss Bauer squeezed my shoulder. "And all this is difficult for you as well, isn't it?"

I stayed silent and Miss Bauer gave me a sympathetic look.

"We'll see you next week?"

"Of course."

I was feeling quite disturbed by the level of deceit I was engaged in and left, managing a polite nod to Mr Fraser as I did. On the trolleybus and tram going home, all the threads of this week drew together. The lies I had to tell, the new school and its demands, losing Willi and Lili, being here in Australia ... everything coalesced into a stomach clenching nausea. I fought to control it all the way home. I rushed into the house past Mutti, scattering *Imbi* as I dumped my duffel bag in my urgency to reach the toilet. My stomach emptied in one vile, lurching cascade and I crouched retching over the bowl, tears streaming down my face.

"Kal, Kal. What's wrong, *Liebling*?"

I half heard Mutti's voice, but felt her caring hands stroke my hair. I glanced up at her but couldn't speak, as my stomach was still churning. I leant over the bowl again, dry retching as my stomach had nothing more to give. Mutti must have left for a moment as a cool, moist cloth wiped my face and arms enfolded me. After a while, I stirred and flushed the toilet.

"Careful, *Liebling*." Mutti supported me as I stood. "Let's get you lying down." She guided me to my room and pulled off my shoes once I was on my bed. "Stay there."

The emotions raging through my body had exhausted me. Lying there half-comatose, I started shivering, despite Brisbane's summer warmth. Through an enveloping fog, I felt a blanket covered me. Mutti lay down beside me, cuddling me to her warm body.

After a while, my shivering stopped and Mutti sat up on the side of the bed. "Here, *Liebling*. Rinse out your mouth and spit into this bowl."

I rolled half onto my side and rinsed my mouth and collapsed onto my pillow. "Thank you."

Mutti tucked the blanket around me and stroked my hair. "What happened, *Liebling*? Do you need a doctor?"

"I don't think so, Mutti. I'm … washed out. I didn't crack my head open like Willi did."

Mutti gave me a half-smile, recalling Willi's collapse at the news of JFK's survival.

"I'm sorry I scared you." I looked up at Mutti's caring face. "On the way home, everything … built up."

"What do you mean – everything?"

I squeezed my eyes closed as I teetered once again on the precipice. "Coming here, Willi and Lili, school, Mr Franks, the Polish Club, the German Club, swimming, the lies, Lizzie … you …" It hadn't worked. Tears slid from my eyes.

Her voice filled with anguish. "Oh, *Liebling*".

I was hurting Mutti and that poured into the seething pool of *angst* and self-loathing that filled me.

"I'm sorry." She scooped me, blanket and all, into her arms, rocking to and fro.

Her tears mixed with mine on our nestled cheeks. We remained still, sharing breath until our faces had almost dried.

Mutti lifted her head. "Can you tell me what you mean by … 'you'"?

Mutti's face showed her hurt, which demanded honesty. "Oh, Mutti, I must remember everything I see – and … and I can't do that. I'm trying, I am …"

Mutti squeezed me. "Oh, *Liebling*. I thought I was helping you." She looked up at the ceiling, tears again filling the corner of her eyes. "But instead, I was pushing you." She took a trembling breath. "It's all too much." She smeared the new tears across her face. "We'll tell … that man … that you cannot do his bidding anymore."

My stomach spasmed in terror, muscles cramping from the repeated strain. "No." I almost screamed. Mutti recoiled in shock.

I sucked in a breath, seeking that island of calm somewhere inside me. "No." Vehement this time, not a visceral shout. "We can't do that, Mutti." I shuddered at the thought. "You know what he will do."

Mutti's gaze strayed through the window to the distant gum trees as she sought a way through the dilemma. "But I can't let you go on like this, *Liebling*."

I lifted a shaky hand and stroked her cheek. "I'll get used to it ..."

"Oh, *Liebling*. You're still a child. You shouldn't have to get used to it."

I sighed. "But you did, in Ravensbrück. And you were younger than me."

Mutti's eyes closed and she gave me a gentle squeeze. "I know, *Liebling*. But that doesn't mean you have to."

"We have to keep going, Mutti." I tried to keep my voice resolute. "We can't risk betrayal."

Another squeeze. "But ..."

I shook the blanket off my shoulder and sat up. "No, Mutti. If we get this wrong, my father will come after us here, as the SS would have come after you in the camp."

Mutti sighed. "But it was different there. My mother and I, we weren't alone." She gave me a fierce look. "Here, we're alone." Her eyes flicked away from me for a moment, returning, narrowed, to mine. "We must be careful not to let our secret slip out the way it did in England."

I could see the admonishment in her eyes – it had been me that had made all the mistakes. I'd taken risks. I told Willi we were from Leipzig, revealed I was a girl masquerading as a boy. Then I slipped up with Lili and that, but for her friendship, would have ended in disaster.

"I'm being careful, Mutti."

Is getting close to Lizzie being careful?

"It's hard to be friends when you keep secrets. Lizzie can sense when I'm holding things back."

Mutti said nothing, gathering me in her arms; but I had seen the worry in her eyes. We stayed like that for a while.

I stirred about to speak.

Mutti placed a finger on my lips. "Lie down and rest. We'll talk about this more later."

"Okay."

I lay on the bed, lassitude flooding me. Mutti covered me with the blanket and I floated, suspended between wake and sleep. I heard scuffling, followed by delicate paws up the bed and "Meep." A small tongue rasped across my cheek. I gathered *Imbi* with a hand and he settled on the pillow beside me. I drifted off to sleep with his dark, watchful eyes gazing from a head resting neatly on his forepaws.

• • • •

THE EARLY DUSK OF THE tropics was drawing the light from my room when I woke. I padded out into the house to find Mutti sitting on the veranda, wreathed in the smoke from a mossie coil.

"How are you, *Liebling*?"

"Washed out, but better, thank you."

Mutti patted the chair beside her and stared into my eyes. "Please, don't let things build up like that again." She grasped my hand. "You must tell me if you feel overwhelmed by things." She raised her chin, glancing at the neighbouring houses, reminding me to be careful with what I said.

I shrugged. "I didn't realise things were getting on top of me until this afternoon."

"Well, we need to lighten your load."

I stared at Mutti in surprise.

I couldn't stop doing the work for Mr Franks.

"There are things I have to keep doing." My tone rose as I realised the enormity of what I thought she was suggesting.

Mutti gave me a comforting smile. "I know, *Liebling*. I know." She looked away for a moment. "But what if you stopped swimming – or running?"

I recoiled in dismay. "That wouldn't work – I enjoy them and they help me settle down and think things through."

"How?" Mutti looked startled by this.

I struggled to explain. "There's something about the rhythms of running and swimming that's settling ... soothing. Stopping those would make things worse." The disgust I'd felt about the deception grabbed my throat and my voice rose. "It's all these lies I must tell. They make me feel ... dirty."

"Shh, *Liebling*." Mutti glanced round at the neighbouring houses. "Let's go inside and get tea ready."

Inside, she put the radio on and we arranged our usual tea of cold meat, cheese, salad and bread.

After we'd eaten, Mutti took my hand. "*Liebling*, you know we can't do anything about the deception we are living."

I sighed in frustration. "I know, Mutti." My voice hardened. "But I don't like the lies I have to tell. It was easier in England once I shared everything with Willi and Lili."

Mutti's hand tensed and she gave me a high-intensity stare. "You're not thinking of doing that again, are you?"

"I wish there was someone I could share with." I slumped. "But there isn't anyone I trust that much."

At least, not yet ...

I could see the relief on her face.

She gave my hand a gentle squeeze. "I think I need to push you less on the details of your days. I think that's all that's left to help take some pressure off you."

Considering this overwhelming week, I glanced at Mutti. "I wonder if the pressure came because everything happened in a few days."

Mutti cocked her head, searching my face. "Do you mean you want to ... carry on and see what happens?" She sounded tentative, surprised ... and worried.

Carrying on was a frightening idea, but I couldn't see a way round it, given the problems we faced with Mr Franks and my father. "I think we have to." A shiver of apprehension coursed through me – and I saw the worry deepen in Mutti's eyes.

"Do you think you'll recognise the pressure building ... before it becomes a crisis?" Mutti gave me a concerned look. "We can't have you collapsing again."

I gulped at the idea of reliving this afternoon. "I think I'll recognise things building up now."

Mutti gave me a penetrating look. "Okay."

I could see she was unconvinced. "I think I'll head to bed and read."

Mutti kissed my forehead. "Sleep well, *Liebling*."

Imbi followed me to my room and scrambled onto the bed, using the coverlet as a ladder: it was too high for him to jump. I lay there reading *Die Blechtrommel* for a while, but the world Grass was conjuring remained disturbing and difficult. I was going to have questions of my own at the next book club meeting.

. . . .

DURING THE FOLLOWING week, Mutti's caring eyes followed me. She didn't push as I recounted my observations of the day, but I was determined to give all the detail I could summon. The Polish and German index boxes added a few cards from a combination of my observations and our newspaper gleanings.

On the Saturday after swimming club, I headed to the foreign language bookshop, where Mr Caune greeted me warmly.

"I'll make us a pot of tea."

"Thank you." I sat and pulled out my copy of *Die Blechtrommel*.

Mr Caune reappeared with the same beautiful tea service. He poured me a black tea and added a slice of lemon, using a delicate, two-pronged silver fork.

"Here you go, Karlota." He passed across my tea. "Have you thought about learning Russian?"

I sipped my tea. What with everything else, I hadn't spent much time thinking about this. I remembered Willi explaining that when he was uncertain, he tried to answer a question with a question. "Why should I learn Russian?"

"Good question," Mr Caune answered with a sage nod. "But one you have to explore yourself." He smiled and I could see a twinkle in his eye. "You seem to be collecting languages – and you already know the Cyrillic alphabet." He gestured towards the counter where the Tolstoy sat from last Saturday.

I took another sip of the tea before replacing my cup on its saucer. "I'm worried about confusing myself."

Mr Caune gave me a questioning look.

I fiddled with my cup for a moment before continuing. "There are times I find it hard not to speak Polish in French classes at school, and on Thursday I started answering a question at my Polish class in French. Adding Russian to the mix might make things worse."

"Perhaps so." Mr Caune drew out his words and gave me a thoughtful look. "And perhaps not. You are a capable linguist – you've mastered English and are acquiring French and Polish. I suspect you will add another language with ease."

He was about to add something when he spied his assistant waving to him. "Excuse me for a moment, Karlota."

I tried to return to *Die Blechtrommel* but Mr Caune seemed set on having me learn Russian.

What was going on here?

I nibbled at that question, but getting nowhere, I sat there, sipping my tea and thinking.

When Mr Caune returned, I had finished my tea. He brought his cup to his lip but returned it to the saucer with a grimace. "Cold tea is uninspiring ... and I didn't make a sale to that customer."

I closed my book. "Please, could you tell me about this Russian lady you want me to meet?"

Mr Caune fussed with some books on the counter. "Well, she's a sort of relative – the great aunt of my wife's cousin. She's been here in Brisbane for about thirty years, but is having difficulty getting around now. My wife and I help her, but she needs someone to talk with – a project to keep her busy. She doesn't do well without regular social contact."

I wasn't sure I wanted to be anyone's 'project'.

Mr Caune must have seen my reluctance. "If you could meet with her for an hour each week, it would give her such a lift ... and I think you'll find her interesting."

My reluctance was growing and, sitting in silence, I sought a way to avoid this added pressure.

Mr Caune must have sensed something and stood up. "Come and meet her." He moved towards the door behind the counter.

I sat there, wondering where he was going.

"Come and meet her ... she has the flat above the shop."

I stood, trapped. He led me through a dim hallway and up a steep flight of stairs to a front door at the top. Mr Caune grasped the knocker and rapped.

"Enter." The door muffled the voice, although still clear and commanding, with no trace of a foreign accent.

Mr Caune opened the door and led me into a room lit by sunshine pouring through the open windows. "Aunt 'Stasia, I'd like you to meet my young friend, Karlota Miller."

A grey-haired woman levered herself out of a chair by the window, unfolding herself with difficulty into an erect figure taller than Mr Caune. Upright, she steadied herself on an ebony cane in her left hand.

"Welcome Lukas." She took several hard steps towards me. "Well, come here, girl."

I glanced at Mr Caune, who indicated with an encouraging smile that I should do as she said. I went and stood in front of her and her eyes travelled over me.

"Hmm ... you're the German girl that wants to learn Russian?"

I blinked, forcing myself not to look round at Mr Caune.

What had he told her?

"Well, I'm not sure about that ... um ...?" I stopped, realising I did not know how to address her.

She smiled over my shoulder. "Lukas, your manners are failing. You did not introduce us." She looked at me. "Please call me Aunt Anastasia. Come and sit in the window with me whilst Lukas makes us tea."

She led me across towards the window to sit in a large wingback armchair, the pair of hers.

"Why are you not sure about learning Russian? Lukas told me you had pulled Tolstoy's book off the shelf."

I looked down at my hands, trying to work out what to say. The problem was that I spoke – and read – Russian; not well but enough to get by and that marked me as a child from East Germany. All school children in east Germany learned Russian from the start of school and Mutti had made sure we kept practicing it.

The ebony stick reached across and prodded my leg, jerking me from my thoughts. "Cat got your tongue?" I looked up and to see a teasing smile on her face.

I returned the smile. "My kitten, *Imbir*, would never do such a thing."

Aunt Anastasia frowned. "Now, why would you have a kitten called 'Ginger' in Russian?"

I blinked – my Russian vocabulary was lacking, it seemed. "It's not Russian, it's Polish."

It was her turn to blink. "You speak Polish?"

My big mouth again …

"I'm learning – I go to class at the Polish Club every week."

"Well, you have some grounding in Russian already, as Polish and Russian are related, like English and German." She frowned. "But why are your learning Polish?"

"One of my school friends in England was from a Polish émigré family. She had spoken Polish from birth." I shrugged. "We swapped languages as we did our homework. I decided it would be a shame to abandon it when we came to Australia."

"A wise choice." Aunt Anastasia agreed. "And now you will come here and you will learn Russian. Lukas tells me you already know the Cyrillic alphabet."

Mr Caune reappeared with another beautiful tea set, placing it on a table beside the old woman. "I must return to the shop. I will leave you to get to know one another." He headed downstairs.

Aunt Anastasia smiled at me. "Please pour the tea, Karlota? I'll have mine black with a slice of lemon."

Pouring the tea allowed me to look more closely at the tea set. Everything was a bluish white, with a blue pattern. It differed from the one Mr Caune had downstairs, but its equal or better in elegance.

Once we settled with our tea, Aunt Anastasia looked across at me. "Please tell me about yourself, Karlota."

As I sat there, my confusion and suspicion about why I was sitting there multiplied. I hated that anything I told her would be the fictitious story forced on me by Mrs Henderson and Mr Franks. Aunt Anastasia watched my silence. Mr Caune's manipulation to get me here was making me rebellious and obstinate; this pushed me to be impolite.

"Why am I here?"

Aunt Anastasia blinked. She picked up her teacup and sipped, watching me over the rim. "You don't want to be here?"

My eyes closed for a moment. "I don't know ..." My eyes opened and roamed the room, not looking, but allowing time to gather my chaotic thoughts. "I'm not sure I have room in my life for anything else."

Aunt Anastasia gave me a sympathetic look. "Why don't you tell me what's crowding your life?"

I took a deep breath. I could walk out now, but the pressure to find a way into the Russian community would still be there. "Well, there's swimming, school ..."

Over the next half hour, Aunt Anastasia drew my story out, encouraging me with comments and insightful questions when I faltered. I found repeating Mrs Henderson's lies was becoming less disturbing – or repetition numbed my disgust.

When I ran down, Aunt Anastasia looked across at me. "I was a young woman when my family fled into China from the Soviets after the revolution. Before that, when I was about ten years old, my father moved us across Russia to Vladivostok as he was to assume management of the family trading business in the east. We fled here when the Japanese invaded China."

Her eyes rested on mine, the sadness of memories visible on her face. "Moving across the world is difficult, isn't it? It tears holes in you where there once were people and places."

I felt the Willi and Lili shaped holes inside me. We sat in silent, shared understanding until the clock on the mantle chimed noon.

I stood up. "I'd better go – it's nearly lunchtime."

Aunt Anastasia shifted in her chair. "Why don't you stay and have lunch with me? I would appreciate the company."

"I have sandwiches in my bag – I was going to eat them in the Botanic Garden."

Aunt Anastasia smiled up at me. "Stay and eat them here with me."

I hesitated and Aunt Anastasia unfolded herself from her chair.

"I would appreciate your company, Karlota." She smiled. "Bring the tea tray into the kitchen, please."

As she watched, I gathered up our teacups and carried the tray into the kitchen.

"Put it on the side over there." She waved at the draining board. "We'll sort it out after lunch."

She directed me to assemble her lunch of tomatoes, pickled fish from a jar and delicate white rolls.

"Bring your sandwiches in and we can put them on a plate."

My cheese and tomato sandwiches looked coarse sitting on a plate that matched the elegant tea set and I cut them into quarters.

Aunt Anastasia inspected the tray I had assembled. "That looks like everything. Take it in and put it on the table."

The table was some rich, dark, polished wood, circular, with a Chinese or Japanese vase sitting on a delicate lace mat at its centre. Four upholstered chairs stood around it.

Aunt Anastasia pulled out a chair and sat, her face showing some relief. "We need mats and cutlery; they are in that drawer." She indicated a drawer in the imposing sideboard, which matched the table. Each mat was a circular Chinese landscape, set in what I assumed was a silver filigree edging. The cutlery was silver, as was the large cruet she had me move to the table. The everyday objects surrounding Aunt Anastasia were things of beauty.

During lunch, Aunt Anastasia regaled me with stories from her time in Vladivostok and Tsientsin. As she spoke, it became clear that her family had been quite wealthy and I realised this was reflected in what I was seeing – the beautiful tea service, the elegant furniture, the silverware. Aunt Anastasia's Russia differed from the austere Soviet version I had grown up learning about in east Germany.

After lunch, I helped her clean up – or rather I cleaned up and washed the dishes and she sat at the kitchen table, directing me.

Once finished, I hung up the linen drying cloth. "I must be going – I have to get to Woolloongabba for my book club meeting."

Aunt Anastasia looked up at me. "I have enjoyed your company, Karlota. Will you come again next Saturday?"

Apart from the importance of finding a way into Russian society, I found this old lady interesting and sympathised with her too. The steep staircase up to the flat must be quite a barrier for her. "I would like that – thank you for the invitation."

Aunt Anastasia struggled to her feet. "In that case, I have something for you." She struggled across the room to a large wooden bookcase, its polished wood glowing in the light. "Now ... where is it?" Her eyes searched the lower shelves. "Ah yes." She grasped the bookcase for support and tapped a book on the bottom shelf with her cane. "Please pull that out for me."

I handed the slim, clothbound book to her and she flipped it open.

"This is the Russian grammar text I used when I was teaching Russian children in Tsientsin. I think you'll find it useful." She closed the book and handed it to me. "When you go downstairs, ask Lukas to find you a Russian-English dictionary. He can put it on my account."

This generosity flustered me. "I ... I can pay for it myself."

"Nonsense, child. These books are repayment for spending time with me."

"Thank you." I stammered.

"Excellent. I will see you after you finish swimming next Saturday. Don't bother to bring lunch. I will arrange that."

I managed another "Thank you," embarrassed at her generosity.

"Off you go. I need my afternoon nap."

Downstairs, I relayed Aunt Anastasia's message to Mr Caune.

He disappeared into the book stacks and returned with a thick, comprehensive dictionary. "Here you are."

"Thank you." I hesitated for a moment, still unsure about Aunt Anastasia's generosity. "I can pay for this."

Mr Caune looked horrified. "No, no, no. She would skin me alive if I let you pay for this."

"Okay."

I wandered in the city to kill time before splurging on a tram and trolley bus to the German Club, where Miss Bauer greeted me. Feeling more accepted by the group, I summoned the courage to ask what 'magical realism' was when it came up in discussion. A sniff greeted my question, but

Miss Bauer silenced it with a look and explained the term and its relevance to *Die Blechtrommel*.

As we had tea after the meeting, Miss Bauer handed me the current copy of the German newspaper. "You seem to enjoy the Grass, Karlota."

"I think it's interesting – but it's difficult sometimes to work out what he's saying ... what's lying under the words."

Miss Bauer smiled. "Indeed – but in part that multi-layering makes it interesting literature."

I headed home, looking forward to relaxing as it had been another busy week. The crushing pressure I had felt last week was now a lingering unease that pulsed with varying intensity in the background. The problems I faced remained, but I was managing better the anxiety they created.

Mutti's face showed her concern as I walked into the house, but relaxed when I smiled at her. I walked over to the radio and turned it up before sitting on the sofa beside her.

"I think I've found a way into Russian society."

Mutti blinked in surprise, but kept her voice low. "That's ... unexpected. How did you do that?"

I told her about Mr Caune, Aunt Anastasia – and pulled out the Russian grammar and dictionary.

"You amaze me, Kal – I'm proud of you." She gave me a hug.

I basked in her praise.

She kept hold of my hands. "I don't think we'll tell that man about this yet. Let's see how it develops, shall we?"

"Okay."

Mutti dragged the German newspaper to her and started leafing through it. I emptied my duffel bag, hanging my swimming things up to dry.

Chapter 10
Early February – early April 1965

The rhythms of school percolated into the rest of my life. Running and swimming were the fundamental beat in my continual search for a calm centre. However, the deceit in my life produced jarring cross-rhythms ... and the aching holes left by Willi and Lili remained. As much as I could, I poured out my heart in my letters to Willi, but the circumlocutions and words unsaid gnawed at the fraying edges of my mind. I talked with Mutti, but it was not the same. I longed to talk freely once again with Willi, but I dared not do so with Lizzie.

Despite being the youngest member of the German Book Club, I felt accepted – or my continued presence no longer raised eyebrows. But I'd gleaned nothing of interest for Mr Franks. I hoped being in the German book club was enough to satisfy him. I was searching, without success, for ways to move more fully amongst the wider club membership. At the Polish club, I always arrived early for class. Mrs Jaworski took advantage of this by asking me to assist her in the kitchen and sometimes in the office. It was there that I found an old membership list discarded in the wastepaper basket when she sent me to empty it into the rubbish bins. I folded it and slipped it into the waistband of my skirt until I could hide it in my bag. It was a small thing, but it made me feel like an actual spy. This delighted Mutti and we created cards for each member – or added their membership details to existing cards. She could now supply to Mr Franks a full name and address for Jan Drozd, the communist sympathiser – along with the membership list.

I enjoyed my hours with Aunt Anastasia. She was such an interesting person, full of stories from her well-travelled life. Every Saturday, I went there straight from swimming and stayed until it was time to head to the German Club. Learning Russian at a reasonable speed would be difficult, but I had seen Willi 'learning' German with me when he already knew it. I wanted to tell Willi about this in my current letter. I ended up writing, "I'm having the same problem learning Russian as you had learning German."

At Aunt Anastasia's flat, I learned how to make tea the Russian way –
in a *samovar* – and serve it in crystal tea glasses held in *podstakannik*, metal
tea glass holders. Aunt Anastasia's *samovar* and matching *podstakanniki*
were of gilded bronze, decorated with a relief of St George killing the
dragon. It had been a wedding gift to her great-grandmother and was, I
guessed, as valuable as it was beautiful. I learned that the tea set we had used
the first day and the 'every day' dinner service were Meissen China, from
Dresden. Mutti explained that the bombing of Dresden in February1945
had destroyed most of the moulds for *Meissen* ceramics. Aunt Anastasia's
tea set and dinner service were probably irreplaceable. I tried not to be
nervous, handling such precious items, but there was always a slight tremor
of trepidation.

At school, I was now a fixture in Lizzie's group, but she still chided me
for the way I remained quiet, listening, but speaking rarely. I was joining
in more, but always had a book in one of my languages if the conversation
drifted off somewhere I found uninteresting. I suppose my close
relationship with Lili and our shared secrets had kept us apart from others
at school in England. As a *Stasi* child in East Germany, I couldn't make
friends. But in spite of my hidden world and strange background, I was
finding things in common with the other girls; we were all teenagers
enjoying the increasing freedom the 'swinging 60s' brought us. We enjoyed
music and all loved the Beatles. Two of the girls in Lizzie's group had
acquired tickets to see them live in Brisbane the previous year, which still
caused some envy within the group. The study habits I had gained with
Willi and Lili meant I kept pace with my schoolwork, including Maths.
I had been hiding behind Willi in this, but was now finding my way,
although not at his level. This meant I could sometimes help members of
the group, who were slowly becoming my friends. They gave me help now
and then, particularly with the baffling Australian slang that peppered their
speech outside of school. Why does 'crook' mean sick here in Australia?

At the swimming club, I still had not made the team, but I was
improving. Coach was pushing me into the 800 m and 1500 m practice
events at the club, although under sixteens didn't compete at these
distances. I found the 1500 m a real stretch and came in a long way last
the first time I tried it at the club. The 800 m surprised me – I beat an

under-eighteen girl, but she'd probably not been pushing herself. I'd been to two competitions as a 400 m reserve and helper and had watched Lizzie collect a second and a third in the 50 m race she delighted in. With the club pushing me to the longer distances, I increased the length of my morning runs. Frequently, I saw Euan standing watching me as I clocked up the circuits, but he was gone before I finished.

Did talking with me stir terrible memories for him?

Each Thursday I brought home the Polish newspaper, which we searched through, gradually expanding our index cards. Despite the information we were amassing, we had turned up nothing of interest beyond Jan Drozd. On Saturdays I brought home the newspaper from the German Club which we subjected to the same treatment. At the end of February, we were sitting on the veranda late one Saturday afternoon, the heat and humidity building towards storms in a day or two. Mutti was idling through the latest German newspaper before we started pulling information from it when she jolted upright.

"What is it, Mutti?" I cradled *Imbi* as I stood and peered down at the paper open before her. On the page was a photo of a group of middle-aged men standing on a jetty, admiring a large fish.

Mutti's eyes reluctantly moved from the newspaper to my face.

"Get the German index cards, please, *Liebling*," she said, a tremor in her voice.

Had she recognised someone?

I carefully deposited *Imbi* on a chair and retrieved the box of German index cards from the bottom of the cupboard in the study. Mutti was sitting at the kitchen table when I returned, the newspaper folded with the photo and its caption displayed.

"Do we have a card for ..." Mutti looked down at the picture. "I think it's Hans Gruber." She reread the caption. "Yes, Hans Gruber."

I opened the box and looked through. "We don't have any Grubers, I'm afraid."

"Hmm ... this man," she tapped the individual in the photo, "is *SS Haupt Sturmführer* Vogel." Her voice was ice cold as she lifted her eyes to stare across the garden towards the playing fields and the stands of eucalypts surrounding them. Her lips pursed and eyes narrowed. "Vogel

was at Ravensbrück for months in late 1944 and part of his duties was ..."
She glanced at me and assessed what she was about to say. "... overseeing the
special prisoners – which included the English girls sent to Europe as spies."

There was another long pause as Mutti revisited these hard memories.

"I went into the block one day, as usual, to empty the slop buckets, with
an SS guard to open each cell for me. As I worked my way down the cell
block corridor, I could see a cell door was standing open with no guard and
my stomach clenched: they had executed someone. As we moved closer,
I could see it was ..." her voice caught for a moment. "It was one of the
English girls. As I arrived at the cell, the door at the far end of the block
opened, the one that led to the yard they used for executions. Vogel strutted
in, replacing his pistol in its holster."

Mutti picked up my hand, her eyes avoiding mine. "I don't think I
should tell you any more ..."

I gave her hand a sympathetic squeeze ... and I guessed why this death
was special, amongst the countless number she had witnessed at
Ravensbrück. "He had executed Colette, hadn't he? The girl I'm named
for."

Mutti's eyes rose to mine, glittering with unshed tears. She took several
uncertain breaths before continuing. "I didn't move away fast enough.
Vogel saw my face and grabbed my throat, pushing me up against the wall.
I reached for the floor with my toes." Her nose wrinkled. "I could smell
the acrid explosives on his hand from firing the pistol. His eyes bored into
mine, revelling in my sorrow. I'll not forget his words or his icy, arrogant
visage." Mutti swallowed, fingers fidgeting at her throat. "He mocked me
for mourning a spy ... and told me he looked forward to scouring the
Reich free of communist ... rubbish ... like me." Mutti's eyes stared into the
distant past. "When he dropped me, I staggered and fell beside the stinking
slop bucket. He strode away, boot-heels smacking his arrogance into the
concrete floor."

We sat in silence for minutes, Mutti lost in her memories. I stayed silent
beside her, concerned at the impact of this photo.

Mutti roused herself and reached for a blank index card to fill out.
"Get the scissors, *Liebling,* and cut out that picture – but make sure there's
nothing important on the other side."

I checked the reverse of the page: it was an advertisement. I carefully cut out the photo and brief article. "Are you sure it's him?" I asked, staring at the picture. He seemed ... ordinary.

"Yes, it's him." Mutti's flat voice showed no uncertainty as she glanced across at the photo in my hand. "Twenty years has done nothing to dim those memories." There was a dark, merciless tinge to her voice.

I looked across at Mutti, startled by her vehemence. "You ... you hate him, don't you?"

Mutti took a deep breath. "Yes." She shook her head. "I thought I was past the hate, but seeing him enjoying a pleasant life here ... rekindled the hatred." Her face was grim. "And I lectured Willi about not hating his father ..."

"What do we do now?" Mutti's conquest over the hatred of her Nazi persecutors was part of what defined her. We were in uncertain territory.

Mutti sat silent for a few seconds before turning to look at me, her eyes echoing her internal conflict. "I'm sorry, *Liebling*. I truly thought I was past this, but I can again feel hate's slow and dangerous burn inside me." Her eyes narrowed. "That man does not deserve a happy life – or any life."

She let out a controlled breath and I saw her contain but not extinguish the sharp emotions.

"What we do now is try to find out more about this Hans Gruber in Sydney and those men with him." Her face saddened. "And I must – fully, this time – find my way through this ... this miasma of hate – and root it out completely."

I gave her hand a supportive squeeze.

You'll find a way, Mutti... won't you?

· · · ·

AS I RAN THE FOLLOWING morning, Mutti's struggle with her hatred of Vogel kept pushing into my thoughts. Euan and Dodger appeared as I slowed, cooling down round the last part of my final circuit. This time he waited, and I walked up to him, regaining breath.

"Ye run 'n breathe well, lassie. 'Tis a pleasure t' watch." Euan's broad Scottish accent was becoming more transparent to me, but I still had to listen with care.

"I've had to increase the length of my runs. The club wants me to swim 800-metre and 1500-metre races."

Euan frowned. "They's a fearful ways t' swim." He looked me up and down. "Reckon ye need to bulk up, lassie. There's no' much meat on ye."

I laughed, self-conscious of my lack of breasts. "Most of my friends are worried about putting on weight."

Euan frowned, shaking his head. "If'n ye goin' t' swim they fearsome distances, ye need resairves." He emphasised the last word, richly rolling the 'r's. "'Tis like runnin' a marathon." The rolled 'r's stressed those words too. "Ye can be a wee bit wiry, lass, but no' skinny."

I could hear his vehemence. This was something to think about, along with everything else. I was about to turn away when I blurted out, "Did you hate the soldiers you fought against?"

Euan's head came up and he gave me a questioning look. "Now, why would ye be askin' that?"

I looked down at my shoes, embarrassed, scuffing them in the loose grass. After a few seconds of silence, I looked up.

Euan had a gentle smile on his lips. "Is ye havin' trouble on account o' being Gairman, eh?" He eyed me thoughtfully for a moment. "No, not hate, lassie." He shook his head. "They was jus' poor buggers like us. We didna' hate each other – least ways not truly hate." He gazed into the past for a second or two. "T'were more like ... respect." He muttered to himself for a moment. "There was terrible stories told about 'em, but they was rubbish." He chuckled. "'Spect they was told how wicked we was." But his voice became more serious as his eyes returned to mine. "Some of your lot did terrible things in the last set to, but most of 'em was rounded up and dealt with, I reckon."

Dodger snuffled against his leg and Euan reached down to caress an ear. Dodger raised his head at the touch and I could see the deep affection between them.

"What if one wasn't?" The question slipped out before I could grab it.

Euan looked at me sideways. He was bent over his dog, eyes holding mine, weighing my worth. "Then, lassie, I reckon ye need to think on't afore ye speak." His gaze pinned me. "There was wicked things done, I ken that, but ... rippin' off t' scabs now, after twenty yairs ... there'll be much pain." He looked away for a moment, before his eyes returned to mine, bright and strong beneath the frosty hedges of his eyebrows. "Aye, much pain an' precious little good to come fra' it."

We gazed at one another for a few seconds before Euan unbent himself and turned away. "You think well on't, lassie." His voice came to me over his shoulder as Dodger waddled to catch up to his sudden departure.

I did not know what to say and stood there watching him for several heartbeats before I set off for home at a gentle trot.

Mutti and I must talk about Vogel.

When I finished showering and put on a sarong, I found Mutti in the kitchen sipping coffee. She was cutting slices of Schwarzbrot while the radio played music. I pulled out the cheese and spreads we liked and poured myself a cold milk.

"How was your run?"

"Good thanks. I met Euan again."

Mutti gave me a querying look.

"The Scottish man who was a runner before the first war."

"Ah, yes. Do you see him often?"

"Once or twice a week and we've talked a few times. Today I think he wanted to talk to me as he waited for me to finish my circuits."

"What did he want?" Mutti's voice was wary.

"He's worried I'm too thin – particularly now I'm swimming longer distances."

Mutti gave me a sideways glance. "Have the swimming coaches said anything?"

"No ... but I should ask them." I stopped, unsure of how much to say. "Euan said it's okay to be wiry but not skinny." I rushed on. "Do you think I'm skinny?" I looked down at my chest where my breasts had, it seemed, stopped developing.

Mutti smiled. "You look fine to me, but I wouldn't know about swimming. Ask the coaches. They're supposed to be the experts."

"Good idea." I munched on a slice of bread, spread with the lime marmalade Willi had introduced us to in England.

"What are you going to do about Vogel?" My mouth seemed to have a mind of its own this morning.

Mutti carefully placed her coffee cup on the saucer. Faint lines appeared around her eyes and mouth.

I blundered on. "Euan said we should think hard before we do anything."

"What?" Mutti was aghast. "What are you doing, sharing our secrets with a stranger?"

I could hear the anger rising in her voice. But as I explained the conversation, I saw Mutti's hackles settle.

"So, what was your friend's advice again?"

"He suggested I think long and hard before speaking to anyone about ... such a person."

Mutti's face was stony.

"He said that there would be much pain and little good come of it."

Mutti reached for her coffee cup, looking over the rim at me as she sipped. "*Liebling,* you must be more careful." Her coffee cup chittered nervously as she placed it on the saucer. "Once again, you've said something that might make people ... wonder about us. We cannot afford to be discovered – again."

My eyes dropped in contrition. "I'm sorry. But I'm worried about you ... after yesterday."

Mutti sighed, her face softening.

"Umm ... Have you decided what to do about Vogel?"

Mutti's face hardened again, her eyes dropping to her hands. She shook her head. "No, I haven't." She looked across at me, uncertainty and frustration in her eyes. "I could speak about this with Mr Franks, but I do not know what he'd do with the information." Mutti stopped and her gaze shifted uneasily around the room. "That means telling him could have unpredicable consequences for us." She raised her eyebrows, grimacing. "It requires careful thought."

I reached a hand out to hold hers.

Her face crumpled. "But if I do nothing about Vogel, that calls into question everything I've tried to do about your father."

I heard the anguish in Mutti's voice and scurried round the table. I hugged her as silent tears ran down her face. After some minutes, Mutti stirred and I reached a box of tissues off the worktop. Mutti pulled out a couple, wiping her eyes and blowing her nose.

"I'm sorry, *Liebling* ... I've made such a mess of things – wrecked your life ..."

I squeezed Mutti's hand fiercely. "No, Mutti. No. We've talked about this and that's not true."

Mutti dabbed at her eyes. "But..."

"No, Mutti." I gave her a fierce look to reinforce my words. "My life now is much richer than it was or could ever be in east Germany. You haven't wrecked my life, you've enriched it."

"By dragging you half-way round the world, away from your friends?"

I shrugged. "Not all the enrichment has been happy... but ... what doesn't kill me makes me stronger?" My voice carried uncertainty about that aphorism.

Mutti laughed. "When did you read Nietzsche?"

"I haven't – but that quote came up in discussion at the Book Club a week ago and I remembered it." I smiled, grimly. "It seems to fit my life."

I pulled my chair over beside her and sat down. "You know, there's someone else you can speak to about Vogel."

Mutti's eyebrows moved into a confused frown.

I leant across and took her hand. "There's always me, Mutti."

"I suppose ..." I could feel her reluctance to burden me further with this. We sat in silence for a while.

"Everyone thinks love and hate are opposites. But I'm not sure that's right."

Mutti gave me a disbelieving look.

I stopped, struggling to grasp this indistinct idea. "Both love and hate are such powerful emotions – their opposite should be no emotion. Umm ... indifference?" I looked at Mutti to see if she understood what I was trying to say, but she remained silent. "I don't hate my father ... I feel nothing for him."

Mutti raised a disbelieving eyebrow.

"Nothing." Frustration blossomed at her lack of understanding. I tried again. "I fear what he might do to us if he found us, but I'm indifferent to what happens to him."

Mutti sat in silent thought before responding. "You mean I should try to be indifferent about Vogel?"

"Yes, but indifference doesn't mean doing nothing. MI6 has your evidence, so we have taken action regarding my father, but those actions are not driven by hate."

Mutti drew in a deep breath. "Hmmm – I need to ponder this." She gave me a brief smile.

We passed the rest of the day quietly, in part filling in index cards from the German newspaper. I wrote some more to Willi, played with *Imbi* and read some more Grass.

• • • •

OVER THE NEXT FEW WEEKS, I worried about Mutti. She did not raise the Vogel issue, but frequently I found her, lost deep in introspection. I slipped away to give her space to think, but I could see she was struggling.

February gave way to March: the nights cooled and the humidity relaxed its sweaty grip. School, swimming club and my activities for Mr Franks continued without problem. March wandered quietly along on until everything that had happened a year ago at the end of the month crashed into me.

Easter was later this year – not until mid-April. Willi's leaving for east Germany was associated in my mind with the Tuesday after Easter, which is why I confused the date. Our English teacher wrote the date on the board.

31st March.

It stunned me.

Willi had left for east Germany a year ago today, triggering the terrible events that followed.

"Karlota?"

I blinked my way into the present, emotion churning through me. "Umm – yes Miss?"

Mrs Somerfield's eyes were hard but softened into concern. "Are you all right, Karlota?"

Had she noticed the incipient tears in my eyes?

From the corner of my eye, I saw Lizzie's worried face. I pulled in a steadying breath. "Yes, Miss."

Mrs Somerfield's gaze lingered on me before she spoke again. "Karlota, please pay better attention. Get out your grammar homework."

"Yes, Miss." I opened my workbook, giving Lizzie a sideways smile of reassurance.

When class finished, Lizzie waited for me. "What was that about, Kal? Mrs Somerfield called your name three times."

"It's all right, Lizzie. I was ... lost in thought..."

Lizzie gave me a quizzical look. "It must have been a serious thought to drown three calls from the teacher."

I stayed silent as we walked to our next class. There was much I couldn't talk about.

Lizzie's look softened. "You can share things with me, Kal. I'm good at secrets."

I shared a tentative smile. "After we leave school ..."

At the end of school, we walked down to the swimming pool. I had sorted through the emotion from the morning and had been my usual self – I thought – for the rest of the day.

"Want to share with me what happened this morning?" Lizzie asked once we were away from the school crowds.

I'd thought about what I could tell her, ready with something that was a partial lie. "I don't know why, but suddenly this morning everything welled up inside me. My father dying, leaving my close friends and coming all the way across the world to Australia ... it all overwhelmed me."

Lizzie's eyes widened in sympathy. "Oh, Kal." She gave my hand a gentle, comforting squeeze. "I can't imagine what all of that was like."

We walked on in silence for a few more steps.

"I've lived in the same house all my life ..." Lizzie's voice trailed off.

I smiled sideways at her as we continued walking. "You've helped me more than you know. You welcomed me as a friend from the moment we met and introduced me to your friends at school."

Lizzie smiled brilliantly at me, a slight blush colouring her cheeks and we walked on to the pool. At the club, the senior coach pulled me aside before we started.

"Karlota, your times for the 800-meter swim are improving nicely. When will you be sixteen?"

"Not until early February next year."

"Well, we'd like you to concentrate on distance swimming – 800 and 1500 meters. By next year, you will be competitive."

"But what about this year?"

He smiled indulgently. "You can't compete at those lengths until you're sixteen."

"I know – but what can I compete in this year?"

The coach blinked. "You want to compete this year?"

"If I'm good enough."

"Well, you're our reserve at 400 meters for the junior girls..."

There was something going on that I didn't understand. "How much faster do I need to be to make the team?"

He looked down at his clipboard, flicking through a few pages. "Well, you haven't swum 400 meters for a few weeks..."

"I know – because you wanted me to swim with the seniors at the long distances. Can I swim the 400-meter trial tonight? Or Saturday?"

He had trouble looking at me. "Hmm...we'll have to see about that."

With that, he brusquely turned away, leaving me standing frustrated and confused.

Lizzie walked up. "What was that about, Kal?"

As I explained, Lizzie's face tightened with anger. "His daughter is a junior 400-meter swimmer. He doesn't want you to swim and oust her from the team. I bet that's what it is."

Of course – I remembered seeing them together.

"Come on – let's get your name down for the 400-meter junior trial. They can't stop you. You are the reserve."

I swam the 400-meter and beat the senior coach's daughter by a body length. After the race, the junior coach came up to me.

"You've improved Karlota. There's a competition coming up before Easter; if you can keep up the time over the next couple of weeks, I think you might make the team." He gave me an encouraging smile and walked off.

I watched the senior coach buttonhole him as he walked away. I now had a target to shoot for, provided the senior coach didn't wreck things.

Lizzie bounced up to me. "Way to go, Kal. You'll make the team if you can keep beating her."

Later in the evening I swam an 800-meter with the seniors. I was getting closer to the leaders and they were two years older than me. They would all be too old for the under-eighteen competition next year, which was why I was being groomed as a distance swimmer.

Thursday morning saw me hit my run with increased determination. After several laps, I ran past Euan, standing with Dodger, where the path emptied onto the field. Giving him a brief wave, I added an extra lap – pushing myself. Euan stood there watching me run. I had the feeling he was waiting for me to finish.

As usual, I gradually slowed to a walk over the last part of the lap, ending up in front of Euan. I sensed his eyes assessing me as I approached him.

"G'day, lassie."

My breath was returning. "Good morning, Euan."

"Ye ken you've a need to work on y' arms as well as ye legs?"

I must have looked confused.

"Y're a swimmer – y' arms are as important as ye legs." The richly rolled 'r's again highlighted his speech.

I hadn't thought about it, but he was right – in swimming we use our arms as well.

"Y're improving t' breathin' an' strengthening t' legs by runnin'. But ye've a need t'strengthen ye arms 'n shoulders."

I could see him determinedly not looking at my upper body, a flicker of a smile touching his eyes. Since my breasts were small, I didn't wear a bra when running – it made me hotter. Glancing down, I realised the damp t-shirt was clinging to me in a revealing way. I needed a baggier t-shirt ... I hunched my shoulders to free the material from my skin.

I gave Euan an embarrassed smile. "How do I do that – strengthen my arms?"

"Ye need to lift weights."

I frowned in confusion. "What do you mean?"

"Strength trainin', lassie, by liftin' weights."

Euan saw the confusion on my face. "Och, I've an old set of weights left by me nephew. I'll lend 'em to ye an' show ye what t' do. Come round after school, an' I'll show ye."

"I can't today – I've my Polish class after school."

Euan raised an eyebrow at that snippet. "Temorra?"

"Umm – I'll have to speak to my mother first. Where do you live?"

"Next street over fro' ye. On 10th Avenue, at number eight."

I loved those rolling 'r's. "Okay – I'll speak to my mother this morning."

"Right y'are." He paused a moment. "Ye've bin thinkin' on t'other matter?"

I tensed and Euan gave me a curt nod of acknowledgement.

"Right, see ye temorra." He urged Dodger to his feet and they set off across the playing field, as always, without a backward glance.

I told Mutti about the weightlifting over breakfast.

She pursed her lips in thought. "I think I'd like to meet this Euan before you go over to his house alone." She paused for a moment. "I'll see if he's at home this evening on my way from work."

When I got home from Polish class, I found Mutti reading a rather dog-eared pamphlet showing diagrams of a man lifting weights in a variety of ways.

"There's a small stack of what I presume is weightlifting gear under the house and this note from your friend Euan." She handed me a sheet of writing paper with tightly written neat handwriting on it. It startled me as I hadn't given him our address – but I realised he knew where we lived from the directions he gave me to his house.

Dear Miss Karlota,

I can understand your mother not wanting you to visit a strange man in his house. So, I put the weights under your house and left this note with the booklet that explains what to do. Be careful and follow the instructions or you could hurt yourself.

I'll talk to you some more when we next meet on your run.

Your friend,

Euan.

"You should write a note thanking him and we can drop it in his letter box tomorrow on the way to the tram." She thought for a moment. "Ask him to come to afternoon tea on Sunday. I could get to meet him and he could help you with this weightlifting thing."

"Okay." And before we left for school and work, I wrote him a note.

Dear Euan,

Thank you for your generous loan of the weightlifting equipment. I will read through the booklet carefully before I try anything. My mother wondered if you would like to visit for afternoon tea on Sunday at about three o'clock, when you could show me how best to use it in person.

Thank you again,

your friend,

Karlota.

Euan wasn't there when I ran on Friday morning, nor did we see him when we dropped off the note – and Saturdays I didn't run as I went straight to the swimming club.

I had lunch as usual with Aunt Anastasia. She expressed her pleasure at my progress, although she chided me for sloppy grammar. I smarted at this, which, of course, Aunt Anastasia noticed.

"Karlota," she sighed. "You are an excellent student and your progress has been quite remarkable."

I could hear the 'but' about to land on me and stiffened.

Nothing slipped past such an experienced teacher and Aunt Anastasia smiled, quirking an elegant silver eyebrow at me.

It was my turn to sigh. "I know ... but I can do better."

Aunt Anastasia looked at me across the richly polished table, where today a crystal vase cast faint rainbows onto the delicate lace mat. "If you think so, it is true." She paused, her pale blue eyes searching my face. She switched to English. "But do not lie to yourself."

Her gaze held mine and all the lies I was telling to live this life forced an embarrassed flush to my face.

Aunt Anastasia's eyes flared, recognising my reaction. A hand reached for mine, her parchment skin lined with blue veins and showing the blotches of age. Light as a butterfly, it landed on my fingers. "We all have to tell lies, Karlota; life pushes us to places where there is no other choice."

I took a deep breath, about to speak.

Aunt Anastasia patted my hand. "No, we'll not speak further of this. There's no need to share secrets that are best unsaid." Her voice and face hardened. "But make sure you are not lying to yourself. Hmmm?"

We sat looking at one another for a few seconds. "I think it's time for a glass of tea, don't you?"

Riding the tram home after the book club, Aunt Anastasia's words bounced around in my brain. I knew I was telling lies almost every day ...

But was I lying to myself?

I knew who I was and where I was from and why I was spying for Mr Franks, but I don't think that was what Aunt Anastasia was talking about. I pondered this as the tram rattled and swayed up Lutwyche Road.

Was I lying to myself about Willi?

At home, I found Mutti baking a fruit cake. Rich aromas of boiled currents, raisins and mixed peel enticed my nose when I opened the front door.

Mutti looked up from beside the stove. "I've not been able to find a cake as moist and delicious as the ones we used to buy from Mr Searle in Herne Bay. I asked around at work and a co-worker gave me this recipe for a boiled-fruit cake." She gave the saucepan a stir with a wooden spoon and turned off the heat. "We needed something for Mr McDonald tomorrow."

Mutti believed shared food strengthened bonds. "It smells wonderful, Mutti." I grabbed a few juicy raisins from the packet and headed to my bedroom. I trod carefully, avoiding *Imbi* at his usual trick of following in front whilst winding between my feet.

Mutti smiled. "That cat is part dog, you know? He was waiting by the door for you to come home."

I bent down and scooped him up rather than trip over him, carrying him through to my bedroom at the end of the hall.

In the kitchen, I watched as Mutti mixed the cake ingredients. "Euan said he's coming?"

"Yes. He left a note sometime earlier today." Mutti spooned the cake into a cake pan and slid it into the oven, setting the clockwork timer. "If you hear the timer ping, let me know. I need to turn the cake and reset the timer."

"Okay. It's good Euan's coming. I think he's an interesting person and I'd like to know him better. I think you'll like him too."

Euan wasn't about when I ran on Sunday morning, but he turned up smartly dressed in a blazer and tie on the dot of three o'clock. We had set the tea table outside on the shaded veranda.

"How do you like your tea, Mr MacDonald?" Mutti asked.

"Frau Miller, t'wa be wrong fer ye daughter to call me Euan 'n' fer ye to call me Mr MacDonald."

Mutti looked up, startled to hear the German honorific.

Euan smiled. "Me name's Euan, Frau Miller."

Mutti glanced at me. "Very well, Euan. I'm Frida." She indicated the tea pot. "Now, tea?"

Euan smiled. "Black for me, thank ye, Frida, wi' a slice of tha' lemon."

Euan knew Mutti was German, but I wondered at him addressing her as 'Frau'. "I didn't know you spoke German, Euan."

Euan chuckled. "No reason ye would, lassie." He looked across at Mutti. "'N I've probably forgotten most of it." He pursed his lips. "I spent t' last eight months of t' Great War in a prison camp near Hanover. Lairnin' Gairman was summat t' keep me mind occupied."

I could see this flustered Mutti. "Please offer your friend a slice of cake, Kal."

I offered the plate of cake slices to Euan, who helped himself to a piece.

"I've read through the pamphlet you left with the weights, Euan, but after tea could show me how to use them properly."

"Aye, lassie. We ca' do that."

I sensed Mutti was struggling to find a topic of conversation that would not be awkward. I flicked her a quick look and turned to Euan. "How long have you been in Australia, Euan?"

"Well now, a fair few yairs it would be." He shifted in his chair. "I was a draughtsman on the ships on t' Clyde a'fore joinin' up ..." He gave an apologetic smile at mentioning the awkward subject of the war. "After I got home, they gae me my ol' job. But in 1929, I and most everyone lost t' job because of the depression." His eyes held a sadness in them. "Them wa' dark, dark days." He seemed lost in the memories for a few seconds.

"I wasna' married and had put a bit by. Seein' t'greyness all around, I recalled some Aussie soldiers tellin' me about t'sunshine in Australia. I got mesel' a spot as crew on a ship headin' t'Australia."

Now on safe ground, we talked about our respective trips to Australia by boat. Mutti noticed Euan picking up the cake crumbs from his plate and offered him another slice.

When he had finished it and his second cup of tea, he looked across at me. "Ready t' lairn t'lift weights, lassie?"

"Yes please – but I don't think a skirt's quite the thing to wear for that. I'll change into gym clothes if that's alright?"

Euan chuckled, glancing at Mutti. "Ye's right about that, lassie."

I slipped into my bedroom and changed into my running gear. Mutti came down under the house with us, where Euan showed me how to assemble and use the weights to increase my upper body strength.

After watching for a while and pointing out things he saw I was doing wrong, he thanked Mutti for the tea and I thanked him for the lesson.

"I'll be seein' ye in t' mornings, lassie." He walked out into the late afternoon sunlight, ramrod straight as ever.

At first, I tried to do weights and run in the morning, but this was too much. I moved the weights to the evening before I showered. At the swimming club that week, I asked the junior coach about what I was doing and he suggested I eat more protein – meat – to give me the building blocks for muscles. I spoke to Mutti about this and the following day, we had steak for tea – and mine was twice the size of Mutti's.

School broke up for the Easter holidays at the beginning of April. The evening temperatures were starting to drop and sarongs were becoming cool. I looked at the woollen jumpers and wondered if it was ever cold enough to wear them here in Brisbane.

Lizzie's family were spending Easter at the Gold Coast and I would be at a loose end. I planned to finish *Die Blechtrommel* and write my ongoing letter to Willi. I'd borrowed several books from the library, including Tolkien's "The Lord of the Rings": over a thousand pages, I thought, would keep me quiet for a while. And there were the weights under the house to use and my daily run. Swimming club was in recess but I still hoped to swim at least once a week.

But Mr Caune stopped me on my way up to Aunt Anastasia's flat the Saturday before Easter. "Hello, Karlota." He paused, his lips fluttering indecisively. "Ummm...could you spare me a moment, please?"

"Of course." I stopped in front of the sales counter. He looked nervous. *Why is he nervous?*

"Please have a seat for a moment, Karlota." He moved to the other side of the counter, his head down, evading my eyes, flicking distractedly at the countertop with a dust-cloth. "Umm *<flick>* Karlota *<flick flick>* could I ask for your assistance with something?"

"Of course ... if I can help, I'd be glad to."

"Yes, yes. Of course." The flicking stopped and he looked up at me. "You see ... um ... my wife and I are going to visit our son in Melbourne over Easter. And ... er ... well, the person who keeps an eye on Aunt Anastasia if we go away is suddenly not available." He stopped and swallowed. "You see ... I was wondering ... if you could stay with Aunt Anastasia for the week?" The end of the sentence came out in a rush.

I was certainly not expecting this. "Do you mean ... come and live with her for a week in her flat?"

"Yes, that's right ... if you can.

"Umm – I think you'd need to speak to my mother about this."

"Of course, of course. When would it be convenient for me to ring her?"

I thought for a moment – I wanted to be home before he rang. "This evening – about half-past six, I think."

He pushed a notepad across the counter and I wrote our phone number on it.

He looked up with a thin smile as he handed me the key to Aunt Anastasia's flat. "Please don't mention this to Aunt Anastasia yet."

"Okay."

Upstairs, Aunt Anastasia was in her usual chair by the window when I let myself in. She had a Russian language newspaper spread across her knees, which I'd not seen before.

"Good morning, Aunt Anastasia."

"Good morning, Karlota".

And we were off into the depths of the Russian language until I was about to leave for the German Club. Before I left, I helped settle Aunt Anastasia into her chair, a fresh glass of water beside her.

"Would you like the newspaper, Aunt Anastasia?"

"No thank you, Karlota. I've finished with it. You can put it in the rubbish."

I moved towards the kitchen, but turned. "If you've truly finished with it, Aunt Anastasia, might I have it, please?"

"Of course, my dear."

"Thank you. I'm sure reading this will help my Russian along."

Aunt Anastasia smiled encouragingly. The folded newspaper went into my duffel bag, beneath *Die Blechtrommel*, to make sure I didn't show it in the German Club.

"Goodbye, Aunt Anastasia. Thank you for the newspaper."

"Goodbye, Karlota."

Downstairs, I returned the door key to Mr Caune.

"Thank you, Karlota. I'll ring your mother this evening."

I still hadn't been able to move deeper into the German Club, which worried me, despite Mutti's reassurance.

How long would Mr Franks' patience last?

I hoped my success at the Polish Club was enough.

As the book club approached the end of *Die Blechtrommel*, I was finding the book increasingly odd. I would not have persisted with it had it not been my entry pass into the German Club. Oskar, making a false confession to a murder and ending up in a looney bin, stretched my willing suspension of disbelief. I thought about this as I sat on the tram. Perhaps I was projecting my issues with lies onto Oskar's character. He certainly had shown no remorse at lying repeatedly.

As soon as I arrived home, I sat down next to Mutti to speak to her about Aunt Anastasia before Mr Caune rang. "Mutti, Mr Caune from the foreign language bookshop is going to ring this evening. He wants me to look after Aunt Anastasia over Easter."

Mutti frowned. "What do you mean, 'look after Aunt Anastasia'?"

As I went through my conversation with Mr Caune, I realised how odd this sounded.

Mutti sat in her chair looking at me when I finished. "Do you want to do this? Care for an old lady for several days by yourself?"

I pursed my lips in thought. "She's a fascinating person and I enjoy Saturdays with her."

Mutti eyed me thoughtfully. "Possibly – but that's not the same as being at her beck and call twenty-four hours a day ... for a week."

"I suppose. I don't know enough about what I would have to do."

Mutti smiled. "I'd better explore that with Mr Caune."

The phone rang after half-past six. Mutti and Mr Caune spoke for some time before I heard her agreeing to meet Mr Caune the following day.

Mutti put down the phone and I looked at her. "Well?"

"I'm going to meet him tomorrow at two o'clock." She saw me open my mouth. "By myself." She added before I could jump in. "He's going to take me to meet this Aunt Anastasia and ... we'll see." She gave me a firm look. "I don't want you there. It might confuse things."

I gave a moue of disappointment.

Mutti patted my arm. "I don't want to hurt the relationship you're building with this woman. Mr Caune told me she thinks highly of you. But I want to say 'no' if I think this is unreasonable – after all, you will be staying with her for about ten days, from what Mr Caune told me."

I blinked. "I thought it was for Easter..."

"Apparently not." Mutti's voice showed her worry. "Which is one reason I want to meet with Mr Caune and this aunt of his."

"She's not his aunt." I reached into my memory. "She's a distant relative of his wife."

I changed and went down to work on the weights, wondering if this was worth it: I hadn't noticed any difference in my arms and shoulders.

Chapter 11
Mid-April 1965

I drifted awake, my hand sliding across the pillow, seeking *Imbi's* soft fur; its absence flicked my eyes open. This wasn't my room; it was one of Aunt Anastasia's bedrooms. I lay there, sleepily wondering if *Imbi* had found his way to Mutti's bed to compensate for my absence. Faintly through the window, I heard pallets clattering down the alley at the rear of the building. Someone was up and moving early in the city, despite it being Easter Sunday.

I glanced at my alarm clock: half-past six and time for me to be up and running. I had put the front door key on a ribbon and slipped this over my head, shuddering from its cold slither down my breastbone under my t-shirt.

Outside, the city was waking as I trotted down to the Botanic Garden. Once there, I did my stretches and set off, enjoying the cool morning air. The trees left the paths in filtered sunlight, though the exotics were shedding their crimson and gold leaves as autumn approached. I completed several circuits before heading to Aunt Anastasia's flat.

By the time I had showered, I could hear Aunt Anastasia moving. I started the *samovar* process and turned on the oven to heat the hot-cross buns I'd picked up yesterday. Aunt Anastasia appeared shortly after, wearing a yellow robe embroidered with red and blue in a Chinese style.

"Oh. That's gorgeous."

Aunt Anastasia smiled, glancing down at the glistening wattle-yellow material with its Chinese motifs. "It is rather gorgeous, isn't it? It's silk, from China. Come and feel it."

I fingered a sleeve, the silk encouraging my fingers to slide until the rich embroidery at the cuff stopped them. "It's smooth."

"Smooth as silk." Aunt Anastasia smiled. "You'll find a similar red one in the wardrobe in your room for you to wear."

"Oh, thank you." I'd seen it hanging there when I unpacked on Friday. That I could use it was overwhelming: a robe like that would be expensive. I turned away to hide my embarrassment and organised breakfast. With the tea poured, I pulled out the hot-cross buns, placing one on Aunt Anastasia's plate. As I munched mine, trying to stop the melted butter from dribbling down my wrist, Aunt Anastasia looked across at me. "I heard you leaving early for your run this morning. You are an unusually committed girl, Karlota. Do you run every morning?"

"Yes." I gave her an apologetic look. "I'm sorry. I didn't mean to wake you. I tried to be quiet."

"It's all right, Karlota. You didn't wake me; I had been awake for a while." Aunt Anastasia paused for a moment. "As I've grown older, I seem to need less sleep." She returned her gaze to me. "But that's not important. We need to talk about the Easter Ball next Sunday."

"Ball?" I almost squeaked with surprise – there was no mention of this when we had talked with Mutti about my staying with her.

"Every Easter, the Russian Club holds a grand ball." Aunt Anastasia's gaze held a certain haughtiness. "You'll be accompanying me and we need to make sure you are appropriately dressed."

Images of grand balls from the previous century flitted through my brain and I shifted uneasily in my chair. "I don't think I have anything ..."

Aunt Anastasia waved a dismissive hand. "Of course you don't." She gave me a conspiratorial smile. "I've arranged for Olga to bring some suitable dresses round after lunch. I'm sure we'll find something amongst them she can alter in time."

This was embarrassing. "Umm ... I don't think we can afford a ball gown ..."

Aunt Anastasia leant across and patted my hand. "It is most kind of you to come and spend Easter with me and this is my treat, Karlota." Her smile was reassuring. "You are my guest and I want you to turn the heads of all the young men at the ball."

"Thank you." I stammered out.

There is only one head I want to turn ...

By the time Olga left that afternoon, I had tried on eight different ball gowns. After much deliberation, Aunt Anastasia selected a full length, high-waisted cream gown. It had a threaded black velvet ribbon motif above the hem, across the bodice and around the half sleeves.

With the choice made, Aunt Anastasia's eyes swept up from my feet. "You have beautiful, dark eyes, Karlota, and the black ribbon enhances them." She paused, looking at my arms. "You have been in the sun too much and your skin is rather dark, but that can't be helped."

I rubbed my arms self-consciously. "I'm out in the sun a lot, swimming and running ..."

Aunt Anastasia pursed her lips. "Well, in my day, we stayed out of the sun to preserve our skin." Her eyes examined my face and arms. "You young things today seem to luxuriate in the sunshine. You should look after your skin."

I'd have to ask Lizzie about this. Her mother would know ...

At breakfast on Wednesday morning, Aunt Anastasia announced we were going shopping. We had to find me a pair of suitable shoes, a clutch bag and a few other things for the ball. I helped Aunt Anastasia downstairs — quite a delicate performance, as she's rather uncertain on anything other than a level floor, but we made it into a waiting taxi without mishap. The taxi took us to Finney-Isles, the most exclusive and expensive department store in Brisbane. I'd looked in their display windows before but never ventured inside. There was never a price on anything displayed, reinforcing its reputation. I was glad to have Aunt Anastasia chaperoning me through the store, as I was awkward amidst its elegance.

Aunt Anastasia led me to the lady's department and sat herself at a counter.

A well-dressed sales lady came over. "Good morning, Miss Zaytseva. How can I help you today?"

Aunt Anastasia was a well-known customer, it seemed. She gestured towards me. "This is Karlota. She is accompanying me to the Easter ball on Saturday and she needs a few things. New lingerie, stockings, a clutch bag, shoes and such."

"Certainly, madam." She turned to me. "Please come with me Karlota and we'll find some lingerie first."

I glanced at Aunt Anastasia.

"Go along, Karlota."

I followed the sales lady into the lingerie section, where she looked me up and down.

"I'm Sandra." She smiled. "Now, what sort of dress are you wearing for the ball?"

I described it and she selected several sets of matching underwear. "Let's try these for a start."

Despite having minimal breasts, Sandra found a delicate bra that "enhanced my assets". I returned to Aunt Anastasia with matching underwear and two pairs of shear stockings with cream elasticated garters to hold them up.

Aunt Anastasia pulled a sample of my dress material from her bag. Sandra soon returned with half-a-dozen clutch bags from which we made a selection.

"Now for shoes." Aunt Anastasia hooked another chair round with her cane. "Sit down and take your shoes off, Karlota."

I sat there with my shoes on the floor, wriggling my freed toes.

Aunt Anastasia smiled, raising an eyebrow. "Give one to the lady."

A discussion occurred about the right shoe colour – to match the dress or the black ribbon? After a while, Sandra returned with several boxes and a junior assistant bearing several more. All had much higher heels than I was used to wearing and I wobbled on them. After some back and forth, Aunt Anastasia decided black shoes would detract from the ribbon in the gown's hemline. We settled on a pale cream pair to match the gown. Sandra placed a Finney-Isles bag on the counter, packing the boxes containing our purchases into it.

Aunt Anastasia waved at the bag. "On my account, please."

"Certainly, Miss Zaytseva," Sandra replied.

"Come along, Karlota." Aunt Anastasia pulled herself up using her cane and the countertop. "We've more to do yet."

Sandra handed me the carrier bag. "Enjoy the Ball, Karlota."

"Thank you." My uncertainty about all this was growing and Sandra must have sensed that.

"You'll be fine," she smiled. "But you should practice at home with the shoes until they feel natural."

I trailed after Aunt Anastasia, worrying about the money she was spending.

The 'more to do yet' comprised having my ears pierced and fitted with gold studs. The piercing hurt for a moment, but I didn't bleed much. We spent about half-an-hour with Michelle, a make-up specialist, who started out by helping me select a fragrance and telling me where to dab it. She called them 'pulse points', places where the blood was close to the surface and would warm and spread the fragrance.

Michelle and Aunt Anastasia debated lipsticks. Aunt Anastasia shook her head at a variety of reds. "Those are too old for a girl. She needs something subtle, delicate..."

Michelle smiled and produced some gentle pinks; we agreed on one of them. She led me through my make-up for Sunday.

"You have a compact?" She asked.

I gave her a blank look.

"Oh, you'll need a compact to touch up your make-up at the ball." She retrieved a silvery compact from under the counter, opened it and slipped in a make-up disc of the same shade she had used on my face.

"Here, let me show you." She drew the puff across the disc and demonstrated on her face.

"Be careful how you use the puff – barely brush the skin." She passed the compact to me. "You try it."

I copied Michelle, using the mirror in the compact lid to watch myself.

"Excellent – remember, only a little make-up on the puff."

Aunt Anastasia lifted my left arm and gestured with it to Michelle. "Do you have something for her skin? I am worried all the sun will damage it."

Michelle lifted my arm and ran her hand softly from wrist to elbow. "You are out in the sun a lot?"

"I swim and run ... and walk to and from the tram ..."

"I can see you have excellent muscle tone." Michelle's thumb massaged the skin near my elbow and she turned to Aunt Anastasia. "Sunlight is good for the skin – and the person – but it can be drying. I would recommend a milk to massage into the skin every night." She looked at me. "Would you like to try some?"

I nervously glanced at Aunt Anastasia – the money she was spending on me was rapidly mounting. She patted my hand in reassurance.

Retrieving a bottle from beneath the counter, Michelle deposited a few drips of milky fluid on my forearm. "You have beautiful skin and this will help it stay that way." Her hand smoothed the milk across my forearm, spreading the milk as the skin absorbed the moisture.

"As you can see, a little goes a long way. Use this after your evening shower on all the skin that sees the sun – not your face. I'll get you cream for that." She dripped several drops onto my other arm. "You do this arm." She reached below the counter, pulling up a container of face cream.

I smoothed the milk out, rubbing it into my skin and glanced up. "It leaves my skin feeling like silk."

"Excellent." Michelle gave me an encouraging smile. "You understand how to do your make-up for the ball?"

My smile was uncertain. I was not used to make-up and was a little unsure if I could replicate Michelle's deft touch.

Michelle glanced at Aunt Anastasia, who smiled. "I'm sure that we'll be fine."

Michelle produced a hairbrush and deftly flicked my hair around, trying various looks before returning to the style given me on the ship. "This style is simple to maintain and it suits you." She turned me towards the mirror where I saw the subtle effects of the makeup and the glint of the studs adding several years to my age.

Aunt Anastasia turned the chair towards her, gazing at my face. "Yes, that is excellent, Karlota." She looked up at Michelle. "Please call us a taxi."

"Certainly, madam." She waved at her assistant, who went to another counter to make the call. Meanwhile, Michelle packed everything into a soft bag. She produced a small bottle of the fragrance we had selected. "Put this in your clutch bag with the compact and lipstick for the ball, Karlota. That way you can refresh your make-up and perfume during the evening." She added the bottle to the soft bag and zipped it up. "Here you go." She handed me the bag with a smile. "Have fun."

"Thank you." My return smile was a little more confident this time.

The taxi was waiting at the front of the store. Helping Aunt Anastasia up the stairs to her flat was awkward, but we made it safely. At the top, I realised it would have been easier had I left the Finney-Isles bag at the foot of the stairs. The outing seemed to have tired Aunt Anastasia; I sat her in her chair and got to work on the *samovar* before serving lunch.

After I had cleaned up the meal, Aunt Anastasia gave me a commanding look. "Karlota, put on your ball shoes. You need to wear them in and get used to them. We can't have you spoiling things by falling over."

"Sandra, the saleslady told me the same thing."

For the next few days, I wore the shoes with their high heels around the flat for several hours and by Saturday, I was walking securely. Aunt Anastasia had me practice the dance steps I had learned on the ship and at school.

Polish classes, swimming and the German book club had all closed down over the Easter holidays. I only left the flat to do some shopping at Aunt Anastasia's direction and for my regular morning runs. We spent the rest of the time in work on my Russian: conversation, taking dictation and reading aloud. Aunt Anastasia pounced on any mispronunciation.

"You don't want to sound like a peasant, dear."

This immersive ten days significantly improved my Russian. By Friday, I had moved from restraining myself to pushing ahead. I could see Aunt Anastasia's pleasure in my rapid progress.

When I returned from my Saturday morning run, Aunt Anastasia was already up and I made tea before heading to my shower. Returning wrapped in the red silk robe, I made breakfast for us both.

"Olga is arriving soon for a last fitting of your gown, Karlota. You will need your ball shoes as well. I suggest you put on the lingerie for the ball and wear that robe for now to make things easier for the fitting."

I went and changed, delighting in the way the bra enhanced my modest breasts. Wrapping the gorgeous red silk robe round me, I caught sight of myself in the full-length mirror as the robe swirled and settled against my legs – such elegance.

Olga arrived with the dress and sent me to get my ball shoes, which I'd forgotten. With the gown on, she fussed with the hem and had me walk up and down the lounge room before looking over at Aunt Anastasia. I angled the full-length oval mirror standing at the front door and inspected myself, surprised by the young woman returning my gaze. I walked towards Olga and Aunt Anastasia, taking small steps rather than my normal walk, which Aunt Anastasia called 'an unladylike stride'.

Aunt Anastasia noticed, smiling in encouragement, and turned to Olga. "Thank you, that will do nicely."

Once I had changed into ordinary clothes, we spent the rest of the morning in more Russian lessons. As we finished lunch, Aunt Anastasia told me she would go to the midnight Easter service at the Russian St Nicholas Cathedral.

"I'll be going alone, Karlota. It would not be appropriate for you to attend. You don't have to wait up for me."

"Okay."

"I will sleep late on Sunday morning." She continued. "I have arranged for us to be picked up at six o'clock tomorrow evening. We will eat early, about four o'clock, before getting dressed for the ball."

We spent the afternoon in more Russian – reading, writing and speaking. I could see the pleasure she had in watching me mastering her language.

"Do you speak other languages, Aunt Anastasia?"

She smiled. "Well – I lived in China for twenty years. I speak and read Mandarin and I learned English from a tutor in Vladivostok as a child." Her eyes looked far away. "I tutored several English children from the community in Tsientsin."

That evening, Aunt Anastasia dressed in dark clothes, leaving in a cab at half-past nine. The cab driver knew her and came up to help her down the stairs. "It's all right, Miss. I'll bring her home and help her up the stairs again."

I went to bed early with Tolkien's Lord of the Rings and didn't wake when Aunt Anastasia returned from the service. As usual on Sunday morning, I was up and running, trying not to disturb Aunt Anastasia's sleep. As I circled the Botanic Garden, I heard a trumpet sounding somewhere in the distance. After a shower at the flat, I made myself breakfast and sat, reading more Tolkien. Aunt Anastasia appeared at about half-past ten.

"Would you like tea, Aunt Anastasia?"

"Thank you, Karlota. But I'll wait to eat until this afternoon. We'll eat early and ready ourselves after that."

For the rest of the morning, we sat reading in quiet company. I was feeling nervous by the time we ate that afternoon.

Aunt Anastasia noticed me nibbling at my food. "You need to eat, Karlota. There will be canapés at about nine o'clock at the ball ... and that's all."

I clamped down on my nerves and – to be honest – a growing excitement. I emptied my plate, gaining a nod of approval from Aunt Anastasia. With our few dishes cleaned and put away, we went to get ready. Reproducing Michelle's subtle makeup artistry took me half an hour, but I was finally satisfied with my appearance in the dressing-table mirror. I wrapped myself in the gorgeous silk robe. I wanted Aunt Anastasia to check my work before I finished dressing. She was sitting in her chair in her yellow robe.

"Could you check my make-up, please?"

"Certainly, Karlota."

I knelt beside her chair and she turned my head left and right, inspecting my work.

"Very good, Karlota." She smiled into my eyes. "I'm sure you'll experiment in the future, but remember, for a young thing like you, less is more."

I grimaced. There'd been women with overdone make-up around the city. I had no desire to look like them.

Aunt Anastasia set her cane securely and levered herself up, towering above me. "Come, Karlota, time to dress."

In my room, I was about to remove my gown from its dust bag but remembered I hadn't put on the perfume. I carefully dabbed it to my 'pulse points' as Michelle had called them, being careful to use it sparingly. As I did, I wondered how I was supposed to freshen some of these spots later in the evening ... and decided I would have to limit it to wrists, throat and behind the ears.

Once I dressed, I walked out, but Aunt Anastasia was not there. *Should I sit down? Would that crease my gown?* I was still pondering this when Aunt Anastasia walked out and sat at the table.

"Come here, please, Karlota."

I stood beside her, still worried about creasing my gown.

"Sit down, dear."

"Won't that crease the gown?"

Aunt Anastasia smiled. "Of course not, dear. Sit down."

I sat down and Aunt Anastasia opened a long black box, revealing a slim gold and diamond necklace with matching earrings.

"Oh," I breathed out softly. "That's gorgeous,"

"Indeed." She glanced down at the jewellery, a wistful look on her face. "My father gave this set to me for my first Ball when I was sixteen." She looked at me, a misty smile in her eyes. "I want you to wear them tonight."

I gasped. "They must be worth a fortune. What if I lose them?"

Aunt Anastasia patted my hand. "You won't." She looked at my throat. "You'll need to take off your gold chain."

My hand found its way to my throat.

Take off Willi's necklace? I hadn't removed it since that morning in Lancaster.

Aunt Anastasia saw my reaction. "It has a special meaning for you? From someone special?"

I couldn't speak.

Understanding filled Aunt Anastasia's eyes and she leaned towards me. "You aren't betraying him if you put it back on tomorrow, Karlota," she whispered.

I took several calming breaths as I examined my feelings. She was right, I realised after a few seconds.

Willi's necklace is a reminder. My feelings for him were the core.

I reached behind my neck and undid the clasp, wondering what to do with it, as its box was at home.

Aunt Anastasia saw my hesitation and gestured at the jewellery case. "Put it there. It will be safe for the evening."

I laid it beside the diamond necklace.

"Put the earrings on, Karlota."

My ears were still a little tender, but I'd been following the care instructions. I removed the studs and put them next to my necklace before fitting the delicate earrings, each with their single glittering diamond.

"Come and stand here."

As I moved round the table, Aunt Anastasia used her chair to help herself to her feet. The necklace glistened as she lowered it over me and drew it up around my neck.

"Turn round, Karlota." Emotion muffled her voice.

I could see in Aunt Anastasia's eyes this moment held great significance for her.

Her lips trembled. "I never had children. This set has been waiting in its box for a girl like you." A trembling hand moved my head slowly from side to side, taking in the earrings. "It is a set for a beautiful young woman like you, Karlota."

Impulsively, I flung my arms round her, hugging her. For a moment, she was rigid. I started to pull away, embarrassed that I'd misjudged her, when her arms came up and pulled me against her. We hugged for several seconds, each suffused by the emotions of the moment before Aunt Anastasia pushed us apart.

She held my forearms and smiled. "You'll certainly turn heads tonight, Karlota. Look at yourself in the mirror."

Were those tears in her eyes?

I spent a minute in front of the full-length mirror. I could scarcely believe this young woman was me. The diamonds in the necklace and earrings caught the light, drawing the eyes. I wasn't beautiful, but with the gown and jewellery I certainly wasn't the flat-chested, ugly duckling I had felt alongside most of the girls at school.

When I turned round, Aunt Anastasia was opening another jewellery case.

"Could you help me with this, please?" She lifted a necklace of what I suspected were emeralds and rubies, holding it against her. "Fasten the clasp for me, Karlota."

Aunt Anastasia wore her hair up and after a second's fumbling with the unfamiliar clasp, I had it fastened. Aunt Anastasia added emerald earrings from the case.

She walked to the mirror and adjusted the necklace. "This was my mother's. It's more suitable for an older woman." She fingered the necklace, inspecting her reflection and turned.

"Come along, Karlota. Get your clutch bag. The taxi will be here in a minute."

Not long after, the bell rang, announcing the taxi's arrival. Getting Aunt Anastasia downstairs was more difficult. I hadn't practiced stairs in my high heels, but we made it safely.

It turned out the Russian Club was on the other side of the Gabba cricket ground from the German Club. I helped Aunt Anastasia from the cab and held her elbow up the steps into the club.

A tall, white-haired man bent and kissed Aunt Anastasia's hand, greeting her in Russian.

"Anastasia, your presence honours us."

"Thank you, Dmitri. This is my guest, Karlota."

He turned to me, speaking English. "Welcome, Karlota. I am the club president, Mr Mikhailov. Have a pleasant evening."

I smiled, answering in Russian. "Thank you. I am sure your club will make me feel welcome."

Mr Mikhailov smiled broadly and turned to Aunt Anastasia. "She speaks excellent Russian, Tasia. You have been teaching her, I suspect?"

"Indeed – and she is an excellent student." She smiled with almost parental pride.

Mr Mikhailov glanced over my shoulder. "Please excuse me, other guests are arriving. I have reserved your usual table, Tasia."

"Thank you, Dmitri. Come with me, Karlota."

We walked through into a long room decked in white, blue and red tricolour ribbons. I recognised these from my east German history lessons as the colours of the Tsarist flag. At the far end was a small stage, set with music stands for an orchestra. A black and gold double-headed imperial eagle hung above the orchestra stage. Beneath the eagle hung portraits of, presumably, Nickolas and Alexandra. Aunt Anastasia led me across to a table half-way along the side wall, set into the central bay window. As we sat, a waiter appeared with two champagne flutes and an ice-bucket containing a bottle of champagne. At a nod from Aunt Anastasia, he carefully filled the two long-stemmed glasses.

Aunt Anastasia picked up one glass and gestured at the other. "For tonight, Karlota, you are eighteen. Be careful. Drink water when you are thirsty from dancing." She gave me a mischievous smile. "Take small sips of champagne."

I followed her advice, taking a small sip. The champagne fizzed on my tongue like sherbet, but with a subtle, dry and delicious taste: I had been expecting it to be sweet.

"The best Russian champagne comes from the Crimea." Aunt Anastasia took another appreciative sip. "Of course, we cannot get that. This is French champagne, but I understand that Australian champagnes showing promise." She looked across at me. "Hold the champagne flute by the stem, Karlota, otherwise you will warm the wine."

I changed my hold on the glass and took another sip. The musicians clattered. settling themselves into their chairs. Shortly, quiet orchestral music played beneath the growing buzz of conversation as more people arrived.

Aunt Anastasia leant towards me. "They won't be playing dance music for the first half-an-hour. That will allow people to arrive and circulate." She pursed her lips. "There will be quite a few people coming to speak with me during the evening. You don't need to say anything unless they speak to you." Her face lightened. "And I suspect that there will be young men coming to meet you." She gave me a serious look. "Please allow me to organise dances for you at first. There is a certain ... hierarchy ... that needs to be observed. Later in the evening, you can make your own choices."

"Yes, Aunt Anastasia."

A stream of mostly older people came past our table and exchanged a few words with Aunt Anastasia, some in Russian but mostly in English. Some asked about me and, if introduced, I responded appropriately. This was a formal affair – at least as far as Aunt Anastasia was concerned. From the deference she received, it was clear she was a person of considerable importance in the Russian community. We'd watched *My Fair Lady* on the ship and I sat there, feeling like Eliza Doolittle at the Ball – out of place and uncertain of my position.

Guests filled the tables around the large room and the orchestra struck up a waltz, bringing a few couples to the floor. A photographer was circulating, his flash bulbs providing occasional accents to the music. I noticed Aunt Anastasia look across the room and give an almost imperceptible nod to someone on the far side of the room.

Shortly after, a slim young man with dark hair presented himself at our table gave a nod of acknowledgement to Aunt Anastasia before turning to me. "Miss Karlota, I am Maxim Korolev. May I have the pleasure of this dance with you?"

I glanced at Aunt Anastasia, who inclined her head in approval.

His Russian was formal and I replied in style. "Thank you. That would be pleasant."

I placed my clutch bag on the table and Maxim held out a hand to help me up and guided me on to the dance floor. We waltzed adequately around the room. At the end, he escorted me to our table and thanked me, nodding again to Aunt Anastasia.

That started a procession of young men wanting to dance with me. They were all apparently selected by subtle glances and imperceptible nods from Aunt Anastasia. After half a dozen dances, I found Aunt Anastasia had obtained a jug of iced water with floating slices of fresh lime. The dancing had warmed me and I poured a glass, draining it.

Aunt Anastasia frowned. "Karlota, sip the water. We are much on show here."

I blushed in embarrassment. "My apologies, Aunt Anastasia. I wasn't thinking of anything but my thirst." I poured another glass and took a sip, noticing my lipstick on the glass.

What about the rest of my make-up?

Clutch bag in hand, I stood. "I'm going to the ladies' room, Aunt Anastasia."

An older couple were showing off their skill in a foxtrot as I walked round the dance floor. Using the mirror in the ladies' room, I checked and freshened my lipstick and make-up and dabbed on some fragrance from the small bottle. The jewellery sent shards of light at me from the mirror. I spent a minute smiling at the sparkle of the diamonds as I turned my head, surprised at how much I was enjoying myself.

On the way back to our table, I could see Aunt Anastasia talking to a man who had his back to me. He turned to survey the dance floor and my heart leapt into my mouth: Mr Franks.

In surprise, I stopped and moved behind a group of people standing at a nearby table. I took a deep breath, seeking my calm centre.

What is Mr Franks doing here? What is his relationship with Aunt Anastasia? Had she told him about me? What did this mean for Mutti and me?

From my hiding place, I watched them talk. I couldn't hear them, but I saw Aunt Anastasia's cheeks flare into fiery points.

Mr Franks is annoying her. What is going on?

After about a minute, Aunt Anastasia waved her hand dismissively. Mr Franks stance straightened and he looked down at her, saying something. Aunt Anastasia remained closed lipped and he turned and walked away, luckily away from me.

My good mood had curdled and I received some odd looks from the people at the nearby table; I mustered what I hoped was an enigmatic smile to cover my anxiety and walked on to our table. The flares on Aunt Anastasia's cheeks and her pursed lips told me she was still upset.

"Are you all right, Aunt Anastasia?"

Her eyes narrowed, staring at some distasteful horizon. "That man is uncouth, uncultured and untrustworthy." The Russian rolled off her tongue softly but with the severity of a judge sentencing a murderer.

Could I get some more out of her?

"What man ... what did he do?"

Aunt Anastasia continued mumbling — she hadn't heard me. "He thinks he owns me." She looked up and saw I was listening. She breathed deeply, looking across at me. "No-one you would know, my dear. No-one you need to worry about." The fiery points on her cheeks faded as she smothered her anger.

Why does Mr Franks think he owns Aunt Anastasia?

I returned her gaze, my brain churning with questions – but most of them would have revealed something about me. I found one that seemed innocent enough. "Who is he?"

Aunt Anastasia's face changed to impassive. "No-one you need to worry about." She said, looking down at her watch. "They will serve *hors d'oeuvres* soon." She tapped the champagne bottle in the ice-bucket. "We need another bottle. See if you can find a waiter – and make sure you tell him it is for Madame Zaytseva."

With that mission accomplished, I returned to the table to find another young man waiting to dance with me. The orchestra retired from the stage soon after our dance and waiters served plates of *hors d'oeuvres*. Aunt Anastasia seemed to have recovered her good mood and insisted I try the caviar – tiny black balls on slivers of dried toast; the caviar exploded deliciously into the taste of the sea on my tongue – and it went well with champagne. After half-an-hour, the orchestra reappeared. I danced several more times, whilst a steady trickle of people visited with Aunt Anastasia. I was keeping a wary eye out for Mr Franks, but I didn't see him again.

At half-past twelve by the ornate wall clock, Mr Mikhailov walked to the stage and the room quietened. The orchestra started playing, and everyone rose to their feet. I followed, wondering what was going on.

Is this the old Russian – the Tsarist – national anthem? It sounds vaguely familiar.

When the orchestra finished playing, there was silence. Mr Mikhailov turned, raising his glass towards the two large portraits hanging on the wall.

"To the memory of our beloved Tsar Nicholas and his beautiful wife, the Tsarina Alexandra."

Murmurs of "The Tsar and Tsarina" ran round the room in English and Russian as people raised their own glasses towards the two portraits. People started moving – clearly the ball was over. I stood looking around, finishing my champagne.

"Come along, Karlota. Our taxi will be waiting for us."

I picked up my clutch bag and took Aunt Anastasia's arm. As we walked towards the door, many people wished us goodnight. I heard a voice remark in Russian, "What was that dinosaur thinking, bringing her pet German to the ball?"

I tried to look round, but Aunt Anastasia's hand became vice-like on my arm, moving me away. Mr Mikhailov caught up with us as we were about to walk down the steps to the waiting taxi.

He bowed over Aunt Anastasia's hand. "Once again, Tasia, thank you for gracing us with your presence tonight."

He awarded me a carefully graduated nod and turned to farewell other guests as I helped Aunt Anastasia down the steps and into the taxi. She leant back into the seat, fatigue thinning her face. I walked round to the other door, gathering the hem of my gown clear of the car door as I sat. Once we were underway, Aunt Anastasia looked sideways at me.

"I know you heard that remark as we left," embarrassment flushed her drawn cheeks. "Please understand that I do not regard you as my pet German." She turned to look through the window beside her and remained silent until we had completed the difficult climb up to her flat. At the table she sat with a sigh and indicated the box for the necklace.

"Please put the jewellery in its box."

I opened the necklace catch after a fumble, carefully laying it in its box, and removed the earrings. Wearing these gorgeous jewels was an experience to savour, but tonight was no Cinderella story. No Prince Charming would arrive in the morning with a glass slipper. Truth be told, I didn't want a Prince. Instead, I picked up Willi's simple gold chain and fastened it round my neck where it belonged.

"Don't forget to put your studs in."

I gave Aunt Anastasia a grateful look. "Thank you."

Aunt Anastasia took the jewellery case and struggled to her feet. "Sleep well, Karlota. We'll talk more of tonight in the morning."

"Goodnight, Aunt Anastasia. Thank you for this evening."

Aunt Anastasia gave me a tired smile and walked into her bedroom.

I undressed and hung my gown inside its dust bag. As I climbed into bed, I thought about cancelling my alarm ... but decided not to. I hadn't been getting enough exercise this week and there'd been no work with the weights at all.

• • • •

WHEN THE ALARM WOKE me, my disorientation from earlier in the week had passed – the half-heard sound of clattering pallets was almost familiar. I'd had barely five hours' sleep, but I was awake and dressed for my run while my brain chewed on Mr Franks' appearance at the Ball. Circuits complete, I headed for a shower and breakfast. I sat at the window, a cup of tea at my elbow and Tolkien open on my lap. But my mind was trying to make sense of Mr Franks' appearance. Aunt Anastasia had said he wasn't to be trusted – which was no surprise to me.

What dealings is she having with an ASIO agent? She certainly isn't a communist. Is she watching out for communists amongst the Russian population in Brisbane?

That was possible, but from what I'd seen this week she was almost a recluse. Hardly a good way to watch what for communist agents.

Is that what the argument was about?

With these thoughts circling, I must have dozed off.

"Good morning, Karlota."

I jerked awake, spilling my book on to the floor. "Good morning, Aunt Anastasia." She was wearing her Chinese robe.

I rescued Tolkien and looked up at Aunt Anastasia. "Would you like some breakfast?" I looked at my tea glass. "I'll make some more tea."

"Thank you – some toast, I think." She smiled gratefully. "But yes, tea definitely."

After a few minutes, I brought through a plate of toast and another with cold meat and cheese to join the jams I had put out while the toast was cooking. Aunt Anastasia came over and sat at the table and I went back for the tea. I was hungry and helped myself to some ham, Italian sausage, cheese and toast.

"You've been for your run, I presume?" Aunt Anastasia was smiling at my plate.

I finished my mouthful. "Yes – at the usual time. I hope I didn't wake you?"

"Not at all. I slept right through until about half-an-hour ago." She took a sip of tea and placed her *podstakannik* on the table with great care. "I'm sorry about that remark you heard last night."

I wasn't sure what to say.

Aunt Anastasia picked up her tea glass, paused, her lips thin, her face showing a slight frown. With a sigh, she replaced it on its mat, her fingers fiddling with the gilded bronze handle for a moment.

"After two wars – particularly the last one – Germans are not well regarded by Russians. We may not like the Soviet regime, but none of us wanted the Nazis to win. Almost everyone here lost relatives in that conflict." Her eyes dropped to her tea glass.

I understand that issue – I had encountered it in England and here in Australia.

Aunt Anastasia took in a deep breath, letting it out slowly. "And now half of Germany is supporting the Soviets." Her eyes lifted to mine, soft with moisture, holding my gaze.

"I'm sorry, Karlota. I have been using you."

My face must have shown my complete confusion.

Aunt Anastasia leant across the table and took my hand. "Clear up the breakfast things and come sit with me." Her face showed embarrassment at ... something. "Bring fresh tea with you."

I cleaned up and returned with fresh tea to sit with Aunt Anastasia in the window. I looked across at this regal woman who was a mentor to me, hoping that whatever she was going to say would not mark the end of our relationship.

Aunt Anastasia's eyes lowered from the window to her hands, which fidgeted for a moment. She drew in a breath. "Karlota ...please, let me ... explain." Her voice faltered before resuming. "That man at the Ball last night was Mr Franks. He ... works for the Australian government."

I sat motionless before Aunt Anastasia, worried that any movement might betray a hint of who and what I was.

"His work is keeping Australia safe from the communists – principally the Soviets, but also the Maoists in China. My position in the Russian community here and experience in China gives me ... insights ... which he finds useful."

Her long, delicate fingers were in constant, uneasy motion, writhing against one another in her lap, twisting a delicately embroidered handkerchief. She glanced down and they stilled. "I need to explain some history to you."

Her shoulders relaxed, difficult emotions no longer to the fore. "After the last war, Australia opened its doors to thousands of refugees – displaced persons they were called – from across Europe. Many of them are from the western Soviet Republics such as Ukraine, which were devastated by the Nazis' advance and again as they retreated in defeat." Her lips pursed, tasting the sour memories of those days. "But the Nazis captured countless thousands of Soviet soldiers who came from all over Russia. Tens of thousands of them died in slave labour camps, but at the war's end, many remained in areas of Germany controlled by the western allies. When they imagined their future in Stalin's Russia, many did not wish to return to their homes."

She gave a thin smile. "Unlike the Americans, Australia welcomed thousands of them. And Mr Franks worries that amongst them are spies working to spread the Soviet empire and damage this country." Her eyes rose to mine. "I have been watching these more recent Russian migrants as much as I can through my position in the Russian community. Passing information to Mr Franks where I thought there might be concerns. But now I am old and no longer as deeply involved in the community. Mr Franks has been asking me to find ... someone ... to take my place."

All my will was focussed on keeping my face blank, staying motionless. *She wants me to spy on the Russian community.*

She leant towards me, her hands resting on her knees, eyes bright and passion showing in her voice. "You have impressed me from our first meeting, Karlota. You keep your thoughtful intelligence shrouded, but I see it. And your language skills are phenomenal. I have never had a student soak up Russian like you have, particularly one learning several other languages simultaneously." Her face held a speculative aspect. "And I feel that you have ... secrets ... that you are careful to keep hidden." She paused, awarding me a respectful look. "You have discretion unusual in a young girl."

I returned her gaze, unable to keep my face from flushing in reaction to her praise and because the lies in my life shamed me.

Her eyes flickered away from me before they returned, narrowing in thought.

"Karlota, I have been grooming you to help me with this work. To become my eyes and ears, particularly amongst the young people." She shook her head. "But last night, that cutting remark you overheard showed how foolish this idea was. As a German, it would be hard for you to be accepted into the Russian community, though you speak better Russian than most of the younger generation."

She sighed. "But Mr Franks is threatening to reveal my long-term ... activity to the Russian community. If I cannot come up with a replacement, I know he will destroy my reputation through rumour and innuendo. I will not be able to show myself at the club ... or anywhere else." Defeat pulled at her face. "I have been looking for more than a year, with no real prospect in view. Then you ... fell into my lap." She sighed, her fingers once again twining the handkerchief. "But lying in bed last night, I realised how wrong I was to be using you – or anyone else in this way."

My mind was racing.

She does want me to help her spy on the Russian community.

The irony of this situation was not lost on me. I had been using her to 'teach' me Russian and introduce me into the Russian community to do exactly that.

"I'm not sure what to say, Aunt Anastasia..."

"Karlota, you don't have to say anything ..." A single tear negotiated the deepening lines on her face. "But ... I hope you will still come to see me ... sometimes."

The silence deepened between us as I thought about how to turn this situation to both our advantages. But foremost, I had deep sympathy for this gentle and generous lady who had befriended me. I slid off my seat and knelt beside her.

"Is it impossible for a Russian speaking German girl to be with you in your community?" I looked up at her, recognising a faint glimmer of hope in her eyes. "If I can, I would like to help ... this is my country now, as well. I want it to be safe."

"Oh, Karlota, you heard what she said last night." Aunt Anastasia reached forwards, pulling my hands into her lap. "You are not responsible for what the Nazis did to my country and should not have to suffer the senseless bile of some of my compatriots."

"But it was only one person..."

"Yes." Aunt Anastasia sighed. "But if one person said it, others would have thought it."

"Perhaps ..."

This was my last day staying with Aunt Anastasia and this unresolved issue hung between us for the rest of the day. Mr Caune arrived as expected during the afternoon, letting us know he and his wife had returned safely, but he soon disappeared downstairs.

Earlier, when I packed my bag, I had stood there for a while looking at all the finery from the ball that Aunt Anastasia had purchased.

What am I supposed to do with it all?

After several minute's indecision, I put it all in the wardrobe and dresser – including the studs from my ears. All that finery was not mine – and, anyway, I told myself, I didn't have room for it in my bag.

At about three o'clock I decided it would be easier if I left for the tram before the rush hour. I made tea and carried it to Aunt Anastasia.

"I've made tea for us."

Aunt Anastasia roused herself from staring at the book that had sat unread on her lap for the past hour. "Thank you, Karlota."

We drank our tea in a strained silence. It seemed Aunt Anastasia felt there was nothing more to be said and I couldn't say anything more until I'd spoken with Mutti. I cleared away the tea things, delighting again in the crystal tea glasses and elegant bronze *podstakanniki* as I dried them. I retrieved my bag from what had almost seemed like 'my' room, but which felt oddly alien after today's events and walked over to stand beside Aunt Anastasia's chair.

"Thank you for letting me stay with you, Aunt Anastasia."

She grasped her cane and went through the awkward process of unfolding herself from her chair, to stand looking down at me.

"My dear girl, it is me who should thank you." She glanced, frowning, at my bag. "But where are the rest of your things?"

I hefted my small case. "This is all I brought with me."

"Where is the ball gown, the shoes...?"

"Well, they're not mine. I left them in the bedroom."

"Nonsense. Come along." She led me into the bedroom.

Half an hour later, I was again standing to say goodbye, but with a case rescued from Aunt Anastasia's box room alongside mine. In the extra case was the carefully folded ball gown and everything else that Aunt Anastasia had purchased, along with the red silk Chinese robe. My ears sported the studs.

Aunt Anastasia cast an eye over the cases. "You can't go on a tram with all that. I'll call you a cab."

"Oh, I'm sure I can manage on the tram." I couldn't pay for a cab.

"I won't hear of it." Aunt Anastasia had seen through my objection and smiled. "It will be on my account, Karlota."

Twenty minutes later, the doorbell rang, announcing the taxi.

The goodbye felt awkward with the Mr Franks issue still between us. "Thank you, Aunt Anastasia."

Aunt Anastasia's arms reached out and pulled me into a fierce hug, before asking, uncertainly. "You'll be here on Saturday?"

"Yes, of course." I could see a glisten of moisture in her eyes.

She sniffed. "Fetch the cabbie to help you with your bags."

I let the cabbie in and he carried my bags downstairs.

Aunt Anastasia walked to her small writing desk and retrieved an envelope. Handing it to me. "Thank you, Karlota."

I looked down at the envelope.

Aunt Anastasia raised an eyebrow. "A small thank you. Now, off you go, the cabbie is waiting."

I stuffed the envelope in my handbag. "Thank you, Aunt Anastasia. I'll see you on Saturday," and pulled her into a hug.

Half an hour later I was in my bedroom, fending off an inquisitive ginger kitten as I unpacked my bags, carefully hanging the robe and ball gown in my wardrobe. I sat on my bed and opened the envelope Aunt Anastasia had given me. Inside were two crisp twenty-pound notes.

Not long after, Mutti arrived home. After we had exchanged a hug, she looked me up and down. "You've had your ears pierced."

"Yes – and Aunt Anastasia lent me a beautiful diamond necklace and earrings to wear to the ball."

Mutti frowned. "What ball?"

"The Easter ball at the Russian club." I jumped up and retrieve the ball gown from its dust bag, holding it in front of me for Mutti.

"It sounds like you've had an adventure."

Chapter 12
Late April 1965

A s we prepared and ate tea, I told Mutti about the ball – but leaving out the appearance of Mr Franks for the moment – I did not want to spoil the meal. As I related the trip to Finney-Isles and described the gown, Mutti frowned and fidgeted with the salt cellar, spilling some grains on the table.

After tea, Mutti's concern came into focus. "Kal, you should have left everything there. She's spent a great deal of money on you ..." Mutti's face mirrored the anxious edge in her voice.

Is Mutti worried that Aunt Anastasia is trying to buy my affection?

The reality of what she wanted was a bigger problem. "Well, I tried to leave everything there, but she wouldn't let me."

Mutti pulled a face.

Is she forgetting why we need her?

"I didn't push any harder as I didn't want to break the relationship when we need her ..."

Mutti was frowning. "Yes, but ... what does she want?" Distrust hovered around the 'she'.

I paused for a moment, thinking over the week I'd spent with her. "I don't think Aunt Anastasia ever had children. I'm not sure if she was ever married."

Mutti gave me a confused look.

"Everyone refers to her as 'Miss Zaytseva'." I went on, explaining about the diamond necklace and earrings. "I think she was sort of ... seeing me as the daughter she never had."

Mutti's concern pushed her eyebrows a few millimetres higher.

I took a deep breath. "But none of that is important..."

Mutti tensed and her eyes flared.

I swallowed, not sure how Mutti would react. "That man ..." I looked closely at Mutti to make sure she understood I was talking about Mr Franks. "... was at the ball."

"What?" Her voice snapped at me, pushing me into my chair.

She glanced away, controlling her surprise, giving herself time to think about what this might mean. "Sorry, *Liebling.*" She returned to me with an embarrassed smile. "Checking up on the Russians?" She righted the salt cellar that she'd knocked over.

"Sort of ... he talked to Aunt Anastasia and she was quite upset afterwards. I'd gone to the toilet and I don't think he saw me."

Mutti's puzzled frown deepened. "What did he want with Miss Zaytseva?"

"This morning, she told me she'd been working for him, monitoring the Russians who arrived after the war."

"And she told you this?" Mutti was incredulous. "She was taking a risk, revealing herself."

"Yes ..."

How is Mutti going to take this next revelation?

"Kal? What else?"

"She's getting too infirm to be active in the Russian community. She's been trying to find someone she can train to take her place – but without luck."

"And?"

"She wants me to help her ..."

Mutti's face relaxed. "She is trying to buy your cooperation. I thought there was some ulterior motive."

"I don't think that's true – but if it is, there's more." What Mr Franks was doing to her made me angry and thinking about him twisted my guts with fear at the same time. "That man is threatening her, like he did us. If she doesn't find someone to help, he'll destroy her reputation in the Russian community."

Mutti mumbled. "He is a disgusting man." She looked up at me. "And what did you tell her?"

"That I wanted to help her if I could. Nothing more."

"Good." She rewarded me with an approving look. "What do you think we should do now?"

I hadn't thought about our next move – but I was surprised and pleased to be asked.

Mutti gave me an encouraging smile. "You know Miss Zaytseva best. Can we trust her?"

"Umm ... the trust thing runs both ways, doesn't it?"

"Yes, it does." Mutti steepled her hands. "And?"

"I think we should help her. I like her and hate what that man is doing to her ... and us."

What do we do next? We need to be careful with Mr Franks.

"We need to work out how best to tell her ... and that man."

"Indeed." Mutti thought for a moment. "Are you sure he didn't see you at the ball?"

"I don't know for certain." The image of him berating Aunt Anastasia was clear in my mind. "I don't think so."

"It probably doesn't matter if he did." Mutti thought for a moment. "But we need to let him know you are working your way into the Russian community. He mustn't be surprised to see you with Aunt Anastasia."

Mutti's eyes lost their focus for a minute and I sat watching, her fingers playing with the spilled salt crystals as she contemplated our move.

After a minute, she breathed in deeply. "I need to set up a meeting with him. There's too much to cover for a coded message." Her eyes returned to me. "You are seeing Aunt Anastasia on Saturday?"

"Yes."

"I need to meet with him before that." She glanced up at the kitchen clock. "Give me ten minutes. Could you clear up the dishes whilst I write something?"

"Okay."

Ten minutes later we walked out into the last rays of the sun, across the park and oval where I ran to the footpath alongside Kedron Brook. We walked to a battered old gum tree stump above the brook's steep-sided gully. Mutti suggested we stop and sit for a moment. As we chatted about the golden light, Mutti checked the area and produced a small metal cylinder from a pocket, slipping it into a deep fissure in the gnarled stump. Shortly after, we returned on a different route, past a phone box. Mutti went in and rang a number, but hung up after a few rings and rang again to hang up once more after several more rings. We walked on in the dusk,

Mutti quietly explaining that the number of rings in the two calls was code for a message to collect from a particular drop location.

As we approached our house, loud meows announced *Imbi*, sitting on the fence a few houses away from ours, complaining about our absence. He jumped down, twined himself around our legs in joyous greeting and scampered towards the house. He did that cat thing of following in front of you, looking to make sure he was following in the right direction.

• • • •

IN THE MORNING, I WENT for my run and saw Mutti off to work after we had breakfast. Once I'd cleaned up, I rang Lizzie to see if we could meet up for a swim, but there was no reply. They must still be on the Gold Coast, although I thought they were returning yesterday. I decided to go later by myself as the rhythms of swimming beckoned me after more than a week away. I spent an hour writing to Willi, telling him about Aunt Anastasia and the ball. I mentioned a strange man that annoyed her as a reminder to tell Willi the hidden part of the story when he read it.

I'd sat down to read some more Tolkien with a kitten on my lap when the phone rang. It was Lizzie and we arranged to meet at the pool at half-past one.

My tram into the city was running late and Lizzie was waiting for me in the stands when I emerged from the changing room.

She bounced up and gave me a hug. "You're late." Softening the accusation with her blazing smile.

"And you're tanned." I replied.

She glanced down at her arms, now sporting a darker shade of bronze than before Easter. "I was on the beach for most of the time – and I've been learning to surf."

My brow crinkled. "What's that?"

"It's where you ride the breaking waves to the beach on a surfboard." Her eyes glazed in concentration and her body moved in memory. "It's quite difficult, but it's amazing to be rushing towards the beach, pushed along by the waves." She breathed the exhilarating memory. "The good surfers stand on their boards, but I can't do that yet – at least not for long."

"I'm not sure I'd like that." I'd never swum in the sea, but I'd watched storm-driven breakers crashing on to the beach at Herne Bay. "Isn't it dangerous in the surf?"

Lizzie gave me a sideways glance. "I suppose it might be in gigantic waves. But you're a strong swimmer – I'm sure it wouldn't be a problem. You could come with us the next time we go there."

"Perhaps ..." I could hear my lack of enthusiasm. I brightened my voice. "Anyhow, let's swim."

It was good to be in the pool, stretching out. I could feel my unused swimming muscles protesting and I didn't push myself hard. Lizzie stormed away from me more than usual. Unlike me, she'd been swimming for most of the two weeks on the Gold Coast. After four lengths, I found Lizzie sitting on the edge of the pool waiting for me.

"Haven't you been swimming while I've been away?"

I hung on to the side of the pool, breathing deeply. "Once – the first week. I was staying with my Russian teacher for the second week and all I could do was run."

Lizzie's eyebrows lifted in surprise. "You're learning another language?"

My big mouth again, but I didn't see any problem in Lizzie knowing this. "Well, yes ... sort of by accident."

Lizzie laughed in disbelief. "How do you learn a language by accident?"

"After swimming on Saturdays, I go into the city and have lunch with this old Russian lady." I smiled at Lizzie's laughter. "She can't get about much – she walks with a stick. I was supposed to be someone different for her to talk with, but when she heard I was learning other languages, she insisted on teaching me Russian."

Lizzie shook her head, still laughing. "How many languages do you speak now?" She counted them off on her fingers. "English, French, German, Polish and now Russian. Five." Her laughter made her splutter for a moment. "Five languages – that's ridiculous. Why would anyone need to speak five languages?"

I pulled myself out, and as we walked over our towels, smiled at her. "You forgot Latin – but no-one speaks Latin anymore."

Lizzie laughed some more. "You stayed with this Russian lady for a week? What did you do?"

"We practiced Russian and ... she took me to the Easter ball at the Russian Club."

Lizzie stopped short. "You went to a ball?"

"Yes."

Lizzie flopped down into her chair, pulling her towel around her shoulders. "That's not you, Karlota. It should have been me." She leant towards me, scrutinising my ears. "Your ears are pierced."

I smiled at her. "So are yours."

"Yes, but when I went away, yours weren't. Was this part of the Ball thing?"

"Yes," I giggled.

Lizzie grasped my hand as if to drag the details out of me. "You're going to have to tell me all about it. What did you wear? Did you dance with some dark and handsome exiled Russian prince? Come on, all the details." When Lizzie was excited, words poured from her.

I rubbed my towel through my hair and gave Lizzie a coquettish glance. "Would you believe I wore a fabulously expensive diamond necklace and earring set?"

"What? Of course not."

"Well, you'd be wrong." I pulled a superior face at Lizzie. "The Russian lady is Miss Zaytseva; but she told me to call her Aunt Anastasia though she's no relation. Anyway, she leant me the diamond set her father gave her for her first ball."

"Real diamonds?" Lizzie's eyes were wide with awe.

I shrugged. "I think so. She has beautiful furniture and elegant things in her apartment. Her family were merchants in Vladivostok before they fled to China with their wealth in 1917 to escape from the Soviets. At the ball she wore a necklace and earrings dripping with rubies and emeralds."

"Ooh. She sounds mysterious and glamorous."

I stopped for a moment, recalling Aunt Anastasia's story, such as I knew it. "I think she's lonely. She has no family here in Australia. She's seen as some sort of matriarch in the Russian community – everyone at the ball treated her with great respect."

That's not quite true, but Lizzie doesn't need to know ...

We sat and chatted about the ball – or rather, Lizzie interrogated me with the intensity of British intelligence. She wanted all the details: the dresses, the jewellery, my dance partners ...

After about a quarter of an hour, I'd had enough. "Why don't you come over to my house tomorrow? You can see everything ... not the diamonds, of course." I stood up. "Come on, let's swim again."

Lizzie followed me, her brow wrinkled by a frustrated frown. "Okay – I'll speak to my mother and ring you this evening."

In the pool, we swam our individual training patterns before Lizzie announced she had to go to meet her mother in the city. I swam for another half an hour before I caught a tram home. As always, *Imbi* greeted me with exuberant enthusiasm. I relaxed for a while playing with him before going down under the house to catch up with work on the weights, under the watchful and critical eye of a ginger kitten. Later, Lili rang to say she'd be over about ten o'clock and we could go swimming again after that.

When Mutti walked in, I leapt up and turned on the radio. "Well? Any news?"

She shook her head. "I don't expect to hear anything until tomorrow."

"Lizzie's coming over in the morning and then we're going swimming."

"Okay."

• • • •

CONSCIOUS OF A WEEK'S lack of swimming, I pushed myself on my morning run.

Euan and dodger arrived and watched my last circuit. "Ye's not bin runnin' for a week, lassie."

I leant on my knees to catch my breath. Euan watched me in silence. After a minute, I stood up. "I ran in the Botanic Garden rather than here. I was staying with my Russian teacher in the city."

Euan stretched fully upright. "Why's ye lairnin' Russian?"

"Because I can, I suppose." I shrugged. "I like languages and I'm good at them."

Euan sniffed. I don't think he approved of Russia – and, by association, of my learning the language.

He pursed his lips. "Anyhow, if'n ye' were in the city, did ye see the ANZAC march on Sunday?"

It was my turn to blink. "What's ANZAC?"

"Ha, ye need to lairn this if'n ye's t'be an Aussie. ANZAC is Australian and New Zealand Army Corps – from the first war. ANZAC day is when we remember the sacrifice of the fallen in the wars." His voice softened. "They let me march as I sairved, same as them."

I could see Euan didn't feel awkward in teaching a half-German girl about this.

"I didn't know about ANZAC day – or a march." A memory surfaced. "Early on Sunday morning, when I was out running in the Botanic Garden, I heard a trumpet call. Was that part of this?"

"Aye, lassie. T'was the last post, I reckon. They play that for the fallen ..." His voice and eyes fell away. After a moment's silence, he looked up. "An' t'other matter?"

My brain cycled a few times before I realised he meant Vogel.

"I don't know. Perhaps you're right ... it's best to do nothing."

Euan's eyes were piercing. "'Tis yer mother not you t' decide, ain't it?"

I pursed my lips. I didn't want my mouth running away from me again.

Euan watched my silence. "Well, I'll bid ye g'day." He turned, walking slowly to allow for Dodger's slow gait. I stood watching them for a minute before turning for home.

I showered and ate breakfast with Mutti before seeing her off to the tram. Lizzie would be round later – and a wicked thought occurred to me. In the meantime, I sat down to add to Willi's letter. When Lizzie arrived, I greeted her at the door, dressed and made up as I had been for the ball.

Lizzie stopped dead. "Wow, Kal." She scanned me from head to foot. "You look amazing. Is this what you wore to the ball?"

"Yes ... except I'm not wearing Aunt Anastasia's diamonds."

Once Lizzie'd inspected everything, we went to my room and I changed into normal clothes. As I hung the gown up, Lizzie saw the red Chinese robe and reached past me, pulling it out on its hangar.

"Where did you get this?" I could hear the awe in her voice as she fingered the material, looking up at me. "It's silk."

"Aunt Anastasia gave it to me. She has a beautiful wattle-yellow one."

Lizzie slipped on the robe, twirling in front of the mirror. "Your Russian teacher is a generous lady."

I waved at the finery in my wardrobe. "I tried to leave all this behind – she must have spent a lot at Fenny-Isles. But she insisted I take everything." I looked at the gown in its dust bag hanging in the wardrobe. "I don't know when I'll ever wear that again."

Lizzie gave me a warm smile. "I do – at the school ball in December."

"There's a school ball?"

"Oh yes – and it's formal. Your gown is perfect for that."

I slipped out to the toilet.

When I walked in, Lizzie was leaning over my desk, reading what I was writing to Col.

"Lizzie, that's private." I pushed past her and closed the journal.

Lizzie blushed. "Sorry Kal. But you shouldn't leave it open where people can read it."

She's right – I should have put it away – but I was all caught up in showing off my ball gown.

"My turn to be sorry, Lizzie. You're right, I should have put it away."

Lizzie glanced at the book in my hands. "Is Willi the boy ... that ... umm ... you did stuff with?" By the end of the sentence, she was blushing through her tan.

"Yes, he was." I blushed as well.

Fortunately, *Imbi* chose that moment to arrive on my bed, demanding cuddles. Once I'd picked him up and he was purring, I passed him across to Lizzie.

"Come and see what I have under the house."

We traipsed down and I showed Lizzie the weights I was working with to improve the strength in my arms and shoulders.

"Where did you learn about this – and where did you get the gear?"

I told her about Euan.

Lizzie shook her head in disbelief. "How have you found such interesting friends – a wealthy Russian and a Scottish soldier?"

I shrugged. "I don't know that I found them – they ... happened."

Lizzie looked at the weights. "Do they make a difference?"

"I don't know."

She looked at my arms and shoulders. "I can't see any difference."

I shrugged. "Come on. Let's get something to eat and head off to the pool. Swimming certainly makes a difference."

We had a good swim. At home, I did my weights exercises, wondering if they were worth it – despite Euan's insistence.

Mutti was later than usual that evening.

Picking up from a dead drop?

The radio went on and she motioned me to sit down with her at the table.

"I'm meeting with ... that man tomorrow evening after work, at a different café, but one I've checked out and will feel safe in."

"Goodness, that was quick."

"My message made it clear the matter was urgent." Her head cocked to one side in thought. "I don't think we should let on we know that Aunt Anastasia has been working for him." Her voice firmed up. "Never divulge information if you don't have to."

Something was niggling my brain, but I couldn't pin it down. "What if she's already told him about me?"

"I don't think that's likely." She gave me a quizzical look. "You told her you'd think about it and would speak to her again on Saturday?"

"Yes ... but what do we say to that man?"

Mutti's smile was a touch predatory. "I'll tell him you are working your way into the Russian community by pretending to learn Russian – he knows you already speak it. We tell him that your teacher is someone well respected in the Russian community and can ease your entry." That predatory edge to her smile grew. "And I'll tell him it will cost him another twenty-five pounds a month, as there are social events that you must attend, requiring better clothes and such."

"Do you think he'll pay?"

"He'll pay." Mutti's voice brooked no nonsense. "Possibly not that much, but he'll pay. He's losing his contact with the Russian community and you're the replacement he needs." Her eyes narrowed in thought. "His threats to Miss Zaytseva show he's getting desperate." Mutti's eyes swivelled to lock with mine. "I don't think Mr Franks is good at his job – and he's probably lazy. He doesn't seem to plan ahead and his ability to cultivate contacts on his own seems limited."

That niggle again, evanescent as smoke in a wind.

"Are you going to tell him about Vogel?"

"No – I'm not." Mutti's tone was adamant. "I don't trust him. He might do nothing, but he might start something that would reveal our identities." Her voice darkened. "But there are other people who might be interested in *Hauptsturmführer Vogel* ..."

Her voice faltered and I went round the table and hugged her. I couldn't think of any words.

After a minute, Mutti held my forearms. "Thank you, *Liebling*." A ghost of a smile flitted across her face. "I'm working on it ..."

I hoped she could find a way through this hatred.

The niggle became large enough to grasp when I was standing looking in the mirror, cleaning my teeth.

Why is Mutti skilled at all this spying stuff?

My toothbrush came to a stop.

Why had she learned all this in Ravensbrück?

• • • •

THE NEXT DAY, I WOKE in tension – and it kept rising through the day. I knew Mutti was meeting with Mr Franks that evening and I couldn't concentrate. I pushed myself hard in my morning run and afternoon weights workout. In part because my mind was elsewhere conjuring possibilities, I lost count of circuits while running and repetitions while lifting. But pushing helped counter the tension and fearful anticipation. My subconscious was not as confident as Mutti of the meeting's outcome.

More than an hour after her usual time and Mutti wasn't home. I caught myself grinding my teeth and chewing the inside of my cheek ... and stopped myself to realise a minute later that I was doing it again. I was cuddling *Imbi* about half-an-hour later when the phone rang, startling me so much I dumped *Imbi* on the floor.

I grabbed the phone, suffering *Imbi's* baleful glare. "Y ... Yes?" My voice was taut and cracked.

"It's alright, *Liebling*. It's me."

I let out a breath full of tension and Mutti chuckled at hearing it.

"Relax, *Liebling*. Everything's fine. A meeting held me up. I'm leaving now. See you soon."

"Okay."

My anxiety ebbed, leaving me oddly uncoordinated to fumble the phone onto its cradle. *Imbi* wound his feathery tail round my legs, looking up with wide eyes, disturbed by my strange mood. I scooped him up and flopped onto the sofa. We calmed each other for a few minutes with strokes, purrs and loving head butts. After a few minutes, he settled on my lap, green eyes slowly closing as he felt my mood ease, purrs softening to an almost imperceptible whiffle. The lassitude of released tension soaked my body and I half dozed.

Mutti's feet on the stairs galvanised me. I rushed over, pulling the front door open to find her standing about to put her key in the lock.

She smiled. "Goodness – let me get inside and we'll talk." She put her bag on the kitchen workbench and turned on the radio. I joined her at the table.

"I told him we were making progress at entering the Russian community but had encountered a problem."

Mutti saw my confused look.

"A problem with the costs involved." Her lips curved up on one side. "After all, you are entering Russian society close to its apex and that means there are ... expectations of you." Mutti's face was serious, indicating that this would be more complicated than what I was doing at the Polish and German clubs. "I could see he was torn between his need for information and a ... disinclination ... to pay us more money. So, I changed tack and asked him if there were people in the Russian community we should particularly cultivate."

I could see where this might be headed. "Miss Zaytseva?"

"He gave me three names that he regards as important. Aunt Anastasia was the last." She raised an eyebrow at me. "Who else?"

"Dmitri Mikhailov, the president of the Russian club?"

"Indeed. What about the third name?"

I racked my brain but came up with nothing. "I've no idea. The people I met at the ball were young men I danced with."

"The third name is Sergei Korolev. I think he's a property developer. And he has a son older than you."

"Umm ..." I thought about the ball. "I danced with a Maxim Korolev."

"He didn't mention the son's name." She shook her head. "It doesn't matter. Your relationship with Anastasia Zaytseva is the key."

"Did Mr Fr ... er ... that man ... want us to pursue that relationship?"

"Ultimately, yes, but it took a while for us to dance into that spotlight." Her lips pursed. Talking about him was distasteful.

I smiled at the strange image of Mutti dancing with Mr Franks.

"I pointed out that the people he wanted us to get close to are wealthy individuals. They would have certain expectations of those around them ... and we could not currently meet those."

"And?"

"We finally agreed on a figure. He will pay us a further twenty-five pounds a month for six months."

I stifled a gasp.

He'd agreed...but why six months?

Mutti's face became serious again. "He made it clear we need to have made substantial progress in the Russian community by that time ... or his support will be withdrawn."

There was something more: Mutti shifted uneasily and her eyes wandered across my face before they settled on mine.

"If we are unsuccessful, I think he will throw us to the wolves."

My stomach flipped.

My father's wolves ...

Mutti leant across, placing a gentle hand over mine. "You know I'll help – but this is a great deal of pressure on you."

I sat there for several seconds as the responsibility settled its crushing weight on me.

This is all Mrs Henderson's fault ...

Mutti stroked her hand across mine and I looked up into her caring eyes. Eyes that had stared year after year across the bleak horror of Ravensbrück and not given up when her friends were executed and her mother died. Something shifted inside me, pushing aside juvenile thoughts of fairness and replacing them with a resolve to ... persevere, to survive. But I needed something, too.

I pulled myself from my reverie with a deep breath. "We can do this Mutti ..."

She raised her eyebrows as she sensed something more in my voice. "But?"

"I can't go on lying."

"*Liebling.* We have to lie – our whole life here is a lie. We have no choice."

"No. With Aunt Anastasia, we have a choice. Anyhow, she's peered past the surface of our relationship, suggesting there are secrets in my life."

Mutti shivered at this. "*Liebling.* We can't risk this – how can we trust her not to betray us?"

How to tell her I need truth in some part of my life? In at least one relationship apart from her. I am drowning in deceit. I'm skilled at it ... and I do not want to be that person: a user of people, like Mrs Henderson and Mr Franks.

"*Liebling?*" I could hear the concern in Mutti's voice.

"I'm worried, Mutti. All this lying – I feel ... dirty. I'm worried I might end up living like that."

I could see the anguish on Mutti's face, her shoulders slumping.

"No, Mutti. You know it's not your fault. Don't blame yourself." I stared into her face, dragging her eyes up to mine. "We've talked about this and we both know you had no choice about my father – you had to act."

Mutti tried to pull her hand away, but I held on. "No, Mutti."

She shook her head, denying what I was saying.

"No." Vehemence coloured my voice. "No. Guilt will destroy us as surely as hate. You bear no guilt for what has happened to us." I grasped her hand, shaking it in emphasis.

Mutti's eyes closed for a long second before reopening. "What is it you want to do?"

I released her hand. "Aunt Anastasia suspects there's something more to me than I have told her. I need to have one relationship — other than with you, Mutti dearest — that is based on truth."

Is that fear – or resignation on Mutti's face? I want agreement, not acquiescence.

"She trusted me – and you; she knows I would tell you enough to reveal her work for ... that man. We've done this before — with Willi and Lili — and we can do it again with someone else we trust."

Mutti dragged in a breath. "You gave me no choice with Willi ... and precious little choice with Lili." There was accusation in her voice and eyes.

"I know, Mutti – I'm sorry." I smarted. "But neither of them betrayed us."

Mutti's shoulder's tensed and her eyes narrowed. "We don't know that."

Does she think Willi betrayed us? Lili?

"Yes – we do." The vehemence returned to my voice. "That woman ... practically admitted it was her that deliberately leaked our whereabouts."

Mutti blinked and her fingers tapped as she tried to recall those conversations with Mrs Henderson in Lancaster. Her eyes were sliding around the room.

"She didn't say it directly, but she'd set someone to watch you while they leaked your contact and whereabouts."

I saw Mutti about to interrupt and hurried on. "And she had everything ready to 'rescue' us and capture father's agents."

Laying it out for Mutti crystallised my thinking: it was Mrs Henderson that betrayed us, using us as bait. Another part of that internal knot come into focus and released.

Willi had nothing to do with it.

Mutti's eyes returned to me. "You're probably right about it being her." She shook her head in disbelief. "How can she ... use people like that?" She murmured before her voice strengthened. "I must have buried those details until you dragged them out again."

For a moment, I was again sitting in the library when Mrs Henderson laid out what was to happen to us. The tableau lifted the hair on my arms. "How can you have forgotten? Those occasions with her are vivid, terrible."

Mutti's eyes wandered again before returning to mine. "They were painful, loaded with my guilt at dragging you down with me."

"No guilt, Mutti. You're not to blame – you had no choice." Mutti leant forward, burying her head in her hands. I wasn't getting through to her.

What else can I say?

"Mutti, what would have happened to me if you'd left me in Leipzig?"

Her hands dropped to the table and her eyes stared into mine. "I could never have done that. I could never have left you with that ... monster." There was horror in her voice.

I sat, breathing softly, hoping she would follow her words.

After I had counted seven breaths, Mutti's mouth worked slowly, at first not forming words but a bitter smile. "You're right. I had no choice."

"There can be no guilt." Not a question – a statement.

"Try telling my subconscious that." Distaste showed in the set of her mouth. "It sees this life we are forced to live and tells me you should have more."

"More? What 'more' would I have that I don't have now if we had stayed in Leipzig – or England?"

Mutti's face softened. "Willi ..."

My shoulders sagged, but I pulled myself up. "I would never have met him if we'd stayed in Leipzig – and losing him is down to ... her, not you."

Mutti huffed out a breath. "True." But doubt suffused her voice.

"And the lies we tell are because of her – and ... that man. They're not your fault either." My look across the table demanded a response.

Mutti's nod was unconvincing, her arms wrapped around her torso. We would have to work on this some more.

"Can I tell Aunt Anastasia about us?"

She breathed deeply several times, looking across at me. "You feel you have to do this for you, don't you?"

"I do."

"Every person who knows about us increases the risk of exposure." Her face hardened. "In England, we were lucky with Willi and Lili. You know that, don't you?"

I remained silent, frightened that any words I used would harm my cause.

Mutti sighed. "I'll want to meet her again. I'll see if I can finish early on Saturday."

"Okay."

Mutti let out a tired breath. "I'm exhausted. I'm going to have a shower and head to bed."

I stood up with her and pulled her in for a hug.

"Thank you for listening to me, Mutti."

Her eyes lingered on my face and she murmured. "You're growing up, *Liebling*. Please don't do it too fast."

I wasn't sure what to say. I gave her another hug and we headed off to bed.

Chapter 13
Late April – mid May 1965

With the Easter holidays ending at the weekend and the swimming club about to start up, Lizzie and I swam twice more during the week. I was looking for an improvement in the strength of my arms and shoulders due to lifting weights, but couldn't feel any difference in my swimming. Euan had said it would take time – but not how much. The next time I saw him on my morning run, I'd have to ask him, but I looked for him each day with no luck.

Mutti had much on her mind – her hatred of Vogel and now my powerful need to tell the truth to Aunt Anastasia consumed her. She was distracted and I sought a way to help her. After thinking about it, I asked her if she'd like to come and talk with Aunt Anastasia on Saturday afternoon when she left work. She was uncertain at first, but finally decided to be there. Part of the agreement was that I wouldn't talk about Mr Franks until she arrived.

As the swimming club was in recess, I ran on Saturday morning, but Euan was still missing. He's not a young person anymore and I wondered if he was alright.

I know where he lives. Should I knock on his door?

I pondered that as I ran, finally deciding I had enough on my plate, but that decision left me uneasy.

Summer had finished, with morning temperatures becoming fresh.

How cold did it get in winter?

Brisbane was subtropical – and there were all sorts of warm climate plants around – including the amazing, delicious, gold-skinned Bowen mangoes we'd enjoyed over summer. These cooler temperatures were welcome after the humid heat, but I'd had enough of European wind-driven rain, sleet and snow.

Am I becoming a hot-house plant, preferring Brisbane's summer heat to northern Europe's miserable winters?

How had Willi managed, thrust from Australia's warmth into one of England's worst winters? He never mentioned it ...

I went into the city early as I wanted to explore the Polish shelves of Mr Caune's bookshop. Polish classes would start up on Thursday. I jotted down a few books to ask Mrs Kowalczyk about on Thursday and I went upstairs to Aunt Anastasia's flat at about half-past eleven.

I knocked on the door and unlocked it with the key she had insisted I take. "Good morning, Aunt Anastasia. It's Karlota."

"Come in, dear." The welcome was clear and bright, mirroring her eyes, belying her age.

Aunt Anastasia was sitting in her usual chair by the window, wearing the dark blue ankle length dress, which was her usual everyday attire. She had the Russian newspaper spread on her lap.

"Come, come." She waved me across the room. "Sit down and tell me how your week has gone."

"Shall I make tea first?"

She beamed. "That would be lovely. Thank you."

Ten minutes later, we were sitting opposite one another at the window. I prattled on in Russian (with Aunt Anastasia correcting my occasional 'peasant pronunciation') about my week, steering clear of the emotional discussions with Mutti.

Eventually, I ran down, and in the silence, we shared a look.

Aunt Anastasia inspected her hands, folded in her lap before raising her head, her blue eyes searching mine. "Have you thought more about helping me?"

I stiffened, despite knowing that this was where the conversation had always been headed. "Yes, I've thought about it a lot."

Aunt Anastasia's shoulders relaxed a tension I'd not noticed before.

"But I'd like to talk to you about this with my mother. She'll be here about three o'clock." I searched Aunt Anastasia's face for reassurance. "Is that okay?"

Aunt Anastasia pursed her lips and her eyes avoided mine. "Your mother doesn't trust me." It was not a question.

"No, it's not that." I leant across, taking her hand as I thought how to reassure her. "It's that ... we both need to talk to you about this."

Aunt Anastasia looked down at my hand and I started to pull it away. Her other hand stopped me. "Alright, Karlota." She looked up, sharing a thin-lipped smile. "We'll wait." She let go of my hand with a gentle squeeze, but I could see she was troubled.

After lunch, Aunt Anastasia had me find a slim volume on her bookshelf titled *The Art of War* by a writer called Laozi.

I looked at the name – it wasn't Russian. "This is translated from Chinese into Russian?"

"Indeed. I think you might find it both interesting and useful if we are to lock horns with Mr Franks."

Hearing his name startled me. Mutti and I always avoided naming him out loud, but I controlled my reaction as I flicked over the pages.

"You think dealing with ... that man ... is like waging war?"

"A little." The murmur firmed. "We need to out-think him, out-manoeuvre him or he will trample us."

I looked down at the slim book. "And this book will help?" I was sceptical.

"Maybe." She looked across at me, a slight frown providing emphasis. "It will certainly make you think – and every little helps."

I couldn't see how an ancient Chinese treatise on waging war would help me in my dealings with Mr Franks, but if Aunt Anastasia wanted me to read it, I would. It was quite a small book. I read it aloud to Aunt Anastasia, with interruptions to check my understanding, make abstruse points about grammar and correct my lapses in pronunciation.

Time crawled round the beautiful Ormolu clock until we heard a knock on the door.

I looked across at Aunt Anastasia. "That'll be Mutti."

Aunt Anastasia started levering herself to her feet. "Well, let her in."

I opened the door for Mutti, who smiled and gave me a hug. As we moved apart, she looked across the room. "Good afternoon, Miss Zaytseva."

"Good afternoon, Mrs Miller." She turned to me. "I think a glass of tea would be welcome, Karlota."

As I headed to the kitchen to start the *samovar*, I heard Aunt Anastasia guide Mutti to a chair in the window. From the kitchen, I could hear them talking, but not make out what was being said, which was frustrating. A few minutes later, I carried the silver tea tray out and set it beside Aunt Anastasia. I pulled a chair for me across from the dining table. Their conversation had stopped as soon as I entered the room. An awkward silence settled over us.

"Tea, Mrs Miller?" Aunt Anastasia passed a crystal tea glass in its *podstakannik* across to Mutti.

"Thank you."

"Here's yours, Karlota."

"Thank you."

Silence descended once more, all of us unsure how to start. Mutti looked at me, gesturing with her eyes that I speak.

I sipped my tea. "Aunt Anastasia, I've told you I want to help you."

"Yes.".

I took a deep breath. "But I haven't told you why." I glanced at Mutti; she was looking at me but holding her face blank. "You see, we are being threatened and used by ... Mr Franks." My eyes flicked to Mutti. I knew she did not like us naming him out loud, but Aunt Anastasia had named him.

Aunt Anastasia's eyes widened, flicking between us. "Go on."

I swallowed, glancing again at Mutti. "I'm not ... quite ... what I seem." I faltered to a stop. This was difficult.

Aunt Anastasia's lips curled into a tiny smile. "I think I can help." She glanced at Mutti before returning her eyes to me. "While you are certainly German, you are from ... the east not west zone ... Yes?"

I blinked and gave Mutti an embarrassed look. "How ... was I that bad at telling lies?"

Aunt Anastasia reached across, picking up my hand. "No, my dear. It wasn't your story that gave you away – although my teacher's nose told me from the first that there was something you weren't telling me." Her smile broadened. "It was your Russian – or rather the speed you picked it up, supposedly from almost nothing." Her eyes smiled at me. "That truly made me suspicious."

"Oh ..."

Aunt Anastasia's voice was a touch patronising. "Karlota, you are talented with languages, but to come from nothing to near fluency in a new language in three months of a few hours a week. Well, I've never heard of such a thing." She looked across at Mutti. "There was some home tutoring as well?"

Mutti remained motionless.

Aunt Anastasia's eyes returned to me. "Then I came across a newspaper article about the education system in east Germany. The article told me that all east German students learn Russian from the start of their schooling – and I began to think." She looked at me. "You've been learning Russian for about six years?"

I sagged, dejected that she had seen through me.

Aunt Anastasia saw my look. "Don't be hard on yourself, Karlota. That you are learning multiple languages concurrently tells me you are a talented and dedicated linguist." She smiled. "It must be hard to pretend you don't know a language while learning it."

Willi had done that with Mutti and me …

Aunt Anastasia's face was puzzled.

"What I do not yet understand is … why Mr Franks can blackmail you." Her eyes gathered mine and Mutti's. "You are defectors, but there are many defectors from east Germany, though probably only a few in Australia." She eyed us, speculation on her face. "What makes you different?"

I glanced across at Mutti. She gave me a nod, encouraging me to go on.

"Well … umm … my father is a *Stasi* … umm … an east German secret police officer and Mrs …" I saw Mutti stiffen. "Er … MI6 used us as bait to trick eastern Bloc agents into the open to kidnap us." I suppressed a shiver at the off-hand way Mrs Henderson had dangled us in front of my father. "MI6 rescued us and they killed and captured agents in England and elsewhere. After that, the *Stasi* and probably the KGB as well wanted us … dead." I stopped, the terrifying detail of the gunfight around us that night pinning me to my seat. I forced myself into the present. "They shipped us off to Australia as the safest place. Mr Franks realised he could blackmail us: if we didn't help him spy on the Poles, Germans and Russians here in Brisbane, he would betray us to the *Stasi*."

Aunt Anastasia's lips pursed as she glanced between us. "Disgusting man … but how did he know you were here?"

Mutti leant forward. "That was my fault, I'm afraid. I insisted to MI6 we needed an emergency contact here in case things went bad. MI6 contacted ASIO and ... that man ... decided he could use us to his advantage as I speak Polish and Russian fluently."

Aunt Anastasia looked at Mutti, her eyes narrowing. "But why is it Karlota doing the work, not you, Mrs Miller?"

I could hear disapproval in her voice and saw Mutti wince at the implication. I jumped in. "We had no choice." I could see the hurt in Mutti's eyes. "If Mutti had tried, our story would not have stood up for long. People would have realised she was from east Germany – and we would have been exposed to my father." Again, I glanced across at Mutti and rushed on. "But Mr ... er ... that man didn't care and we came up with a way for me to do the work. Mutti helps – a lot." By the end, I could hear the pleading in my voice.

Mutti had no choice ... she's not abusing me ...

Aunt Anastasia frowned over this for a few seconds before her face relaxed. "I understand." She looked at us. "You had no choice." Her glance at Mutti was full of empathy. "He put you in a desperate position, didn't he?"

Mutti sighed. "I ... well, we ... couldn't see any other way." She glanced at me, loaded with love and pride. "It was Kal that came up with the ideas that made this possible and it is her that carries out our plans. I help when it's needed."

Aunt Anastasia acknowledged me with a smile filled with respect. "Well done, Karlota."

I blushed at the praise.

Aunt Anastasia gave me a confused look. "But why did you feel you had to tell me all this? You could have continued as before – I had my suspicions, but that's not proof ..."

I huffed out a breath. "Because of me." I looked down at my feet for a moment before looking up, glancing in apology at Mutti. "In every part of my life I was having to tell lies and it was ... is wearing me down." I shot Mutti a regretful look. "I persuaded Mutti that I ... we ... could have an honest relationship with you because you would not betray us."

Aunt Anastasia considered this in silence before looking at both of us with deep gratitude on her face. "Thank you for your trust." She picked up her tea, took a sip and frowned. "I think we need fresh tea. This is barely warm."

I gathered up the tea things and made us another round.

Mutti came into the kitchen as I was finishing. "Aunt Anastasia says there are some lamingtons in a biscuit tin in the pantry. Can you find them?"

"I'll look."

There were several biscuit tins, but I found the correct one on my second try. I arranged half a dozen of the small chocolate and desiccated coconut-coated lamingtons on a plate and added that to the tray, which I carried out.

After the rather intense conversation, I relaxed, watching Mutti and Aunt Anastasia chat – in Russian – about Aunt Anastasia's experiences in China; they got on well.

Aunt Anastasia turned to me a few minutes later. "What do we tell Mr Franks?"

I gathered my thoughts for a moment. "Tell him you haven't been able to find anyone suitable in the Russian community. But you've been teaching Russian to a German girl who's agreed to help you." I turned to Mutti. "We'll tell him I've attached myself to a highly placed member of the Russian community by pretending to learn Russian." Mutti's smile had that predatory touch. I turned to Aunt Anastasia. "We need to make sure that he doesn't realise we both know the truth about each other." I was feeling devious. "That way, we both get credit for the same thing."

Aunt Anastasia laughed. "That's excellent, Karlota – I like it. Perhaps reading Laozi helped after all."

I smiled at Mutti. "Mutti is teaching me about this sort of thing: always seek a way to take advantage of a situation."

Mutti returned the smile. "You're learning, Kal." She looked at the clock. "But we must be going, Miss Zaytseva."

I gathered up the tea things. "I'll wash these up."

"Thank you, dear." Aunt Anastasia smiled.

Ten minutes later, as we were walking down to the tram, Mutti took my hand, giving it an encouraging squeeze. "You handled that well."

"Thank you, Mutti."

"I think this will work well for all of us."

"I do, too."

• • • •

ON MONDAY, THERE WAS still no sign of Euan. After spending time with Aunt Anastasia and the excitement of the ball and Mr Franks, school and my usual activities felt humdrum. I'd asked Lizzie not to mention the ball, as I didn't want to attract attention. I could see that she was bursting to share my experiences with her friends, but she agreed to say nothing.

Euan was still absent on Wednesday morning.

What was going on?

I decided that I'd go to his house on Friday after school if I hadn't seen him.

At swimming on Wednesday, Lizzie blitzed the fifty-meter field, much to her delight. My time for the 800m swim improved by several seconds: the weightlifting was helping, it seemed.

As always, my improvement thrilled Lizzie and she berated me when I downplayed it. "Kal, you're good and getting better all the time. I'm sure you'll be beating people in the long swims by next year. Remember, you're at least a year younger than all of them."

I hugged her in thanks before we headed for our trams. She's such a caring, supportive person and I'm truly lucky to have found her as a friend.

I hate lying to her ...

On Thursday after Polish class, I showed Mrs Kowalzcyk my list of books. She looked at the list and frowned. "I think you might find them dry." Her lips pursed for a second. "Umm ... have you read any Science Fiction?"

"No. What's that?"

Mrs Kowalczyk laughed. "I don't know myself. But there's a new Polish author that is being spoken of highly – Stanislaw Lem – and he writes this science fiction, sort of ... futuristic fiction. Ask the bookshop if they can get you a copy of his novel *Solaris.* If you can get a copy, please let me know what you think of it."

I jotted down the name and book title in my exercise book. I'd speak to Mr Caune about it on Saturday.

At home, Mutti told me she was still waiting to set up a meeting with Mr Franks but had heard nothing. Euan and Dodger were still absent on Friday morning and I went to his house straight from the tram home from school. The blinds were down – but that could be to keep out the sunlight.

I knocked on the door and waited. I didn't hear any movement and knocked again. After a minute, I heard movement and the door opened. Euan stood there blinking in the sunlight.

"Ah ... Karlota." His shoulders were drooping, not in his usual upright soldier stance.

"Good afternoon, Euan ... er ... I called round to see if everything was okay. I've not seen you and Dodger for quite a few days."

His shoulders slumped further and he looked away. "I'm 'fraid Dodger is n' longer with us."

"Oh, Euan."

Without thinking, I pulled him into a hug and I felt his hands come up and rest on my shoulders. After a few seconds, he gave my shoulder a gentle pat and pushed me away.

"Thank ye, Karlota." His eyes lifted over my head. "We'd been t'gether nigh on sixteen yairs. I ken this day was approachin', but ..." His voice drifted away.

My single experience with death was the *Stasi* agent getting shot in our car when Mrs Henderson rescued us and that was totally different. I didn't know what to say to comfort Euan and, in my desire to help, blundered on. "Can I come in and make you a cup of tea?"

Euan's eyes locked with mine. "'N yer mam? She'd approve of ye comin' inta m' house – alone?"

I stood there, uncertain how to answer.

Euan smiled and gestured to a bench on the veranda. "Sit yesel' on that. I'll fetch out tea."

A few minutes later, Euan brought out two mugs of tea, handing one to me and sitting himself in silence at the far end of the bench.

"Thank you."

We sipped our tea in silence for a few minutes before Euan spoke. "I buried him over yonder, by t' fence." He pointed to some freshly turned earth. "I've a mind t'plant a tree o'er him."

I searched for something to say. "I knew Dodger whilst he was old. What was he like as a puppy?"

For a moment I thought I'd said the wrong thing; Euan leant his head back against the house, eyes squeezed shut before chuckling. "He were a terrible chewer – shoes, chair legs, ye name't and he'd chew on't. He fair wrecked a few things 'til I trained him."

Once started, Euan reminisced about Dodger for some minutes as we finished our tea. Eventually, he glanced down into his empty mug. "Ah, lassie. Ye should'na let me prattle on — but thanks."

I smiled. "I miss you out on my runs."

"Weel now, suppose I still need t' walk." He sized up my shoulders. "'N I see ye's been usin' them weights."

I glanced down at my arms. "I can't see a difference. But I shaved a bit off the eight-hundred-meter swim this week."

"'Tis na more muscle ye want, but stronger muscles. Anyhow ye shoulders have grown, I reckon."

"Thank you for lending me the weights."

"'Tis ma pleasure, lassie." Euan stood. "'N thank ye fer coming round t' brighten ma day.

I stood up. "I was worried about you, Euan."

Euan huffed. "Away wit' ye, lassie. Ye should concairn yersel' wi' lads, not old codgers likes o' me."

There's only one lad that concerns me ...

I could see the twinkle in Euan's eye. "See you on my run, on Sunday?"

"We'll see."

At home, I rushed to get tea ready for Mutti. When asked about 'that man', she shook her head.

"I went round to Euan's house this afternoon."

Mutti raised an eyebrow. "You need to be careful ..."

I wrinkled my forehead. "Euan's not dangerous."

Mutti's gaze was disapproving. "That's not what I was suggesting. But what would the neighbours think of him, seeing you, a young girl, go into his house?"

"Oh ...But I didn't go in. I sat outside and Euan brought tea out."

"Alright. But why did you go there?"

"I haven't seen him and his dog on my morning runs. I was worried about him. It turns out Euan's dog – Dodger – has died."

"Oh, the poor man. How is he?"

"He was down, but I got him reminiscing about Dodger and that seemed to cheer him up."

Mutti smiled with approval. "Do watch out for him – but remember, you shouldn't go into his house unless I'm there. We don't want the neighbours gossiping about him." She thought for a moment. "We should ask him round for a meal one weekend?"

"That's a marvellous idea. I think we should leave it for a week or two, though."

"Probably a good idea."

• • • •

AT SWIMMING, I HELD my improved time for the 800 m. Coach told me I could try the 1600 m on Wednesday. Lizzie gave me an 'I told you so' look. We parted with a wave after swimming, with her heading home while I walked into the city.

Mr Caune noted down the Stanislaw Lem book. "I'll see what I can do, Karlota ..." He looked up, a twinkle in his eye. "This might test my contacts in the publishing world," he said, relishing the challenge.

"Good luck." I smiled. "Mrs Kowalczyk, my teacher at the Polish club recommended it."

Upstairs, I went to make tea once I'd greeted Aunt Anastasia. As I sat down with the tea tray, her unusual fidgeting warned me she had something on her mind.

Mr Franks?

She sipped her tea through narrowed lips, replacing the *podstakannik* on the mat with an uncharacteristic clumsy clunk, nearly sloshing the tea over the rim. "Have you spoken with Mr Franks yet?"

Indeed, Mr Franks.

"Not yet, I'm afraid. Mutti is trying to set up a meeting, but it hasn't happened yet." I pondered this for a moment. "What about you?"

She shook her head. "I've left a message but heard nothing yet."

I gave a dry laugh. "He's playing hard to get. Mutti says he plays games to prove he's in charge."

Aunt Anastasia didn't react and we both sipped our tea as the silence deepened around us.

After a while, Aunt Anastasia shifted in her chair. "Would you mind sharing with me the sort of thing you are doing in the German and Polish clubs?" Aunt Anastasia sounded diffident.

"Well ... I'm not doing anything in the German Club. I told them my mother doesn't want me speaking German, but I don't want to lose my heritage. They let me join the book club on Saturday afternoons. I keep my ears open and take home a newspaper which we read, but I haven't seen or heard anything that might interest ... that man."

Aunt Anastasia looked up. "Why do you refer to him as 'that man'?"

"Mutti is worried that someone might overhear us talking; we try to keep things anonymous."

Aunt Anastasia frowned.

"In east Germany, the *Stasi* planted bugs – listening devices – in people's houses. Mutti has the radio on while we talk, in case."

"I see ..." Aunt Anastasia looked across at me. "I can understand why the two of you are careful, given the danger you face if you're discovered." She paused for a moment. "Your mother seems quite adept at this sort of thing."

"Mutti learned this in Ravens ..." I snapped my motor mouth shut.

Aunt Anastasia sat motionless for a second. "Ravens ... brück?"

I dropped my head, annoyed that I'd revealed more about Mutti than I should.

Aunt Anastasia's gaze was piercing. "Your mother was in a Nazi death camp?"

I stared at my hands, taking several deep breaths.

When I raised my head, Aunt Anastasia's face was full of understanding. "It's not your story to tell, is it?" Her eyes stayed on mine. "And that's important to you, isn't it?"

I jerked a nod, angry that I'd slipped up – again.

"Thinking before you speak is difficult, isn't it?" Her eyes were full of sympathy. "It's alright, Karlota. I'll keep that to myself." Her eyes drifted away from mine but settled on me after a moment's thought. "You should tell your mother that there are a few people here in Brisbane that survived those ... places. I don't know if any of them were at Ravensbrück, but perhaps some were."

My stomach sank at the thought of another way we could be exposed. "I'll let her know ..."

For a moment, I tried to fit this fresh problem into all the others Mutti and I faced. I couldn't see anything we could do about it. We must hope these people would not recognise a middle-aged Mutti as the girl and teenager they had known.

Aunt Anastasia leant across and patted my hand, dragging my attention to her. "So, tell me about the Polish Club."

I dragged my mind from the swamp it had been contemplating – and realised that Aunt Anastasia had switched subjects deliberately. My eyes squeezed shut for a moment. "I had a Polish friend in England, Wi... er ... we did our homework together and swapped languages." It seemed she'd not noticed me pull myself up and I pushed on, hoping she'd say nothing. "I went to the Polish club as I heard they had a library and I wanted to borrow Polish language books to help me keep my Polish alive. They let me join the Polish classes they run on Thursday after school for the children of members." I was quite proud of my achievements there. I told her about helping in the office and finding a membership list – and about Jan Drozd.

"Mutti and I have a card index we add to each week using the German, Polish and now Russian language newspapers to keep track of people."

"My dear, you and your mother seem to be meticulous about this."

There it was again, that niggling, out-of-reach thought about Mutti.

Aunt Anastasia waved across at her desk. "Please pass me my diary. It's that green book on my writing desk. Oh – and the fountain pen as well."

The diary was tooled leather with "1965 *Дневник*" and the Russian eagle in gold on the front. A leather clasp held it closed. I handed it and the pen to Aunt Anastasia and she flicked open the clasp.

"Now ..." She leafed through the pages. "Ah yes, here we are." She looked across at me. "On Saturday, the twelfth of June, the Korolevs have invited me to a cocktail party at their house. I'd like you to come with me." She looked up. "You danced with Maxim, their son, at the Easter Ball."

I shrugged. I had danced with nearly a dozen young men at the ball.

Aunt Anastasia smiled. "Maxim was your first dance partner ... taller than you, with dark hair and eyes – more brown than nearly black like yours."

His face floated up from amongst the others I'd danced with that night.

"He's nineteen, studying law at the University." Aunt Anastasia pursed her lips. "I expect he thinks you are older than you are, thanks to your makeup and the champagne you were drinking." She gave me a calculating look. "I think you should get close to him."

I wasn't sure where this was going and I remained silent under Aunt Anastasia's penetrating gaze.

After a moment, she quirked a smile. "Do you have much experience with boys?"

Willi's gentle breath on my neck, our arms around one another, hands sliding over our bodies ...

My face flushed and I dropped my eyes. "Um – no."

"But there was ... someone special?" Her eyes were soft, understanding.

I couldn't speak, squeezing my eyes shut, clamping down on the sudden tears. After a moment, Aunt Anastasia's hand slid across mine.

"Your gold chain?"

My hands flew to my neck, the tears now beyond suppression trickling down my face. Through my misery, I heard Aunt Anastasia shift in her chair and a soft handkerchief dabbed my cheeks. My eyes flew open to find her leaning forward, her eyes glistening as a single tear spilled from an eye, called from her own deep sorrow. I reached up and moved her hand across to her face, our tears together darkening the snowy cloth.

We shared our sadness for several seconds until I summoned enough strength to speak. "They dragged me away without a goodbye." I smothered the emotion. "I tried to send him a message – but she didn't pass it on."

Aunt Anastasia's pale blue eyes watched as we moved our shared hands and handkerchief to collect the tears on our faces. "Yuri was a cavalry officer. So gay, so alive." She shook her head as if trying to deny what had occurred. "He died fighting in Manchuria in the war with Japan ... in 1904."

Her eyes closed and I saw her swallow, still feeling the loss across the decades. She struggled to her feet and I leapt up to help, worried that the emotion we were sharing was painful for her.

She read the care on my face. "It's alright, Karlota." She patted my shoulder. "Stay here. I want to show you something." She disappeared into her bedroom, her cane clicking on the polished boards when she reached the edge of the carpet. After a minute, she returned, clasping a large, inlaid Chinese box to her chest. Sitting down, she arranged the box on her lap and shared a watery smile.

"This is a Chinese puzzle box. Parts of the pattern slide and unlock the box." Her hands moved over the dark lacquered surface, recalling its feel.

I sat, waiting for her to continue.

"Like this ... I think ..." a section of one end slid sideways, followed by one that slid down. "That's right ... was it here next?"

I watched as she manipulated the box, eventually freeing the top, which she laid on the side table with great care. She took a deep breath and retrieved a thin packet of letters held by a green ribbon. "Yuri wrote to me when he could after he joined his regiment ..." Her hand shook as she placed the bundle on the lid beside her. Next, she pulled out a small black box, placing it on her lap. She scrabbled to pull out the last item – a large leather photo frame, a tight fit in the box. She sat lost in silence, gazing at the closed cover for a while before she opened it. Her breath a barely suppressed gasp as she stared at the photo.

After a moment, her eyes rose to mine. "I have not opened this for many years." She blinked, controlling the tears I could see shining in her eyes. "Oh, I had forgotten how beautiful he was." Her voice a distant wail, heard through layered years. Her hand caressed the photo and her breath shuddered for a moment. She turned the photo to me. It showed the face of a young man with an expansive, curled moustache.

Modern standards were different – I found the moustache off-putting. "He's handsome," I managed.

Aunt Anastasia placed the photo on the arm of her chair, lost in it for a few seconds. "He was a good man, the second son of another merchant family. It was an arranged marriage – a family alliance – but we were in love. We were engaged a few weeks before he left." She opened the small black box in her lap to reveal a filigree diamond and sapphire ring. "After news came he had been killed, father made me return his ring. But Yuri's mother visited me a few days later and pressed it into my hand." Tears brimmed in her eyes. "She insisted I had something to remember him by ..." Aunt Anastasia's eyes clamped shut.

I knelt and hugged her, the loves we each had lost overwhelming other thoughts.

After a time, she took several deep breaths and stroked my hair. "Tea, I think, Karlota."

I looked up to see her smiling at me, tears staining her cheeks. "Thank you for sharing Yuri with me."

"I had not realised how much I still loved him. I had buried him in that box until you revealed your loss." She looked into my eyes. "You must tell me more about your love." She shared a sad smile. "But make the tea first."

As I made the tea, I thought about what I could say. Willi's origin from the future would have to stay hidden. I longed to tell Aunt Anastasia of his foreknowledge about the collapse of Soviet hegemony. But if it happened as Willi remembered, it was over twenty years away, probably beyond Aunt Anastasia's personal horizon.

As I set the tea tray down, I noticed Aunt Anastasia was wearing Yuri's ring.

"Please, tell me about your lost love."

As we sipped our tea, I told her the story of Willi, the abused son and Col, the defector, daughter of a feared *Stasi* officer. Aunt Anastasia laughed when I told her of Willi's confusion as I revealed myself to be a girl, not the boy he thought and I frowned.

"No, no, Kal. I am laughing with you, not at you." Her face echoed the concern in her voice. "Your telling was excellent and full of the strange comedy that surrounds us humans as we struggle to communicate between the sexes." Her smile was interested and supportive. "Please, continue."

I sipped my tea to settle myself. I told her about our Polish friend, Lili, and my hand in the essay competition Willi won rather strangely and the circumstances that trapped him into taking the prize trip to East Germany. And how the whole thing turned out to be an MI6 operation to retrieve Mutti's evidence that father was a Nazi war criminal.

Aunt Anastasia's eyes hardened. "Your poor mother ..." Her voice trailed off before her curiosity reasserted itself. "You told me that MI6 used you as bait." Aunt Anastasia's blue eyes held my dark ones. "But earlier you said something about 'she did not pass on a message'."

Mrs Henderson's seamed face filled my memory. How her supercilious looks on every occasion sapped my self-worth. The sting when she slapped in the garden in Lancaster. Her dismissal of our fears and concerns as she bundled us off to Australia.

"Karlota?"

I found my eyes had closed as I relived those scenes. Aunt Anastasia's voice startled them open and I cleared the thick emotion from my throat. "Sorry."

"Karlota." She leant across to take my hand. "You don't have to tell me if it's painful."

I closed my eyes again for a second.

I have to tell her about Mrs Henderson...

"When we defected from east Germany, Mutti made sure we got to the British zone. It was British Intelligence that interrogated us, first in Frankfurt and then in a house somewhere in England." I could still see the room they kept me in for nearly a week, separated from Mutti. "The person who was in charge was Mrs Henderson – a person lacking almost all emotion. A person who uses everyone around her ..." I stopped to find some saliva to clear the distaste from my tongue. "... uses them until she drains them of use before casting them aside."

Anger blossomed in me. Aunt Anastasia watched as I sipped my tea.

"Willi's father had abused him and ... well ... he almost killed himself, twice." Shame surged through me from that time under the cedar tree. "When Mutti and I disappeared, I was frightened that he would blame himself and ..." my voice trailed away at the visceral emotion.

"And?"

The gentle prompt pushed me on. "... and I tried to send him a message that we were safe, but Mrs Henderson would not deliver it." Pain in my left hand drew my attention: my fingers clamped, white-knuckled, round the armrest; I forced them to relax. "By chance, Willi had bumped into my father in Leipzig and I knew he would think that – somehow – he had inadvertently betrayed us." All my uncertainty about Willi erupted inside me. "I don't know if he's still alive ..." I collapsed forward, sobbing, my head on my knees.

Minutes must have passed before the storm cleared. Aunt Anastasia's hand stroked my head as she murmured, "You poor little bird."

I raised my head and a gentle hand helped, lifting my chin.

Aunt Anastasia's eyes held mine. "You must hold him alive in your heart."

My tear-filled eyes bleared her face, but I could still see the fierce strength in her gaze. I blinked several times and wiped my eyes, trying to clear my sight. Aunt Anastasia produced the tear-moistened handkerchief and I wiped my eyes and blew my nose.

"I am sure he will not have forgotten you." Aunt Anastasia's voice held a calm certainty.

But the darkness in my head whispered, *"If he's still alive ..."*

"Your friend – she will help him." Her voice held certainty.

Of course.

I felt a burst of warmth. "I told her that Willi was ... unstable ... and to tell me at once if she thought Willi was acting strangely."

Why hadn't I thought of this before?

"Yes, I'm sure she will help him." My anxiety lessened.

Aunt Anastasia patted my hand. "Don't let the dark voices in your head pull you down." She shared a knowing look. "I was only a year or two older than you when Yuri was snatched from me ..."

Our shared look was of understanding; Aunt Anastasia looked over at the clock. "What time is your Book Club?"

The clock showed after half-past three, telling me I had well and truly missed it. "It started an hour ago. Never mind, I'll ring and find out the book for next week."

Aunt Anastasia glanced at the phone. "You can ring now. I'm sure the club is in the phone directory."

"Are you sure?" I didn't want to impose.

"Of course."

After some to-and-fro on the phone, I discovered they were reading Thomas Mann's *Der Tod in Venedig – Death in Venice*.

Aunt Anastasia smiled at the news. "I'm sure Lukas will have that downstairs."

When I looked at the German shelves after saying goodbye to Aunt Anastasia, I picked up a copy that I started reading on the tram home.

Is this on the 'to read' list Willi and I shared? ... the title was familiar.

Once home, I settled on the sofa with *Imbi* and the book to wait for Mutti.

She arrived home about half-an-hour after me, turning on the radio as usual. "I'm meeting 'that man' on Monday after work."

I tensed. "Do you want me there?" I didn't want to be there – Mr Franks disgusted me, but if Mutti needed me, I'd go.

"I don't think so, *Liebling*." She shared a pensive look. "I don't want you to be seen with him. It's safer that way."

I gave her a relieved smile and changed the subject. "Aunt Anastasia wants me to go with her to a cocktail party in June."

"Yes?"

I wasn't sure how to say this next bit. "Umm ... she wants me to attach myself to the son of the Russian property developer that's giving the party – Maxim Korolev. I danced with him at the ball."

Mutti's face softened and she tilted her head. "How do you feel about that?"

"I'm not sure ..."

Mutti's eyes held mine for several seconds. "You know you can talk to me ... about anything."

I blushed. "Mutti. I'm not Mata Hari."

Mutti blushed in turn. "I know. But ... be careful about what you are getting into."

I must have been mulling this over in my subconscious, as this clarified things. I gave Mutti a reassuring smile. "He may already have a girlfriend and, if he doesn't, I'm going no further than a friend." My voice darkened. "After all, I already have a boyfriend."

I could see a worry line on her forehead.

As I trotted down to the oval on Sunday morning, I hoped Euan would be there and my heart sank when there was no sign of him. But as I ran my last lap, I heard a peel of excited barking. Euan appeared with a young black and white dog straining at the leash and barking at the magpies carolling in the trees.

Euan has another dog already?

I slowed my pace for the last part of the lap, starting my warm down and came to a halt a few paces from Euan. The dog – a border collie puppy – pulled at the leash, trying to reach me.

Euan reeled it in. "Sit. Sit." The puppy looked up at Euan's gentle commands. "Stay." The puppy was quivering with excitement, but stayed sitting, focussed on Euan but darting quick glances in my direction.

"Good mornin', lassie. I'd like t' introduce ye to ma neighbour's new pup, Simon."

Not his dog ...

"Good morning, Euan." I smiled down at the puppy. "May I introduce myself to Simon?"

"Aye, go ahead, lassie." Euan chuckled. "But I'm warnin' ye, Simon'll lick ye left ear through ye right."

I knelt and Euan let out the lead. A bundle of black and white fur with a pink tongue launched at me. Simon was trying to prove Euan right.

After half a minute, Euan gently pulled on the lead and Simon walked across to him, tail whipping back and forth. "Here, boy. Sit."

"He's beautiful, Euan."

"Aye lassie, he is." Euan's voice was distant, thinking perhaps of a young Dodger. He looked down at Simon. "I'm to help train the wee beastie, as my neighbour knows precious little about dogs."

I shivered and Euan frowned. "Ye need to keep movin' or ye'll stiffen up. Off home with ye, lassie."

He was right. I bent down and stroked Simon's head. "Bye, Simon. Bye, Euan."

"Get yersel' home and into t' shower." The smile on his face put the lie to the growl in his voice.

"I'm going, I'm going." I laughed and I trotted off up the track through the trees. Over my shoulder, I saw Euan walking off round the oval, teaching Simon to 'heel'.

After breakfast, Mutti and I went through the Russian paper I had brought from Aunt Anastasia – and I explained why the lack of a German one, telling her about Yuri. I'd see if I could pick up old copies next Saturday. I spent an hour doing the small amount of homework set during the week before doing my weights in the afternoon.

· · · ·

I WOKE WITH A START on Monday morning. *Imbi* jumped to the end of the bed and began washing himself, occasionally awarding me a reproachful glance and flick of an ear.

Mutti is seeing Mr Franks this evening.

I sat up and *Imbi* deigned to allow me to stroke him.

That meeting was never far from my thoughts throughout the day: dealing with Mr Franks always had its dangers. I did my best to hide it, but at lunch, my moodiness got to Lizzie. "What's up with you today, Kal? You're all sharp corners."

I took a deep breath, thinking at high speed. "My friend Euan's dog died and I'm worried about him." It was sort of the truth, but a lie as well. It worried me I was finding it ever easier to do this.

Lizzie looked into my eyes, full of caring friendship.

But is there a touch of suspicion there as well? Am I seeing that because I know I am lying?

"Oh, that's a shame." Lizzie patted my arm. She held my gaze for a second before turning to the rest of the group. At moments like this, I knew I differed completely from the other girls.

Like in east Germany.

When I arrived home, I changed and tried to lose myself by pushing hard with the weights. I kept going until my arms felt like wet string and sweat was sticking my t-shirt to me. I clambered up to shower, change and prepare tea.

As Mutti was meeting with Mr Franks after work, I expected her to be late. I eventually heard her coming up the stairs about an hour later than usual and met her at the front door. She responded to my anxious, questioning look with a smile, put her bag on the counter and turned on the radio.

Her nose twitched at the aroma coming from the beef stew staying warm in the oven, but she could see I was on tenterhooks. "Come and sit down – we'll have tea in a minute."

I plonked myself into a chair next to her. "Well?"

Mutti raised an eyebrow at my impatience. "He doesn't like us much ... but he needs us."

I sighed in relief and Mutti gave my hand a squeeze.

"It was clear, mostly from what he wasn't saying, that finding a link into the Russian community is important to him. The news that you had turned 'learning Russian' into a way into the community was what he wanted to hear."

"Did you tell him who my contact is?"

"Indeed. I impressed on him you had become attached to one of the most highly respected elders in the Russian community – and she took you to the Easter Ball."

"And?"

"Well, he didn't see you at the ball and asked who took you. His reaction to Miss Zaytseva's name was almost comical – part disbelief and part embarrassment."

"Does he suspect I saw him?"

"Maybe ... maybe not. But I don't think that matters much. He's focussed on retaining visibility into the Russian community. He must be under pressure from his superiors."

"I wonder when he'll be in contact with Aunt Anastasia – and how that will go?"

Mutti patted my hand. "I think Miss Zaytseva scares him because of her wealth. I'm sure she'll continue to manage him expertly." Mutti's look was reassuring. "Come on, let's have tea – I'm hungry."

Now the worry of the meeting with Mr Franks was over, my hunger asserted itself as well.

For the rest of the week at school, I tried to be more outgoing with the group of friends that had Lizzie as its bubbly centre. As we walked to swimming on Wednesday after school, Lizzie and I shared a laugh about our English teacher fluffing some lines of poetry several times.

"You seem much happier, Kal."

I walked on a few steps before replying. "Well, my friend Euan is getting over the loss of his old dog. He's helping train his neighbour's collie puppy. I saw them on my run again this morning. He's loving that."

"That's good."

As promised, coach let me swim the 1600-meter race. I was unsurprised to come in last but delighted it was by a small margin. Coach talked to me later, giving me some things to work on to improve at that length. Lizzie was getting better and better, coming in ahead of most of the under eighteen-year-old girls. She looked at me where I sat in the stands and I gave her a congratulatory wave.

Her chest heaving from the exertion, she walked over to me. "Wow – we're both getting better. I'm sure swimming those longer races with you helps."

"The weights are helping me."

We parted after practice and I headed home, doing some reading for homework on the tram. The rest of the week settled into the usual rhythm. At the Polish Club on Thursday, I spotted a letter as I helped in the office. Someone was complaining about Jan Drozd.

Was he going to be expelled from the club?

I swam both the 800- and 1600-meter races on Saturday morning. I pushed hard in the 800, beating two of the older girls, but dragged in the 1600, coming in equal last. I walked to the stands on wobbly legs, collapsing on my chair next to Lizzie.

"What are you trying to prove, Kal?" Lizzie's voice was fierce. "You shouldn't be swimming both one after the other."

I looked at her, trying to connect my thoughts. "Umm ... coach told me to swim them both."

Lizzie's eyelids drooped. "He's up to his games again – probably trying to get you injured." She sprang to her feet and marched off and I didn't have the energy to follow her.

I don't need this drama along with everything else.

Steam fizzed from Lizzie's ears as she plonked down beside me. "I was told to go away and mind my own business."

"Don't get yourself into trouble trying to protect me." I smiled, squeezing her arm in gratitude.

Lizzie fizzed with exasperation. "He knows you shouldn't swim long races like those one after the other." Her eyes flashed. "What's he trying to do?"

I shrugged. "Still trying to protect his daughter?"

Lizzie laughed. "Well, you still beat her in the 800-meter race. That idea didn't turn out well."

"If he tries to do this to me again, I'll speak to the junior coach. I should have done that today."

I could see the approval on Lizzie's face. "Good for you, Kal – assert yourself."

We parted with a hug outside the pool and I walked into the city. Although the walk was familiar, the cooler weather gave the city a different feel: more European and less exotic. Brisbane is bigger than Lancaster but somehow felt smaller, less cosmopolitan. Perhaps it had something to do with its age. Brisbane was about 100 years old whereas Lancaster castle is 1000 years old – and my research into Roman England told me they built the castle on the site of a Roman fort. I thought there was nothing that old here until I learned a little about the first Australians who had been here for at least forty thousand years. But there was no trace of them in the city – except for some strange street and suburb names.

At the bookshop, Mr Caune waved to me. "I think I've found your Lem."

"That's great. When do you think you'll have the book?"

He frowned. "Well – I'm not sure I've found a copy yet – but I may have a lead to one."

"Okay ... next Saturday?"

Mr Caune laughed. "We'll see."

Upstairs, I let myself into Aunt Anastasia's apartment to find her asleep in her chair, the Russian paper spread as usual on her lap. Trying to keep the clatter to a minimum, I made tea and carried out the tray and set it down beside her. I sat down, sipping from my *podstakannik* and watched. After a minute, her nostrils flared at the aroma and her eyes opened.

"Good afternoon, Karlota. I must have dozed off for a minute." She picked up her tea glass. "Thank you for the tea."

"Good afternoon, Aunt Anastasia. Are you well?"

She sipped her tea. "Quite well, thank you."

"Have you been in contact with ... that man?"

Aunt Anastasia gave me a broad smile. "Oh, yes." The smile became conspiratorial. "Between us, I think we have him contained – at least for a while." She saw the question on my face. "He thinks he's the master spy. He has no idea that we know the truth about each other." She leant across and her voice dropped. "As we get you established, we will both send him the same information — different versions, of course. That way, it will reinforce your reliability when you take over completely."

"Um ..."

Aunt Anastasia saw my worried look. "Don't worry Karlota, that won't be for a while yet. I have some work to do to secure you a membership." She folded up the Russian paper and passed it to me. "Here's this week's edition for you and your mother to squeeze dry for information."

"Thank you."

"Now, have you thought about Maxim?"

I fingered my necklace, forcing myself to engage Aunt Anastasia's eyes. "I can be his friend, but not his girlfriend."

She gave an almost imperceptible nod. "I understand ... but I do not think you have much to worry about."

"You mean he already has a girlfriend?"

Her eyes drifted away for a moment before returning to mine. "See what you think of him when you spend time with him at the party. Mr Korolev has made it clear that he expects Maxim to be your host."

"I see."

"Now, let's have some lunch."

After we had eaten, Aunt Anastasia had me finish reading *The Art of War* before I left for the German book club. I'd read the first two chapters of *Der Tod in Venedig* and hoped that would catch me up. At the German club, I walked up the stairs to our usual meeting room.

Miss Bauer saw me walk in and came straight across to me. "Welcome, Karlota." A slight frown wrinkled her brow. "When you weren't here last week, I was worried your mother might have discovered your activity and forbidden your return."

"I'm sorry about last week. I was helping a friend."

It was sort of true ...

"Come and sit down. We're up to chapter two – were you able to get a copy?"

I pulled my copy from my bag and we sat talking about the first chapter. Miss Bauer was uneasy talking about Gustav and Tadzio. I agreed Gustav was creepy in his growing fixation on Tadzio – but Miss Bauer's attitude suggested there was something I was missing. During the discussion that became clear: Mann was dealing with his own struggle with homosexuality through that relationship – and some people in the group were uneasy about this.

My mind returned to Herne Bay one gloomy November evening: seeing Willi's shock at my emotional declaration when he still thought I was a boy.

"Karlota, could you give us a young person's reaction to a relationship between an old man and an adolescent?"

What does she see on my face and in my eyes?

I was lost again, reliving my awful reaction to Willi telling me he was a seventy-year-old man, somehow transported into his twelve-year-old body and brain.

"Um ..." I tried to cover my absence as if delving deep for my answer, which was true in a way the book group could never understand. "I'm not sure about the ... um ... homosexuality. I'd not thought of that." I looked round the group, their faces showing disinterest in what this slip of a girl thought. "But I don't see a problem in a friendship between an old man and a teenager. Isn't that called mentoring?"

My suggestion caused a minor stir and the discussion spiralled off in several directions. One of those was disgust at any acceptance of homosexuality, let alone suggestions of paedophilia. Helmut Neumann, a bald man tending to stoutness, stood and announced that he could not condone the reading of a book with such a disgraceful subtext. He stormed out, tossing his book in the wastepaper basket as left. An embarrassed silence followed for a few seconds before the conversation restarted.

The discussion wound down and we had tea. I noticed Miss Bauer watching me, ignored on the outskirts of the group. I finished my tea and decided I would leave without the newspapers rather than face questions from Miss Bauer. But she intercepted me.

"Karlota, don't you want the old issues of the newspaper?"

My footsteps stuttered to a halt. "Um ... thank you Miss Bauer."

She pulled Mr Neumann's book from the wastepaper basket. "This'll go into the school library," she muttered before straightening up. "Come with me. I have the papers safe downstairs."

I followed her out and down to the ground floor, where we went into the office area.

"Hello, Karin ..." Miss Bauer stopped short. Karin waved and carried on with her phone call. Miss Bauer pulled open a file drawer and retrieved half a dozen newspapers. She gestured me outside to talk.

"You seemed to lose yourself once or twice today, Karlota. Are you sure everything is alright with your mother?"

"Yes, everything's fine."

Miss Bauer cocked her head sideways. "If you're sure." She pursed her lips, her eyes shaded by doubt. "I am still uneasy at helping you go against your mother's wishes."

I didn't know what to say and we stared at one another in shared awkwardness.

Miss Bauer sighed and passed me the small stack of newspapers. "Here you go, Karlota."

"Thanks, Miss Bauer." I gave her an uncertain smile and scurried away, her unspoken questions trailing in my wake. I didn't stop to put the papers in my bag until I was outside the club.

On Sunday, Mutti and I worked through the papers and she found an article about a missing businessman: Hans Gruber hadn't been seen for a week.

Chapter 14
Mid May – late September 1965

The newspaper article contained no detail; Mr Gruber had disappeared on a business trip to Newcastle and his car hadn't been found. The New South Wales police were asking the public for help.

Mutti stared at the full-face picture in the newspaper. "Vogel ..."

I remembered Mutti had mentioned she might send information to someone about Gruber/Vogel.

Is this disappearance a result of Mutti telling someone about him?

Mutti's gaze narrowed, fixed on Gruber's photograph.

A hint of a grim smile?

I watched Mutti concentrating on the photo, thoughts swirling inside me.

Had she contacted someone? How did she know people that might make Gruber disappear?

Mutti shook herself and reached for Gruber/Vogel's index card, adding the information about the article. "Cut out the article and photo please, Kal." She flicked through the rest of the pages and passed the paper across to me, picking up the next one.

After I checked the reverse of the article, I cut it out to add to Gruber/Vogel's file. We kept working at it for about an hour until we'd finished the German papers and Mutti started on the Russian one.

"Look, *Liebling,* there's a photo of you at the ball." She frowned at me. "You should have told me there were photos. Please, get me a copy of this one and any others of you."

I looked over her shoulder. It showed me dancing with Maxim Korolev. The caption said: "Maxim Korolev, son of well-known property developer Sergei Korolev, enjoying himself at the Brisbane Easter Ball". I didn't rate a mention.

Mutti chuckled. "His face is not showing much enjoyment – but you look lovely, *Liebling.*"

"It was formal, Mutti ... structured. I think we were both conscious of the many eyes on us as we danced. That doesn't make for much enjoyment."

"And this is the young man that Aunt Anastasia wants you to ... um ... cultivate?"

My face flushed. "I've told Aunt Anastasia that I can be his friend, but not his girlfriend." The emotion I had shared with Aunt Anastasia felt comforting. "I told her about Willi and she told me about her fiancé, Yuri – a cavalry officer, killed in 1904." I sniffed, sudden moisture in my nose, surprised that her story affected me. "She still has his letters and a photo. Her father made her return their engagement ring – but Yuri's mother gave it back to her, ensuring Aunt Anastasia still had something of his."

Mutti shook her head. "The poor woman."

I blinked. "That's what she called you."

Mutti looked confused, raising a questioning eyebrow.

I realised that once again I'd let my mouth lead me. "Umm ... I let slip that you had been in Ravensbrück."

Mutti sighed. "*Liebling*, I know you trust Aunt Anastasia, but you must be more careful." She stared from beneath her eyebrows. "Please ..."

I shared a contrite look. "Yes, Mutti ... Oh, but it's probably helped us I slipped up. Aunt Anastasia says there are a few survivors of the death camps here in Brisbane. She's not sure if any were in Ravensbrück, though."

Mutti blinked several times. "I'd not thought of that – but it seems unlikely as the Russians arrived there, not the western allies."

"I'll see if she can find out more, shall I?"

"That's a good idea."

Lying in bed that night stroking a purring *Imbi*, my questions about Mutti kept circling. That Mutti was hiding some part of herself from me seemed possible. I was dozing when I sat up, disturbing *Imbi*, who retreated to the foot of the bed.

During my interrogation when we defected, my interrogator had been asking about my parents when she stopped and left the room. She had realised something didn't seem right. I let out a frustrated breath – but they'd let us into England and moved us here.

It can't have been about Mutti – it must have been about my father.

I struggled to remember what we had been talking about. I knew I'd written about it in my diary – but they'd taken that from me as a security risk.

Come on, Col – think.

But while I could see my interrogator's face – Jennifer, the name leapt out at me – I couldn't remember the detail of that talk. *Imbi* walked up my body, standing on my chest, staring into my eyes. I reached up to stroke behind his ears. He settled, sliding down beside me as he drifted off to sleep. Despite my questions about Mutti, I soon followed him.

• • • •

MAY TRAVELLED INTO June, the temperature in the mornings falling. I needed a thin jumper over my T-shirt when I ran: runs that started in the darkest greys of almost dawn. Sometimes Euan was there at the end – but as the cold weather took a deeper hold, his appearances became scarcer. Swimming stopped as the pool became too cold and wouldn't start again until late September. I pushed harder in my runs and with the weights, trying to keep my fitness at a reasonable level and build strength in my shoulders.

My time at the Polish and German clubs produced nothing worth a report. I was worried that Mr Franks might get impatient, but Mutti reassured me that all was well there – no news was good news. Mr Caune found me a copy of Lem's *Solaris* and it felt as if my life was finding a settled rhythm after the vast changes in the previous twelve months.

My Saturdays with Aunt Anastasia were part of that continuing rhythm. She'd been teaching me about the important people in the Russian community. She surprised me with two photographs of me taken at the ball. These delighted Mutti and aroused Lizzie's envy when she came round one day. Aunt Anastasia's diamond necklace was notable in both.

Two weeks before the Korolev's party, I went to Finney Isles again – this time without Aunt Anastasia as she was suffering from a severe cold. I'd felt uneasy spending her money, but she's assured me that this was part of our work and told me to enjoy the shopping.

I was under orders to find a 'suitable outfit' for an afternoon cocktail party. As I walked into Finney-Isles, I still felt like an imposter, with everyone's disapproving eyes following my gauche moves. Aunt Anastasia had organised Sandra to take care of me again. She helped me select a blue floral dress that was quite short, with half sleeves and a square neckline. It was not a miniskirt, as Sandra said that would not be appropriate, but still well above the knee. To go with the dress, we found lingerie, a small handbag and shoes that matched the blue in the dress. Michelle helped me with a blue eyeshadow, mascara and a new fragrance. Apparently, daytime fragrances differ from evening ones.

With my dress in a dust bag and everything else in a Finney-Isles carry bag, I walked through the city up to Aunt Anastasia's flat.

"Come in, come in, Kal." She smiled at the bags I was carrying and sneezed.

"Bless you."

A lace-edged handkerchief appeared from the cuff of her cardigan and she dabbed her nose. "How did the shopping expedition go?"

I laid the dust bag over a dining chair and put the Finney-Isles bag on the seat. "I think it went well, thank you. Here, I'll show you." I picked up the dust bag to open it.

"No, no, dear." She waved me off with a smile. "Dress. I want the complete picture."

"Okay."

I picked up everything and changed in 'my' bedroom, touching up the makeup sitting at the dressing table. From the bedroom, I walked towards Aunt Anastasia, who smiled and indicated I should do a twirl. The dress lifted and my hands moved to my thighs to control it.

Aunt Anastasia chuckled. "That's not as short as many I've seen, but you need to be careful."

Clearly.

"Now sit down."

I dropped into the other chair in my usual way – and the skirt rode a long way up my thighs.

"That won't do at all, Kal." She shook her head. "You look lovely, but you must sit more gracefully. Sit at the front of the seat and slide back a little once you are seated."

I tried again.

"Better – again."

After several more tries, Aunt Anastasia looked satisfied. "Remember not to move fast – and watch out for the wind."

I stood up. "I'd better change."

"In a moment, Kal. There's a box on the dining table. Please bring it here."

I'd not noticed the box – a jewellery case. Inside was a gold necklace with a delicate gold pendant in the shape of the double-headed Russian eagle, two small diamonds glinting in its claws.

"Kneel, Kal."

I did so, removing Willi's chain and leaning forward to make it easier.

"There." Her hands left my neck and I straightened.

Aunt Anastasia smiled, but with a misty look in her eyes.

"Yuri gave me that for Christmas in 1903." She sighed and lifted my chin. "It suits a youthful neck."

I reached up and took her hand. "Thank you for letting me wear this."

Aunt Anastasia held my hand between hers. "It's my pleasure, Karlota. Jewellery exists to be worn and this," she reached out to touch the pendant where it hung below my throat, "has waited many years." Her smile was wistful. "Look at yourself in the mirror."

I walked across to the mirror, tilting it to see myself from head to foot. As I found when wearing the finery for the ball, I barely recognised myself in the sophisticated reflection. I tried several poses, admiring myself. With a twirl, my panties appeared; Aunt Anastasia had not exaggerated the problem. A much slower turn lifted the dress, but it was no longer immodest.

"I'd better change and get lunch."

Aunt Anastasia smiled and picked up the Russian newspaper. After changing into my usual clothes and removing the make-up, we spent lunch and an hour after talking about the Russian community. Aunt Anastasia told me who would be at the party and why they were important.

"Hang your new things up in the bedroom, Karlota."

Leaving them here made sense.

In the sitting room, Aunt Anastasia looked across at me. "As you're not swimming next Saturday, can you get here earlier?"

"Of course."

"Good. We'll have an early lunch before we dress. We should arrive at the Korolev's house about half-past three."

I glanced at the mantelpiece where the invitation card leant next to the elegant clock. "I thought the invitation said three o'clock."

"It does. But we are important guests – and we need to let the less important people arrive before us."

I frowned in confusion. "I don't understand – and anyway, I'm not important."

Aunt Anastasia frowned. "Sergei Korolev asked for you by name – that makes you important. But," her face relaxed into a smile, "you are arriving with me and that alone makes you important. After the ball, you are a person of some interest in the Russian community."

I made a sour face. "Your pet German."

Aunt Anastasia fixed me with her pale blue eyes. "You know that's not true. The woman who said that wants my position and is angry because I refuse to die." She waved a dismissive hand. "Her jealousy is of no account."

"Why am I interesting to the Russian community? I'm boring me."

Aunt Anastasia pulled me in front of her. "But you are interesting — young, beautiful and mysterious." Her eyes twinkled at this. "You are my protégée and ... you danced with the sons of all the important Russian families here in Brisbane." She gave my hands a gentle shake. "Add to that, you speak better Russian than those sons – and some of their parents."

I shook my head in disbelief.

Aunt Anastasia smiled. "Yes – you are all of those. Believe me." Her demeanour became serious. "At the party, you need to be self-assured and a touch mysterious. Listen, but speak little." She raised an eyebrow. "I don't think people will be indiscreet – but you never know; listen to the conversations around you and remember them. Some guests will not know you speak Russian." She raised an eyebrow. "We still have a job to do."

"Yes, of course." But it was easy to forget that when being treated as someone special, like at the ball. I started as a thought occurred to me. "That man's not going to be there, is he?"

Aunt Anastasia sneezed again, her silver hair catching the window light and the handkerchief appeared again. "I doubt it, Karlota, but if he is, it doesn't matter. We know what's going on – he only thinks he knows." She looked up at me. "But we still need to satisfy that man to keep all three of us safe."

"Okay."

"Off you go. Take care and I'll see you early next Saturday."

"I hope you are over the cold soon." I turned at the door and gave her a wave. On the ferry, I refreshed my memory about the next chapter of *Death in Venice*.

The German book club was more relaxed this week with no Mr Neumann creating a scene. I sensed unease at the homosexual undercurrent in the book, but the more we read, the more sympathy I had for Gustav.

Is this because I had already struggled, knowing Willi was a seventy-year-old mind in a teenage body?

This sort of echoed Gustav's feelings in reverse. Of course, I could not explain that to the book club. Over a cup of tea once the discussion wound up, I told them I would be absent next week as I had a personal engagement.

Miss Bauer raised an eyebrow. "Is everything all right, Karlota?"

"Of course. I have another engagement."

Miss Bauer almost asked for more information. Instead, she pulled this week's German newspaper from her bag. "I'll save next weeks for you as well."

"Thank you, Miss Bauer."

During the week, school was school and my slow integration into Lizzie's group continued. The girls accepted I was a private person, reluctant to share much about myself. I watched as the lies slid from my tongue when sharing became necessary, leaving a greasy feeling in my stomach.

On Saturday, I ran and then travelled into the city with Mutti. I spent some time browsing, ending up in Mr Caune's shop before walking up to

Aunt Anastasia's flat. I found her sitting in the window chair, wrapped in the beautiful silk robe, but with a rug around her legs.

"Good morning, Aunt Anastasia. Are you feeling better?"

"Yes, thank you, dear."

"Tea?"

"Please."

Ten minutes later, we were sipping tea, talking about the day ahead. Aunt Anastasia quizzed me about the important people from the Russian community that would be there. "When we arrive, these people will greet me. Make sure you remember their faces and their names."

I'd lean on Mutti's training for this.

"Of course, you met all these people at the Ball."

"But I wasn't introduced. I never heard their names."

Aunt Anastasia's voice hardened. "Don't make excuses, Kal. I'm sure you'll recognise these people; you're an observant person. All you have to do is to link their names to their faces."

"Yes, Aunt Anastasia."

She smiled with approval. "Now, I think it is time for you to read to me and practice your pronunciation." She passed me the Russian newspaper. "There's an interesting article on page four about buying houses in Australia. Start with that, please."

I read that and several related articles out loud, recognising some names that were involved from the card index Mutti and I were building — amongst them, Sergei Korolev.

After the fourth article, I stopped and looked at Aunt Anastasia. "Is this paper doing a special on property?"

She smiled. "Indeed. It's quite serendipitous, given this afternoon's party."

I folded the paper. "Can you tell me why you are interested in Sergei Korolev?"

Aunt Anastasia's eyes became distant. "I'm not sure why. He's tried unsuccessfully on several occasions to involve me in projects as an investor." She stopped for a few seconds before continuing, her voice softer. "There was nothing I could put my finger on but ... they did not feel quite ... right." She shrugged. "I prefer to be in control."

Her eyes refocussed on mine and she pursed her lips. "How he got his start-up funds is a mystery. I believe he arrived as a displaced person from Europe in 1948 with his wife, young son and the clothes he was wearing ..." Her eyes lost their focus again.

"What are you hoping I will discover by associating with Maxim?"

Aunt Anastasia stiffened in surprise. "I'm sorry, Karlota. I was deep in thought. What was that?"

"You want me to get close to Maxim Korolev. What are you hoping I will find out?"

She shook her head. "I don't know..." her eyes narrowed. "... anything you can. If there's anything to find out, it will be a jigsaw piece at a time, I'm afraid – and those pieces may never form a picture."

It all seemed vague, but Mutti had schooled me that what we were doing involved the accumulation of detail.

Aunt Anastasia roused herself. "Come on, let's have lunch. There's a beef stroganoff simmering in the oven – just the thing to give us the stamina to last through one of Sergei's parties."

I gave Aunt Anastasia a confused look. "If it starts at three o'clock, when will it finish?"

"They will usher out most guests by about half-past six, but we will stay much later. Didn't I tell you?"

I frowned. "No, you didn't. How much later?"

Aunt Anastasia saw my frowning face. "Oh, I'm sorry, Karlota. I sometimes forget details. We'll be there until late – around midnight. I meant to tell you to bring overnight things ... and, of course, your mother doesn't know."

I could see she was getting quite upset with herself. "It's all right, Aunt Anastasia. I'll ring Mutti at work and tell her I'm staying with you tonight."

"But you've nothing here."

I chuckled. "For one night, I'm sure I can survive."

Aunt Anastasia shook her head at her forgetfulness. "I'm sorry, Karlota."

"It'll be fine." I gave her a reassuring smile. "Can I ring Mutti from your phone, please?"

"Of course."

Ten minutes later, I'd got through to Mutti at the Ladies Fashion counter by pretending to be a customer and asking for her by name. Once she realised it was me, I explained what had happened and that I'd be staying with Aunt Anastasia overnight as the party would run late. I could hear Mutti was not happy and would quiz me about this tomorrow, but she agreed to let me stay overnight.

The aroma from the Stroganoff was now permeating the flat, encouraging my appetite. I set the table and retrieved the casserole from the oven, placing it on a cork mat.

"This smells wonderful, Aunt Anastasia. Did you make this?"

She smiled. "It's my mother's recipe – but no, I did not make it. I have an arrangement with a group of Russian ladies who prepare many of my meals."

We ate in silence for a while. I noticed that Aunt Anastasia's portion was spare compared to mine.

"Eat up, Karlota. There will be some *hors d'oeuvres* at some point, but supper will be late." She looked across at my emptying plate. "Some more?"

"Yes, thank you."

We finished eating and I cleaned up, putting the remaining Stroganoff in the fridge.

"The necklace for today is in the box on the table, Karlota."

"Thank you, Aunt Anastasia."

My make-up skill were improving. I dressed and was ready well before Aunt Anastasia returned from her room, supported by her silver-topped cane. She had an embroidered dark blue brocade jacket over a cream blouse and black silk skirt, carrying a silk shawl over one arm.

"Come here please, Karlota. I'm worried that you might be cold today." She held up the cream shawl to show me the delicate Chinese landscape at its centre. "This is hand painted silk and the blue exactly matches your dress."

She draped it over my shoulders, showing me how to catch the ends over my arms. She indicated I should turn. "Excellent."

At a quarter-past-three, the doorbell rang. "That will be the taxi. Help me downstairs, please Karlota."

We descended the stairs and into the taxi, Aunt Anastasia supporting herself on my shoulder.

The Korolev's house was in Hamilton, looking down across the river – and it was huge, several stories high. As planned by Aunt Anastasia, we arrived about half-an-hour after the party started. The taxi stopped at the gates, guarded by a large man in a suit.

He held the door for Aunt Anastasia as I went round to help her. Once Aunt Anastasia unfolded herself from the taxi, she steadied herself on the cane and took my offered arm.

"Thank you." We walked up to the front door, where Mr Korolev himself greeted us. Someone must have been watching out for Aunt Anastasia and alerted him.

"Welcome, 'Tasia, you are looking well."

"Thank you, Sergei."

"If you go through the house, Karlota, you'll find the young people out by the pool." His face and voice revealed nothing.

I looked at Aunt Anastasia, who smiled. "Off you go, dear. Have fun."

I set off through the house, passing a large room filled with older people talking. Deeper into the house was a kitchen on the left, bustling with caterers. I came to a games room with folding doors opening onto the pool area where about twenty young people were talking. Maxim was with a small group of young men and didn't notice me.

I picked up a coke from an esky loaded with bottles sticking up in the crushed ice and stood listening to the conversation from a nearby group of girls. It took me a few minutes to work out they were trying to impress one another. I'd heard talk like this from the 'in' group at school, but I didn't recognise any of these girls. I was the subject of a few sideways glances from the girls as they tried to work out who I was, but none of them approached me.

After about a minute, Maxim noticed me. "Karlota, welcome." He walked across to me. "My apologies. I didn't see you there."

From the corner of my eye, I noticed my name meant something to at least one girl, who turned and started whispering to her group.

"Good afternoon, Maxim."

He took my hand and his eyes swept across me. "You look lovely."

"Thank you."

He guided me across to the group of young men and – as if this was a signal – several girls moved to join the group. Introductions were made and I worked on fixing names with faces as the conversation flowed around me. The role of the girls was to stand, look beautiful and nod in agreement with their men and this made the task easier. Several of the surnames were in our index files, but linking them to their parents was important.

It was easy for me to stay mute and listen, which I did for some time. I finished my drink and wandered over to the esky. I crouched to acquire another coke, Aunt Anastasia's warning about my skirt sounding in my head. As I stood, a shadow fell over me.

"You're this mystery girl we've been hearing about." The voice belonged to a red-haired girl taller than me, wearing a pale green pants suit and large, gold ring earrings.

I sipped my coke, returning her gaze. "I don't think I'm mysterious. I'm me."

She reached across and held the Russian eagle hanging at my throat with her fingers. She let it go and looked with narrowed eyes. "Well, despite that, I know you're not Russian. Where are you from?"

I let my much-suppressed teasing side out and answered her in Russian. "I'm Karlota, half English and half German".

She blinked – not a Russian speaker.

My tease took over and I tried her again, in Polish, German and finally French. I was smiling as I finished.

"You're Karlota and you're ... English and German?" Her head was on one side as her eyes narrowed again, trying to size me up.

I raised my eyebrows in acknowledgement.

She regarded me for a few more seconds before her shoulders relaxed and she took a sip from the wineglass in her hand. "Do you speak all those languages?"

"Yes, I do – and English."

She laughed and put out her hand. "I'm Deborah. Pleased to meet you." Her face changed. "You speak French, German, Russian and," her voice had a touch of wonder. "... what was the other one?"

"Polish."

"Goodness. And you're a friend of Madame Zaytseva?"

I smiled. "Do you speak Spanish?" My tease still in command.

Deborah blinked in confusion. "No ... what makes you think I do?"

I awarded her a mischievous look. "All these questions made me wonder if you were from the Inquisition."

Deborah's eyes crinkled into a smile. "Very good."

We shared the smile for a moment.

"Call me Deb. And ... Karlota ..." She stumbled over the multiple different pronunciations she'd heard, particularly the way I had emphasised my Rs. "... is quite a mouthful..."

"I'm Kal to my friends."

"Well, I hope we can be friends, Kal, as I can't see myself rolling my R's the way you do." She took another sip of wine. "You didn't answer my question."

"Which one was that?"

"Madame Zaytseva..."

I wasn't sure where this was heading. "Yes – we're sort of friends."

"You were at the Easter Ball with her, weren't you? There was a photo of you dancing with Maxim in the Russian newspaper."

I gave her a non-committal nod.

Deborah's eyes narrowed. "The ball and that photo caused a stir. Maxim is the most eligible Russian bachelor. My mother's always trying to push me into his path," she sniffed. "Like all the other mothers."

Maxim must be quite a catch to be the matrimonial target of the Russian mothers.

"Your mother's Russian."

Deb chuckled. "I'm a half-breed, like you. My father's Irish."

"But you've not learned Russian from your mother?"

She frowned in surprise. "Why would I do that? This is Australia and we all speak English." She paused, subjecting me to a speculative look. "But I think I understand about your languages. You had to learn English, didn't you?"

"We lived in Germany when I was little – I learned English when we moved to England."

How easily the lies slip out ... but at least that was a half-truth.

"That explains English and German. What about the others?"

I shrugged. "I had a Polish friend in England and we swapped languages. I'm learning French at school and Madame Zaytseva is teaching me Russian. She thinks I have a talent for languages."

"I'd say she was right," Deb smiled, looking across the pool. "You've been hanging around in the background – come and meet some of the girls."

With that, she whisked me over to a group of half a dozen girls, all in their late teens or early twenties. After Deb introduced me round, the conversation soon veered to gossip about who was going out with whom and which couples had split up. I noticed Maxim arrive from deeper in the house and walk over to the group I was in.

"Please excuse me, ladies. My mother wishes to meet Karlota."

He took my hand. "Is that all right, Karlota?"

I allowed myself to be led through the house.

Maxim glanced into the large reception room. "Hmm ... mother and her friends must have retreated upstairs to her sitting room for a while."

Maxim pulled on my hand, heading for the stairs. "Let's get this over."

What is going on here?

Upstairs, I heard conversation as Maxim led me along the first-floor landing and into a sitting room where a group of ladies – including Aunt Anastasia – sat talking.

One of them rose to her feet. "Maxim, thank you for bringing Karlota to meet me." She smiled at me. "Come here and sit down, please." She waved a hand at the sofa where she had been sitting.

I glanced at Maxim and his nod suggested I should do as his mother asked. She sat down, patting the cushion beside her. I walked across and sat gracefully, I hoped, on the edge of the cushion.

Her eyes inspected me, lingering for a moment on the necklace before quizzing me in Russian. "Maxim tells me you speak excellent Russian."

My eyes flicked to Aunt Anastasia.

Is this some kind of test?

"Thank you, Madame Korolev. I have an excellent teacher." I answered in Russian, glancing at Aunt Anastasia.

She then interrogated me — in Russian. My answers were short and I allowed my nervousness to show. Madame Korolev would, I hope, interpret that as resulting from her questions, rather than me being circumspect with my answers.

Maxim stood by the door, embarrassed at what was occurring.

After about five minutes, Madame Korolev gave me a thin smile. She looked over at Maxim. "I've kept you and Karlota from your young friends for long enough. Off you go. Enjoy yourselves." She turned to me "It's been lovely to get to know you."

I could taste the insincerity in her voice. "Thank you, Madame Korolev." I stood up and walked across to Maxim, who guided us out into the corridor, but instead of heading downstairs, he turned us down a corridor, where he stopped. He looked at me, his body tense with acute embarrassment.

"I'm sorry, Karlota. I did not know she was going to interrogate you like that." His voice was low and intense.

I gave him a dark look. "What was that all about?"

He shushed me with his hands. "Keep your voice down." He looked along the corridor. "I think you've been interviewed as a potential companion."

"For your mother?" I gasped with surprise.

A smile flickered across Maxim's face. "Of course not – for me. And I think you passed."

Careful, Kal. Don't be eager. "I have a boyfriend."

Maxim gave me a quizzical look.

I used a breath to push down thoughts of Willi. "... but he's in England."

"So, it won't be awkward for us to be seen together around town?"

I stayed silent, giving him no encouragement.

His hand almost reached out to me. Instead, he started twining his tie round a finger. "Can I explain what I think is going on?"

I raised a questioning eyebrow.

"Mother, well, father, is concerned about finding the right partner for me. I won't marry ..." a strange expression passed across his face at this thought. "... for a few years, as my parents want me to concentrate on my studies." His discomfort grew more palpable. "I think they want me to use you as a ..." he searched for the right word. "... a placeholder, to keep the Russian mothers at bay ... until I am few years older."

A placeholder?

"Won't they be worried that you'll end up with me?"

Maxim's eyes dropped to the carpet for several seconds before he looked up at me, his facing pleading for forgiveness. "No." He swallowed several times. "They know I could never marry a ... a German."

I thought for a few seconds, astounded at the manipulative way this society operated, thankful Mutti was different.

"I promise all we'll do is be seen around town. I won't make any other ..." he gave an embarrassed laugh "... demands of you."

Memories of cuddling up with Willi on the sofa in Herne Bay flashed through me. "You'd better not."

He shook his head, a smile touching his lips. "Believe me, I won't."

What am I missing?

"All right – but I have a busy life and you'll need to fit in around that."

"Fair enough."

"And right now, I would like you to show me where the toilet is."

"There's one down here." He pointed to a door further down the corridor. "Will you be able to find your way downstairs?"

I gave him a guarded smile. "I think I can manage that."

The door led into a palatial bathroom. I did my business and freshened my lipstick in front of the huge mirror. Staring at myself, I thought over the conversation with Madame Korolev and Maxim's strange explanation. Much of the girl talk I heard at school was about trying to hold boys' wandering hands at bay. I had not experienced that with Willi – in fact, it had been me that wanted to explore faster. I was glad Maxim was not interested in that.

Why isn't he interested?

The memory of Lili's Christmas party bubbled up. I was still masquerading as a boy; Lili saw Willi and I kissing and assumed we were homosexual. That could have exploded our friendship and our cover – but we convinced her I was a girl and our three-way friendship deepened.

Is Maxim interested in boys, not girls?

Something to watch, anyway.

I checked my dress was hanging correctly. Why I opened the door with care, I couldn't say. Perhaps it was because I was in the depths of a strange house. With the door open a few centimetres, I heard the voices of two men.

"...need the government's approval."

"Yes. And we know how to get that."

That's Sergei Korolev's voice.

"Fair enough. And the finance?"

"I'm still working on that."

"You don't sound confident about it."

"Leave it with me."

"Hmm ... we have to move soon."

Footsteps headed off down the corridor. I waited, listening at the crack of the door. I inched it open and peered out. The corridor was empty – but I could see a door further down that was closed earlier was now ajar.

Dare I look?

I walked down the corridor and paused, listening.

Nothing.

I pushed the door open –an office with a heavy dark wood desk, bookshelves and leather chairs. Indecision held me at the door for a moment before I moved to the desk. Papers lay in a tray with a couple lying on the desk. The Soviet hammer and sickle on one caught my eye. It was from an undersecretary at the Soviet embassy in Canberra, confirming the in-principal agreement with Jacaranda Constructions, the Korolev company. Unfortunately, the letter gave no more details. The other loose papers on the desk gave no clue about the agreement.

I could feel my heart beating faster: time to leave.

At the door I paused, listening, but all was quiet. I glanced at the tray full of papers.

No – too risky.

I slipped into the toilet to give myself time to calm down. This was the first time I'd taken such a risk; I was pleased with myself but not sure about doing it again. After a minute, I washed my hands and walked out along the corridor and downstairs to Maxim.

At about six o'clock, people started to leave. Maxim told me to go upstairs to the room where I had met his mother. Aunt Anastasia was there and I sat down next to her, itching to share what I had seen, but it would have to wait until later.

The rest of the party was boring. We sat down to a formal dinner with polite conversation that did not involve me, giving me plenty of time to observe people. I identified the other voice I had heard upstairs as a man called Alex. People also addressed him as 'minister' – but he was no priest.

The evening wound down before ten o'clock, which was much earlier than Aunt Anastasia expected. I helped her into a taxi. Once we'd made it – with great care – up the stairs and I'd helped her sit in her favourite chair, she gave me an exhausted smile.

"A glass of tea, perhaps?"

Some minutes later, I brought out a tray with two tea glasses and we sat, sipping in silence. I could see Aunt Anastasia was tired and decided what I had discovered could wait until morning. Tea finished, we headed to bed. Lying there, I tried to put the information into some context, but I didn't know enough.

I woke at my usual time, without the help of my alarm that sat at home. Without my running gear, I walked in the Botanic Gardens, arriving as the sun rose. The air was still and wisps of mist writhed above the river's surface in the chancy air. Back in the flat, I showered and dressed. It was too chilly for a robe. I sat, reading the last part of *Der Tod in Venedig*.

Aunt Anastasia stirred about an hour later and I prepared tea. I heard her stick tapping on the floor and she found me in the kitchen. "Excellent, Kal. I thought I smelled the aroma of tea." She headed to her usual chair in the window.

I carried in the tray, passed a tea glass to her and sat sipping mine.

After about a minute, Aunt Anastasia smile at me. "How was the party?"

"Pretty boring." I saw her wince at that assessment. "But I have some information that I don't understand."

Aunt Anastasia raised an eyebrow, leaning forward. "What information?"

I told her about what I'd overheard and seen in the study – and that the other voice I'd identified as 'Alex' or 'minister' during dinner.

Aunt Anastasia relaxed into her chair. "Hmm ... Sergei has some sort of deal involving the Soviets. The 'Alex' you identified is Alex Dewar, the Queensland Minister for industrial development." She looked across at me. "Do you think he's involved in the deal?"

I shrugged. "I don't know. But wouldn't it be odd for there to be those papers on the desk if he wasn't involved?"

"Indeed. And how are we going to report this to 'that man'?"

I smiled at her picking up the way we referred to Mr Franks. "We'll have to do it separately. We still want that man to think we don't know about each other, don't we?"

"Of course." She pondered for a moment. "I'll tell him about the closeness of Sergei with the minister at dinner. You can tell him about the letter you saw and identify the other voice as 'Alex' and 'minister' – but not know who he is." She looked at me for agreement. "How does that sound?"

And that's the way we played it, with Mutti putting in a report via the dead drop system. I wondered how Aunt Anastasia sent in her reports.

Once our report was in, I discovered a major frustration as the weeks passed. We did not know how they used our information; nor did Aunt Anastasia when I asked her. Mutti reminded me we had a tiny piece of the story — and it might all be completely innocent. It was the same with the occasional bit of information from the Polish club and I still had nothing of interest from the German club.

I accompanied Maxim to several posh dinner dances over the rest of winter and although we danced many times, he was as good as his word: his hands never wandered. Despite this, the unfriendly gaze of quite a few mothers of eligible daughters seemed to follow me. Spending time with Maxim, I got to know Paul well, Maxim's close friend from university.

My suspicions about the pair grew – but I had nothing concrete. My time with Willi when he thought I was a boy ... and what I'd read in the literature of Europe was not enough to challenge them. It was none of my business, anyway.

As winter warmed into spring, I saw Euan more regularly on my runs, accompanied by the growing and obedient puppy. Swimming started again and I found my work on the weights had born fruit – or I'd grown. Whichever, I was now a definite long distance 'prospect' for the coming season, according to the coach. My birthday was late in the season, but he thought he could swing it for me to swim the 800-meter and 1500-meter races from the start in early October.

On the tram home, I realised that in a few weeks we would have been in Australia for a year. Despite being uneasy about all the unavoidable lies, I was feeling safe. We were keeping Mr Franks at bay. My father had not found us.

Nor had the police found any trace of Gruber.

Chapter 15
Late September 1965 – early February 1968

September – spring in Australia – brings brilliant colours to Brisbane, at least to my European eyes. They have planted the city and suburbs with thousands of Jacaranda trees that blossom before their leaves appear. It was that pinkish purple haze colouring the city I had seen from the window of the plane as we arrived a year ago. The trees shed their blossom into a carpet under the trees – but if it's wet, I'd discovered the carpet becomes a skating rink that will dump you on your behind. Late spring – October – brings the flame-red Poinciana blossom against the brilliant green of their new fern-like leaves; this lasts through into January. After a thunderstorm, the Poincianas are dark-trunked monks under thick green cowls. They stand in pools of steaming blood – the blossom stripped from the tree glistening as the sun heats the rain to vapour.

The first weekend of the new school term, I looked over my "Willi letters". I had filled one and a half bound A4 notebooks and my determination not to edit them was proving difficult. I had described Aunt Anastasia when I first met her as "an old-fashioned schoolteacher, stuck in her ways" – which embarrasses me each time I read it. My times with Maxim worried me. I was writing about them, but what would Willi think? I was as clear as possible Maxim meant nothing to me, but still …

That had me thinking about Willi and other girls – such as Lili.

Would they tempt him to forget about me?

Perhaps, but the gentle and unhurried way he had dealt with me and my confused desires gave me confidence.

With the start of school, all my previous activities had started again. On top of those, Aunt Anastasia expected me to accompany her to various Christmas events and the New Year ball. I was expecting Maxim (or was it his father) to require me for a variety of appearances. To prepare me for these social demands, Aunt Anastasia arranged for us to visit Finney-Isles one Saturday in late October. This allowed us to arrange a suitable set of outfits for the Christmas party season. The wardrobe in 'my' bedroom at her flat was becoming extensive. Leaving these clothes and accessories in Aunt Anastasia's flat helped my unease at the money she was spending on me. Mutti had tried to contribute, but Aunt Anastasia had always refused the offers with firm but gentle grace. Mutti told her about the money we received from Mr Franks, but Aunt Anastasia still refused.

The Polish and German Clubs had events in December to which I received invitations – invitations that included bringing a partner.

They left me in a quandary.

Should I ask Maxim to accompany me?

He was Russian (well, in heritage) and that would be unwelcome at both places and raise uncomfortable questions about how we met. I spoke with both Mutti and Aunt Anastasia and they disagreed. Aunt Anastasia believed I should take Maxim to 'my' events. This horrified Mutti, as it would cause problems for me at the clubs. We couldn't risk that and I explained the problem to Aunt Anastasia. She finally agreed that taking Maxim was not a good idea. I think she's fixated on the Soviets and doesn't understand that, for Mr Franks, information on the German and Polish émigré communities was as important. If we stopped being his link because I the clubs barred me, he'd threatened to expose us to the *Stasi* and KGB.

My lack of a partner was on my mind as I drank tea and chatted with Miss Bauer at the German book club in November. After talking about the current book, I overcame my nerves and asked her if I could come alone to the German Club Christmas party, as I didn't have a partner.

"Surely there are young men chasing you?" She asked, surprised.

"Not one. I'm at a girl's school. There are young men at the swimming club, but they're not interested in the German girl." I pulled a face.

"Hmmm." She gave me a sympathetic look. "It would be a shame for you to miss out. I'm sure you'll find some other young people to be with at the party." She thought for a moment. "I am going alone this year." She raised a questioning eyebrow. "You could sit with me and my friends, if you like?"

"Oh – thank you."

"Consider it settled. We'll sort out the arrangements nearer the time." She smiled and looked me up and down. "It's quite a formal affair. Do you have something to wear ... a cocktail dress?"

For the Polish and German clubs, I was planning to wear the dress I had worn to Maxim's party. "I think so." I described the dress to her.

"That sound perfect. Oh, before I forget ..." She reached into a carrier bag. "Here's this week's paper for you."

"Thank you. These are a great help." Of course, I didn't explain that they helped with much more than my German reading skills.

She glanced across the room – the organiser of the book club, Mr Fraser, was waving at her.

"Excuse me, it seems John needs me for something."

"That's fine. See you next week, Miss Bauer."

"Indeed." She smiled and I headed home.

On Thursday at the Polish Club, I spoke to Mrs Jaworski about the Christmas party and coming alone.

She cocked her head sideways. "Ha – no need for you to come alone. I will find a nice Polish boy to escort you."

This was awkward. I couldn't say no and risk the relationship I had with her and the club. "Um ... I'm quite shy with boys ..." It was the best I could come up with on the spur of the moment and had the advantage of some truth.

Mrs Jaworski pursed her lips, smiling in understanding. "Don't worry, Karlota, I will find you a nice, polite Polish boy."

Her matchmaking antennae twitched in anticipation, but she could see I was uneasy.

"It's okay, Karlota." She smiled. "You wait, I'll find you someone nice."

All this build-up had me feeling quite anxious about Christmas and it was only early November. Mutti noticed my tension and sat me down. When I explained what was going on, she gave me a wry smile.

"If I didn't know better, I'd call you a social butterfly, flitting from one party to the next." Her smile was full of understanding. "But I know that's not the way you are."

We shared a moment's silence and Mutti leant across to take my hand. "Is this about the lies you have to tell?"

I took a deep breath, thinking. "Yes ... no ... well, yes ... I suppose underneath everything else it is."

"What do you mean, *Liebling*?"

I had been trying to work out why I was feeling anxious and in a flash of insight, I knew. "Control – I have almost no control over my life."

Mutti thought for a moment and gave my hand a squeeze. "I'm not sure what we can do about it."

"We have to keep that wretched man happy." My shoulders slumped and the silence extended.

The weather continued to warm as November progressed, but somehow it didn't seem as hot as last year. We were becoming acclimatised, I suppose. End of year exams at school arrived and I was confident walking in – and remained so walking out.

Lizzie and I grew closer during the year – thanks to our shared time at swimming and school. I was still 'the quiet one' in her group, but a few asked me for assistance in French, which helped.

I arranged with Aunt Anastasia to stay with her the nights of the German and Polish club parties. The Polish club Christmas party was the first Saturday in December, followed a week later by the German club. I planned to catch the tram as I always did, but Aunt Anastasia wouldn't hear of it. She arranged a taxi to take me and gave me the number to call for the taxi at the end of the evening.

After I changed, Aunt Anastasia looked up from her book. "Do a twirl, Karlota."

Mindful of the shortness of the skirt, I rotated slowly.

Aunt Anastasia chuckled. "Very good." She looked me up and down. "I don't think the Russian eagle would be appropriate for tonight."

"Neither do I." I smiled. "Tonight, I will be happy wearing Willi's gold chain."

When I arrived at the Polish club, Mrs Jaworski took me by the hand and led me across the room. "Karlota, this is Janusz. Janusz, this is Karlota. I would like you to look after her this evening."

Janusz looked younger than me, with dark hair and brown eyes hiding behind thick glasses. He did not seem thrilled to be with me. We sat next to one another for a few minutes in an awkward silence. I had to find something to do and saw Mrs Jaworski bustling around with platters of food.

I stood up. "Excuse me, Janusz, I need to help Mrs Jaworski."

He gave me a blank look. I walked into the kitchen. "Can I help you, Mrs Jaworski?"

"Oh, Karlota. Would you? Thank you." She pointed to a fridge. "There are sandwiches in boxes that need to be arranged on the platters over there." She whisked an apron off a hook. "Here you are – you mustn't get spills on that beautiful dress."

Sometime later, she chased me out. "Thank you for your help. Now find Janusz and have some fun."

I wandered through the club without finding him, but I saw a group of young people out on the unlit veranda. I slipped outside and ambled towards them, looking for Janusz but not wanting to be seen if he wasn't there.

As I approached, a voice lifted over the others. "Janusz, what are you doing with that German girl? Won't any of the decent Polish girls dance with you?"

I stopped, staying in the shadows.

"She's not German, she's English." At least he was trying to defend me.

"Rubbish, Janusz. She's half German and that makes her a Nazi. Why they let her in here is beyond me." The speaker towered over Janusz, pushing him and forcing him against the wall. "You stay away from her."

Janusz stayed silent and the large boy grabbed him by the shoulder. "Stay away from her, or else."

"Yes, Szymon." Janusz quaked.

The large boy pushed Janusz back into the wall and turned, laughing, to his friends.

I slipped inside, anger and shame warring inside me; anger at the bully and shame at what my father and his generation had done to Poland and its people. I wanted to find somewhere to be alone and lick my wounds, but running away would risk my connection here. I retreated to the safety of Mrs Jaworski's kitchen.

"Karlota. Why are you here?"

I tried to plaster a more cheerful aspect on my face, but Mrs Jaworski saw through it.

"What's happened, Karlota?" Her expression was a strange mix of sympathy and frustration at the interruption.

"It doesn't matter, Mrs Jaworski." My eyes were pleading. I couldn't go out there. "Let me help you with the food."

I received a long stare before her face relaxed.

"Okay, but we'll talk later." She reached up and a fresh apron flew off the hook towards me.

I spent the next hour helping prepare and carry platters of finger food into the bar and the tables set up in the room we used for Polish classes, then a further hour washing platters and cleaning up the kitchen. Once we were done and aprons doffed, Mrs Jaworski sat on one chair, dragged another across with a foot and pulled off her shoes to rest her feet.

"Ooh ... that's better." She wriggled her toes and pointed to at another chair. "Now, sit down, Karlota and tell me what happened." Her face darkened. "Janusz behaved himself, I hope?"

"Oh yes, he didn't do anything wrong."

"Good. But you didn't spend the evening with him."

I sighed and explained. "You and others here are kind to me ..." I came to a stop. I didn't know how to explain without giving offence.

"But..." Her eyes were penetrating. "You're German ... and not everyone accepts you?"

"But it's not Janusz's fault. A boy called Szymon bullied him."

She sighed. "Karlota, I'm sorry that's happening to you." Her eyes drifted away from mine. "There are people here who had," her lips pursed for a moment, "a terrible time during the war ... and their feelings have trickled down to their children." She frowned. "But that Szymon Nowak is a real bully. I'll speak to his parents ... again."

I sat ... I'd been here before.

Mrs Jaworski's eyes returned to mine. "But you should know that many people here at the club are impressed with the help you provide me." She smiled. "And you are doing well in your Polish class, too."

I dropped my eyes, embarrassed. "Thank you."

"No, thank you, Karlota." She thought for a moment, before slipping her feet off the chair and into her shoes. "Come along. I'll introduce you to a few more of the senior members of the club."

Rather against my will, Mrs Jaworski escorted me into the bar, where she introduced me around, in Polish, as her best helper. Mr Taciak and Mr

Franc remembered me from the time they interviewed me and they were polite in their thanks but guarded. I met several other people – a few were parents of students in the Polish class – and Mrs Jaworski was effusive in her praise. All the same, I sensed uneasiness at the idea of a German girl being involved in their club.

I ended up standing next to my Polish teacher, Mrs Kowalczyk, who had an amused smile on her lips. "Mrs Jaworski has been singing your praises, Karlota."

I blushed. "I wish she hadn't."

"She had her reasons, I think." She raised an eyebrow. "Some people here harbour ill-will towards Germans and that must make things ... uncomfortable for you?"

I sighed. "It was like this in England."

Mrs Kowalczyk's smile was sympathetic. "I expect all this will fade as the years pass, but that doesn't help you now."

I smiled wryly. "It could be worse."

"Worse ... how?" Mrs Kowalczyk sounded bemused/

I gave her a mischievous smile. "If I was half German and half Japanese."

Mrs Kowalczyk chuckled. "Very true."

We chatted about books for a while. I glanced at the clock above the bar – it was fast approaching ten o'clock. "I have to go."

"Are you coming to Polish classes next year, Karlota?"

"Yes, of course ... if that's all right?" Keeping Mr Franks at bay required I attend.

Mrs Kowalczyk smiled at me. "You're one of my best students, but your Polish is not yet perfect. I'd be delighted to have you there."

My smile was part relief and I summoned my best Polish. "Happy Christmas. Mrs Kowalczyk. See you in the new year."

"You too."

I found Mrs Jaworski and she let me phone for the taxi, which deposited me at Aunt Anastasia's flat. She was still up, although wearing her Chinese robe.

"Shall I make tea?"

"Thank you, Karlota. That would be nice – and you can tell me all about the party."

A few minutes later, I brought out the tea glasses. As we sat there, I recounted the evening's events.

"I'm afraid there are people like that boy ... what was his name?"

"Szymon ... Szymon Nowak."

Mutti's memory training at work...

"Ah yes ... there are people like Szymon Nowak in every nationality, wishing to dominate others." She looked over the rim of her tea glass. "We know of one Australian right here in Brisbane."

I smiled in agreement.

Aunt Anastasia finished her tea, placing her tea-glass on the tray. "But we're trying our best to outsmart him – or at least keep him at bay, aren't we?" Her look held the fierce determination that had seen her through many vicissitudes across the decades.

"Of course."

I helped her stand and we headed off to bed.

• • • •

IN THE COOL OF THE early morning, I ran several circuits in the Botanic Gardens before returning to shower and prepare breakfast for the two of us. We lingered over our tea, chatting about the upcoming social events.

Mutti was sitting listening to the radio when I arrived home.

"Did you have fun?"

"No, it wasn't a fun night."

She gave me a sympathetic and questioning look; I sat down next to her and explained what had happened.

When I finished, Mutti pulled a glum face. "I'm sorry, *Liebling*."

"Oh, Mutti. It's not your fault everyone hates Germans. You are a victim of the Nazis, too." I closed my eyes for a moment, sighing in frustration. "I wish I could tell people that you and thousands of other Germans were in the death camps – along with the Jews, the Romani, the Russians, the Poles, the homosexuals – and some English girls."

Mutti leant across to pat my hand. "But you can't – and you know why."

I sagged into my chair. "That man." I looked across at Mutti. "How can we ever free ourselves from him?"

Mutti shook her head. "I don't know ... if the KGB and *Stasi* ceased to exist..." her voice trailed off.

It had happened in Willi's world, but not until the late eighties, when the whole of the Eastern Bloc collapsed like a house of cards.

Would that man run our lives until then?

For the Christmas party at the German club, I again stayed the night with Aunt Anastasia. Miss Bauer met me outside the club. She had arranged a table comprising members of the book club and their friends. Literary discussion made the evening pass pleasantly, warding off the darkness I felt.

Christmas came and went – as did the Russian New Year ball. For that, Maxim sat with me at Aunt Anastasia's table and I felt the heated glowers of the Russian mothers focus on me. It seemed word had gone out and not one young man I danced with at Easter approached our table. I noticed the occasional speculative glance in my direction as they passed in a waltz or quickstep. I hated being the focus of such ill-will.

Aunt Anastasia sensed this and leant across, taking my hand. "Don't worry, Karlota. You are doubly protected sitting here with me and Sergei's son." Her gaze swept round the hall, her ice-blue eyes quenching the mothers' ire – at least for the moment.

• • • •

AFTER NEW YEAR, LIZZIE again departed for the Gold Coast with her family and I leaving me to my own devices. I ran, worked on the weights each day and swam several times a week, but those rhythms could not dissolve the grey surrounding me. It sapped more of my will as each day passed. Mutti watched and I knew she was worried, but we both knew she was powerless to change our situation.

When Lizzie returned, we met at the pool, but her bubbling personality could not rouse me. She persuaded me to race, but I let her power away from me.

She was standing waiting for me when I reached the wall and leant down, pulling me out. We walked over to our towels and I saw concern and questions on her face.

"What's wrong, Kal?"

I sat, trapped in my fog, looking across the pool as it sparkled in the brilliant sunshine. She was my best friend and I must keep lying to her.

"I'm fine." It was almost a whisper.

She grabbed my arm, turning me towards her. "No, you're not." Her voice held a fierceness I'd not heard before. "You haven't been fine for ... well, since before Christmas."

I dropped my eyes from hers, but she bent forward, holding my shoulder, looking up at me.

"Something's not right, Kal. I'm worried about you." Her face softened. "Please, let me help."

I squeezed my eyes shut, my hands crushing my wet hair across my scalp.

What could I say?

Finally, I shrugged.

Lizzie's eyes demanded more.

I stumbled, searching for a response that would satisfy her. "I ... umm ... my life's ... flat ... at the moment."

"I don't understand." Lizzie frowned. "You're being squired to posh parties and balls by a handsome Russian, wearing gorgeous jewels and clothes ... and you're not enjoying that?"

I examined my toenails. They needed trimming. "You'd love that – but it's not me." I gave her a thin smile. "I want to sit at home, cuddle *Imbi* and read."

Lizzie opened her mouth – but closed it again. She gave me a sideways look. "You mean that?" She held my eyes, searching, confusion in her voice. "You do."

We sat in silence for a while before Lizzie grabbed my arm. "Come on, Kal. You're going to race me." Her face hovered a few centimetres in front of mine. "And this time you're going to beat me."

She tossed my towel down onto the chair and led me to a pair of empty lanes.

"Four lengths – your distance." She stood me at the head of a lane. "... ready ... go." She dived and I teetered for a moment, almost diving, but stood there.

After a few strokes, Lizzie realised I was not swimming. She turned and swam towards me.

"Snap out of it, Kal." Fiery spots of frustration stood out on her cheeks. "Swim."

She turned and powered down the lane. I watched for a few seconds before turning to pick up my towel and head for the changing rooms. I knew I was hurting her, but all the lies were crushing me. I half expected her to find me before I walked out to catch my tram, but she didn't.

Mutti watched me pick at my food that evening and had to chase me out of bed for breakfast.

"You didn't run?"

I shrugged. When she asked me what I was planning for the day, I sighed. I could see her struggling with my attitude, but she left me to my mood. I sat on the veranda with *Imbi,* unable to summon the effort to read. About an hour later, the phone rang. Deciding to answer or ignore it was beyond me. I sat until it stopped. A minute later, it rang again and I fled inside myself.

I don't think I slept, but I wasn't aware of anything until a shadow fell on me – Lizzie kneeling beside my chair.

She watched me fail to meet her gaze and enfolded me in a deep hug. After some time, she leant away. "I don't know what's wrong, Kal. But I want to help." She was hesitant, tentative. "If I can."

I could not respond, head down and hair cloaking my face.

Lizzie's hand brushed the hair from my eyes. "Well, if I can't help, I'll be your friend."

The tears trickled down my cheeks.

"Oh, Kal." Lizzie pulled me into another deep hug and we stayed that way for a while before she rocked onto her heels. "My knees are killing me."

She pulled a veranda chair round in front of me and sat, our knees almost touching, red spots on hers from the kneeling. She looked around, searching for understanding, stroking *Imbi,* who stretched luxuriously.

"I'm here, Kal, whenever you need me ..." Her eyes were full of care. "For whatever."

"Thank you, Lizzie." A surge of gratitude came close to bursting the dam holding in our secrets. I shivered in fear, causing silent questions to scurry over Lizzie's face.

We sat in silence before Lizzie gathered herself.

"I have to get home before my mother or she'll be mad at me." Lizzie crushed me in another hug. "Please take care of yourself, Kal."

I could see the lines of worry on her face as she turned away.

Once she'd gone, I sat there with *Imbi*, thinking over Lizzie's visit. She had the same worries about me that had tortured me with Willi. He was unstable and had come close to killing himself twice and I'd set Lili to help watch over him. Now I was feeling something similar and Lizzie had appointed herself to that role for me.

I'd made Willi promise to talk to me if he ever felt like that again – and now I travelled that same path, some distance behind him, but in his footsteps. Willi had promised me – but that promise worked both ways: it locked me into being there for him wherever he was: I must step off the path as Willi had done. The grey fog persisted in my mind, sapping the colour from my world. But I would push it away – somehow.

When Mutti arrived home, I hugged her. "I'm sorry about this morning."

Mutti's hand stroked my cheek. "You don't have to apologise, *Liebling*."

"But I do." I huffed out a breath. "I shouldn't let things overwhelm me."

Mutti placed her bag on the sofa and drew me into her arms. "We rely on one another, *Liebling*. Alone, we might not make it. We can do this – if we talk."

Supporting her was the resilience from surviving ten years in Nazi death camps.

If she could find her way through those years, I can do this. Can't I?

The following morning, Euan was there as I dragged myself around the oval. I pulled up a lap short of my usual run, struggling to find the will to push myself into the final circuit.

"Eh, lassie, ye's draggin' today."

I bent forward, catching my breath, resting my hands on my knees.

"The world's pressin' on ye?"

I stood up, nodding.

"'Tis nae good." He huffed. "Ye have ta press back, else ye'll be crushed." His 'r's rolled over me, breaking waves surging against my gloom.

I pulled a wry face, still sucking in deep breaths.

Euan sniffed. "Ye's young and fit. Ye have t' choose – push or gae under."

"And if I have no choice?" I tried to keep my voice neutral, but I heard the tinge of self-pity there.

From the look on Euan's face and the snap in his voice, he heard it too. "Ye've always a choice." His eyes drifted away over my head and his voice came from the distance of decades. "Ye can gi' up 'n run – or stand wi' ye mates as the guns thunder around ye ..."

I watched as he brought himself back into the present.

He stooped to fondle the collie's ears. "'Tis nae gunfire pressin' on ye. But whate'er 'tis, ye's not alone." His voice held fierce conviction. "There's alus people standin' with ye." His eyes gripped mine until his gaze forced a nod from me.

"Now, gae run another lap – and do this one proper, wi'out the lead in ye boots I saw afore."

A shiver ran through me as I set off. Euan was right – I was not alone: Lizzie, Euan, Aunt Anastasia and, of course, Mutti; they all stood with me, despite my secrets. When I looked up halfway through the lap. Euan was gone, his job done.

• • • •

MUTTI AND I KEPT GOING through the rest of 1966, with its switch from pounds to dollars in February, and on into 1967, much as we had our first year in Australia. Aunt Anastasia understood and helped. While Euan's words were sparse, he understood my life from watching me run, offering encouragement in his gorgeous Scottish accent. Lizzie did not know what my problem was and accepted I couldn't tell her; but she always supported me if I quavered, providing strength from beneath her bubbly encouragement.

In late September 1967, a knock on the door disturbed me from my Maths homework. When I opened it, a grey-haired woman was standing there.

"Karlota Miller?"

"Yes?"

"I'm Mrs Fraser, Euan MacDonald's niece from Melbourne. May I come in?"

I opened the door, leading her to sit down in the lounge. Euan had never mentioned other family. "How can I help you?"

She was silent, looking me over before speaking. "Euan passed away three days ago."

Oh, Euan.

I sat, disorientated by the news. "I didn't know he was sick – I saw him on my morning run a few days ago."

"It was quite sudden ... he would have been eighty-one next year."

She seemed unperturbed by losing her uncle.

Eighty was a wonderful age ... but I'll miss you, Euan.

"Anyway," she said. "You are mentioned in his will." She folded her hands in her lap. "Can I ask how you knew my uncle?"

Why would Euan mention me in his will?

"Oh ... umm." I dragged my attention to Euan's niece. "I run every morning on the oval where Euan walked Dodger, his dog. He had been a runner and ... we started talking."

"I didn't know that about him." There was curiosity in her voice.

"He told me he was training to race in the 1916 Berlin Olympics. They were cancelled because of the war. He helped me with my running."

And many other things ...

Mrs Fraser's face showed her surprise. "He must have been quite good if he was training for the Olympics." She looked down at her hands. "Umm ... his will gifts you a set of weights ... but I've no idea what that means. Can you help me?"

I smiled. "I can do better than that – I can show you." I stood up. "They're under the house where I use them."

Mrs Fraser followed me down and I showed her the weights.

"Oh – weightlifting weights." She glanced at me in understanding. "And you use these?"

"Oh yes – every day. I'm a swimmer and I use them to build my upper body strength."

"I'll let the solicitor know you already have the weights." She gave them another glance and turned to me. "The funeral will be in a few days. Would you like me to let you know when it is?"

"Yes, please."

When Mutti arrived home, I told her about Euan.

"I'd like to go to his funeral. Mrs Fraser promised to tell me when it would be."

"You'll need a black dress. And shoes."

Aunt Anastasia had insisted I have a black cocktail dress as more befitting my approach to womanhood. "I've a black cocktail dress and shoes at Aunt Anastasia's flat. Would that be suitable?"

"As long as it's a reasonable length."

I indicated two inches above my knee. "About there."

"That should be fine."

"Can I give Aunt Anastasia a ring and see if it's convenient for me to drop in after swimming tomorrow?"

"Of course."

I rang Aunt Anastasia. She said she would be delighted to see me.

I explained about Euan to Lizzie before school.

"Oh, Kal. That's sad." She pulled me into a hug before pulling away to peer at me. "Are you okay?"

"His niece told me would have been eighty-one next year – which is a good age."

"I suppose ..."

As we walked down to the pool after school, I told her about Euan leaving me his weights.

"It's good you have something to remember him by."

My fingers traced Willi's gold chain.

After swimming, I caught a tram into the city and walked up the stairs to Aunt Anastasia's flat, knocking on the door and announcing myself.

"Aunt Anastasia, it's me, Kal."

"Come in, Karlota." She waited for me to enter. "You should have let yourself in as usual." I could hear the half-scold in her voice.

"I thought it was too late to do that."

Aunt Anastasia shook her head. "I want you to think of this as your second home, Karlota."

"Thank you, Aunt Anastasia. But I didn't want to scare you by walking in unannounced."

"Nonsense, Karlota." Aunt Anastasia glanced at the clock. "Do you have time for a glass of tea?"

"Of course ... I'll get it."

Five minutes later, we were sipping our tea. The beautiful crystal glasses in their elegant, gilded holders never failed to enhance the experience.

Aunt Anastasia placed her tea on the table beside her. "I'm sorry to hear about your friend."

I took a deep breath. "Thank you, Aunt Anastasia. It's ... it was a strange friendship. Euan came to afternoon tea a couple of times, but usually we saw one another when I ran and he was walking his dog. Most days we would nod to one another in passing, but sometimes we would have a longer conversation."

"But he was important to you."

"Yes, he was." I took a stuttering breath. "He seemed to know when he needed to talk to me from how I was running. He helped me several times – and he's left me the weights in his will." Tears dribbled down my cheek.

Aunt Anastasia pulled a lace-edged hanky from her cuff and passed it to me. "Now you need to say goodbye to him at the funeral and pay him the respect he's due by dressing well."

We sat in contemplative silence for a while before I roused myself, returning the hanky. "I'd better put the dress and shoes in a dust bag and find a tram home."

Aunt Anastasia started to stand up. "I'll call you a taxi. You shouldn't be alone on the streets this late."

I knew better than to argue with her. I helped her stand and went into 'my' bedroom to organise the cocktail dress, handbag and shoes, adding my makeup bag as well.

The taxi deposited me home, where I hung the dust bag in my wardrobe.

Euan's funeral was on the following Monday. Mutti rang the school and told them I would be absent for the day. The funeral was a strange experience. I knew Mrs Fraser, but no-one else. Looking round, the chapel was filled with men of Euan's age. I could see a row of medals lying atop Euan's coffin. The men were wearing medals too, but Euan had served in the British, not Australian army.

Outside after the service, Mrs Fraser acknowledged me with a nod. A man of Euan's vintage approached me.

"Excuse me, Miss, would you like to write in the memorial book for Euan?"

I was startled at this. "I'm not his family – I'm a ... a friend, I suppose."

"Most of us here are not his family – but his friends," he explained. "This book will go to his family, but it's about Euan and his life." He paused for a moment. "Could I ask you how you know Euan?"

I could hear the uncertainty in his voice and thought for a moment. "All right – if you could explain why all these men are here?"

He smiled. "That's a deal." His gaze swept around the gathering. "As an ex-serviceman, Euan was a member of the RSL – we're here to pay our respects to a fellow soldier."

"Um – what's the RSL?"

The man cocked his head sideways. "It's the Returned Services League. An English girl doesn't know that?"

"I'm only half English and I've not been in Australia long."

"Oh. You're a new Australian." He questioned me with a look. "What's the other half?"

"German," and I waited for him to turn away.

He raised eyebrow. "Euan knew this?"

"Yes." I waited for the rejection.

His head tilted the other way. "You haven't told me how you knew him."

"I met him running."

"Euan was running?" he asked, astonished.

I blinked. "Err ... no. I was running, Euan was walking his dog."

"And you got talking?"

"Yes." All I wanted was to end the conversation and leave.

He must have heard the terseness in my voice and seen the tension in my body. "Please Miss, I don't hold it against you that you're part German – and it's clear Euan didn't."

I remained silent as our eyes engaged.

"Can we start again? Please?" That eyebrow lifted again. "I'm Major Jennings. Pleased to meet you, Miss ...?" He held out his hand.

Still unsure of where this was going, I shook his hand. "Karlota Miller."

"Pleased to meet you, Miss Miller. I would be grateful if you would write something about the Euan you knew in the memorial book." He gestured at a table to the side.

"All right." It was grudging, but it seemed I wouldn't escape until I did.

Once he had me standing in the queue beside the table, Major Jennings went in search of others. This gave me time to think about what I might write that would be meaningful to Euan's family. After a few minutes, I reached the front of the line and wrote, in German,

Dear Euan

Thank you for the advice and help you shared with a confused young German girl.

Karlota.

I wanted people –Euan's family in particular – to know that he had befriended and helped a lonely and confused German girl. It spoke volumes about Euan ... once they translated it.

I turned and made my way out, but Major Jennings stopped me.

"You wrote something in Euan's book?"

"Yes."

"Thank you."

I made my escape, wondering what they'd make of what I'd written.

At school the next day, Lizzie gave me a hug. Friendship that accepts secrets is rare.

• • • •

THE YEAR WOUND ON, with all my usual activities – school, swimming, the German and Polish clubs, accompanying Maxim to parties and accompanying Aunt Anastasia to functions at the Russian club. Within myself, I had pushed away the grey wall of fog, but its presence clouded any thought of the future. And it still worried me I had nothing of the slightest interest to report to Mr Franks, despite Mutti and Aunt Anastasia's reassurance.

Lying in bed one night, I remembered what Willi told me about the *Stasi* files being full of nothing more than reports of ordinary, everyday life. It seemed I was experiencing the same thing. When I had talked about this with Aunt Anastasia, she added that possibly the rise of Communist China was now of greater importance to Australia than the more distant threat of the Soviet empire.

Would Mr Franks end up releasing us because we were of no more use?

Imbi shifted against my side and I stroked him before we both descended into slumber.

For the Christmas party at the Polish club, I persuaded Mrs Jaworski to let me help her and not try to set me up with anyone. I spent much of the party in the kitchen or handing round platters of *hors d'oeuvres*. I caught the occasional glare, but most members accepted me. Several engaged me in brief conversations — in Polish and English. At the German club party, I sat with Miss Bauer and her friends again. We had a fun and literary evening ranging across English and German books. I was asked to dance by some of the young men, but I was careful not to dance with anyone more than once; I didn't want to lead anyone on. If pushed, I fingered Willi's necklace and told them I had a boyfriend who couldn't make it to the party.

Well – that's not a lie.

During the year, my suspicions about the relationship between Maxim and Paul had grown. Maxim squired me to the Russian ball on New Year's Eve and I tested him by dancing close. He moved me to a 'respectable' distance without changing his expression, which proved nothing. It caused baleful gazes from the mothers.

• • • •

THE END OF JANUARY 1968 saw me enter my final year of school. I was doing well in all my subjects, including in Maths – not at Willi's level to be sure, but a solid B to go with my A's. I now faced a real dilemma – what to do after school? And what to do about Mr Franks? After this year, I couldn't continue in the Polish classes. I'd had to persuade Mrs Kowalczyk to let me stay another year. According to her, my Polish was more than good enough. We discussed that and she relented, telling me she would expect me to help with teaching as much as sitting there learning. With no Polish classes, I would have lost my connection to the Polish community. Next year, I'd need to find another way to stay in touch for Mr Franks. I could stay at the German book club and Aunt Anastasia would keep me attending the Russian club.

Sunday afternoon, I was relaxing with *Imbi* lying beside my feet as it was too hot for both of us for him to sit on me, when the phone rang.

I glanced at Mutti sitting in the other veranda chair, who smiled and flicked her eyes from me to the phone.

Sighing – and to *Imbi's* meowed protest – I levered myself up to answer the phone.

"Hello, Karlota speaking."

"Karlota – it's Mr Caune." His voice was guarded. "Umm ... is your mother there?"

I looked towards the veranda. Mutti turned towards me. "Yes, she's here."

"Umm ... May I speak to her?"

Something in his tone clutched at my stomach. "Mr Caune, what's happened?"

I imagined him fidgeting with something to cope with his nervousness. "Well ... er ... Aunt Anastasia ..."

The line went silent.

"What about Aunt Anastasia?"

"Er ... I'm afraid that she died during the night."

I gasped, steadying myself as my world shifted. When I was there yesterday, she'd seemed unchanging, indestructible.

Mutti sensed that something was going on and came to stand next to me, her face questioning me. I put my hand over the mouthpiece. "Aunt Anastasia died during the night." I heard my voice crack with emotion.

Mutti's face morphed into concern and circled an arm round my shoulder.

"Karlota ... are you there?" The tinny voice came from my trembling hand. I lifted the handset up to my ear.

"Yes, Mr Caune. I'm sorry to hear that. Is your wife all right?"

"Umm – yes, she'll be fine, thank you."

"Is there anything I can do to help?"

"Err ... no, I don't think so, thank you."

"You'll be in touch with the funeral arrangements?"

"Of course."

I could think of anything else. "Thank you for letting me know, Mr Caune."

"Umm ... I'll be in touch soon. Goodbye."

"Goodbye."

I put the phone down and looked at Mutti.

"Are you all right, *Liebling*?"

Mutti pulled me into a comforting embrace.

After several seconds, I took a deep breath, seeking my centre of calm. "She was another mother to me – like you were for Willi."

"I know, *Liebling*. I know. Come and sit down."

Mutti's arms folded me into her. We sat on the couch in silence for a while as I remembered Aunt Anastasia's countless kindnesses. Another implication struck me. "What are we going to do about Mr Franks now we've lost the link to the Russian Club?"

Mutti shook her head. "I don't know. I'll send him a message and see what he says. We still have the Polish and German communities."

My sleep that night was disturbed and fitful. The rhythms of my morning run failed to soothe my inner turmoil. Losing Aunt Anastasia reinforced Euan's absence. As I slowed after the last lap, I could almost hear his voice chiding me... "Ye've people around you. Ger on wi'it."

I met Lizzie as usual outside the school and told her about Aunt Anastasia.

She pulled me into a hug. "Oh, Kal. I know she meant a lot to you."

I sighed. "She did."

"Will you be okay today?"

I hugged her back.

"I'll see you at lunchtime?"

"Of course." Our timetables didn't link up on Monday mornings.

Lizzie must have spread the word as several members of the group gave me a hug at lunch. I had not expected support from the wider group and it made me stop and think. Death was a difficult topic and I could see that, despite the hugs, they were uncertain and didn't know how to act or what to say.

The awkwardness built: wary glances and suppressed chatter. The hugs showed me they cared and I knew I should try to relieve their unease at death's intrusion into their lives. At the second break, I spoke up. "You've all heard that my friend, Aunt Anastasia, died yesterday." I gave a lopsided smile. "Well, she wasn't my aunt, but she was important to me — a second mother." My gaze traversed the group. I could see the tension remained. "Thank you all for your kind words and hugs. They're helping. I'll be down for a while, I expect, but if you carry on as normal, that will help me the most." There were a few tentative smiles in return, but the tension was releasing.

Lizzie pulled me into a hug. "Thank you, Kal."

Everyone else joined her and they surrounded me with their arms, love and compassion for a few unexpected seconds. They broke away and the usual chatter about school, boys, pop music and clothes started up, but I saw several glances in my direction.

It would take a while.

• • • •

ARRIVING HOME, I LET *Imbi* out and wandered into my room. Opening the cupboard, I fingered the clothes that Aunt Anastasia had bought for me, remembering each occasion I'd worn them. There were many more in 'my' room in Aunt Anastasia's flat.

Mr Caune might want me to return everything; I should speak to him about this. I did not feel anything Aunt Anastasia had purchased for me was mine. They were costumes I'd worn to play a role. I also had a key to the flat, which I should return. I was about to ring him when I stopped – he would have much more important things to worry about. There was no hurry with this.

I skipped swimming on Wednesday, asking Lizzie to apologise for me. Mr Caune rang after I arrived home to tell me the funeral would be on Saturday afternoon at two o'clock at St Nicholas' Russian Orthodox Cathedral. I jotted down the details on the pad we kept beside the phone and told Mutti about it when she arrived.

"You have a black dress to wear to the funeral?"

"Yes, but that outfit is at Aunt Anastasia's flat." I gave Mutti an anguished look. "Now what do I do?"

Mutti raised an eyebrow. "You'll have to ring Mr Caune. You can't walk in and take it."

"Of course not." That would feel like theft.

I rang Mr Caune's number, but his wife told me he was out. I explained who I was and asked if Mr Caune could please ring me, before or after school. She promised to pass the message along.

I was in the shower after my run when the phone rang on Thursday morning.

A minute later, Mutti stuck her head round the bathroom door. "Mr Caune's on the phone. Do you want me to tell him you'll call him?"

"No – I've finished."

I wrapped myself in a towel and padded into the lounge, dripping a little.

"Mr Caune, it's Karlota."

"Good morning, Karlota. You wanted me to ring."

"Yes ... it's awkward. Aunt Anastasia bought me lots of clothes and things and many of them are in my ... er ... a bedroom of her flat. The outfit I should wear to her funeral is in there. Please, can I come and collect it today after school?"

"Of course, Karlota. You have a key, don't you?"

"Yes ... and I wanted to talk to you about that – and all the clothes, shoes and things I have here. I'm not sure what to do. Should I return them all to her flat? I don't think they're mine to keep."

"Umm ..." There was silence for a second or so. "Don't worry about that right now." There was another long pause. "Please come and collect your outfit for the funeral ... and drop by and ... er ... have a word with me in the shop, please."

"Thank you, Mr Caune. I will."

"Er ... I'll see you this afternoon after school."

After I hung up, Mutti wrapped me in a hug, then held me at arms' length. "I think you are probably right about returning all the things she gave you," her voice became pensive. "Though I don't know what they'll do with them." She clapped her hands. "But right now, you need to get dressed."

After school, I headed straight to Mr Caune's shop. He was on the phone, but waved me through to the corridor and stairs that lead up to Aunt Anastasia's flat.

I stood on the threshold, half expecting to find her seated in her chair at the window. I walked across the room and sat opposite her chair, letting Aunt Anastasia's ambience settle on me. She had been such a large part of my life and I was already missing her strength. I wandered through the flat, running my fingers over the beautiful objects she had lived amongst – the ormolu clock, the crystal tea glasses with their elegant, gilded holders, the samovar, the Meissen China, her books. They all evoked vivid memories of her understated elegance, taste and intelligence. With a shake of my head, I went into 'my' room. I gathered up the outfit I needed for the funeral: black cocktail dress, stockings, black stilettos and matching handbag. I wondered if I'd need a hat.

Ask Mr Caune about that.

I pulled the small case from on top of the wardrobe and folded the dress and stockings, put in the shoes in a shoe-bag, added my makeup kit and the handbag

In the centre of the lounge-room I stood, capturing its scent, bidding its memories farewell. I doubted I would be here again. Downstairs, Mr

Caune was off the phone and he started fiddling with things on the counter as soon as he saw me.

"You collected your outfit?"

"Yes, thank you."

Ask about hats.

"Mr Caune, should I wear a hat for the funeral?"

He shook his head, hands brushing invisible specks of dust off the small stack of books at one end of the counter. "Older women will wear hats, I expect." His nervous glance flicked across me before returning to the desk. "But not you young things."

My key clicked on the glass counter. "Here's my key."

Mr Caune was still for a moment, his eyes holding mine. "Thank you for helping to look after ... after her." His eyes dropped away and his hands straightened several books on the counter stack before his eyes darted up to mine. "I know she valued your company highly." A reluctant hand reached out to pick up the key.

"Thank you, Mr Caune." I turned away, feeling that an entire episode of my life was ending.

"Don't be a stranger, Karlota." The words tumbled over one another in a nervous rush. "There are many books here that would like to be your friends." His eyes held mine for an unusual moment.

My throat was choked with emotion. All I could to was nod and walk out into the street. For a moment I thought about going home instead of to the Polish club, but the spectre of Mr Franks pushed me onto the tram to Milton.

• • • •

AUNT ANASTASIA'S FUNERAL on Saturday afternoon was ... difficult. I had half-hoped Maxim would phone and ask me to accompany him, but he did not call. I arrived early and found a seat in a corner of St Nicholas, trying to be inconspicuous — but Mr Caune noticed me and smiled. Sitting there, I realised a hat would have helped me remain inconspicuous. I wanted to pay my respects to Aunt Anastasia but was unsure of my reception from some in the Russian community. The lack of a call from Maxim presaged that now Aunt Anastasia was dead, I would no longer be welcome.

The service was quite long, with much ritual. At one point, they invited people to rise and walk past Aunt Anastasia's coffin. I stayed seated – she would have understood. At the end of the service, I slipped away, although I saw Mr Mikhailov, the president of the Russian club, look in my direction. I decided I would say my personal goodbye to Aunt Anastasia at her grave in the South Brisbane cemetery in a week or two.

At home, I changed and sat on the veranda with *Imbi,* worrying about the Mr Franks implications. But the deep sadness at the loss of my friend occupied most of my thoughts. This woman who had started as my teacher and became my mentor, friend and second mother. Her passing signalled that my time as an interloper in the Russian community was at an end – and warned of problems with that man.

This all became much more complicated on Wednesday. An invitation to visit a solicitor in the city to discuss my inheritance from Miss Zaytseva arrived in the mail.

Chapter 16
Early February – late December 1968

I arranged to visit the solicitor's office on Friday afternoon after school. On Thursday I struggled at school and in the Polish class but disappeared before anyone could ask me questions – although I caught a puzzled look from Mrs Kowalczyk. I was more distracted at school on Friday.

What does 'my inheritance' imply? Euan had gifted me his weights ...

The solicitor's offices in Eagle Street made me feel small: high ceilings and dark polished wood with an enveloping silence barely disturbed by the click of a typewriter. A thirtyish woman sat typing at reception, hair pulled into a tight bun above a pinched face. Her eyes flicked to me in my school uniform when I walked in, but she returned to her typing.

I stood for a moment, summoning the confidence to interrupt her. "Excuse me, I'm Karlota Miller. I have an appointment with Mr Jameson." My words vied with the rapid clack of the typewriter.

The sound continued for some seconds before she glanced at me. "Take a seat, please." She dialled a number and spoke into the phone.

I sat there for several minutes as she continued typing before standing up. "Come with me, please."

I followed her to a door with "Mr Jameson, Senior Partner" lettered in gold script. The woman knocked, waited for a moment and opened the door.

"Miss Karlota Miller to see you, sir."

A lean, balding man in his fifties stood up. "Come in, please, Miss Miller."

He indicated a chair in front of his desk and sat after me. He glanced at a file open on his desk and steepled his hands. "Miss Miller, I hope you don't mind me asking, but how old are you?"

"I'll be eighteen in about three weeks."

"Hmm ... that makes things more complicated." It seemed he was speaking to himself more than me. He turned a page in the file.

I sat in silence, waiting for him to continue.

He took a deep breath. "Madame Zaytseva was a wealthy woman who had no heirs. Her most recent Will is clear about what she wished to happen with that wealth after her death."

I didn't know what to say.

"There are several bequests to various people and one to the Russian Club here in Brisbane, subject to certain conditions." His eyes were boring into mine. "But Miss Zaytseva has left a large part of the estate to you."

I blinked.

Mr Jameson's keen eyes inspected me for a long second.

"I do not know the exact value of the estate and there are death duties to pay, of course. But I estimate that your share will be around a million dollars."

The hair rose in a wave across my arms and head. That sum was beyond immediate comprehension.

Mr Jameson steepled his hands again, fixing me with a penetrating gaze. "Did Madame Zaytseva know your age?"

I fought my way out of its daze to bring my mind to his question. "Yes. Yes, she did."

A million dollars?

"Hmm." He paused, looking down at the file. "Knowing your age, it seems strange that she did not make provision for a trust." He looked up at me. "But you are underage, which I had not realised. I will need to speak with your father about this."

I was confused and for a moment. Momentary panic threatened at the thought of him contacting my father in east Germany. "My father is dead."

"Hmmm – your mother?"

"My mother's Frida Miller."

"Very well. Please ask her to phone this office to make an appointment. I will need to draw up fresh papers." He looked up. "There are a few other matters to discuss and that discussion is best done with your mother present."

I was still trying to come to terms with what was happening.

Mr Jameson gave me an appraising look. "Young lady, this is probably quite shocking news for you – not bad news, but nonetheless …

unexpected. I would suggest that you do not discuss the matter with anyone apart from your mother."

It didn't feel real to me, anyway.

Why had Aunt Anastasia done this?

Mr Jameson stood up. "Please ask you mother to contact me as soon as possible." He handed me a business card.

I stood up. "I will."

He walked round the desk and opened his office door. "I will see you soon. Good afternoon, Miss Miller."

On the street, this news had dazed me, but I mustered enough brain power to get myself home. I was still trying to come to terms with this when Mutti arrived, turning on the radio as usual and kissing me on the forehead.

"What did the solicitor want, *Liebling*?"

"It was about Aunt Anastasia's will. I knew she was well off but didn't realise that she was truly wealthy." I could see confusion on Mutti's face. "She has left me a huge amount of money."

Mutti blinked. "By huge, what do you mean?"

"The solicitor said it would be around a million dollars."

Mutti turned and plonked down beside me. *"Liebe Gott. Ich glaub' ich spinne."* She almost fell onto the sofa, shaking her head in disbelief.

"Quite." I gave her a quirky smile. "And Mr Jameson, the solicitor, needs to speak to you because I'm underage." I passed her his business card.

Mutti looked down at the business card. "Is this real?"

I shrugged. "I don't know – but I think it must be."

Mutti took a deep breath. "Well, first thing, this stays a secret – we're not going to tell anyone about this." She gave me a serious look. "Not the slightest hint."

"Mr Jameson suggested that as well."

We sat in silence for about a minute before Mutti stood. "Come on, *Liebling*, let's get tea.

At swimming in the morning, Lizzie noticed I was out of it – and my swimming was well off the pace.

"What's wrong with you this morning, Kal? Your mind's not on the job. Are you sick?" Coach was aggressive and I flinched at his outburst.

Lizzie was on to him. "Go easy, coach. A friend of hers died this week."

His face flushed with embarrassment. "Sorry, Karlota. I didn't know." He stood for a moment and turned away to harass some other poor swimmer.

Lizzie gave me a hug. "Are you okay, Kal?"

"Sorry, Lizzie." I sighed, looking down. "It takes getting used to." My eyes moistened. "After swimming, I used to go straight to her flat." Lizzie drew me into another hug.

After some seconds, I pulled away. "Thank you, Lizzie."

"Come and sit down." She led me towards where our towels were. "I have to go – my race is up next."

"I'm coming with you, to cheer you on." Staying involved would stop my thoughts from spiraling off.

Lizzie smiled – and blitzed the field. She's getting better all the time.

When we changed and walked out, Lizzie turned to me. "What are you doing now?"

"I thought I'd head into the city and browse the bookshops."

Lizzie gave me a diffident look. "You can come home with me, if you like."

"Thanks Lizzie," I gave her hand a squeeze. "But I need to spend some time trying to sort my head out."

Lizzie looked unconvinced.

I squeezed her hand again. "Thank you for the offer, but I'll see you at school on Monday."

She drew me into a hug. As I walked into the city, an aching, empty tract of time opened before me. My steps pulled me towards Mr Caune's bookshop, but I forced myself past. I couldn't visit right now. I bought a sandwich at a milk bar and walked down to the Botanic Gardens and sat there eating it before catching the ferry to the German club.

I was early and we sat around for a while.

Miss Bauer picked up my mood. "Is everything okay, Karlota? You weren't here last week."

"I'm sorry Miss Bauer. I completely forgot to phone and let the club know I wouldn't be there." I paused for a moment, wondering if I should say more. "I was at a friend's funeral."

Miss Bauer took my hand. "I'm sorry to hear that, Karlota. Please let me know if there's anything I can do."

"Thank you."

After the book club meeting, Miss Bauer produced two weeks of German papers and passed them over with an encouraging smile. "Take care of yourself, Karlota."

"Thank you, Miss Bauer."

At home, I sat reading with *Imbi* until I heard Mutti on the stairs.

"I've had a message from that man." Mutti pulled a face. "We are to continue on as before for the moment."

"What do we do now that I've lost my Russian contact?"

Mutti shrugged. "Nothing, it would seem." She sat for a moment. "I contacted the solicitor's office. We have an appointment at four o'clock on Monday – and I was told to bring our passports, for identification, I suppose."

I pulled out the German newspapers and we set to work on those before tea. The meeting on Monday afternoon was a distraction for me for the rest of the weekend. The solicitor had mentioned he had 'a few other matters' to discuss and I wondered about those. This distraction continued at school on Monday and I drew several disapproving looks from my teachers.

I walked to the solicitor's office after school, arriving early. The secretary directed me to sit and wait. Mutti arrived and at four o'clock the secretary showed us into Mr Jameson's office.

"Good afternoon, Mrs Miller, Miss Miller. Please take a seat."

After we sat, he smiled at Mutti. "Mrs Miller, did you bring your passports?"

Mutti retrieved them from her handbag and passed them across.

Mr Jameson paged through them, glancing up to check our faces against the photos. He made a note on a pad of paper and returned them to Mutti. "Thank you. Those seem in order."

He turned the pages of a thick file on his desk. "Madame Zaytseva's Will is explicit in a number of places concerning your daughter, Mrs Miller. Please allow me to detail these and then I will be happy to answer questions."

I looked at Mutti, who gave Mr Jameson a nod.

"Very well. The contents of Madame Zaytseva's flat are to go to Miss Miller, but not the building itself." He looked up from the papers. "You will need to arrange clearance of the flat at a later date with this office."

I am to have all of Aunt Anastasia's beautiful possessions?

"Except for a ruby and emerald necklace and earring set, all Madame Zaytseva's jewellery is willed to Miss Miller."

That's the one she said was for an older woman ... Mrs Caune?

"Madame Zaytseva's other assets are an extensive share portfolio and various properties here in Brisbane. To meet death duties and the other bequest, we will need to sell some of these assets." Mr Jameson looked up. "I would suggest that we handled this through the sale of one or more of the properties rather than shares; the commercial property market here in Brisbane is quite buoyant at present." His eyes returned to the file and he checked some detail. "The last item is a bequest to the Russian Club here in Brisbane – but it is conditional and involves you, Miss Miller."

I shifted in my chair. "Involves me?"

"Indeed. The bequest is not small and has two conditions. First, the Russian Club must grant you, Miss Miller, life membership. Second, they directed all expenditure from the bequest to the creation and maintenance of Russian language skills in Brisbane." He raised his head from the file to look at me. "And that expenditure is subject to Miss Miller's approval."

I blinked.

Aunt Anastasia has set things up to let me continue in the Russian club as a member — and one with some influence. But would the club accept the conditions that placed a German in a position of influence?

Mr Jameson looked up. "If the Russian Club cannot accept the conditions, the bequest returns to Miss Miller."

Mutti and I shared a rather confused look.

"You have questions, I suspect?" Mr Jameson steepled his hands, waiting for us.

Mutti leant forward. "When you say, 'not small' – how much is the bequest to the Russian Club?"

Mr Jameson pursed his lips. "Hmm ... as you are involved, it seems reasonable that you should know. The amount is fifty thousand dollars."

I glanced at Mutti and turned to Mr Jameson. "Please, could you tell me what 'shares' are – shares of what?"

Mr Jameson gave me a small, patronising smile. "Shares are shares in publicly traded companies on the Australian stock exchange. Their value changes with the profitability of the company. Shares generate income each year through their dividends – a particular amount of money per share depending on the company's profits. Last year, Madame Zaytseva's share portfolio generated about thirty thousand dollars in dividends. From this year, that money will be paid to you, Miss Miller, once Madame Zaytseva's affairs are settled."

Mutti's eyebrows went up. "Is that the amount for this year? What about other years?"

Mr Jameson smiled at her. "The amount varies from year to year depending on the profits made by the companies. Madame Zaytseva has ... er ... had a well-balanced portfolio and I expect it to continue to produce similar income in future years."

Mutti sank into her chair.

"Do you have any other questions?"

I looked at Mutti, giving my head a shake. She turned to Mr Jameson. "What is my daughter to do with all this money?" She looked across at me. "I don't mean how is she to spend it, but how does she look after it? We know nothing about shares ... or commercial property ... or anything to do with this."

"An excellent question, Mrs Miller." He considered this for a moment. "Madame Zaytseva used a well-regarded firm of stockbrokers to manage her shares. Another company specialising in that area managed her properties. She engaged a well-known accounting firm to see to her taxation affairs. We will continue with those arrangements as Madame Zaytseva's executors and can arrange meetings at the appropriate time. You can continue with them for your daughter if you wish."

That sounded sensible. "What about the Russian Club?"

"With whom do you think I should speak at the Russian Club?"

"The club president is Dmitri Mikhailov. He and Aunt ... er ... Madame Zaytseva were friends. I think he would be the person to speak to."

Mr Jameson blinked at the name and passed me a piece of paper. "Please, could you write that name down for me?"

I wrote the name in both English and Cyrillic scripts and handed it to him.

Dmitri Mikhailov

Дмитрий Михайлов

Mr Jameson looked at the paper. "You speak and write Russian?" I could hear an edge of disbelief in his voice.

"Yes. Madame Zaytseva taught me."

"I see." An eyebrow lifted as he regarded me. "That illuminates the conditions on the Russian Club bequest."

He seemed to be talking to himself more than Mutti or me.

"Very well, I will contact him and progress the matter." He stood up. "My secretary has some papers for you to complete and sign."

He came round his desk and shook both our hands. "I will be in touch with you once we can finalise Madame Zaytseva's estate."

"Thank you, Mr Jameson."

In the outer office, they sat us down at a desk and asked us to complete a small stack of typed forms. Once the secretary checked we had filled them in correctly, we left the office and caught a tram home, both of us silenced by events.

Two weeks later, Mr Jameson rang me at home after school to advise me that the Russian Club had agreed in principle to the conditions on the bequest, but that agreement could not be put into effect until the estate was finalised.

After swimming on Saturday, I purchased a bouquet of white roses and visited the south Brisbane cemetery. It has a large section of Russian graves and I found Aunt Anastasia's. I laid the roses on her grave and sat beside it, tears rolling down my face as I thanked her in silence for everything she'd done. After a while, the tears stopped and I could speak.

I placed a hand on the headstone. "Dearest Aunt Anastasia, you know I'm not religious, but I hope that, if there is an afterlife, you have found Yuri waiting to envelop you in his loving arms and you find the bliss you were both denied." I took a settling breath and sat. "You have showered money on me and I have no idea what to do with it, but I will find something useful, something you'd be proud of."

The silence of the cemetery engulfed me. After a time of contemplation, I rose and stood in front of her grave. "But there is one thing I can tell you I will do – and that is find Willi – and my real self."

She would approve of that.

The thought of walking away from her brought fresh tears to my eyes. "I love you, Aunt Anastasia." My throat worked as I turned and walked away. My pace quickened as I feared going slower would end up with me returning to her grave.

• • • •

I TURNED EIGHTEEN IN February and joined the Polish and German clubs as an adult member. This caused a small amount of consternation at the former and smiles at the latter. Mutti and I decided I should stay away from the Russian Club for the moment.

Despite the wealth about to descend on me, life continued as before; the German book club was reading Schiller's poetry, Polish classes continued and swimming ended in early June as the pool was now too cold. School progressed, aiming at the Matriculation examinations in late October. I would take English literature, French, Maths B, History and German. I'd had a fight to be allowed to take the German exam. My school did not offer German, but they had finally relented and I studied from the language textbook, reading the set texts in free periods. I was lucky with these - Goethe's *Iphigenia auf Tauris* and Thomas Mann's *Der Tod in Venedig.* I'd pulled apart the Mann in the German Club and still had my much-annotated copy. Miss Bauer helped with the Goethe. She pointed out Goethe's depiction of Iphigenia as the ideal of a strong, independent woman, a perspective I took to heart. I saw echoes of Iphigenia in Aunt Anastasia and Mutti.

Then in August everything changed in Europe.

The Soviets tried to suppress moves towards freedom and democracy in Czechoslovakia by rolling their tanks into Prague. Mass protests and civil disobedience erupted across eastern Europe. Within a month, the Warsaw

Pact governments had all resigned and unrest spread to the USSR itself – and the Soviet Union was no more by early October. Willi had told me this collapse had happened in 1988 in his world. Perhaps his experiences with young people in east Germany had hinted at things happening faster than in his world. But as he hadn't been to East Germany in his previous life, it was just a feeling.

Mutti and I listened to the news every night. At first, the suppression of Czechoslovakia spread a dismal pall over us. But with each succeeding day, the situation improved and by the middle of September it was clear that the Eastern Bloc had disintegrated. The countries were making advances to the western European nations about joining the European Community. The collapse and splintering of the Soviet Union in October made the changes certain and marked the end of an era.

For Germany, the situation was more complex. Germany existed as two separate countries stained with Nazi guilt. But both east and west Germany wanted to re-unite. In Australia, there was some concern about a re-united Germany. Australians had volunteered in their tens of thousands to serve in 1914 and the death toll had been horrific for such a small country, over sixty thousand. The toll for Australia in the second war had not been as great in Europe, but my experiences had shown me that Germans were still regarded with lingering distrust.

Would the European powers allow them to re-unite?

The news one evening in early September reported they had disbanded the Stasi. People could view their own *Stasi* file. The breath whooshed out of me and it took seconds for me to gasp in a fresh supply. I needed several other deep, centre-seeking breaths.

"Mutti." The hope was almost strangling me. "If they have disbanded the Stasi, that means father can't hunt us down." I shivered as weird feelings of entwined hope and fear coursed through me. "Doesn't it?"

She sat there, silenced by the news. Finally, she turned to me. "We need to be careful about this, but I think you're right."

"And ... that man can no longer blackmail us."

Mutti pursed her lips in thought. "Well, not about telling your father. But remember how he controlled Aunt Anastasia – by threatening to reveal her to the Russian community? And there's still the KGB – at least for the moment."

My mood sank.

"He might try that sort of blackmail with us." Mutti thought for a minute. "But I'm not sure he'll want us – or can afford us – anymore." She looked across at me with a faint smile on her lips. "If there are any communist agents in the Russian, German or Polish communities, I suspect they are feeling quite lost and isolated."

A flutter of hope began deep within me again. "You think we can be free? We can be ourselves – not his ... and her ... pawns?" Underneath the hope was a flicker of anger at Mrs Henderson – but the hope was flooding through me, its blaze suffocating the anger. "We can return to England?"

Mutti's eyes held mine. "Home is Leipzig, *Liebling*, not England ..."

I pursed my lips. "But England first."

"I understand." Mutti took in a lengthy breath. "But we must sort out that man before we can do anything."

My lips thinned at that thought.

"And you need to finish school."

I grimaced at that – I wanted to leap on a plane to England now.

"*Liebling.*"

I could hear the warning in Mutti's voice and my unwilling eyes turned to her.

"*Liebling.* We have survived these years by being careful and cautious, and you have done this well." I could see the love in her eyes – it reached inside me and calmed my impatience as her hand stroked my arm. "We must continue like that. There is still no-one on our side ... except us."

"I have to keep living and telling the lies?" That familiar, greasy darkness was there, trying to smother the hope.

Mutti sighed. "Yes – both of us must, for now." I could see the distaste on her face. "And we have to do that until we re-establish our real identities." She paused for a moment and a dark look passed across her face. "If that's possible."

"What do you mean?"

"Who knows what bridges that woman burned in building these identities for us?" She shook her head. "We may never reclaim our real identities ... I don't know."

I shivered again at that thought. After a moment, I pulled Mutti's left arm to me – she always wore long sleeves. I undid the cuff on her left sleeve and slid the sleeve up to her elbow, revealing the blue numbers tattooed on her forearm. "You have these to prove who you are."

Mutti's breath was stuttering as she hugged me with intensity. We stayed clasped in each other's arms for a while. Sitting up, she released me, keeping my hands in hers.

"It's time you knew the truth about your mother." She looked at me, tension building throughout her body. "You know I trained as a translator?"

"Of course." My voice echoed my sudden insecurity.

What had she hidden?

"But I trained for another job as well."

The hands holding mine were now grasping almost painfully. Those puzzle pieces that had lingered in the deep recesses of my brain clicked into place, pulled by their mutual magnetism.

"You were a spy."

Mutti blinked in surprise. "How did you know that?"

I sat in wonder at what my brain had done. "I didn't – until now." My tension seeped away. "It's lots of little things – like how you handled that woman ... and that man, the way you knew how to go about the tasks we had to do for him. The ways you could help me." I smiled at Mutti. "You were so clever, so subtle that all I had was odd, disconnected, little thoughts – until they clicked."

Her hands were still holding mine, but the fear-driven clasp had relaxed. "But I lied to you." She pulled her hands away.

"No, you didn't." I grabbed her hands. "Not telling me is not a lie. And you couldn't tell me." I gave her a look of admiration. "You used all their training to deceive ... that woman and that man ... to protect us and allow us to survive in this new place." I squeezed her hands. "Thank you, Mutti."

"But, *Liebling,* part of the reason your father was desperate to find us, was what I could reveal to that woman." Her hands gripped mine. "You

see, it was my job to spy on the Soviets and Poles whilst being a translator."
She sniffed. "Your father didn't realise that I had to bury it deep when we
defected: that woman would never have allowed us a normal life."

I could see guilt written in the lines around her eyes, at the corners of
her lips.

"I risked you, *Liebling*. If I'd stayed in Leipzig, you would have been
safe." Anguish tortured her voice. "I'd been through the camps; I knew I
could deal with ... failure. But I put you in danger by taking you with me."

Realisation hit me. "You were thinking of leaving me behind?"

Mutti dropped her eyes. "But I couldn't do it. I couldn't leave you
behind. I knew I was being selfish ..." Emotion stopped her, tears streaming
down her face.

Anger bloomed inside me and Mutti read it on my face, from the
tension in my hands holding hers. She collapsed onto the couch, sobbing.
"I know, I know. I should have left you behind."

"No." I shouted. "No." I grabbed her hands, pulling Mutti towards me
with such force that her eyes opened wide in fear. "I'm not angry that you
took me with you."

Her mouth half-opened in confusion.

"I'm angry that you thought about leaving me – that you think I would
hold it against you for bringing me with you." I pulled her to me. "I'm
proud of you, Mutti. I love you."

We embraced until Mutti whispered in my ear, "Can you forgive me for
what I did — for exposing you to danger?"

I pushed her away and I saw the fear of rejection on her face. "There's
nothing to forgive, Mutti." I reassured her with a smile. "You weren't selfish
in taking me with you; you saved me from a terrible life and a dismal
future."

Her face changed. "You forgive me, *Liebling*?"

I caressed her cheek. "There is nothing to forgive. It is for me to thank
you – for saving me."

Some soft music was playing on the radio and we sat, allowing it to calm
our emotions.

After some minutes, Mutti turned to me. "We have to continue as we
have been. You understand that?"

"Yes." I sighed. "But I know what I'm doing when I finish school."

Mutti gave me a puzzled look.

"I'm going to England, to find Willi ... and Lili."

"Oh ..." After a brief pause, "I'll come with you."

This was hard. "No, Mutti, by myself."

I held her eyes and could see her thinking. "I understand."

We sat in silence for a while before Mutti turned to me.

"What am I going to do?"

"What do you want to do, Mutti?" I had assumed she would continue as before.

She looked around our house and out to the gum trees beyond. "I don't know. Despite the lies, our life here is good – in a friendly country." Her eyes returned to me. "I need to meet with that man to discuss this new situation. I'm hoping he won't need us anymore. Without him threatening us, we can relax."

I understood, but anguish laced my words. "But we won't be ourselves. We'll still have to tell that woman's lies."

Mutti's eyes sought mine and smiled a thin smile of understanding. "Well, we don't have to decide now."

"I'm going to England after school finishes."

Mutti sat in silence, her gaze lingering on me. "Christmas is months away. Concentrate on school for now."

A few days later, Mutti was home late. I'd had tea ready for over half an hour when I heard her coming up the stairs. As usual, she turned on the radio.

"I'm sorry I'm late. I was meeting with that man."

My stomach didn't lurch – but it tightened. "What did he want?"

"He's cutting us loose." Mutti laughed. "I'm not sure exactly why, but I think finding Soviet agents has fallen off the priority list. So, no more money from him and no more reports from us."

"And he can no longer blackmail us?"

"I don't think we are on the *Stasi* or KGB priority list anymore. They have other concerns – such as their own survival against retribution."

"No more lies?"

Mutti pulled a face. "We must keep living as we have, at least for now. I don't know what would happen if we revealed our true identities ..."

"What do you mean?"

"We came here on false passports with false names. What would the Australian government do if that came out?"

I could see the questions on her face. "They wouldn't kick us out, would they?"

"I don't know, *Liebling*. And I don't know how to find out without risking that very thing."

In bed, I cuddled *Imbi,* trying to find a way round this problem – for Mutti.

I was going to England.

· · · ·

IN EARLY SEPTEMBER, Mr Jameson contacted us again. Aunt Anastasia's estate had been finalised and we needed to go in, sign more papers and meet with the stockbroker and accountant. As the meeting would be lengthy, he suggested we come to his office at half-past ten in the morning. This was a problem in terms of school and Mutti's work, but we settled on the next Saturday. Mutti took the day off. I told Lizzie I had something on and let the swimming and German clubs know I would be absent.

When we arrived, they ushered us into a meeting room where Mr Jameson joined us. A small mountain of paperwork waited for our signatures. Mr Jameson explained things – with patient repetitions when we became confused. All that took until midday, at which point Mr Jameson smiled and suggested we break for lunch.

Mutti and I headed off to the toilets and when we returned, two other men had joined Mr Jameson. He introduced Mr Thorndyke, the stockbroker, and Mr Parkinson, the accountant. Both were wearing old-fashioned suits and looked to be in their sixties – if not their seventies.

As we ate lunch, these two gentlemen explained in patronising terms what they did. The assumption that they would continue to do this was clear in their attitude. They directed most of their words to Mutti, ignoring me. Once they cleared away lunch, the stockbroker went through what were now my holdings in overwhelming, endless and boring detail. Much of the explanation seemed directed at Mr Jameson and not Mutti and me.

After an excruciating hour of this, I interrupted Mr Thorndyke. "Please – I'm sorry to interrupt, but this is all going over my head."

Mr Thorndyke stopped mid-sentence. "I beg your pardon, Miss?" His indignation at the interruption was quite apparent.

I let out a frustrated sigh, looking between Mutti and Mr Jameson. "Mr Thorndyke. I'm an eighteen-year-old schoolgirl. I have limited understanding of the world of finance."

Mr Thorndyke blinked at me, looked towards Mutti and opened his mouth.

I jumped in. "What I need is someone who can spend the time to help me understand what I need to know about what I own and how I should manage it."

Mr Thorndyke's impatience with me showed on his face and in his voice. "My dear girl, that is exactly what I am doing."

"But not all at once – I don't understand most of what you're saying." I gave Mr Jameson a pleading look. "I know I need to learn, but I can't do it this way."

"Hmm – I think I understand." Mr Jameson looked at Mr Thorndyke and Mr Parkinson. "Madame Zaytseva would have given you general instructions on how to operate her investments?"

The two men glanced at one another. "Yes." "Of course."

"I suggest you continue with those general instructions for the next couple of months – and bring to me any significant issues; I can discuss them with Miss Miller." Mr Jameson smiled at me. "Would that be satisfactory?"

I interjected. "Yes, but I still need to understand..."

"Of course." He held up a finger to stop me and turned to Mr Thorndyke. "Would that work as a temporary measure for you, Mr Thorndyke? Mr Parkinson?"

They both showed their agreement.

"Excellent." Mr Jameson thought for a moment. "I realise your time as senior members of your firms, Mr Thorndyke, Mr Parkinson, is valuable.

So, would you have a junior member of staff who could spend time with Miss Miller over the next few weeks explaining the financial system in general and her holdings in particular?"

Mr Thorndyke's eyes travelled between Mr Jameson and me. "Possibly."

Mr Jameson raised an eyebrow in question at Mr Parkinson.

"I think so," Mr Parkinson replied, grudgingly.

"Excellent." He turned to me. "Would you be able to meet these representatives here next Saturday, Miss Miller?"

"I could be here after swimming – about ten o'clock."

"Excellent, excellent." He looked at Mr Thorndyke and Mr Parkinson. "Can you ask your junior staff members to be here at that time?"

They both agreed and Mr Jameson stood. "Thank you for your valuable time, gentlemen. I won't keep you any longer." He ushered them from the room, closed the door and returned to his seat.

He gave me a lengthy look. "To safeguard your interests, you will need to understand all of this to some extent, Miss Miller."

I sighed. "I know – but I was drowning in all that detail."

"We'll see how things go next week, shall we?" Mr Jameson shuffled some papers on his desk and produced a large manilla envelope. "Here are the cheque book and bank account documents for Miss Miller. At present, it requires both of you to sign each cheque and withdrawal."

Mutti opened the envelope and pulled out several documents, including a cheque book.

"That is a statement of the opening balance." Mr Jameson pointed at a sheet bearing the bank's logo.

Mutti turned it the right way up – and her eyes widened. She passed it to me without comment.

Twenty-five thousand dollars?

I gave Mutti a stunned look.

"That is the cash-in-hand after settling Madame Zaytseva's affairs." Mr Jameson read our faces but misunderstood our reaction. "Of course, that does not include the share portfolio," he pulled out another bulging envelope. "The details of that are here. The property portfolio was liquidated to settle the death duties and some ten thousand dollars remained. I moved it into the brokerage account." He passed the envelope to Mutti. "You'll see that listed in the recent transactions."

Mutti opened the envelope, pulled out several papers and read them. I saw her chest rise as she took a deep breath. She passed one to me. I read the current valuation: $1,109,256.25 and we shared a dazed look.

I realised Mr Jameson was watching us.

He cleared his throat to gain our attention. "On your behalf, I have engaged a well-respected firm of removalists to assist with clearing Madame Zaytseva's flat. They have storage facilities for larger items, should you need that. I can arrange for items to be sold at auction if needed."

Aunt Anastasia's beautiful things ...

I looked across at Mr Jameson. "How soon do we need to do that?"

"The building of which the flat is the top floor contains a bookshop. Madame Zaytseva left the building to the owners of the bookshop."

"That's Mr Caune and his wife. I think his wife is some sort of distant relation to Aunt ... er ... Madame Zaytseva."

I thought for a moment, glancing at Mutti. "There are one or two things I would like to have in our house, but I think we can pack the rest up and put into storage for now." I turned to Mr Jameson. "Can we go there now? You can have the removalists pack up the rest and store it."

He smiled. "I can do that."

"Please tell them to treat everything with great care. Aunt Anastasia's possessions are beautiful and delicate."

"Of course, Miss Miller." He pulled another envelope from his file and passed it across. "This is an itemised inventory of the contents of the flat, along with their valuation."

I didn't open it.

"If you open it, Miss Miller, you will find it includes a listing of the jewellery found in Madame Zaytseva's bedroom safe." He paused. "In finalising the estate, I had these items valued. Once that was done, I placed them in a safe deposit box at your bank. The details of that are in the envelope."

I passed the envelope to Mutti, who added it to the others in her bag.

"If you'll give me a moment, I will arrange for one of my staff to accompany you to the flat." He slipped out, returning after a minute. "Miss

Lambert will accompany you – she is waiting in reception." He turned to me. "I look forward to seeing you next Saturday morning, Miss Miller."

Mutti shook his hand. "Thank you for your help, Mr Jameson."

"A pleasure, Mrs Miller."

At the flat, I packed the crystal tea glasses and their holders in a suitcase amongst my clothes. Making tea in these would remind me of countless teas with Aunt Anastasia. I looked with longing at the ormolu clock but decided it wouldn't fit our ordinary house – best for it to go into storage. We had few visitors, but anyone seeing that valuable clock would wonder about us. I filled another large suitcase with the remaining clothes, shoes and other items. Looking at everything, I asked Mr Caune to call us a taxi as the phone in Aunt Anastasia's flat had been disconnected.

For the next few Saturdays, the hours I had spent on previous weekends with Aunt Anastasia were now spent with a junior accountant and stockbroker. I learned one unexpected thing – I did not want a career in finance. That said, I could lose everything though my ineptitude: I persevered. By the time matriculation exams happened, I could have passed one in economics.

I knew I'd done well in my exams – now we all had to wait for our results. In the meantime, the formal end of our years of school arrived. I stood to one side, watching Lizzie's group talk about what they were doing next as we gathered on the lawn after Speech Day. Many had jobs lined up and a couple were heading to university.

Lizzie turned to me. "Are you going to Europe after Christmas?" Her voice was tinged with envy and disbelief. Some of this year's sixth form were heading to England – but they were the daughters of wealthy families. I hadn't told Lizzie about Aunt Anastasia's money.

"I need to visit where I was born, to explore, to find out more about my German background."

How much would Leipzig have changed in the six years? But first – first I am going to England.

"Do you remember much about Frankfurt?" Lizzie asked.

"What?" I dragged my mind into the present. "Oh ... no ... I was young when we left."

Lizzie raised an eyebrow. "How long will you be away for?"

"I don't know." I shrugged. "A year ... maybe."

I stifled the 'more' that was poised to follow.

Lizzie's eyes held mine, her friendship shining but clouded by questions. She was the single close friend I had in Brisbane – and I didn't know how to tell her I was probably not returning.

Our eyes stayed locked as I measured the extent of my debt to her. She had taken me into her circle, standing up for me when her other friends regarded me as an interloper, encouraging their acceptance of me. She had hugged and helped me when I struggled and we had shared our laughter. I realised I knew her better than I knew Lili or Willi, but I was still going to walk away from her — over to Europe to seek them out. I owed my English friends after my abrupt and unexplained disappearance.

All this ran through my brain and I pulled her into a hug as tears ran down my cheeks. She deserved to know the truth about me. But not here, not now surrounded by her peers and their parents: later, somewhere she could walk away from me if the lies I had told proved too much.

After a minute, I pulled away to see tears on her face too. "Lizzie, there's much I need to tell you. Can we meet tomorrow?"

"Okay ... my house, yours?"

"No." It needed to be neutral territory. "How about the Botanical Garden?"

Lizzie's face was puzzled, but she accepted my unusual suggestion. "Okay — near the pavilion at ten o'clock?"

I could see her brain turning over this strange request, but her mother arrived.

"Hello, Karlota." She seized Lizzie's arm. "Come along Elisabeth, there are several people I want you to meet."

Lizzie gave me a quick, apologetic smile. "Tomorrow, Kal."

Sleep that night was hard to find as I sought for the right thing to do. I owed her my truth – but all of it? And what of Mutti and her half-expressed desire to stay here in Australia?

• • • •

I PACED UP AND DOWN, pretending to look at the plants; standing still was not possible as I waited for Lizzie. The fear of breaking this friendship was knotting every thought and roiling my stomach. I saw Lizzie approaching and she pulled me into a hug that I could not fully return – which Lizzie noticed.

She arched an eyebrow. "What is this all about, Kal?"

"Let's sit over there in the shade."

We walked across the lawn and sat in the spreading shade of a Poinciana.

Once settled, I looked at Lizzie. "Please don't interrupt me – if you do, I'm not sure I would have the strength to continue."

I saw Lizzie open her mouth and I held up my hand. "No, Lizzie. Please."

With reluctance, Lizzie closed her mouth and I started.

It took a few minutes to give her a potted history of myself, laying bare the lies. Several times I saw her stop herself as she witnessed my anguish at the telling.

Finished, I sat, searching for her reaction.

She was silent for some seconds before her eyes focused on mine. "Kal ... er ... what did you say your real name was?"

"Colette Hilda Schmidt – my friends call me Col."

Is she still my friend?

"Er ... Col, that's quite a story."

I swallowed in relief at her use of my name. "It's not a story, Lizzie. It's who I am."

Lizzie smiled. "But it's still quite a story – escaping from east Germany, being sent here with a false identity and being blackmailed into spying." She laughed. "It's like you're a female James Bond."

"But I told you so many lies, Lizzie."

Lizzie cocked her head to the side. Several strands of blond hair fell across her face and she brushed them away. "It's not like you had any choice, Kal ... er, Col. If you hadn't, you'd have been ..."

She stumbled into the truth. Her eyes widened. "Oh, Kal. They might have killed you." She pulled me into a crushing hug.

When we separated, Lizzie sat for a few seconds and took my hand. "You're worried that because of the lies, I won't want to be your friend, aren't you?"

I closed my eyes, afraid of what I'd see in hers. "Yes."

"Oh, Ka ... Col. Why ever would you think that? If you'd told me the truth, I might have let it slip and you'd have been ... dead." Her horror powered the grip on my hand.

I opened my eyes. "You don't mind I lied about myself?"

"No — I'm grateful that I didn't know the truth." Her grip loosened.

As the tension drained from me, I squeezed her hand. "Thank you, Lizzie,"

A smile flickered across her lips. "This trip to Europe of yours, would that include England?"

My eyes wandered to the greenery above us. "I must find him – and Lili. We three were close and one day I ... disappeared." I let my eyes find hers, searching for her understanding. "I owe them an explanation."

Lizzie's smile broadened. "And you want to know if ... what's his name ... still wants you."

I blushed, nodding. "There are a couple more things, Lizzie."

"Yes?"

"Please keep calling me Kal. I don't know when – or if – I can become Col again."

"Okay, Kal."

"And as my friend, please, could you not tell anyone else about me?"

Lizzie pursed her lips. "I'm sort of OK with secrets, Kal, you know that. But this is something else. Why on earth did you tell me?"

"Because you are my friend and I owe you the truth."

"But surely, it doesn't matter anymore. You're no longer threatened by ... whoever."

"That's true, but we came here on false papers and we don't know what the government would do if they found out."

Lizzie frowned. "They might throw you out?"

"We don't know and can't ask anyone."

"Well, I certainly don't want you thrown out. I want you to come home after your trip ...with your lost love."

Australia's not my home ...

After a while, we wandered into the city and enjoyed a pot of tea before going our separate ways, arranging to meet at the pool later in the week.

• • • •

AS THE END OF THE YEAR approached, another segment of my life was ending. Loose ends required attention, though.

I met with Dmitri Mikhailov at the Russian Club. The meeting had moments of tension around my participation and membership. We agreed the club would set up Russian language classes using the income from Aunt Anastasia's bequest to pay the teacher. The club would provide the room. At the end of the meeting, he asked me to wait a moment and left the room. On his return, he handed me an invitation to the Christmas ball.

"Thank you, but I don't think I should attend. Perhaps we should let things settle down a bit."

Mr Mikhailov's lips pursed. "Tasia would be unhappy with your refusal, Miss Miller."

"On the contrary, I'm sure she would understand. My attendance would be divisive. Besides, I have no-one to bring as my guest."

Mr Mikhailov gave me a long look. "Easter, perhaps?"

"I'm afraid I won't be in the country for Easter."

"I see." His eyes lingered. "I hope to see you on your return."

"Thank you."

And we left it there.

I attended the Polish and German Club parties, though, and felt welcome at both.

Mrs Jaworski was quite upset when I told her I was travelling overseas after Christmas and wasn't sure when I would return. "Make sure you visit Poland, now it is liberated."

"I will."

To my surprise, I received an invitation to the Christmas party at Lizzie's house.

I rang her as soon as I saw what the envelope contained. "Hi Lizzie. Thanks for the invitation, but how did you get your mother to agree to this?"

Lizzie chuckled. "I told her I wouldn't go if I could not have my best friend there. She could not face the embarrassment. You must come — and wear some of those smart clothes I know you have in your wardrobe. That will completely floor her."

I laughed. "Okay."

Some of my new wealth purchased an outfit at Finney Isles. I remembered I needed winter clothes and some remained from the last winter season. Enough to keep me from freezing to death when I arrived in an English winter.

Lizzie's party was a scream. Lizzie's mother blinked several times when I arrived, wearing a shimmering blue Thai silk, backless cocktail dress. My outfit was gorgeous, but Aunt Anastasia's diamonds caused her the greatest trouble.

Halfway through the evening, Lizzie whispered to me. "Mother wants to know if the diamonds are real."

"You know they are. What did you tell her?"

Lizzie laughed. "I told her I couldn't ask that."

"Good for you."

When I thanked Mrs Robinson at the end of the evening, she kept glancing at the diamonds. I could see she was bursting to ask about them but couldn't let her superior façade slip. Lizzie and I shared a delicious, wicked smile.

Mutti and I spent Christmas together and, on December 28th, she took me to the airport for my flight to London.

"Be careful, *Liebling*. Send me lots of postcards and letters."

"Of course, Mutti. Look after *Imbi*." We hugged for one last time and I headed through passport control, brandishing the British passport in my fake name courtesy of Mrs Henderson. I blinked away tears.

Chapter 17

Late December 1968 – early January 1969

As there were no flights from Brisbane to London, I flew to Darwin to join the flight from Sydney. I sat in the Brisbane departure lounge sipping an orange juice to steady my nerves, reading about the Apollo 8 trip round the moon.

Willi could tell me every detail of this.

I had wanted to travel by myself, but the reality now descended on me: I was alone for the first time in my life. Added to that, I was still nervous about flying, despite its glamorous image. My flight was called and a bus took us to the aircraft. We'd sailed for several days round the south of the continent when we first arrived, but this flight impressed on me the vast size of Australia. The in-flight magazine map showed we were flying over Australia's northeast corner, but it took four hours – in a jet plane.

Clouds hid Darwin when we arrived and I caught only a momentary glimpse of the city. I walked down the steps from the plane and I gasped; I thought Brisbane was hot and humid, but Darwin in the middle of the wet season was ridiculous. Within minutes, my blouse was sticking to me and the rest of my clothes felt damp. The hour I spent waiting to board the flight to London was uncomfortable.

How do people live in these conditions?

From the bus, I could see that the London bound aircraft was much bigger with four engines – a Boeing 707 I learned; I was certain Willi would quiz me. I sat, sweating in my window seat, until the aircraft started its engines and the air cooled and become dryer. Despite its glamorous image, flying half-way round the world was boring. There were moments of interest as we flew into the various airports on our route – at least during daylight – but the rest of the time I read and slept.

Once through passport and customs control in London, I caught the airline bus through the winter rain to the Victoria air terminal. I checked into the hotel my travel agent had booked for me. In the morning, I dressed in the winter clothes I had acquired in Brisbane and checked out of the hotel. I visited the bank and arranged access to the money that had been transferred for me, withdrawing some cash to supplement my travellers' cheques. The walk into Victoria Station was trying, straining my arms from carrying my cases.

The departure board showed a train to Herne Bay in half an hour, but instead of the ticket office, my feet led me to the cafeteria. I sat nursing a cup of coffee until that train had left and the coffee sat, cold and ignored. Now that I was about to see Willi and Lili again, fear gripped me; they might not want to see me, might hate me for deserting them. My greatest fear returned: they might have been pushed into each other's arms by my disappearance ... and my diaries in the suitcase would be unread and valueless.

I sat, lost in my circling thoughts, until a voice disturbed the fugue.

"You goin' ta drink that? Must be stone cold b' now."

I looked up at the waitress. "No – thank you."

"Can I get you summat else?"

Some courage?

"No, thank you."

It doesn't matter how long you sit here. The fear's not going away ... and you have a hotel reservation in Herne Bay for tonight.

With a deep, centre-seeking breath, I gathered my bags and myself. The departure board showed the next train to Herne Bay left in ten minutes. I bought a ticket and found a seat. The journey passing unnoticed as I struggled to hold at bay the rejection I feared.

At Herne Bay station, I caught a taxi. It appeared little had changed as we passed through the town. I checked in at the Pier Hotel with a bored young man behind the counter: winter would be quiet in a seaside hotel.

"Your reservation is for two nights, but with an option to extend." The man at the reception counter gave me a questioning glance. "Do you know if you will stay longer?"

My fears and uncertainties welled up. It took a moment to control them. "Umm ... not yet."

He raised an eyebrow at me. "We can't hold that room open forever, you know."

In a seaside hotel in the middle of winter?

I smiled and turned away to my room. Once there, I dumped my bags and headed out to Lili's house, not far along the seafront. As I approached, it looked the same and I walked up the path and rang the bell. After a minute, the door opened, revealing a middle-aged woman.

"Yes?"

It wasn't Mrs Wisniewski.

"Umm ... I'm looking for Lili Wisniewski ..." My voice trailed off in uncertainty.

The woman looked at me. "I'm sorry, I can't help you."

My fear pushed desperation into my voice. "But she lived here, four years ago."

The woman shook her head. "Sorry, love, I do not know who lived here before. We've only been in the house for a year."

Disappointment now tinged my fear, pushing it in a new and unexpected direction.

What if I couldn't find them?

I moved off the doorstep, embarrassed at the intrusion into her life. "Oh, thank you."

I turned away, heading for Willi's house. He would know what had happened to Lili. I walked up the Downs with the memories of Willi swirling round me. I could almost reach out and touch the two of us, laughing on the sled as we descended the hill that first snowy winter. In Seaview Road, I paused outside the house MI6 had put us into; it looked much the same but held no interest now. Turning the corner, I came to a stop: Mr Searle's corner shop was closed, the display windows showing a dusty 'For Lease' sign.

After my failure at Lili's house, this almost drained me.

Was everything changed?

I steeled myself to continue walking. Willi's house looked the same as I approached. I lingered at the open gate, searching the house for reassurance, as crows cawed from the fir trees across the road. The gravel driveway crunched with reassuring familiarity as I walked towards the front door. That hadn't changed, nor had the sound of the bell. I waited, but there was no movement. I pressed the bell again and stood waiting. About to turn away, a car turned into the drive, stopping outside the garage. A young woman and two small children climbed out, eyeing me with curiosity. It was not Dr Johnstone. My stomach flipped and my breath quickened.

The woman walked across to me, the children lagging behind her. "Can I help you?"

I mastered my breathing with difficulty. "I am looking for Dr Johnstone and her son, Willi ... er ... Will."

Her head angle to one side as she caught my unthinking German pronunciation of his name. She frowned. "I think the previous owners were the Johnstones ... but I don't remember one being a doctor." She gave me a tentative smile. "We never met them."

"Do you know where they went?" I was grasping at straws now.

The youngest of the children came up behind her, pulling at her skirt. "Mummy ...."

She took the child's hand. "No, I'm afraid not." She glanced down at the child. "I have to go now."

"Thank you."

I started walking towards the town but turned towards the house, hoping for some miracle. The woman was pulling shopping from the boot of the car. As she turned towards the house, she saw me looking and almost stopped. But the youngest child pulled at her skirt and the woman went on into the house. My disappointment was a crushing load, sagging my shoulders beneath the winter coat.

I walked into the town as dusk was falling, returning to my hotel. The bored young man was still at the reception counter and I walked past, avoiding his eyes. Both families had moved house and I'd not thought past knocking on their doors.

What am I going to do now?

One thing was certain: I was not giving up.

I ate alone in the hotel restaurant and spent the evening in my room, thinking. As far as I knew, Willi had no relatives outside of his immediate family, but Lili had an uncle ...

Wujek Brajan, wasn't it?

The phone directory listed no Wisniewskis. It must be a maternal uncle if he was still in town. I flipped towards the front of the book – no Johnstone either, which I had expected.

Fear and frustration bubbled up.

Think, Col.

Lili had been well known at the art supplies shop; they might know something. Better, *Wujek Brajan* had worked as a car salesman at the garage where I had taken Willi to see an E-Type Jaguar. There were leads to follow in the morning.

· · · ·

I STARTLED THE YOUNG man at reception when I went past him in running gear at six in the morning. I set off along the seawall, the rhythm of running helping me quell the worry I was feeling. I would have preferred to swim, but the cold, grey sea surging and sucking on the shingle was not inviting.

At breakfast, the young man at reception reminded me that today was New Year's Eve and the restaurant would be closed that evening. When I asked him where I could eat, he shrugged.

"Everyone is going out this evening."

"I've recently arrived from the other side of the world and I know no-one in this town." I gave him my best stare, feeling the rawness of that statement in my throat.

He dropped his eyes. "We could organise a plate of sandwiches for you," he mumbled.

"Thank you ... Oh, and I will stay for two more nights, at least." Whatever happened this morning, I needed more time to investigate around town ... and there was Willi's school in Canterbury.

I walked to the art supplies shop ... now a bicycle shop. Standing outside, the sea wind wrapped its chill, moist fingers round me as tears of frustration and fear filled my eyes. I was down to the last of my local leads: the car showroom. I turned the corner and gusted out a relieved sigh. It looked much the same, though there was no E-Type in the front display.

I pushed the door open and walked across to a young, dark-haired woman sitting behind a desk and stopped, unsure how to ask for 'Uncle Brian'.

The young woman looked up. "Can I help you, miss?"

"Well ... I'm not sure. I'm trying to find the uncle of an old friend of mine – his name's Brian, or *Brajan*, as he's originally Polish.

The young woman blinked. "Er – can you describe him?"

"He's big – and he has this scar on his face – he was a pilot in the war." I traced a finger across my cheek.

A strange look came over her face. "I see ... and what would be the name of your friend?"

"Lili – er Liliana Wisniewski."

The young woman stared at me for a few silent seconds before standing. "Please take a seat." She turned and almost ran through the door behind her.

I sat there, feeling confused. She knew the Brian I was looking for, but there was some undercurrent here I did not understand.

After a minute, the young woman reappeared. "Would you come with me, please?"

Still confused, but now hopeful, I followed her and she ushered me into an office. Standing behind the desk was *Wujek Brajan*.

My relief launched me into Polish. "Uncle Brian, I'm trying to find Liliana."

He looked at me for a few seconds, his eyes narrowing in puzzlement. "You were a friend of Liliana?"

Realisation hit and the words tumbled out. "Oh ... when you met me, over four years ago, I was a boy ... er ... pretending to be a boy. My friend Willi – er Will – brought me here to look at your E-Type Jaguar. We met again at the Christmas party at Lili's house." I paused. "I went there, but they don't live there anymore. Can you please give me her address?"

He gave me an appraising look before answering in English. "Please, young lady, sit down and tell me your name."

"I'm Colette Schmidt – known as Col when you met me."

His gaze held mine, memory returning. "Your friend ... Will? ... wanted to be a fighter pilot?"

"That's right – but I've been to his house and he isn't there either."

Uncle Brian pursed his lips. "I remember now – you and your mother disappeared without trace about four years ago." His eyes held mine and his voice hinted at disapproval. "Lili worried about you, a lot. She was quite upset."

"It's a long story." I shook myself – I couldn't go there right now. "Please, can you tell me where I can find Lili, because she will know how I can find Willi."

Uncle Brian took a deep breath and sighed it out. "I'm afraid she won't be able to tell you anything." I could see moisture in his eyes. "You see, my sister's family were all killed in a terrible car smash, four years ago before Christmas."

"Lili's dead?" My voice squeezed past the horror choking my throat.

His face filled with remembered grief.

For seconds, I sat there, lost to the world.

Lili – beautiful, talented, joyous Lili was dead.

The tears came and I sat, letting them run down my face. I realised someone was talking to me.

"Miss Schmidt, Miss Schmidt – drink this." The receptionist was crouched beside me, holding a glass of water and a box of tissues.

I grabbed several tissues, cleaned myself up and sipped some water. "Thank you." My voice was unsteady.

Her eyes were full of sympathy. "It was a terrible shock to all of us – Brian's my father, Lili was my cousin."

I sniffed and blew my nose. "And now me coming here has raised all these terrible memories for you."

She squeezed my hand. "Not at all. We understand how this must be a shock for you."

I sat there, not sure what to do or say.

"I'm Alicia, by the way." She gave me a tentative smile. "Would you like to wash your face?"

"Thank you."

Alicia showed me to the women's toilet and was waiting when I came out. "Father would like to talk to you again – if you're feeling up to it?"

We returned to the office, where Uncle Brian rose to his feet as we entered.

"Miss Schmidt, I want to talk with you, but today is not a good day. We are about to move cars around and decorate the show room for tonight's New Year's Eve party. Are you staying here in Herne Bay?"

"At the Pier Hotel."

"I would like to invite you to tonight's party – if you'd like to come, that is?" He looked at me, unsure of my reaction.

"Thank you, that is most kind."

"*Świetny*. Excellent." He relaxed. "Tomorrow, would you to come to our house? You can tell us that long story of yours – all about Liliana and yourself. Would that be all right?"

"Yes, that would be fine." I realised I didn't know his name – and that calling him Uncle Brian was rather forward. "Er ... Mr ...?"

Uncle Brian smiled at me. "It's Nowak. But at that Christmas party, I told you to call me Uncle Brian. May I call you Col?"

"Of course."

"Alicia, please give Col an invitation for tonight." Uncle Brian smiled at me. "I'll see you this evening."

Alicia led me out to her reception desk and from a drawer produced a beautiful invitation on heavy card. "Here you go, Col."

I looked at the classy invitation. "What will people be wearing tonight?"

Alicia smiled. "Oh, it's smart. The men will wear dinner suits and the women long dresses." Her smile faded to a concerned look.

"Hmm..." I pondered what I had in my bag, thinking of all the clothes I had packed into a trunk that was coming by sea and wouldn't be here for weeks. "Is there a decent dress shop in town?"

Alicia shook her head. "There's several in Canterbury ... but they're quite expensive." She looked me up and down, her voice trailing away.

I smiled at her. "I think I can stretch to a long dress."

Thank you, Aunt Anastasia.

"Is there enough time to get a bus to Canterbury?"

"Bus?" Alicia snorted. "No, I'll drive you. Hang on a minute." She disappeared into the offices, reappearing wearing a coat and swinging her handbag. "Come on. Let's go shopping – much more fun than putting up decorations for the party."

She dragged me through the rear of the showroom and we piled into a smart, bright red sports car. "This was my Christmas present – an MGB GT. Like it?"

The car started with a throaty exhaust sound. Forty minutes later, we walked into the Lefevre department store in Canterbury city centre. "I'm sure we'll find you something that will fit you here," Alicia said.

Lefevre was an upmarket department store. I had wandered through it with Lili, admiring the fashions on several occasions. I tried on several dresses, picking one in my favourite blue – the colour of the dress Lili gave me to wear for Willi that last Christmas Eve. It seemed an appropriate way of acknowledging Lili – at least for the moment.

Alicia noticed my wistful expression and distracted me by looking at the price tag. Her face changed to concern. "Umm ... Col ... can you afford this? It's a hundred pounds."

"Last year my aunt died." I gave Alicia a sadness-tinged smile. "Well, she wasn't my real aunt, but anyway, she left me some money and that's what's paying for this trip."

I was still good at producing half-truths on demand, it seemed.

"Now, I need a clutch bag, shoes and the right makeup." I smothered my memories of Lili and Aunt Anastasia with action.

An hour later, we were at the car, fitting my packages into the rather limited luggage space.

Once we were underway, Alicia glanced sideways at me. "You spent two hundred pounds. How much money did your aunt leave you?"

I gave her an enigmatic smile. "Enough."

Alicia raised her eyebrows but kept her eyes on the road.

As well as the dress, shoes, clutch bag and makeup, I'd bought an ankle length, midnight blue cloak with a red silk lining to wrap around me against the chill wind off the channel. This was the first time I'd splurged on myself. It left me feeling euphoric – until I remembered Lili was gone.

Alicia stopped at the hotel and helped me carry my packages up to my room. "See you this evening at half past seven."

"Thank you." I smiled and shut the door behind her.

I bathed, did my usual minimal make-up (sending silent thanks to Michelle at Finney-Isles for her guidance) and dabbed perfume onto my pulse points. The dress and cape cried out for Aunt Anastasia's diamonds, but I hadn't wanted to risk them in my luggage on the plane. After a moment contemplating myself in the mirror, I realised that wearing them could well be over the top for Herne Bay. I thought about the Russian Eagle necklace, but that could cause problems at a gathering with lots of Poles. In the end, I chose a thin gold choker and two studs with tiny diamonds that I'd brought with me from Aunt Anastasia's collection.

When I walked up to the reception desk at twenty past seven, the young man on the desk blinked out of his boredom and I smiled at his reaction.

"Please, will you call me a taxi?"

"Er ... yes Miss Miller."

I waited whilst he did that. "I don't expect to return until well after midnight. How do I get into the hotel?"

He pulled a key from under the desk. "This is a night key. It opens the door across the way there." He pointed to a door on the other side of the foyer.

"Thank you." I slipped the key into my clutch bag.

"When you return, please drop the key into the box." He pointed to the box on the reception desk.

I turned away to watch for my taxi. The Nowak car showroom was a brief ride and a large man in a suit opened my taxi door.

They had security here?

I pulled the invitation from my clutch bag.

The man glanced at it and waved me towards the door. "Thank you, Miss."

Uncle Brian's family were greeting people. He turned towards me and stopped dead. Behind him, I saw Alicia smiling at the effect I had on her father.

After a moment, Uncle Brian grasped my hand in both of his enormous ones. "Welcome, Col." He leant in to kiss me on both cheeks. "Thank you for coming." He turned to the woman at his side. "This is my wife, Mary – and you know my daughter."

Mrs Novak took my hand as soon as Uncle Brian released it. "Alicia tells me you were friends with our poor Liliana." Her eyes filled with care and sadness.

"Yes, Mrs Nowak. Lili and I were close friends. We met at school here and both went on to the grammar school in Canterbury."

"Please call me Mary, Col. I want to hear all about Liliana from you." She turned to her daughter. "Alicia, dear. Please show Col to our table."

A small dance band was setting up in a corner as Alicia lead me to her family's table. I glanced round the large space; it was hard to believe this was a car showroom – there was even a glitter ball hanging from the ceiling.

"Where did you put all the cars?"

Alicia laughed. "The workshop is stacked. There are cars on the lifts to make more room." She gave me an appraising look. "You look sophisticated, Col."

"Thank you, Alicia. As do you." I pulled off my cloak. "I need to find somewhere to put this."

"Put it in my dad's office along with ours. Come on."

When we returned, Alicia's parents were seated along with an older couple – Mary's parents, Mr and Mrs Gordon.

During the evening, Mrs Gordon turned to me. "I'm a little confused as to who you are," she said with a smile. "Colette isn't a Polish name and yet you speak Polish – fluently as far as I can make out. How come you speak Polish?"

"I was friends with Liliana Wisniewski. She and another friend of ours had a ... a language club, I suppose you'd call it. We did our homework and learned each other's languages as we went – English, French, German and Polish."

"Ah, Colette is a French name." She paused for a moment. "But where does German come in?"

I smiled. "That's me. I'm German – Colette Schmidt."

Mrs Gordon's eyes narrowed as she tried to work things out. "Who was French?"

"No-one was French – but we were all learning that at school and that became our secret language as none of our parents spoke it." I smiled at her. "Willi was learning Latin as well and we shared that too."

"Goodness me."

"Willi and I learned each other's languages, mostly before we met Lili. We persuaded Lili to teach us Polish if she learned German. We used to travel on the bus to and from school in Canterbury and do our homework at Mrs Wisniewski's kitchen table."

"I see." Mrs Gordon smiled. "Lili did well, teaching you Polish."

"She did."

No need to mention Mutti – or the Polish classes in Brisbane.

"I know about Lili and her family." She glanced across at her son-in-law. "Where's ... er ... Willi now?"

I drew in a breath. "I don't know ..."

Mrs Gordon's eyes lingered on my face, searching. "And he was your boyfriend?"

I clung to the edge of control.

Mrs Gordon saw my struggle and reached across to pat my hand. "I won't tell you it will all turn out right, because ... part of it already hasn't." She stopped and Lili's death lay between us. "But if you care about both of your friends, keep looking."

I sat, muted by my emotions.

Alicia looked across. "Come with me, Col. Let's powder our noses." She grabbed my hand and led me into her father's office.

"Oh Col, this has been such a terrible couple of days for you, hasn't it?"

I tried to blink away the tears.

Alicia handed me a tissue from a box she pulled from a drawer. "Do you want to go back to your hotel?"

I took several deep breaths, seeking my centre of calm. Death had been an occasional fellow traveller these last few years – Dodger, Euan, Aunt Anastasia. But Lili's death was different, snuffed out before she found herself and her talent – and I had spent years thinking of her as alive, yearning for a reunion. Thinking of her as dead felt ... unreal.

Alicia watched me in silence.

"No – I'll stay, thank you. I think that's what Lili would want me to do – to get on with life."

Alicia let out a breath. "You'll want to fix your makeup before we go out."

I dabbed my eyes with the tissue and pulled my compact out of my clutch bag. Surveying myself in the mirror, I sorted things out.

Alicia pulled me into a hug. "All right?"

I took Alicia's hand and gave it a grateful squeeze. "Thank you."

For the rest of the evening, I felt her caring eyes on me.

The events of the last two days had drained me and did not stay long after midnight. Alicia arranged to pick me up in front of the hotel at eleven o'clock and I said my thanks to Uncle Brian and his wife. The cloak swirling round me flashed crimson as I walked out to the taxi. At the hotel, I dropped the night key in the box and headed to my room, where I found a plate of sandwiches that I'd forgotten to cancel.

* * * *

I ABANDONED MY MORNING run and hid in bed, trying not to let the loss of Lili and my failure to find Willi push me down. After about half-an-hour, I roused myself and was waiting for Alicia when she arrived. Their family home was a large house on Beltinge Road, looking towards the sea.

When we arrived, Uncle Brian welcomed me. "Good morning, Col." He showed me into the lounge room. "Would you like a drink? Alicia is having a sherry, but Mary and I are having a gin and tonic."

Alicia saw I was lost. "Here, have a taste of sherry and see if you like it."

She handed me her glass and I took a small sip – sweet with nutty undertones. "That's nice, thank you."

Uncle Brian poured me one and sat down beside his wife. "You know a side of Liliana that we did not." He looked at Alicia and his wife. "We'd be grateful if you'd share with us."

I took a sip of sherry and paused in thought. "I need to start a little before I met Lili."

Uncle Brian relaxed into the sofa. "Tell the story in the way you want."

I took another sip of sherry, placed the glass on the table and licked my lips. "My name is Colette Hilda Schmidt, born and raised in Leipzig, in what was until recently, communist east Germany." My voice held a nervous tremor and I could see the surprise on their faces. Taking a breath, I pushed on. "My father was a senior officer in the *Staatssicherheitsdienst* – the *Stasi,* the east German secret police. But if you look in my passport, it will tell you I am an English girl called Karlota Miller ..."

Despite my best endeavours, the story came out disjointed, with side-tracks – Mutti's time in Ravensbrück, her discovery that her husband was a Nazi war criminal, our escape to the British zone in West Germany. MI6 settling us in a safe house in Seaview Road caused some surprise at such goings on in provincial Herne Bay. I told them about becoming friends with Willi, Dr Johnstone's son.

Mrs Nowak looked up. "I remember her. I was pleased to have a lady doctor and was sorry when she left. Do you know what happened to her? When I asked at the practice, they said she'd moved."

"I went to their house as soon as I arrived, but the current owners had no idea where they'd gone." A slight shiver ran through me at the memory. *How much should I say?*

"Umm ... I think Willi's parents might have separated. I know he was worried that might happen."

Mrs Nowak changed from such an awkward subject. "Brian tells me he first met you at the car showroom."

I smiled. "Yes. I'd seen an E-Type jaguar driving around town and chanced across it, walking past the showroom. I badgered Willi to come and see it with me." I smiled at Uncle Brian. "That's when we first met – but I was masquerading as a boy still because MI6 thought that was safer."

Uncle Brian smiled. "You did well – I did not know you were a girl."

I told them how I met Lili at junior school – but we were enemies before joining to beat back the racist bullies. After a shaky start, Lili, Willi and I became friends, spending a great deal of time together – usually with Willi or I reading aloud from a book and Lili sketching.

"Later that year, things became complicated as I had strong feelings for Willi – and when I revealed to him I was a girl, I found he reciprocated them. But Mutti would not let me tell Lili I was a girl."

I recounted what had happened at Lili's Christmas party – and how that resulted in us trusting Lili with our secret.

"For *Heiligabend* – Christmas Eve – Mutti invited Willi and Lili to join us. I had no girls' clothes and buying a dress for me was impossible. Lili found a dress she'd grown out of but would fit me with some alterations, which Mutti did. The dress I wore last night was almost the same colour as that dress of Lili's – that's why I chose it."

I stopped there to steady myself with a sip of sherry.

The story flooded out about Willi's prize trip to East Germany that was a setup by MI6 to smuggle to England Mutti's evidence about my father's Nazi past. The memories of our disappearance – kidnapped by *Stasi* agents were challenging, but I made myself explain what had happened. "Once again, this was a play by MI6 – to flush out Eastern bloc agents. We were rescued by MI6 and shipped off to Australia, as my father now wanted us dead." My throat closed. After a second to gather myself, I looked up. "I tried to send Willi and Lili a message that I was safe – but she refused to deliver it."

Alicia gave me a confused look. "Who's 'she'?"

I'd been so involved in telling the story, I hadn't spoken about Mrs Henderson. "She is Mrs Henderson – a person at MI6." I heard the distaste in my voice and paused in thought. "She has to be someone senior, as she wields considerable power."

I looked around their faces, showing a mix of amazement and some disbelief.

"Oh my, that's quite a story." Alicia sighed. "Why are you telling us this? Isn't it dangerous for you?"

Uncle Brian laughed. "Alicia, dear. You must pay more attention to the news. The Soviet Bloc collapsed last year." He looked at me. "That freed you, didn't it?"

I nodded. "I wanted to come here straightaway, but Mutti made me finish my final year at school."

Mary took a deep breath, shaking her head in wonder. "Your story's almost unbelievable, Col."

I shrugged and sipped the last of my sherry. "I have a favour to ask, if I may."

Aunt Mary glanced at her husband. "Yes?"

"Lili made lots of sketches of Willi and I ... amongst many other subjects. After ..." I cleared my throat. "When their house was sold, what happened to all of Lili's paintings and drawings?"

Uncle Brian shook his head. "I don't know. I was incredibly busy sorting out the business – Mr Wisniewski and I jointly owned it." He looked across at his wife. "Do you have any idea?"

She shook her head.

"But I do." Alicia smiled at me. "I put all of Lili's artwork into two large boxes. I meant to sort it all out later, but never got round to it."

"Where are they now?" Uncle Brian asked.

"I think they're with several other things stacked in the garage."

A current of hope sent a shiver up my spine. "Please, can we look?"

Mrs Nowak rose to her feet. "After we've had lunch, I think. Come on, Alicia."

I stood as well. "Can I help?"

Mrs Nowak smiled at me. "Thank you, dear. You can help Alicia set the table."

We enjoyed an English lunch of roast beef with all the trimmings. My appetite was suppressed in part by Lili's loss and by the exciting thought of finding a portrait of Willi in Lili's drawings. After lunch, Uncle Brian, Alicia and I went to the garage.

After shifting some clutter, Alicia pointed to a large cardboard box. "I think that's the main one."

Uncle Brian extricated it and Alicia opened it. "Yes – that's it. The other one has paints, crayons and things in it."

Uncle Brian smiled. "Let's take it to the sunroom. You can go through it there."

The large box seemed much smaller in Uncle Brian's huge arms. He placed it on the floor next to a rather battered table.

Alicia gave me a nod. "Go ahead, Col."

I unfolded the cardboard flaps. There were about half a dozen of the sketchbooks Lili used, along with a cardboard portfolio secured with a ribbon. I picked up a picture frame wrapped in corrugated cardboard.

"It's okay. Open it." Alicia encouraged.

I opened it – and gasped: a charcoal, pencil and crayon portrait of me.

"Oh. I'd forgotten about that. It was on the wall by her bed." She looked in the box. "There should be another one ... yes, here it is."

She handed me the package and I sat with it on my lap, scared to open it in case it wasn't what I hoped for. I willed my trembling fingers to behave and removed the wrapping: Willi returned my gaze. I sat for some seconds, allowing my eyes to engage his and letting my emotions settle. I knew he would not look like this now – four years had changed me and would have changed him, but the essential Willi would still be there – the crazy mix of seventy-year-old maturity and teen insecurity, the talented mathematician, the considerate lover, the abused child.

"That's your Will, isn't it?" Alicia's voice drew my attention and I nodded, but I kept my eyes on Willi's portrait.

"I wonder what else is here?" Alicia pulled out the cardboard portfolio and undid the ribbon holding it closed, allowing it to open on the table.

My eyes clouded – the first sheet was a self-portrait of Lili, a half-smile on her lips. I retrieved a tissue from my bag.

"Are you all right with this Col? Do you want to stop?" I could hear the worry and concern in Alicia's voice.

"No ... that is, no, I don't want to stop."

There were pictures of Lili's cat, Rupert, and several sketches that were clearly studies for Willi's and my portraits. There were a few sketches of sites around Herne Bay – the clock tower and one of a raging storm surging around the pier.

Alicia pulled out the sketchbooks. Her hand slipped, allowing the last one to gape open. A small shower of envelopes fell out. I recognised Willi's handwriting as they lay on the floor: five envelopes.

Alicia gathered them up, noticing the consistent writing. "I wonder who these are from – a boyfriend, do you think?"

My suppressed fears that Lili would scoop up Willi crystallised.

I must have gasped, for Alicia swivelled towards me. "What's wrong, Col. You've gone as white as a sheet."

I could feel my breath stuttering, my skin cold and clammy and I swayed.

Alicia rushed to my side. "I think you need to lie down, Col." She pushed me onto the sofa, swinging my legs up and giving me a worried look. "Stay there."

I closed my eyes and tried to still the darkness swirling in my head and stomach.

Col had been writing to Lili.

I had to read those letters, but when I tried to sit up, my stomach lurched. A moment later, Alicia returned – with a glass of water and her mother.

"What's wrong, Col?" Mrs Nowak knelt beside the sofa.

"I'm sorry. I'm sure I'll be all right in a minute." My voice was no more than a whisper.

Mrs Nowak held the glass to my lips. "Take a sip."

I leant forward. The water slid across my tongue, sweet and cold.

"I'll put it here beside you, dear."

Lying against the cushions, I closed my eyes to help still the gyration in my head.

I heard paper rustle, opening my eyes to see Alicia had taken the letter out of one envelope. She scanned through it.

Alicia looked up. "It's from Willi." Her eyes held mine. "Shall I read it to you?"

I squeezed my eyes shut for a moment, sucking in a quick breath. "Yes ... please."

"All right ... the handwriting is hard to read, though."

Willi's handwriting had always been terrible.

Dear Lili

School continues as usual – I'm enjoying the work, but there's a mountain of it. My fault, I know – but I couldn't bear dropping more than Latin. Studying the languages helps me stay close to Col ...

I sighed, the tension washing from my body.

Alicia looked up, her face full of concern. "What, Col?"

I scrabbled for a tissue and blew my nose, shaking my head.

"It's all right, Alicia." I closed my eyes in shame that I'd thought Lili or Willi would betray me.

The sofa shifted as Alicia sat beside me, taking my hand.

"You were worried that your disappearance had pushed them together?"

Embarrassment pulled my hand from hers.

Alicia grabbed it again, her firm but gentle grip providing unconditional support. "And you've had that fear since they kidnapped you to Australia."

Alicia reached across to the table with her free hand, gathering up the envelopes. "Here." She placed them in my lap. "I'll let you read through them in peace." She stood, giving me an encouraging smile. "But I want to read them – as will my parents – to hear about Lili."

When the door closed behind her, I looked at the envelopes and sorted them into date order from the postmarks. Reading them was like hearing one side of a conversation: frustrating. Through her letters, Lili must have kept reminding Willi of his promise to speak to me before he 'did anything'; when his letters drifted towards darkness, he pulled himself up by recalling that promise – but he had a continuous struggle. His letters referred to me as 'her' and mentioned several times 'sitting and staring at her'.

Lili must have made another portrait of me and given it to Willi, keeping the small one for herself.

In a later letter he referred to 'the large picture' – he did have a large picture of me. The portraits of Willi and I that Lili had kept for herself were not large.

Was there a larger version of her portrait of Willi that she had been going to give to me?

I carefully rifled through the cardboard portfolio – if there was such a portrait, it wasn't there. I still felt shaky, but I gathered the letters and opened the door to the house, following voices to the lounge room.

Mrs Nowak was on her feet as soon as she saw me. "How are you feeling, Col?"

"Better, thank you." Willi required some explanation before they read the letters. "The writer of these letters is Willi – my boyfriend. His father abused him physically and emotionally for years and Willi struggled with suicidal thoughts. You'll see this in the letters." Sharp memories halted me for a moment. "Willi promised me he would speak to me if he felt that darkness encroaching. I involved Lili in watching him as well – and you'll see she did that for him after I disappeared."

I passed the letters to Alicia. They weren't long, but there was silence in the room as the letters passed between them, with Uncle Brian and his wife reading them together.

When Alicia finished the last letter, she leant across to me. "Thank you, Col. Hearing your story, going through the box and reading the letters has helped me feel much closer to Lili." She picked up my hand. "But it's been an emotional maelstrom for you, hasn't it?"

I gave her hand a squeeze of thanks for her understanding. I could see Alicia thinking.

"Umm ... would you like to visit her?"

I looked at her, not understanding.

"Lili, would you like to visit her grave?"

I swallowed. "Yes, please." It was almost a whisper.

Alicia's parents had been watching this exchange across the room.

Uncle Brian lifted himself to his feet. "We'll all go." He offered a hand to his wife, lifting her effortlessly.

We gathered our coats and uncle Brian brought out his Jaguar Mk 10. Alicia and I sat in the roomy rear seat as he drove us across the Thanet Way. The cemetery was at the foot of the hill where the Herne windmill stood. Lili, Willi and I had passed it every day on the bus. Uncle Brian swung the big car into the car park and we gathered our coats around us against the wind.

"This way." Alicia said, taking my hand and walking through the gates into the cemetery.

After a short walk, we arrived at the Wisniewski family's grave. They had all died on the same day, December 7th, 1964. Memories of Lili swirled about me and tears ran icy tracks down my face. An arm curled round my shoulders and strands of Alicia's dark hair flung themselves at me.

"Sorry, Col." She pulled a beany from her coat pocket and tamed her hair beneath it.

We all stood there, becoming ever colder. After a while, I started shivering.

Alicia grabbed my hand. "Come on, let's get in the car. I forgot you're from an Australian summer." Alicia's parents followed us.

Sitting in the car, Alicia turned to me. "I'm sure I remember some poster tubes from Lili's room. They must still be somewhere in the garage."

Alicia poked around in the garage, finally appearing triumphant, with two long cylindrical tubes. We took them into the family room and opened them. When we carefully unrolled the first, it was of a storm around the pier, the grey sea roiling beneath it. The one in the sketchbook must have been a study for this larger and more detailed work. As we unrolled the second one, my heartbeat rose – it was Willi.

Uncle Brian looked at me. "I think you should have this one, Col."

I squeezed my eyes shut for a moment. "Thank you ... but could you keep it here for me, please? I'll be living out of a suitcase for a while."

"Of course," Uncle Brian smiled.

"You should take this one with you, Col." Alicia handed me the small version that she had taken from the wall beside Lili's bed.

"Thank you."

We rolled up Willi's portrait and slid it into the tube. As we did that, Alicia sensed I was drained. "Would you like me to take you to your hotel?"

"Yes, please." I realised this might sound rude and turned to Uncle Brian and his wife. "Thank you for lunch ... and everything. But I need some time alone ... to think."

Aunt Mary folded her arms around me in a hug. "Of course you do, Col. We quite understand."

Alicia drove me to the hotel. When she stopped, she pushed a piece of notepaper into my hand. "Here's our home phone number and address and for the car showroom. Please, stay in touch."

"I'll be here for another couple of days and go to London after that – there's someone there I must see, whatever happens." I leant across and kissed both her cheeks. "Thank you for everything."

I scurried out of her car and into the hotel, the wind of a building channel storm slapping my coat against my legs.

. . . .

IN SPITE OF THE STORM, I ran again in the morning, the rhythms tamping down but not stilling my swirling emotions. After breakfast, I caught a number seven bus to Canterbury – the same bus that the three of us had taken to school. This time, though, I left the bus at the stop Willi had used. I was hoping to find a clue to Willi's whereabouts at his school.

Willi's school was in the cathedral precincts. The uniform hadn't changed from what I saw of the students – boys, in pinstriped trousers and boaters. I stopped one and asked for directions to the school office. He pointed across the open grass. "Go round the Green and it's that house next to the undercroft."

I had no idea what an 'undercroft' was, but I could see a house. I walked onto the grass.

"Miss, you can't walk across the Green. That's for masters and prefects."

I could hear the shock in his voice. Smiling, I set off round the path circling the grass to the school office.

Inside, I could hear a typewriter clacking away in a room to the left. I knocked on the open door.

"Enter."

Sitting at a desk behind a typewriter was a thin lady, whose greying hair was pulled into a tight bun.

"Excuse me, I'm trying to find out some information about a student – well, a past student."

The woman looked at me with disapproval in her eyes. "And you are a relative of this gentleman?"

"Er ... no. I'm a close friend, but I've been out of the country for four years and we lost touch."

The woman sniffed. "Clearly not such a close friend."

I swallowed my annoyance at her attitude. "His name is William Johnstone – he was quite a special student."

A brief flicker of recognition?

"We cannot give out any information about past student unless you are a relative. If this William Johnstone was a student."

"Oh, he definitely was a student." I curbed the irritation I heard in my voice. "He excelled in Maths and Physics but was studying languages as well."

She did not recognise the name as her face remained blank – or she was an excellent actor.

"As I told you, if this person was a student, we could not give you any details. You are not a relative."

I stood there, trying to think of a way round this uncooperative woman.

"Is there anything else?" Her eyes were telling me to leave. "I have much work to do."

I turned on my heel and controlled the urge to slam the door. Looking over the Green, the cathedral towered above the buildings clustered around it. I'd seen a gift shop catering to tourists on the far side. I should let Mutti and Lizzie know how things were going: a postcard first and I'd write an airmail when I was in London.

Walking round the Green, I passed a building labelled 'Staffroom', stopping to look at it. Something tried to surface in my memories, but it eluded me. I walked round the cathedral and found the tourist shop, buying some postcards. I took them into the tea shop and sat writing them over a cup of coffee.

"Pollock". I must have said it aloud, as I was the recipient of strange looks from the few customers and staff. I dropped my head and looked at my coffee.

Mr Pollock – Willi's maths teacher. If he was still teaching at the school, I'm sure he'd remember Willi. He might find me some information about Willi. Approaching him required careful thought as this felt like the final, faint thread of a lead to Willi – at least one not involving Mrs Henderson.

I finished my coffee and walked through the city centre, posting the cards to Australia at the post office. The number six bus took me to Herne Bay, surrounding me in remembered snatches of conversations in the various languages we had used.

At the hotel, I found the school's number in the phone book. If that unhelpful woman answered, I'd have to hang up.

"Hello. I'd like to get a message to Mr Pollock, please."

"Certainly, who shall I say called?"

It's not her and he's still a teacher there.

"My name's Kal Miller. I'm from Australia and my mother asked me to get in touch with Mr Pollock. I'm some sort of cousin." The lies slid out – a polished skill thanks to Mr Franks and Mrs Henderson.

"I see. Mr Pollock is teaching at the moment. How can he get in touch with you?"

I gave her the hotel phone number and she assured me she would pass the message on.

That evening, Mr Pollock returned my call.

"Miss Miller?"

"Yes."

"I'm Charles Pollock. I understand we are related."

"Er yes. My mother was quite insistent I get in touch with you. Would it be possible to meet with you – say, on Saturday?"

There was silence for a moment. "There's a tea shop in the cathedral precinct – across from the West Door?"

"Yes."

"We'll meet there at half-past three on Saturday." His voice was precise.

"Thank you, that's most kind."

I heard a grunt and the line went dead.

That was abrupt.

Willi told me Mr Pollock seemed to spend most of his time thinking about maths. He wasn't good at relating to students, but was, in Willi's estimation, an excellent maths teacher.

That meeting meant spending at least two more days in Herne Bay and there were things to be done before I left. In the morning after a run and breakfast, I walked into the town centre to the florist. There wasn't much choice in the middle of winter and I selected a bunch of chrysanthemums. A number six bus took me to the cemetery and I found my way to Lili's grave.

The chilling wind had died and occasional glances of sunshine limned the bare-branched poplar trees along the boundary of the cemetery. On the hill above, the windmill stood arms spread aloft: a motionless supplicant to the silent sky. I placed the golden and russet chrysanthemums on Lili's grave, a lonely splash of colour amidst the stone-greys and faded winter grass. Coming to terms with her death was hard. I'd spent years in Australia imagining her bright artist's eye capturing the world as her skill blossomed. We had shared as girls for such a short time, but in those few months, we had shared everything.

I sat on the wide stone edge of her grave. Amongst the three of us friends, I had contemplated the death of two of us – mine, at the hands of my father and Willi's by suicide. But Lili's death was not part of that world. But the universe had snuffed her out with no reference to who she was and what she might become. If my father had killed Mutti and me, at least our deaths would have had meaning for him. If Willi was dead at his own hand, I understood how that could happen; I'd been part of his struggle to hold back the dark tides that lapped at his mind. But there was no sense to be found in Lili's death.

After a while with these dark thoughts, the cold roused me. I stood, looking round the cemetery: its bare trees and grey stone pocked with lichen, a complete contrast with my farewell to Aunt Anastasia. But this time I could not bring myself to speak into such bleakness. I laid my hand on her headstone and thanked her for being a friend to the friendless, awkward boy who turned out to be a girl, for the joy she brought to our three-way friendship, for sharing her talent, visible in our portraits, and for the support she gave Willi after I disappeared.

I walked away, blinking away tears under the dun, indifferent sky.

At the hotel, I wrote a long airmail letter to Mutti and a shorter one to Lizzie. I shared Lili's death and Willi's disappearance with Mutti. It didn't feel it was right to burden Lizzie; I told her about the flight to England and what I'd seen of the places we'd stopped. I wrote to the Nowaks, thanking them for the kind hospitality and assuring them I would give them an address once I had one. I took these to the post office in the High Street as dusk enveloped the town.

On Saturday, I decided I would spend the day in Canterbury shopping for more winter clothes before meeting with Mr Pollock. Off the bus, I window-shopped and people-watched, trying to come to some idea of winter fashion. The 'mini-skirt and knee boots' look I had seen in magazines in Australia had been replaced by knee-length shift dresses and coats. But knee boots were still much in evidence. After a coffee to warm me up, I gravitated to Lefevre, where the staff in ladies' fashions spent an hour updating my winter wardrobe. I arranged for my purchases to be held for me to pick up after my meeting with Mr Pollock.

How am I going to get past the lie and engage his help?

Chapter 18
Early January 1969

As I approached the tea shop, I realised I did not know what Mr Pollock looked like – nor he me. Once inside, I stood looking around, trying to imagine what a middle-aged, I presumed, Maths teacher looked like. I could see no middle-aged men by themselves and secured a table with a view of the door and ordered a coffee.

About five minutes later, a middle-aged man with a somewhat unruly head of black hair flecked with grey entered.

Mr Pollock?

But he waved across the room and joined another table.

Following him was a couple – a tall, stringy man with glasses and a much shorter woman. The man looked around and nudged his companion towards me.

"Excuse me, but would you be Miss Miller?" His manner was diffident, almost apologetic.

I stood up. "I am. You must be Mr Pollock."

"Indeed." He looked me over. "You claim to be some sort of distant relative from Australia?"

I summoned up a smile. "Why don't you sit down? Would you like a pot of tea – or a coffee?" If I pinned them down with a pot of tea, it would be more difficult for them to walk away.

Mr Pollock glance at his female companion. "Tea, my dear?"

She nodded. I went across to the counter to order a pot of tea for two. Remembering how tough conversations around the table with Mutti, Willi and Lili had been eased by cake, I ordered the cake selection plate as well.

When I sat down, I could see suspicion in the woman's eyes.

Mrs Pollock?

I breathed deep. "Mr Pollock," I began. "Please forgive me. I've called you here under false pretences."

He blinked and glanced sideways at his wife. Her eyes narrowed.

"I am not a distant relative and I apologise for the deception. But speaking with you away from the school is important and that was the best subterfuge I could think up." I gave them a lopsided smile. "But I am recently arrived from Australia."

I could see Mrs Pollock's hand tighten on her husband's arm and she seemed about to stand.

"Your pot of tea and cakes." The waitress placed the plate of cakes on the table along with small tea plates for the three of us. I indicated the tea was for the Pollocks and she set up the cups and saucers, standing the teapot between them.

"Thank you," I smiled.

Would the tea and cakes anchor the Pollocks to their seats for long enough for me to persuade Mr Pollock to help?

I offered the cakes across the table. "Cake?"

Mr Pollock chose a chocolate cupcake and gave me a piercing look. "Hmm ... why did you need to speak to me?"

I took a steadying breath. "Do you remember a talented Maths student who was also an excellent linguist? He would have completed his A levels in 1965, I think."

Mr Pollock's forehead wrinkled. "Perhaps ..."

"He won a German essay competition in 1964. The prize was a two-week trip to East Germany."

"Ah yes, that boy." He glanced at his wife.

He had talked with her about Willi?

"I am hoping you can help me find him. I lost touch with him when my mother and I moved to Australia."

"You don't know where he lives?"

"No, not now." The fear and loss pushed towards the surface.

Breathe, Col.

"I went to his house, but they had moved away some time ago." I paused for another breath. "I tried to find him through a mutual friend, but she was killed in a car accident not long after we left for Australia."

Mrs Pollock looked at her husband and poured two cups of tea. "I think I remember you telling me about this boy." She glanced across at me, her eyes softening. "You were close friends with him?"

"His name was William Johnstone." The name registered with Mr Pollock. "I asked at the school office, but they told me they could not give me the private information of students as I wasn't a relative."

Mr Pollock glanced at his wife. "He was a remarkable young man. Not a brilliant mathematician, but certainly talented." His eyes wandered into the distance above my head. "I seem to recall that physics was his primary interest though ..." there was silence for a few seconds before he leant forward to pick up his cup and take a sip of tea. "He was into nuclear physics, I think." He pondered for a moment. "Did he go to Imperial to study in their nuclear engineering program?" he mused. He took another sip of tea and fixed me with his eyes. "You would like me to check the school records and pass the information to you." He clattered his cup onto the saucer and I could hear disapproval in his voice.

Mrs Pollock gave me a thin smile. "Why did you not stay in touch by letter?"

What should I tell them?

"Because I couldn't." I picked up my coffee, stalling as I took a drink.

I replaced the cup, delaying further as I took a breath. "My name is not Karlota Miller, though I have a valid UK passport in that name."

I could see surprise and confusion on their faces.

"I am Colette Schmidt, born in Leipzig – east Germany as it was until recently. My mother and I defected to the West in 1962. British security hid us here at first but then in Australia, as our lives were under threat." I couldn't bring myself to name my father. "We could not stay in touch with anyone here in England. That would reveal our location."

Mr Pollock's narrowed eyes regarded me. "Why should I believe you, help you?"

I dredged my memory, trying to think of something that might convince him I was Willi's close friend.

"Um ... I think I remember Willi telling me you helped him on one occasion – with something other than Maths ... was it in the library?" The memory was vague, blurred. I struggled to retrieve it.

Mr Pollock fixed me with a stare, his brows furrowing in concentration before they relaxed, releasing his bushy eyebrows. "Yes ... Yes, I did. The newspapers were still in the librarian's office and I retrieved them. He was anxious about something ..."

Got it.

"He was. It would have been in February 1964 when the Soviets shot down a US plane that had wandered into East Germany. He was worried that it might disrupt his trip to East Germany at Easter."

Mr Pollock's head bobbed. "Yes, that was it."

I looked across the table at him. "Willi held you in high regard, Mr Pollock. He thought of you as someone occupying the lofty heights of mathematics."

That's true – but Willi had included a reference to 'ivory tower' – which was a touch less complimentary.

Mr Pollock ducked his eyes from me in embarrassment and glanced at his wife; she was squeezing his forearm in delight at hearing this. He cleared his throat. "It's always good to hear that one's students respect you." His eyes returned to me. "What information are you seeking?"

He was going to help.

"Anything that would allow me to find him. His mother's address, the university he's studying at. Whatever you can get me that would help me find him."

He looked at me in silence before reaching into his pocket to pass me his card. "Ring me here on Monday night after six o'clock. I'm not promising anything, mind you."

I smiled, putting the card in my handbag. "Thank you. That's wonderful."

Mr Pollock wagged a finger at me. "No guarantees, young lady."

But I could see a faint smile on his lips.

"Can I order you another pot of tea?"

Mrs Pollock smiled. "Thank you, that would be lovely."

When I sat down, Mrs Pollock leant across, almost conspiratorially. "Could you tell me about Australia? It sounds wonderful."

"Well – I know Brisbane – that's the capital of Queensland. I've not been anywhere else."

I spent the next fifteen minutes as we finished the tea and cakes answering Mrs Pollock's questions about Brisbane and Australia.

Mr Pollock nudged his way into the conversation. "It's been most pleasant meeting you, Miss Miller." He frowned for a moment. "Or should that be Miss Schmidt?"

I smiled. "At the moment, I think I'm still Miss Miller, although Mutti and I are hoping to reclaim our real identities."

"Well, Miss Miller, thank you for the tea and cakes, but we must be moving on. We'll speak on Monday evening."

After they left, I settled the bill. At LeFevre, I looked at my packages and realised that managing everything on a bus would be a problem. I arranged for a taxi to pick me up. Dusk was falling as the taxi left the city – and for a second, frissons skittered across my skin as my previous taxi ride out of Canterbury flooded my brain.

Breathe, Col. Breathe.

When the taxi pulled up outside my hotel, I was still feeling shaky. The taxi driver helped me carry my purchases into the hotel lobby. The eyes of the young man behind the reception desk followed me. He was examining the bags bearing the Lefevre name. My elegant New Year's Eve outfit and now these bags were causing a reappraisal from me as an ignorant colonial, perhaps.

"May I help you with these, Miss Miller?"

I smiled at him. "Thank you."

He was about to turn away when he picked up an envelope. "There's a message for you."

He handed me the envelope and produced a luggage trolley. With my purchases loaded, he followed me to my room, unloading the trolley. Once alone, I opened the envelope: the Novaks had invited me to lunch the following day. I rang, thanking them for the invitation and Alice arranged to pick me up at eleven.

After eating in the restaurant, I spent the evening going over my purchases; I would need another suitcase.

I spent a pleasant few hours with the Nowaks on Sunday.

It horrified Alice to discover I didn't know how to drive. "Once you've completed your search, get yourself some lessons and find a car." She looked across at her father. "I'm sure Daddy would help you with this."

Uncle Brian smiled. "An E-Type Jaguar?"

• • • •

I HAD ALL DAY MONDAY to myself and was at a loose end after my morning run. Eventually, I dressed in some of my new warm clothes and headed out along the coastal path into the territory that Lili, Willi and I walked many times. The wind was blustery and the thin sunlight held no warmth – the antithesis of the Australian blaze. Few other people braved the cutting wind. The solitude of the cliff-top path drifted memories before my inner eye.

Almost without realising it, I ended up at Bishopstone Glen, where we three had stood on that first day together. I stared over the stream-cut gash in the cliffs, hoping the call with Mr Pollock would provide the information to find Willi. If that failed, there remained one possibility – Mrs Henderson and I quailed before that thought. If she consented to meet me, she would tell me whatever fitted her ends – with no regard to the truth or my needs.

Mr Pollock had to help me.

On the return, the wind cut deeper with a frozen edge because the spectre of Mrs Henderson dogged my steps.

In my hotel room, I tried without success not to watch the hands of my alarm clock creep away the afternoon. Frustrated with its glacial movement, I wandered down to the TV lounge. I sat watching children's programming for an hour but was in my room well before six o'clock with Mr Pollock's card in front of me, a notepad and pen at the ready.

I delayed dialling until five past six. The phone rang for a while before they picked it up.

"Hello?" It was Mrs Pollock.

"Good evening, Mrs Pollock. It's Karlota Miller. Is your husband home?"

"He is. I'll get him."

I heard her call out and put down the phone. Long seconds later I heard it scrape across a surface as Mr Pollock picked it up.

"Miss Miller? It's Mr Pollock."

"Good evening, Mr Pollock." I could feel my hand sweating where it gripped the phone. "Were you able to find anything?"

Mr Pollock cleared his throat. "Yes, indeed." He paused. "Before I tell you anything, you must promise me never to reveal how you came by this information. It would embarrass me or worse, if it came out I had passed on student information."

"I understand, Mr Pollock. I'll tell no-one."

"Very well." Another pause and I heard paper rustling over the thump of my heartbeat.

"As I thought, William Johnstone went to Imperial College to study nuclear engineering."

I scribbled the information onto the pad.

Mr Pollock continued. "The most recent address I found is in Honiton, Devon. Twenty-five School Lane, Honiton, Devon. Unfortunately, there was no telephone number listed with that address."

I repeated the information back to him.

"That's correct, Miss Miller. I wish you success with your search."

"Thank you for your help, Mr Pollock."

We hung up and I looked at the pad, hoping that this would be the link to Willi. I went down to the restaurant for dinner. A young woman at reception told me for Honiton I would need a train to London and another to Devon from Paddington Station. She showed me a listing for hotels in Honiton and I rang to book for the following night at the Old Pig Inn.

I started packing – and realised I'd forgotten all about picking up another suitcase. I'd have to do that first thing in the morning.

• • • •

A SHOP IN THE HIGH Street provided a suitcase. I raced through the rest of my packing and caught a train up to London. When I asked at Victoria Station for directions to Paddington, the porter cocked his head on one side, looking at my cases.

"Well now, missy. You could catch the Underground, but you'd find it difficult with them cases." He gave me a gap-toothed smile. "Why don't you let me get you a cab?"

I dithered for a moment, Aunt Anastasia's money warring with my careful upbringing. "Okay."

He loaded my bags onto a trolley. "Follow me, missy."

He found me a black cab, loaded my cases and stood there, smiling at me expectation on his face.

He wants a tip.

I blushed with embarrassment. "Thank you. Er ... I've recently arrived from Australia and I have no idea how much to tip. We don't do tips in Australia. Could you please help me?"

The porter gave me an incredulous look. "No tips?"

I shook my head. The cabby pricked up his ears – he'd want a tip too, I supposed.

He pulled his earlobe in thought. "Well, for carrying your cases across 'ere and finding you a cab, I'd suggest two bob." He saw my confused look. "That's two shillin's."

I opened my purse and found a pair of shillings, dropping them into his hand. He touched his hand to his forehead. "Thank you, Missy." And closed the door to the cab once I'd climbed in.

The cab drove into Paddington Station and dropped me. I paid and tipped the cabby what he suggested and he waved to a porter, who came over.

"I need to buy a ticket to Honiton, in Devon."

"Aye, miss." I followed him to the ticket office, where I discovered the train was quite full.

The porter leant towards me. "You'd better get a first-class ticket with all this luggage, miss."

Thank heavens for Aunt Anastasia's money.

"Thank you."

A few minutes later, he saw me and my cases into a first-class compartment. About fifteen minutes later, the train accelerated out of London and swept through the vivid green countryside. I arrived in Honiton in mid-afternoon. Another cab saw me to the Old Pig Inn. Once in my room, I had a quick wash and headed downstairs to ask directions to School Lane.

It wasn't far – but, once there, I couldn't find a number twenty-five. The numbers stopped at thirteen on one side of the road and twelve on the other. I walked along the street again, checking the numbers: no twenty-five.

Had Mr Pollock made a mistake?

At the hotel, I checked the phone book for Willi's mother, Dr Johnstone: nothing. At the hotel, I asked if Honiton had two School Lanes. There weren't. I went to my room and rang Mr Pollock. He was adamant that the information he had given me was correct – and please stop bothering him.

Mrs Henderson's work muddying the trail?

Her presence in my head disturbed my sleep. Over breakfast, I decided there was no point staying in Honiton. I would have to return to London and try to find him through the university – but that was probably a false lead as well. Living out of a suitcase was getting me down and it seemed my search for Will was going to take longer than I had expected. I needed something more permanent than a hotel room. At Paddington station, I asked a porter about renting a flat in London.

"Get yerself a copy of the Evening News," he saw my questioning look. "It's a newspaper – lots o' flats advertised in that."

He brought my cases to a taxi, which took me to the Victoria Hotel and I checked in for two nights. After talking to the receptionist about maps of London, she directed me to a nearby newsagent for a copy of the London Street Directory and the newspaper. The Evening News had many ads for flats. I made several calls and booked an appointment with an agent to look at apartments near Willi's university – perhaps.

After breakfast, I caught a taxi to the agent's office in South Kensington. The office seemed posh, but I went in and was shown to a small back office that was dimmer and much more downmarket than the offices we passed on the way.

A young man stood up behind the cluttered desk. "G'day," he glanced down at his diary. "Karlota Miller?"

He looked me up and down, making me feel uneasy. "I'm Jake Walker. Youse arrived from Oz? I'm from Sydney."

I shook the proffered hand. "I'm from Brisbane."

"Right ho." He looked sideways at me.

Assessing my smart clothes?

"These flats I was going to show you are basic, you know." His frown added emphasis.

"What do you mean?"

"Well, they're glorified bed-sits ... a hot plate and grill, shared bathroom." His eyes swept over me again. "You might prefer something ... um ... better?"

I thought for a moment. "How about you show me the best of the ones I asked to see and we'll take it from there?"

"Right you are." He stood up. "I'll get the keys." He darted out, returning with several keys with cardboard labels.

Jake was right. If a dowdy room in a musty smelling house was the best he could offer, I wanted something better.

On the street, I turned to Jake. "You're right. I want something better than that."

"Anything better is going to cost more, you know." Jake frowned. "Can you afford that?"

I looked him in the eye. "Why don't you take me to the office? We can go over what's available."

Jake's shoulders slumped. "I'll have to hand you over to Mrs Sanders. I deal with the cheap bedsits." He must get commission on rentals he arranges.

Mrs Sanders eyed me with suspicion as I sat in her much more salubrious office. I don't think she thought much of a teenager from Australia trying to rent one of her flats. She showed me her file of flats in the area with reluctance. I stifled my reaction at the rents. Converting pounds to Aussie dollars, I realised the rents were over three times what Mutti was paying for our house in Brisbane.

Thank you again, Aunt Anastasia.

I told Mrs Sanders I would like to look at two of them.

She shifted in her chair. "Even if you can afford them, the owners will require references. Do you have any?"

What's her problem? Does she think I'm going to have raucous parties every night?

I summoned my best posh look and voice. "Mrs Sanders, I'm an eighteen-year-old girl fresh out of one of the best schools in Australia. I've lived with my mother all my life. I have an excellent reference from my school, but that's all."

Her closed expression told me it would not do. I thought for a moment. "Could I pay a larger security deposit instead of references?"

She smothered a snort of derision and a thin smile of satisfaction appeared on her face. "If you cannot supply references, I cannot help you." She snapped her file closed and stood up, giving me a glare to chase me out of her office.

A minute later I was standing outside on the pavement, smarting at the patronising and dismissive handling I'd received.

I don't want to keep living out of a suitcase in a hotel.

I vowed to keep trying. Looking along the street, I noticed another agent store front and wandered down to look through the window. It contained colour pictures of flats for sale and thanks to Aunt Anastasia, I could afford them. I recognised one as being in Mrs Sanders' rental file.

We had a somewhat confused start when the agent could not believe I was a real purchaser. I had her speak to my bank and that sorted things out. I had looked at the two-bedroom flat, bright even in the thin January sunshine.

When we returned to the office, the agent, Mrs Brooks, sat me down. "Do you intend to stay in England long?"

I sighed. "I don't know."

She smiled. "The owner is in no hurry to sell the flat. It's available to rent, you know."

I explained about my lack of references, but Mrs Brooks thought that would not be a problem if she told the owner I was thinking of buying the flat. She pulled out a rental agreement and promised to phone me once she'd spoken to the owner.

I walked up Exhibition Road past all the museums to what was, perhaps, Willi's university. I received a firm rebuttal from the student records office when I asked about Willi: if he was a student, they could not share his information with me. But they told me he couldn't be studying nuclear engineering as that was a post-graduate program.

It had to be Mrs Henderson falsifying Willi's information.

But why would Mrs Henderson tamper with Willi's information? She hadn't passed on my message either.

Lying in bed that night, I wondered about Lili's death.

Was that Mrs Henderson as well – tying up loose ends?

Shards of violent, angry dreams accompanied my waking in the morning, with Mrs Henderson's presence looming over them.

She wouldn't arrange for Lili's death – would she?

I sat in bed, thinking over everything I knew about Mrs Henderson – which was not much.

Had she been involved in the shooting during the rescue? She'd been icy calm and matter of fact in the car on the way to Lancaster.

Recalling our few meetings, she had shown the slightest hint of emotion but once – when she'd slapped my face. I concluded she could contemplate Lili's death – but I doubted MI6 would allow it, let alone the erasure of a complete family. That she could think about arranging Lili's death didn't mean she had done it. What was that aphorism my history teacher quoted? *Never assign to malice, that which is adequately explained by coincidence.* Accidents happen.

But I had no answer to the fundamental question. Why is she hiding Willi from me?

I was dressing when the phone rang. Mrs Brooks confirmed the owner would rent me the flat and I went in to finish the paperwork. I now had a part-furnished flat and I spent the day buying everything else I'd need. This provided enough activity to prevent me from deciding about finding Mrs Henderson. I was rearranging the sitting room furniture for the third time when I stopped and sat on the edge of the sofa, cradling my chin in my hands.

I had to find that woman and make her tell me how to find Willi.

Sitting there, I confronted the fear she conjured in me. Mrs Henderson lurked behind everything I had been through, starting with my interrogation in that house 'somewhere in England'. Mrs Henderson would have directed Jennifer's interrogation of me while Mrs Henderson interrogated Mutti. After that, she'd used Willi to secure the evidence against my father and used Mutti and me as bait in the trap to round up

Eastern Bloc agents. Finally, she shuffled us off to Australia, as we were a danger to those around us and no longer useful to her.

Did she set us up with Mr Franks?

I shivered. She could have suggested to him we might be useful. I closed my eyes and pushed myself back into the sofa. Wherever I looked, I could see her manipulation of our lives. My eyes flicked open.

What about Vogel's disappearance?

Mutti had hinted she'd passed information to someone – but who would Mutti know that would be interested in killing an ex-SS officer? That role didn't fit what I knew about Mr Franks and I couldn't see any benefit to Mrs Henderson from such an action. Who might Mutti have contacted that wanted to eliminate Nazi war criminals? I contemplated this, but nothing came to mind.

His disappearance could be a coincidence ...

But this was more distraction and procrastination. On a whim, I checked the phone book and sat up in surprise: it gave a phone number and the address of the MI6 headquarters building.

The following day, I was on a bridge over the Thames, staring at the MI6 building as the grey-brown river slid beneath me. My hands curled round the stone parapet, knuckles whitening at the thought of facing Mrs Henderson. I must have been there for about ten minutes, oblivious to the people walking past me, trying to summon the courage to enter.

"Good morning, Karlota – or should I be calling you Colette?"

The voice startled me from my fugue and I turned to find Mrs Henderson's cold, judging eyes staring into mine from beneath a fedora.

Chapter 19

Mid – late January 1969

My stomach flipped and my body backed away from the danger. As always, Mrs Henderson's gaze sapped me of value, but as the shock passed, my anger rose.

Those eyes maintained their unwavering, superior gaze. "Nothing to say for yourself, Colette? That's unusual." The statement was barbed, aimed to goad and reinforce my inferiority.

I suppressed my desire to lash out. Our eyes stayed locked.

"You've done well." The same sardonic tone and her face remained hard, giving the lie to any approval. "I had not expected you to rise so well to the challenges that you faced."

What did she know?

I shook myself, struggling to hold my focus as her cutting scrutiny fanned my anger; I wanted a single thing from her. "Tell me where William Johnstone is."

Her head cocked to one side as she leant on her furled umbrella. "But it seems your manners have not improved."

I knew she was goading me, but I could not prevent my fingers from curling into fists at my side. "What you've done to me ... us ... has erased any niceties." I swallowed, struggling to hold myself in check. "Where can I find him?"

A gust of wind fidgeted her hat and she reached up to steady it. "I don't carry such trivial details in my head." Her eyes remained fixed on mine, revealing nothing. "Come with me. We may have that information." She stopped, a deliberate pause. "Or maybe not."

After a moment, she walked past me, her swinging umbrella tapping out alternate steps as she headed towards the MI6 building. She kept walking with her nearly imperceptible limp, her gaze fixed firmly forwards. I hated she was in control again – still – but swallowed my fury and followed. I had no other choice.

She was at the traffic lights, waiting to cross the road. I stood beside her, but she didn't acknowledge me, walking across the road and up the steps into the MI6 building without a sideways glance. I followed her, but stopped as she walked across the foyer to a security gate. She spoke for a second with a guard and then disappeared into the building.

The guard beckoned me over. "Take a seat, please, Miss. Someone will come for you shortly." He pointed at a bench seat.

I walked towards the bench and stood. The exit beckoned – an escape from Mrs Henderson's pitiless gaze. But if I did that, I wouldn't learn how to find Willi. I walked to the bench and sat, clutching my handbag as I tried to contain the froth of anger, fear, hatred and hope swirling inside me.

This was classic Mrs Henderson, to make me feel yet more insignificant. After about ten minutes, the fight to contain myself was slipping from my control. A balding man in a suit came through the security gate. The guards pointed me out and he walked across.

"Miss Miller? Would you come with me, please? I'm Mr Pritchard."

I stood, wary of anyone associated with Mrs Henderson. He shepherded me through the security gate and into the building. After riding up several floors in a lift and down a corridor, he showed me into a room containing a table with chairs on either side.

"Please take a seat."

I walked towards the table and heard the door click shut as he slipped out behind me. When I tried the doorhandle, the door was locked – of course. The phone on the table was dead when I picked it up – no dial tone and no response to a jiggled cradle.

The wretched woman was imprisoning me again –as she did when Mutti and I first arrived in England.

With nothing else to do, I pulled out a chair and sat where I could watch the door. Another ten minutes passed, but it could have been longer. I was deciding I should buy a wristwatch when the door opened and Mrs Henderson walked in, closing the door behind her. She walked across to the table, placed a thick file on the table and stood looking down at me.

My file – or was it Willi's? Surely, his wouldn't be that thick?

I tried to read the name upside down – but it had a file number, no name.

The chair scraped across the floor and she sat, one hand resting on the file.

"You want to know where your friend is."

A statement, not a question.

"Yes."

Mrs Henderson sat, unmoving, her eyes slicing through my tiny store of anger-bolstered confidence, peeling away the puny defences I possessed.

"What do you have to trade for that information?" Her eyes were unwavering.

"What?" My brain was reeling.

She raised a disapproving eyebrow. "Manners, Colette." The admonishment was flat and hard.

We sat, her eyes conducting an assay of my value. "You want information. You've been involved in this for long enough to know that everything has a price. What can you offer in exchange?"

I swallowed my confusion as best I could. "I don't understand."

"It's simple, Colette. You want something from me. I want something in return."

This was crazy. "Do you know where Willi is?"

"Perhaps." Mrs Henderson's face gave nothing away.

I gritted my teeth in frustration. "But I don't have anything to give you." A thought occurred to me and my eyes narrowed. "You want me to give you ... money?"

"I'm aware of your recently acquired wealth." Mrs Henderson's lips curved, but her voice held no warmth. "No. Money is not what I'm after." A finger moved on the file, tapping it once. "And now you've tried to bribe a public servant."

I sat there. She'd reduced me to nothing – again. My shoulders slumped in defeat and my eyes fell to my hands, limp in my lap. "Please tell me what you want." My voice was barely above a whisper.

There was silence from across the table and I dragged my eyes up to hers.

Had she heard me?

The eyes were waiting – judging, dismissive, devoid of empathy. The silence stretched. Mrs Henderson pulled the file towards her, leaning it against the table's edge, denying me any view. She turned pages before stopping at one. "Your language skills have flourished in Australia." She was speaking in French.

Now what?

"English, French, German, Polish and Russian." She flipped another page. "What are you going to do with those languages?" She mused, then looked up, holding my eyes for a second, before leafing on through the file again. "Then there's everything you learned from your mother while you worked for Mr Franks." Her eyes rose to mine, lingered and then returned to the file.

I sat, stunned.

She knew I'd been working for Mr Franks. She knew they trained Mutti as a spy.

Her eyes lifted from the file, hard and uncompromising. "With the collapse of east Germany, all sorts of interesting information became available from the *Stasi* files." She smiled wryly. "Those colonials in Australia never realised the resource they had in your mother." She sniffed. "But then, neither did we. Your mother dissembled with admirable skill during her interrogation. Our contacts in east Germany gave us no hint she was not what she said – a simple translator."

The file closed with a snap. "But that's all water under the bridge." She came upright in her chair. "Work for me and you'll get to read our file on William Johnstone."

"What?"

Mrs Henderson's gaze was unchanged. It stripped the years from me and again I sat before her as in Lancaster, a naïve and powerless child.

"You have skills I would find useful."

Confusion suppressed my ability to think. "You want ... me ... to come and work for you?"

She sat, unmoving.

Another question surfaced in my whirling brain. "Doing what?"

Those eyes lingered on me. "What you were doing in Australia – watching out for potential dissidents."

I was dazed. "Here in London? How would I do that?"

Mrs Henderson's eyes narrowed and I wilted under her disdain. "Of course, not here. In Germany – in your hometown of Leipzig, at least at first."

My mouth dried at the thought of having, again, to live a lie. My tongue sought some saliva and I swallowed before I could speak. "You'll let me read Willi's file if I do that?"

"Eventually." Her unblinking eyes held mine and her voice drew out the word.

"What does that mean?"

Mrs Henderson watched me for several breaths. "Once we have established mutual trust and understanding."

"Mutual trust and understanding ..." I almost spat out the words; anger and fear were bubbling in a dangerous cocktail close to the surface. "You expect me to work for you in the hope that, one day, you'll tell me what I want to know?" My voice was rising with the anger. "You want *me* to trust *you*?"

Mrs Henderson's face was unmoving.

I knew she would pull any trick to get what she wants.

A thought bubbled through the emotional turmoil. "Is he alive?" The words came out in a horrified gasp.

She sat motionless in unblinking silence and the room compressed around me – trapped with this hateful, manipulative woman.

"Your father is alive ... somewhere."

She was threatening me again.

The chair crashed against the wall as I stood.

"Let me go." I almost shouted it.

Mrs Henderson's eyes remained on me as she raised the phone, speaking a single word. "Now." Without taking her eyes off me, she replaced the handset.

The burst of anger that had got me to my feet faded and I stood, feeling foolish under the gaze of this puppet master. The door opened and Jennifer, my original interrogator, walked in. She handed Mrs Henderson a fat package, gave me the briefest acknowledgment with a glance and left.

Mrs Henderson placed the package on top of the file. "Sit down, Colette."

Not sitting was the one thing I controlled. I remained standing.

Was that a hint of a frustrated sigh from Mrs Henderson?

Mrs Henderson opened the package and pulled out the Matryoshka, the Russian doll my mother gave me after a trip to Russia and ... my old diary. They had taken both items from me when we defected. I'd thought them lost forever.

With surgical precision, Mrs Henderson eviscerated the Russian doll, revealing the next smaller one. That precise disassembly continued until she had all six dolls lined up in front of her. Her eyes returned to mine with a simple message: to her I was less than the least of the dolls. Without looking down, she slid the diary across in front of where I had been sitting.

"Consider this as a gesture of good will." But her eyes held no hint of any such thing. She pushed herself up from the chair and walked to the door. Placing her hand on the doorknob, she spoke without turning. "Contact me when you're ready to start."

She was that certain I would submit.

The door opened revealing a waiting Jennifer, who stood aside to let her superior leave. Jennifer's face remained blank as she walked across and reassembled the doll. She held it out to me. "Come with me." I picked up my diary and squeezed that and the doll into my handbag.

Jennifer's eyes held something unexpected.

Sadness? Pity?

A few minutes later, I was again on the bridge, watching the river slip away beneath me as frustration and disappointment warred with fruitless anger. There must be a way to get the information I needed. Living the lies Mrs Henderson would require of me was a price I couldn't pay.

I trudged through London to my flat, isolated and lost. I set my Matryoshka on the mantelpiece, pulled my diary from my handbag and dropped them both on a chair.

Trying to make some sort of personal connection, I wrote a long letter to Mutti, telling her about my encounter with Mrs Henderson, asking for her advice. I'd picked up some postcards earlier and tried to write a cheerful one to Lizzie. After staring at a card showing Tower Bridge, I managed a few words, telling her about my flat and inviting her to come and stay.

Willi's small portrait reminded me to write to the Nowaks, giving them my address and phone number.

That evening, I was sitting, not watching some drama on the TV, when the story caught my attention: a character was hiring a private investigator. A few minutes with the telephone directory showed London had quite a few. I did not know how to choose between them and selected one at random.

In the morning, I ran as usual in Hyde Park before heading out to meet the private investigator. But my resolve started to waiver.

What could an investigator do in the face of MI6? Should I tell him about MI6?

I found a café and had a coffee to settle myself. Sitting there, I racked my brain trying to think of some other way to find Willi. An hour later, I walked up the stairs beside a greengrocer in Wood Green. Several office doors lead off the landing; one proclaimed itself to be "Wallis Investigations".

I knocked – without reply, but the door opened when I tried it. I found a desk with a typewriter and another door, through which I could hear an indistinct voice.

Someone on the phone?

A minute later the door opened to reveal a fair-haired man with an open and innocent face. He was in his early thirties.

He blinked. "Ah – right." He waved at the desk and typewriter. "Let's see if you can do better than the last one."

I gave him a blank look. "Sorry?"

"You're here about the secretary job – although I asked for an older woman, not some wet-behind-the-ears dolly bird." He sniffed. "Well, sit down and I'll give you some dictation."

I smiled at him. "Mr Wallis, I think we are at cross-purposes. I'm not looking for a job."

He blinked. "You're not?"

"No, I'm not." I gave him what I hoped was a reassuring smile. "I'm thinking of hiring you to do some work for me."

He blinked again, his fair complexion showing a faint blush. "Er ... sorry." He gestured to his open office door. "Um ... please come in."

He directed me to one of a pair of chairs beside a low table. "How can I help you ... er, Miss?"

"Miss Miller. I'm trying to find someone I've lost touch with."

He reached round to his desk, grabbing a spiral notebook and biro off the blotter. "Go on."

"He's a young man, my age and probably studying physics at university somewhere in England, but we've been out of touch for several years."

He raised an eyebrow.

"I've been in Australia."

"I see. Please go on."

"Before we go further, I need to find out if you can do this sort of work.

He gave me a confused look.

"Please tell me about your organisation." I looked towards the empty outer office.

He looked at me for a few seconds. "It's only me at present – but as you know, I'm trying to hire a secretary." An embarrassed smile flitted across his face.

"How much experience do you have?"

"Oh – I have lots of investigative experience ... with the Met."

"The Met?"

"The Metropolitan Police. I left them last month to set up my business."

This sounded fishy.

"When you say left, were you sacked?"

Mr Wallis frowned. "No, absolutely not. I still have good contacts in the Met." He gave me a thoughtful gaze. "The job ... frustrated me."

He considered what to tell me.

"You see, there's an increasing number of young people running away from home and turning up in London – and the Met can do little for the parents looking for them unless they're in danger. The Met can't help those, so I will – for a fee."

I smiled at him. "How much are your fees?"

"They're one pound ten shillings an hour." He paused for a second and added. "Plus expenses."

"Umm ... how many hours do you think it would take to find my friend?"

He shook his head. "I don't know. Tell me more about him and I'll do some research."

"How much will that cost?"

He smiled at me. "Pay me twenty pounds as an advance and I'll start. When it runs out, I'll let you know."

I pulled my handbag up from the floor beside me and he stood up.

"Where are you going?"

He sat down. "Umm ... I thought you were about to walk out."

I opened my bag and pulled four five-pound notes out of my purse. "Here you are."

Mr Wallis' eyes widened in surprise. "You're hiring me?"

I waved the notes at him. "What does this look like?" I softened the words with a smile.

He reached across and took the notes. "Umm ... thank you." He folded the money and stuffed it into a trouser pocket. He seemed dazed.

"Aren't you going to give me a receipt?"

"Umm ... right." He went behind the desk and rummaged in the drawers, returning with a receipt book. He slipped the carbon paper behind the first page and started writing. "Miss Miller, is it?"

"Karlota Miller."

He finished writing and tore out my copy, handing it to me. "You'd better tell me about this young man you want me to find."

Over the next ten minutes, I gave him a carefully edited background for Willi, leaving out all references to MI6.

He looked down at his notes. "Er ... what school did he go to?"

"I've tried there – but they won't give information about students unless you're a relative."

"But tell me anyway, for completeness."

Now what do I do?

He picked up my hesitation. "What aren't you telling me?"

"You can't tell anyone this, but I contacted one of Willi's teachers, who passed Willi's information on to me. But it must have got jumbled up as the address doesn't actually exist, nor does the university course they said he was studying."

Mr Wallis gave me a lengthy look. "Okay – one last question. Why do you call him Willi? Johnstone isn't a German name."

I smiled. "No – he's not German, though he speaks German fluently. It's me that's German – on my mother's side."

The fluent half-truths keep coming…

Mr Wallis looked through the notes he'd made.

"What happens now?" I asked.

"I search for him, starting with births, deaths and marriages."

He picked up my stifled reaction, awarding me a considered look. "What now?"

Perhaps he needed to know.

"Willi was close to suicide – twice." I saw again the scene under the cedar tree: Willi with the knife poised over his wrist and a shiver of shame passed through me.

Mr Wallis sat in his chair, watching, encouraging me to continue.

I sighed – he was good at this.

"You think he might be dead?"

I fought the tears. "No …" He must have heard the hint of misery in my voice.

Mr Wallis leant forward, a reassuring look painted on his face. "I'll contact you in a few days. I should have some idea about things by then."

He showed me out of his office. I caught the Tube and returned to the flat, my fears about Willi curdling my stomach.

He has to be alive; he has to be.

After a run in the morning, I sat in my flat trying to work out what to do. After a while, my mind was circling and I sat up with a jerk.

If I don't find something to do, I'll go mad.

London is full of museums. I'd start with the ones close to what wasn't Willi's university. I grabbed a coat and almost fled from the flat. I started with the Natural History Museum, amazed to find that entry was free to its vast collection. I was still there when it closed and there was still more to see. Next day, I explored the rest of the Natural History Museum and moved to the Science Museum. Willi would love the top floor of the Science Museum, dedicated to aviation: as I walked in, I recognised a

Spitfire from the model that had hung in his bedroom. But the Victoria and Albert Museum captured me – it's collections of clothing in particular.

On Friday afternoon, I rang Mr Wallis' office and a woman answered. He had found a secretary. Mr Wallis was out and I left a message for him to call me, please. He returned my call as I was preparing supper.

"Hello."

"Miss Miller? It's Brett Wallis."

"Good evening, Mr Wallis. Have you made any progress?"

"Some – William Johnstone is still alive –"

My breath caught and my eyes closed for a moment.

"At least, there's no death registered in the name that corresponds to the information you gave me – nor a marriage. He has a passport, though."

"Of course he has. He won a trip to East Germany a few years ago."

"Right." He seemed annoyed I hadn't told him this.

"What's next, Mr Wallis."

"Um … I need to ferret around in Herne Bay and Canterbury." He paused and his voice sounded hesitant. "That will incur some travel expenses. I might need to spend the night away."

"You will provide me with itemised expenses and receipts, Mr Wallis?"

"Of course. I'm used to that from the Met. We could meet at my office on … Wednesday morning?"

"Okay."

He said goodbye and hung up. I wasn't at all sure what he would find by 'ferreting around' in Herne Bay and Canterbury, but he thought it important. I was at a loose end for a few more days.

Keep busy …

On Saturday, I returned to the museum strip, exploring more of the collection of clothing at the V & A, as it's known. The museum has something of everything – from Elizabethan attire, Edwardian wedding dresses frothing with lace, to a collection of Victorian ladies' underwear. Imagining being tied into a corset made me shiver. In the foyer, I picked up a pamphlet about some other museums in London. I visited one on Monday that has an impressive collection of mediaeval arms and armour – the Wallace Collection. Tuesday saw me at the Tower of London, viewing the British Crown jewels while wondering how Mr Wallis was going.

On Wednesday, my nervousness about the upcoming meeting saw me pushing hard in my run. Running better than nothing, but it lacked the rhythmic stroking through a pool. Finding a pool was high on my to-do list. I rushed my breakfast and was outside the Wallis office before nine o'clock – but no-one arrived. After ten minutes, I walked downstairs and found a café opposite from which I could watch.

Two cups of coffee later, Mr Wallis arrived and disappeared upstairs. I abandoned my third coffee and hurried up to his office.

Mr Wallis was pecking on the typewriter when I walked in, frowning when he saw me. "Miss Miller." He almost spat out the name.

What was going on?

His eyes held the fire of anger – and something I couldn't identify. "Thanks to you, my secretary has resigned and I expect it will be difficult to replace her."

"What?"

"I don't think she liked the idea of becoming caught up with the Secret Service – and nor do I." His frown deepened. "We tried to stay as far away from the spooks as we could in the Met."

Mrs Henderson ...

I stifled a sigh.

He picked up my reaction. "I see the involvement of MI6 is not a surprise to you." He pursed his lips, his problems bitter in his mouth. "Thank you for nothing. Taking on you and your security issues as a client may well have wrecked my business before it had truly started."

"What happened?"

His hand smacked the desk. "MI6 happened." It was an angry shout. "I arrived in the office yesterday and was dictating my report for you when this woman limps in and tells me to stop working for you, if I knew what was good for me."

"Mrs Henderson ..." I grimaced in anger and frustration.

His eyes narrowed. "You know this woman." He came round the desk, rage simmering on his face. "Please leave and don't come back. Ever." He half pushed me to the door. "Goodbye Miss Miller ... if that's your name."

The door closed and I heard the lock click. Mr Wallis wanted nothing to do with me. I leant against a wall, eyes closed, trying to pull myself from the consuming gyre of frustration and anger.

"Gottverdammter Scheiß auf diese elende, sich einmischende Schlampe." My voice rose as I spat out the words, slapping the wall to emphasise them.

I heard a gasp and my eyes flew open: a middle-aged woman was standing in another office doorway, mouth gaping at my incomprehensible outburst. Embarrassed but shaking with anger, I raced down the stairs, almost bowling someone over as I flew through the entrance.

Now what?

Lost in my anger, I strode along the pavement, oblivious to my surroundings until I crashed into a barrier round an open manhole.

A head appeared. "'Ere. Watch out." The workman growled at me, snapping my attention out of my anger.

I took several breaths, finding myself weak and shaky. Looking around, I saw a park with an empty bench. I staggered across and flopped onto it. Wherever I turned, Mrs Henderson was there, blocking my path, herding me towards her chosen destination.

My single path to Willi was to submit to Mrs Henderson: to return to the life of lies I had escaped.

I slumped down, defeat crushing me into the seat, squeezing bitter, futile tears down my cheeks. I'd lost Lili and now my road to Willi lay through Mrs Henderson. Its surface thick with the falsehoods I would have to live, the fabrications, half-truths and outright lies I would have to utter. I knew what would be required of me – the same as Australia, working for Mr Franks, but now in Europe, working for her – with no end in sight.

Submit to Mrs Henderson or lose all hope of finding Willi.

Sitting there, viewing my choices, I realised how Willi could decide to end it all. When no good choices exist, only bad or horrific, what's the point of continuing? I could give up on Willi by refusing her or I could submit to Mrs Henderson's will, return to a life of lies and find Willi ... when she let me.

But if I did that, could I live with myself? Could Willi live with someone whose existence was a lie?

The chill and a drizzle forced me to move after some uncounted time. I struggled home to my flat and collapsed on the bed.

The shivering cold woke me. I headed into the bathroom and stripped out of my clothes. Stepping into the shower, I let the water chase away the cold that had settled bone-deep, but it could not rinse the darkness out. Some of the water swirling into the drain was my helpless tears and I stood there until the water cooled. After, I wrapped myself in a warm robe and stood, surveying my flat with blurred eyes.

What now?

I sat on the couch, tucking my feet under me to keep them warm, my thoughts writhing in desperation, seeking for some way past Mrs Henderson, but found nothing. I fell to the side, sobbing in abject despair.

I woke to daylight this time, shivering with cold – again. A hot shower later and dressed, I stood in my tiny kitchen trying to persuade myself to eat something, but the thought of food brought waves of nausea.

I slumped onto the couch and noticed my handbag, half hidden beneath a cushion where I had dropped it last night. There behind it lay my diary, where I tossed it days ago. I picked it up, but in my torpor, it slipped from my hand and fell open – a piece of paper fluttered to the floor.

It held a London phone number – 01 363 1879.

That had not been in there when Jennifer took the diary from me six years ago. I reached across to my phone, but stopped before picking up the handset.

Think, Colette.

The slip of paper must have been put there by someone in MI6. I couldn't call from this phone – it must be monitored by Mrs Henderson's minions ... that's probably how she discovered Mr Wallis ... or was I being followed?

Perhaps both.

I thought over my recent visit to Mrs Henderson's lair.

Jennifer?

There had been something other than pity in that glance. Did she put the number in there? Does she want me to contact her? A fierce hope blossomed inside me: she's going to tell me how to find Willi.

Donning a coat, I grabbed my bag and set off to find a phone box. I remembered seeing one in the area ... somewhere. I walked for about five minutes but carried on past it. Mutti had been careful with phone boxes when calling Mr Franks, never using the same one and always checking to see if she was being followed.

I stopped to look into the window of a second-hand furniture shop, scanning the surrounding people in the reflection. I was on a busy street with no idea how to work out if anyone in the crowd was following me. It had been much easier on the less crowded streets of suburban Brisbane where Mutti had shown me this.

Go somewhere less crowded.

Half-an-hour later, I emerged from the underground and walked into Hyde Park at Marble Arch. A few people were about on this cold and overcast morning. After walking into the park, I sat for a while on a bench, watching people as I looked round the park. Everyone I could see was heading somewhere. At least that was the way it appeared. Taking my time, I walked through the park, pausing again to look round from the bridge as I crossed the Serpentine.

No followers.

From there, I headed to the Science Museum. I had noticed several pay phones in the foyer. Once there, I pulled the slip of paper from my coat pocket and dialled – but it rang out. Dialling again brought the same result = Jennifer would be at work. I'd have to try calling this evening – or it might be better to try early tomorrow morning on my run. I wandered down into South Kensington, sitting in a café to warm myself with a hot chocolate and pondered what to do.

What if the phone number wasn't Jennifer?

I frowned.

But who else could it be?

Someone sitting down opposite me startled me.

"Mrs Henderson has been waiting for you to contact her."

Jennifer.

She unwound a blue and grey striped woollen scarf from her neck. She had followed me and hadn't noticed. Mutti would be horrified at my poor trade craft.

A shudder passed through me. "I've nothing to say to her – or you."

I rose, but Jennifer reached across and grabbed my hand. "Sit down, Colette. You need to listen to me."

We engaged in a silent tug of war for a second.

"I'm not your enemy, Colette." Her eyes were pleading. "Please, sit down and hear what I have to say."

I stopped struggling, but Jennifer didn't let go despite my glare. "There's one thing I want from you."

Jennifer sighed, her eyes soft with regret. "And that's the one thing that I can't give you."

"Because you're her creature." My voice was dismissive, venomous.

Jennifer glanced round and shook her head. "Please sit down. People are looking at us and neither of us wants that."

I jerked my hand. Jennifer rose before dropping my hand and collapsing into her seat.

Was that a tear in her eye? What's going on?

I frowned in confusion and sat down.

Jennifer let out a ragged breath. "Thank you."

Arms folded, I sat, waiting.

"I don't know where William Johnstone is. I don't have that clearance."

My confusion deepened. "Why is his location secret?"

Jennifer shook her head. "I have no idea." Jennifer's hand gripped the table-edge. She was tense.

Why?

I leant forward. "What's going on, Jennifer?"

"I'm supposed to persuade you to join us." Her other hand joined the other, gripping the table as if to steady herself on her chair. "But I don't think you should do that." She took a sharp breath. "I know you shouldn't."

I blinked. "You don't want me to join ..."

What had they called it in Lancaster?

"... um ... the firm?"

"I know you from before." A grim smile acknowledged her interrogation of me as a twelve-year-old. "And I've read your ASIO file."

I stared at her for a moment. "That's why my file was thick ..."

"That wasn't your file." Jennifer sniffed. "Mrs Henderson said letting you near your file was ... problematic." She half-smiled. "She knows you're strong from all the exercise and she was worried you'd grab it from her."

"Oh." I twisted my brain around to what she had been saying. "What did my ASIO file tell you?"

Her gaze steadied and held mine for a breath. "It told me you had ... have ... enormous potential as an agent."

I frowned. "But you don't want me to join you ... I don't understand."

"Those Australians didn't read between the lines – and they didn't have access to the diaries you wrote for Will."

I leant forward. "You've read my diaries?" I could hear the affront in my voice.

"Of course. They were in your hotel room, unattended while you were out and about."

Jennifer seemed surprised this intrusion offended me.

I clamped down on my anger. "What did they tell you?"

Jennifer's eyes ran across me again. "That you'd be an excellent field agent, with some more training. But ..." she trailed off, her lips pursing and relaxing as if she was having problems releasing the words.

"But what?"

"The life of an agent would cause you ... serious problems. You'd become ... unstable and useless after a while."

We looked at one another across the table and a hand reached out to mine.

"You were having difficulties with the lies in Australia."

I gave her the briefest nod of acknowledgement.

"It would be worse and for longer if you joined us."

My eyes closed as I imagined Mrs Henderson's path of lies, half-truths and subterfuge winding into the recesses of my mind. In the solitary darkness they carried with them, I shivered, alone.

I couldn't go there ...

My chest was collapsing under the emotional load. My eyes flicked open and I drew in a ragged breath. "But Willi ..." It was almost a wail and I saw heads turning towards us again.

Jennifer's hand found mine again, her voice low but intense. "If you work for her, it will kill you." Her eyes were pleading. "You'll have to give him up."

Brief anger surfaced. "Why do you care? This is some double bluff, isn't it?"

"No bluff. I'll lose my job if she finds out what I'm telling you to do." Jennifer shrugged. "I'm helping you because you've been badly used by us. I want that to stop."

The momentary rage evaporated and I whispered. "There must be some way for me to find him."

Jennifer squeezed my hand. "Look at me, Colette." She waited until she held my gaze. "She'll never let you find him – your hope is her unbreakable hold on you if you join us. If you don't, whatever you try, she will be one step ahead. She can falsify any record that you seek and she has powers and resources that you cannot match. Your newly acquired wealth is nothing in comparison."

I closed my eyes for a moment, wishing my ears could shut out her voice. When I opened them, her face showed sorrow and pity and her voice came softly through the café background. "Time to walk away, Colette. Go to Germany and pick up your real life. Time to move past these last six years and get on with the rest of your life." Her eyes hardened. "If you don't, she will drain you until all that's left is a husk."

"Why does she hate me?"

Jennifer almost laughed. "She doesn't hate you. I think she sees something of herself in you – your linguistic skills in particular." Her eyes became distant. "You're a useful tool she wants to have at her disposal." Her focus returned to me. "She doesn't want to leave that tool lying around for someone else to use, someone who does not share England's interests."

I pursed my lips. "But I'm not English."

"Quite." She pursed her lips. "Go back to Germany and pick up your life." She reached into her bag. "These might help." She slipped two small, dark blue covered booklets across the table.

My eyes widened: our east German identity cards.

Jennifer stood up, intensity flaring in her eyes. "Go to Germany, Colette. Rediscover your life – and live it." She swung the scarf round her neck. "And if Willi is the person you think he is, he'll come looking for you."

I watched her pick her way through the tables and chairs out into the drizzle.

Why was she doing this? To salve her conscience?

Our old ID cards secured in my handbag, I headed to my flat, my thoughts a swirl of confusion.

Chapter 20
September 1969 – August 1970

I left the Munich University bookshop, walking into the sunshine of an Indian summer and stood, savouring the view. I'd seen photographs of the wrecked city of 1945 and today's cityscape astonished me. Restoration work was not yet complete, but the careful blending of old and new delighted me. Mutti and I had seen the concrete bleakness of Leipzig's reconstruction under communism. Despite this, there had been a sense of people shaking off twenty years of restrictions, seeking a new identity. Willi's remarks about the young people he had met on his visit to east Germany seemed almost prescient.

Where are you Willi? I tried searching for your doctor mother – but still nothing. Jennifer said you'd come looking for me ...

Walking away from Mrs Henderson had meant walking away from my single remaining link to Willi. Reliving that decision caused emotion to slice through me. I needed the rhythm of movement to soothe me.

I strode for a tram, my textbook-loaded bag's gentle thud on my hip helping me contain my inner turmoil. In our apartment, I started preparing tea with *Imbi* threading through my legs, purring happily. Aunt Anastasia's money had allowed me to fly him here and he was settling in, although I expected he would find the upcoming winter challenging. With the shepherd's pie in the oven, I sat with *Imbi* sleeping on my lap, glancing through my Russian textbook whilst at least half my mind gnawed at the fruitless search for Willi.

Always there, coiled like a serpent waiting to strike, was Mrs Henderson's offer: acquiesce and Willi would be mine. Jennifer's warning of what this would do to me had been stark. I would have to ignore that if I were to succumb to Mrs Henderson's blandishments. The endless, self-destructive lies required for Mrs Henderson carried more weight than Jennifer's warning.

I shuddered and forced myself to concentrate on the textbook. I had chosen Russian and Polish as my specialist languages for my undergraduate linguistics degree; English and French had tempted me, but it seemed most people from the old West Germany spoke English to some extent. Mutti had suggested that having deep knowledge of Russian and Polish would probably benefit me more in the job market after I graduated. But she'd smiled, advising me to keep my French and English going. The English would be easy: Mutti and I moved fluidly between English and German in our daily conversation. French was my weakest language. I wasn't sure how I would keep that going, let alone improve it until Mutti pointed out that France was less than four hundred kilometres away from Munich. In the meantime, there were always books and newspapers.

Should I learn to drive and get a car as Alicia suggested?

Mutti opening our apartment door roused me. I carefully placed *Imbi* on the sofa and greeted Mutti with a hug. "How's it going?"

Mutti smiled as she hung up the coat she'd had draped over her arm. "I'm still in the orientation and training program, but it's feeling less bizarre to be working for the security services here in the west."

I had felt some of that oddness, too, when Mutti told me she'd been offered a job as an analyst/translator for the security service.

Our return to a reunited Germany had been simple. Mutti joined me in London and after a few days, we flew to Berlin as tourists on our British passports. From there, we caught a train to Leipzig. But the day after we arrived there, a man and a woman from the *Bundesnachrichtendienst (BND)*– the Federal Intelligence Service – knocked on our hotel room door before breakfast. We think that was thanks to a tip off from Mrs Henderson, but don't know for sure. The *BND* agents knew our real identities and asked us – politely – to accompany them to the local *BND* office. We had two days of – well, let's call it interrogation. It was civilised compared to the grilling British security had given us after we defected. They let us return to our hotel that first night, although Mutti suspects they were watching to see if we would try to abscond. Late on the second afternoon, they gave us new German identity cards in our original names. They suggested we surrender our British passports. I pointed out that I had significant assets in Australia tied to my British identity and could not abandon it – at least not yet. In the end, we both kept our British passports on the understanding we returned them 'soon'. We kept our now useless east German identity cards.

There thing of interest on both sides of the interrogation table: the whereabouts of my father. He had 'dropped off the *BND's* radar'.

Their interest confused me. "Why are you looking for him? Has he committed a crime?"

The two agents shared a brief sideways glance.

"There are some ... issues ... from his time during Nazi rule when he was in the *Orpo* that we wish to discuss with him. Then there are his more recent activities in the Stasi, particularly at Leipzig Prison."

Mutti sighed. "You have the evidence that I assembled about his wartime activities?"

There was another sideways glance between our interrogators. "We have evidence provided by MI6."

It seemed Mrs Henderson was trying to take credit for Mutti's careful work.

"Mutti assembled that evidence." My voice was angry. Mutti's hand held my arm, trying to restrain me. I frowned at her. "No, you did the work and you should get the credit."

I turned to our interrogators. "Mutti left the evidence hidden in Leipzig when we defected. It was our insurance if they captured us. MI6 had it smuggled out – unwittingly – by my English friend when he visited east Germany in 1964."

"I see." She looked at Mutti. "Thank you for that work." Her eyes flicked between the two of us for a second. "And what do you know about his activities at Leipzig Prison?"

I shrugged and looked at Mutti.

She glanced across the table and turned towards me. Her lips worked, finding the words. "As part of his duties with the *Stasi*, I ... think ... your father was involved with interrogations and ... executions there."

I could see the pain in her eyes.

"Leipzig Prison was where all the executions took place in the DDR." Her voice became harder. "They executed many for the crimes they committed under Nazi rule." Her hand grasped mine and her voice dropped. "But they executed political prisoners as well."

The man leant forward. "You knew of his activities there?" There was an accusatory undertone in his voice.

"Knew?" Mutti shook her head. "No." Her hand tightened on mine. "But I linked some of his absences with announcements of executions."

There was silence from the other side of the table.

Mutti's face was grim. "It seems he had a ... taste ... for participating in such activities."

Was this what had caused my interrogator's strange reaction to something in my file when we defected? What did his disappearance mean? Was he dead? MI6 didn't think so.

"Col? Col? Hello?"

I shook myself into the present. "Sorry, Mutti. I was miles away."

Her hand stroked my face. "Is everything all right?"

I sighed. "I was thinking about father."

We shared a worried look before Mutti turned away. "Let's have tea."

As I lay in bed with *Imbi* purring beside me, the large portrait of Willi graced the wall. His eyes engaged mine as they did most nights.

Was he trying to find me? Thanks to Mr Wallis, I knew he was still alive ... somewhere.

The language studies were easy, but the linguistics part was almost philosophical. Within both the Russian and Polish contexts, the hand of the Soviet state had played a significant and, according to some of my lecturers and tutors, sinister role. According to them, it had warped the language to political and social ends. An academic war was playing out between several professors, with a desire for vengeance underlying the academic discussions.

That desire for retribution for past crimes committed by the east German regime and its organs of power like the *Stasi* played out in the wider society. Frustrations were building. There was an insistence by the government that the rule of law be applied, which resulted in a glacial slowness in dealing with what many saw as the criminal oppression by the east German regime. Senior members of the east Germany regime were being investigated, but run-of-the-mill informants and *Stasi* officers seemed immune.

Was my father 'run-of-the-mill'? He had Nazi war crimes to answer for as well.

Mutti and I established new rhythms and rituals in our new life. I swam in the university aquatic centre pool and every morning I ran in nearby Sendlinger Park as temperatures fell through Autumn. I wondered how I would cope with running in the snow.

Autumn finally shuddered into the freezing arms of winter. Mutti and I were used to Brisbane, where winter temperatures rarely fell to ten degrees Celsius; we both felt the bite of Munich's winter. *Imbi* went joyously berserk in the first snow on our balcony, leaping, rolling and lashing the powdery snow into the air with his tail. When he finally came inside, his paws clattered on the floor tiles from the ice that had frozen on them. He sat for some time, chewing it out. Mutti and I survived outside in warm coats, woollen leggings, hats, scarves and thick gloves. Thankfully, our apartment was centrally heated and *Imbi* frequently sprawled in sybaritic pleasure on the shelves above the radiators. My runs in the park stopped with the snow after a single slippery attempt. I resorted to going into the university early to swim for longer.

My fellow students regarded me as an oddball. I was by nature solitary and studious. I did not participate in their undergraduate frivolity nor engage in the seemingly endless political discussions. To make matters worse, I didn't have a boyfriend and had rebuffed the few approaches I had received. After that, I noticed a few girls giving me covert looks.

I missed Lizzie. I stayed in touch with her, exchanging letters every few weeks. She was trying to persuade her parents to let her visit Munich for Christmas. Her mother was proving difficult, but Lizzie was working on her father.

My life in Australia still called for my attention: I had Aunt Anastasia's inheritance to manage, however loosely. Now I was in Europe, that presented a problem: I was unlikely to return to Australia – at least to live.

Should I sell up and move the money here?

I had people I trusted looking after the money in Australia and I had no-one like that here.

I'd need to work on this.

Then there was Aunt Anastasia's bequest to the Russian Club. Extricating myself in a way that honoured Aunt Anastasia's intentions would be hard. There had been letters going back and forth, but it was difficult to manage at a distance and that was not what Aunt Anastasia would want.

I arranged driving lessons and, much to my delight, passed my driving test in late October. I wanted to buy an E-Type Jaguar but baulked at the cost and the cost of insurance. Instead, I found myself a low mileage VW *Karmann Ghia*. Mutti talked me out of buying a soft top when she pointed out it would be cold in winter. With this freedom, I could spend several weekends in France before Christmas, keeping my French language skills alive. Mutti had never learned to drive and was quite happy with public transport around the city.

In late November, Mutti finished her orientation and started working as a translator/analyst at the *BND*. Once teaching ended, I headed to Luban by train for a long weekend. I wanted to take photographs of what had been Mrs Jaworski's hometown in repayment for all the kindness she had shown me. They had fought over it as the Russians advanced towards Berlin, but much of the old town remained. I shot off a roll of colour film and chose about a dozen of the best which I sent to Mrs Jaworski, care of the Polish Club in Brisbane as I didn't have her address.

Lizzie's mother refused to let her visit. I know they could afford the airfare – I suspected she did not want her daughter so far beyond her control. The student Christmas parties did not entice me – Christmas evoked mixed emotions, many of them sad. A day or two after Christmas, I asked Mutti if there had been any news of father.

She came and sat beside me on the sofa. "*Liebling*, if I heard anything, I would let you know."

"Would the *BND* tell you if they heard anything?"

Mutti looked away for a moment. "Yes, I think they would. I've told them he holds grudges and would come after me if he could."

"We won't be safe until he's locked up."

Mutti stared at her hands before looking up. "I understand, *Liebling*, but you can't spend your life like that. If he's out there, the *BND* will find him."

Mutti's arm crept round my shoulder. There was nothing I could do about father; I leant my head against Mutti's shoulder, drawing solace from the love we shared.

Once the snow melted, I resumed my early morning runs in the park, though it was still dark. There were occasional streetlights and I knew the paths. When I let my running habit slip in conversation at university, the other girls were horrified, giving me all sorts of dire warnings about rape. I hadn't considered that and resolved to be more aware of my surroundings as I ran, but kept the morning runs going.

I was planning to spend the Easter long weekend in France to help keep my French up to scratch. Mutti decided to come, too. An immersive weekend would help boost her French language skills. The weekend before Easter, Mutti and I headed into the centre of Munich for some quality browsing at the Karstadt department store. Neither of us needed anything, but looking is always fun. We spent several hours viewing and commenting on the Spring fashions. I saw some beautiful clothes, but I didn't have a good reason to buy anything; I hadn't had another opportunity to wear the outfit I'd purchased for the Nowak's New Year's party at the car showroom in Herne Bay. Alicia had sent me an invitation for this year's party, but I'd declined as flying to England for a party seemed, well, self-indulgent. I had invited her to visit me in Munich – and sent her a picture of my car, which she liked. Mutti and I ended our visit trying fragrances and looking at makeup, something that I had a minimal interest in, despite Michelle's endeavours in Brisbane.

We walked out into a squally Spring shower, pausing in the doorway's shelter. People were hurrying past, battling recalcitrant umbrellas in the gusty wind. We fastened our coats and stepped out, turning left for the trams.

Right in front of us was my father – Axel Schmidt.

His gaze was predatory. I froze. He pulled his right hand from a pocket. It was holding a pistol, which he levelled at us. "Goodbye Frida, Col."

I heard someone shouting and father's eyes flicked past me. Mutti pushed me sideways and I heard several shots. She landed in front of me as the glass display window beside us collapsed in a cascade of glass shards.

There were more shots. More glass and a display mannequin fell on us. I heard people screaming.

"Stay down." A man with the pistol was pointing it at someone on the ground past us.

I shifted carefully, conscious of the glass all over us. There was an indistinct shout and another shot, its sound shaking out more glass from the window.

"Stay down." A different voice growled at me from behind me.

After a few seconds, the first man walked into view, a pistol in each hand. "He's dead."

A gloved hand started brushing glass off Mutti and I realised blood was pooling beside her head.

"Mutti." I screamed, scrambling towards her through the glass.

A hand grabbed my coat collar and hauled me to my feet, depositing me inside the store. "Stay there."

I tried to push past him. "Mutti."

He pushed me into the crowd gathered in the store's entrance. "Hold her."

Arms went round me, turning me.

"She's bleeding." Hands grasped my wrists, turning them palm up.

Confused, I looked down and pain blossomed. Blood was dripping from several deep cuts in my hands – some showing slivers of glass.

A chair appeared and hands guided me onto it. In the distance, I could hear sirens as someone wound a cloth round my hands, staunching the blood.

"She's cut her knees, too."

They pressed more cloths to my knees and I hissed in pain. The people around me were a blur.

What's happened to Mutti?

A man pushed through the crowd. "Give her some air." He crouched in front of me, staring into my eyes. "Your mother's hurt, but alive. The ambulance is on its way."

I tried to stand and get to Mutti, but hands pressed on my shoulders. "Stay here. Help is coming."

Sirens howled close by and moaned to a stop. The crouching man stood and moved people away, then crunched through the glass in the entryway. I could see Mutti's feet, but the surrounding people blocked my view. Shortly after, they lifted her onto a stretcher and disappeared.

An ambulance man loomed over me. "Can you walk?"

I looked at him blankly.

He helped me to my feet. "Come along. Lean on me." With him on one side, they walked me through the glittering carpet of glass. He half lifted me into the ambulance and seated me, calling to the driver to go.

Everything was blurred after that. I remember people fussing round me at the hospital and sharp pain as they unwrapped my hands and knees before it all faded.

My father grinned at me from behind a pistol, skin taut across his skull.

"Mutti." I jerked upright and a nurse arrived beside my bed.

"It's all right. Your mother's here." The nurse pushed me back onto my pillow.

I tried to resist but had no strength. "I have to go to her."

"Soon."

"No. Now." I tried to sit up, but she pushed me down onto my pillows.

"Stay here. I'll fetch the doctor." Her hand held me to the bed. "Okay?" She gave me a questioning look until I relaxed into the pillows.

Had I heard the man say my father was dead?

The doctor agreed to let me visit Mutti, provided I did as I was told. A few minutes later, the nurse helped me into a wheelchair. There were bandages on my knees and hands. The nurse fussed over getting me settled, finally pushing me past the police officer outside my room and along the hospital corridors. There was another police officer outside Mutti's room.

Mutti was unconscious, her head bandaged, her face pale on the white pillow. I manoeuvred the wheelchair beside her bed and reached out a bandaged hand, stroking hers with my protruding fingertips.

A doctor arrived and gave me a disapproving look.

I returned the stare.

"Colette Schmidt?"

I suppressed a wave of nausea when I tried to nod.

He glanced at my mother. "A bullet grazed your mother's head. It required stitches, but she will be fine."

"When will she wake up?"

"When she does." His voice was arrogant and he swept out of the room as if Mutti's care was insignificant to his other duties.

Once he'd left, I pulled a spare pillow from the other bed, putting it beside Mutti's arm and rested my head, my fingers tips stroking her hand.

Lying there, I dozed until Mutti moved. I sat up and swayed as giddiness swirled through me.

"*Liebling?*" Mutti's voice was thick with sleep.

I sat for a moment, letting the giddiness pass.

"Are you all right, *Liebling?*"

"Yes, Mutti, I'm fine. What about you?"

Mutti's hand grasped mine and I stiffened in pain. With some effort, she raised her head and saw the bandages. "Oh, *Liebling.* You're hurt." Her head slipped down onto the pillow.

"Cuts on my hands and legs, from the glass. It's not serious." I stroked her hand. "How are you feeling?"

Mutti's eyes closed. "My head's sore and I have a terrible headache."

"The doctor said a bullet grazed your head."

A nurse appeared. "Come along, Colette. Now your mother's awake, the doctor needs to examine her."

I protested, but Mutti waved a limp hand. "I'll be fine, *Liebling.* You need to rest, too."

The nurse wheeled down the corridor to my bed and I surprised myself by drifting off to sleep. The following morning, they let us go home with a large packet of painkillers, anti-biotics, a page of instructions and a female police officer.

Waiting for us, we found a detective from the Federal Criminal Office and a woman from the *BND*. They had us sit on the couch and the woman sent our accompanying police officer to make a pot of coffee.

I leant forward. "Is he dead?"

The detective glanced at the BND woman. "I can confirm that a man we think was Axel Schmidt was shot dead."

I sagged into the couch.

But why do they only think he's dead?

Once the coffee was poured, they asked us to go through what we remembered of the incident.

"Axel tried to shoot us," Mutti said.

"It was his bullet that grazed your head." The detective added.

They want us to know it wasn't one of them ...

Mutti and I gave them as much as we could. It surprised me how disjointed we were, despite our training in observation and reporting. For me, the incident was a set of jagged stills, images lit by the strobe of fear.

When we finished, the detective consulted his notes and glanced at his BND colleague.

She looked at both of us for a moment before speaking. "We need you to make a formal identification."

Mutti sighed.

Ah ... they need this before they can say it's him.

I turned to Mutti. "I have to come too."

"There's no need for you to do that, *Liebling.*"

I shuddered. "Yes, there is." I took a conflicted breath: I didn't want to see him, but ... "I must see his dead body – to know all this is finished."

Mutti's eyes held me as all that had happened over the years passed unspoken between us. She turned to the agent. "When can we do this?"

"Today – now? We can take you there if you feel up to it. Otherwise, tomorrow would be fine."

"Now would be good."

An hour later, we arrived at the morgue in a police car and they led us through to a viewing room where a shape lay beneath a sheet. The place smelled of disinfectant overlaying unpleasant odours. A man wearing rubber boots joined us from a side room.

The BND officer moved in front of us. "We're here to view Axel Schmidt's body."

The man moved to the shape, folding down the sheet to reveal the head. From this distance, I could see it was him – my father. A strange shiver of combined fear, disgust and hope lifted the fine hairs on my arms.

Mutti took my hand and we moved closer.

There had always been an aura of brooding intensity about my father. But now he was different, shrunken from the tall, distant, commanding figure haunting my memory. Lying there covered by a sheet, it was hard to believe he had ruled my life half a world away in Australia, chaining me to all the lies that came close to tearing me apart.

Mutti looked at the agent. "That's Axel Schmidt."

"Thank you."

Mutti turned to me. "Enough?"

I released Mutti's hand and moved closer to the body. For several seconds, I stared down into its face, printing the dead features into my memory. I wanted my subconscious to be certain he was gone and I was, finally, free.

Then I drew the sheet up, closing off the years he had dominated my existence.

When I turned, Mutti was watching me, her face full of concern. "It's all right, Mutti. It's over." I pulled her into my arms and we hugged.

"Let's go home, *Liebling*."

We walked away but found we were at the centre of a small media storm. Several journalists tried to interview us, but Mutti refused them. It was an unreal experience to read about myself and Mutti in the newspaper. Somehow, they had information about us and much detail about father, including his wartime activities.

Mutti snorted when she read the articles. "Someone at the *BND* has leaked – probably with official approval."

"What do you mean?

"The *BND* want to cast their shooting someone dead in the centre of Munich in the best possible light. The blacker they paint your father, the better it looks for them and the fewer questions there will be about how they let it get that far."

After a few days, we were no longer news and the media left us alone.

Slowly, our wounds healed, but we stayed home over Easter as neither of us was in the shape to travel. The side of Mutti's head had been shaved to allow the surgeon to stitch the bullet's graze. She rearranged her hairstyle to compensate as best she could – and it was still cool enough for her to wear a headscarf outside. When our stitches were removed, they told me that my hands and knees were coming along well. There would probably be faint lines on them once the scars fully healed.

They were right, but those faint lines stood as mute reminders. When my father's memory troubled me, I stared at those lines.

Life returned to normal – or rather, a new normal. My doctor forbade running and swimming until the wounds were fully healed. That meant I was denied the calming, rhythmic exercise I needed. In response, I dived into my studies as exams were in June.

During this convalescence, I realised that much of the underlying darkness in my life had ebbed: no longer did I fear my father would find and kill us. Losing that large strand looping through the knot diminished it, but did not unravel it.

As my wounds healed, I had plenty of revision time. I was confident about the written and oral language exams, but the sociolinguistics presented a problem. I was unsure of the approach to take, given the conflicting perspectives we had discussed in tutorials. Mutti's advice was simple: pick a side and justify your position. It was time to revisit the texts and papers we'd read during the year.

Exams finished in mid-June and with my head out of my books, I looked around for something to do during the summer. A longer trip to see more of France ... or maybe into Poland for longer this time. With Aunt Anastasia's capital earnings piling up in my account, I didn't have to work, but I couldn't sit idly by.

I considered my options that first week. On the Tuesday, I was preparing dinner when I heard Mutti's key in the door.

She dropped her bag on a chair and sat at the table. "Come and sit with me, please, *Liebling*."

I wiped my hands and sat facing her. Memories of troubling conversations in Australia surfaced and she must have read anxiety in my reaction.

Mutti smiled. "It's nothing serious, *Liebling*."

The tension left my body.

"Would you be all right by yourself for a week in August?"

"Of course, Mutti. I was alone in England for weeks." I gave her an interested look. "Where are you going?"

"There's a fusion conference in Leipzig. Because of the nuclear content, my boss wants someone there to keep an ear on things. She wants me to be one of the translators."

Mutti saw my raised eyebrows and patted my hand. "They're going to give me some training on the specialist language and I'm told no-one expects the translators to be experts in the field."

"How long's the conference for?"

"I'd be away for most of a week." Mutti's face was full of love. "Would you be all right by yourself?"

"Of course, Mutti."

"Okay. I'll tell them I can go." She stood up. "Let me help with dinner."

My results arrived a week after the exams finished – A's in everything, including sociolinguistics. With nothing better to do, I made a few brief trips into France and the low countries and spent the rest of June and into July reading through the texts for next year's. I spent some time thinking about Aunt Anastasia's inheritance and my promise to use it for something she would deem worthwhile.

Something in the old east Germany?

Mutti's conference was to run from Monday 3rd August to Thursday, 6th. She had to be there from the Saturday afternoon for the translator briefings and technology run through. I dropped her off at the station on Saturday morning and returned to the apartment. I lazed around with *Imbi*, planning a longer trip to the south of France until the phone rang early in the afternoon.

"Hello."

"*Liebling*, it's me."

"You're there safely?"

I heard her chuckle. "Yes – but there's a problem. Three of the translators have pulled out – they've got food poisoning or something and we're having trouble replacing all of them at such short notice."

"And?"

"I suggested you could help. Herr Danzer grabbed at the offer."

"But I'm not a qualified translator … yet."

"He knows that. You'd do the written translations which someone else will check over – not live translations. That will free up someone who can do live translations."

"I see."

"Will you come? It'd be fun to have you here with me."

"I'd love to. Where do I have to be?"

Mutti gave me the information and I scribbled it on the telephone pad.

"I'll have to pack and arrange with our neighbours to look after *Imbi*; I won't be there until late."

"You'll drive?"

"Yes – it should take me about five or six hours on the autobahn ... I'll need to stop to eat something."

"All right, *Liebling*. I'll wait up for you – we'll be sharing a room."

"Okay – see you soon."

"Drive carefully."

The next forty-five minutes flew by as I packed and arranged for our neighbour's daughter to look after *Imbi*. Although it was summer and many people were on holiday, I made good time, stopping to buy fuel for the car and myself outside Bayreuth. I arrived at the hotel before ten to find Mutti sitting in the foyer.

"Drop your cases here and park the car. I'll wait for you here."

Five minutes later we were up in her – now our – room.

"Tomorrow is a full day. I expect you're tired – shower and bed?"

After breakfast, I completed the forms allowing me a 'temporary translator permit'. A whirlwind of briefings followed, one of which provided me with a multilingual dictionary of fusion terminology. By Sunday evening, my brain was spinning.

I would be based in the translator room, providing written translations as requested – not that I would be typing. Instead, I would read the paper and dictate the required translation into a Dictaphone. specialist typists would do the typing. Someone else would look over the typed copy before it went out.

I had a short training session on the Dictaphone that afternoon and did a trial run of one paper in French into my other four languages. The unfamiliar vocabulary required I stop and consult the multilingual specialist dictionary. This made the process painful, but I suspected I'd pick it up during the conference. There were a few minor suggestions about wording from the trial, but apart from that, I received smiles, which helped calm my nerves.

Mutti would be live translating the opening session from German into English; the other live translated languages were French, Spanish and Russian. Then she was working on specialist breakout sessions for the rest of the conference until the final plenary session. It was clear we'd both be busy.

I was translating from the start of the conference as people had already requested translations of several papers ahead of time. I didn't see Mutti until Monday evening when we met at the hotel for dinner.

"How's it going, *Liebling*?"

"Good, I think." I stretched my shoulders, cramped from hunching over the Dictaphone. "I've not had any complaints. But the workload is insane. I have a stack of papers already waiting for tomorrow."

Mutti massaged her ears. They had spent most of the day under a headset.

"Are the headsets uncomfortable?"

"A hazard of the job, I suppose."

"I think I'll come in early tomorrow and try to get ahead of things."

Mutti frowned. "Don't overwork yourself, *Liebling*. If you can't get everything done, you can't."

"Things might slack off tomorrow. Won't people have requested the papers they want today?"

"Perhaps ..." Mutti shrugged.

When I arrived at the translators' room early, the pile of papers had grown, but I waded in and the pile shrank through the day, with only a few additions. By late afternoon, I had it down to a couple when Mutti arrived.

"That's me done for the day." She wandered over to look at my much lower in-tray. "You've done well, *Liebling*."

"I need about twenty minutes to finish this one."

Mutti poured herself a glass of water and sat down by the window. I continued working and when I looked up five minutes later, her eyes were closed. My limited exposure to live translating at university had shown me how tiring it was. I spoke my translation into the Dictaphone, checking some of the specialist vocabulary. I looked up when I heard the door open.

A solid, grey-haired man poked his head round the door, speaking Russian. "Excuse me. I need a translator."

Mutti roused herself. "Carry on, *Liebling*. I'll see to this."

She turned to the man, guiding him out. "How can I be of assistance?"

I lost myself in a complex translation that seemed more electromagnetic theory than fusion. I turned to a general dictionary for this as the fusion glossary did not cover it. After a while, the door opened and I looked up, expecting Mutti. Instead, a young man walked in, giving a confused look to someone behind him.

What?

I looked at this intruder again and wonder blossomed inside me. "Willi?"

The young man cocked his head on one side and I saw past his straggly beard.

"Col."

The knot inside me unwound and I found myself in a laughing, crying, three-way embrace as Mutti joined us.

Epilogue
June - August 1975

I looked down at the letter in my hand. It invited me, Frida Schmidt (née Karpinski), to attend the rededication of the Ravensbrück Concentration Camp memorial. I watched, detached, as the letter wobbled, exaggerating my trembling hand.

Seeking the chair, I groped behind me and fell on to the seat.

As a nearly sixteen-year-old, I had run from those gates into the cold spring of 1945. The SS guards inexplicably herded several thousand German nationals from the camp. I'd never returned; nor did I wish to. I knew too well its miasma of suffering, cruelty and evil. The camps had drained the life from my mother through a decade of imprisonment, forced labour and starvation as she struggled to keep me alive.

I dropped the letter on my desk; the memories spread the trembling across my body.

Breathe, Frida, the way Col does.

They moved us to Ravensbrück from the Lichtenburg prison in May 1939. My mother and I were amongst the first prisoners to walk through the gates into the camp. We'd been imprisoned since May 1935 when they arrested my parents, members of the communist party. I learned after the war they executed my father within days of his arrest. There is no grave to visit and I have only shadow memories of him – no face, but a smiling voice heard by a young child's ears through decades of distance.

When they opened the Ravensbrück gates and pushed us towards them, we ran, terrified, into the woods. We expected to be shot down as escapees – but there was no gunfire. After two days in the woods moving further north, away from Ravensbrück, a Soviet unit scouting ahead of the main advance found me. I was lucky not to be shot out of hand, but the unit commander was NKVD. They had briefed him about the camp and recognised the red triangle on my 'striped pyjamas' as signifying a political prisoner. Some weeks later, I ended up in my hometown of Leipzig, a city I barely recalled. It was now shattered beyond recognition in heaps of charred rubble.

Much has happened since. I married unwisely, but was gifted a beautiful daughter. She gave me the strength that enabled our incredible journey: defecting to the UK, hiding from the *Stasi* in Australia and, when the Eastern Bloc collapsed in 1968, our return to a re-unified Germany.

I folded the letter into the envelope, placing it on my desk – time to think about this after the weekend. Nothing must dampen the joy of the next few days: Colette, Willi and their three-year-old daughter, Liliana, were visiting from Leipzig, with some news. I knew they were expecting another child in October. It wasn't that ...

Time to clean and prepare their rooms.

• • • •

THAT FIRST EVENING once we had bathed Lili, read to her – in English today as her parents were intent on raising a multilingual child – Col sat beside me.

For several long seconds, we sat in silence, eyes engaged. "Well, Mutti, are you going?"

I gave her my best blank look – to no avail; we knew one another too well.

She took my hand, stroking it in loving support. "To the Ravensbrück rededication?"

"How did you find out about that?" I sent a sharp look in her direction and tried to jerk my hand away, but she held on.

"I wasn't snooping, Mutti. Lili poked about in your desk and she dropped the letter on the floor."

"Why would I want to return to that terrible place? It robbed me of my childhood and my mother – the grandmother you never knew."

Col's eyes echoed my pain. "I understand. I do." She stopped, worried eyes staring across the room. "No-one would want to visit such a place. But

... perhaps you need to?" Her eyes returned to mine. "Perhaps ... we all need to."

I flushed with shame. I'd been thinking only of myself – I'd not thought about her needs ... or Willi's. Ravensbrück was an important part of this family's history.

She looked across the room at Willi, who had his head in an engineering journal. "Willi ... Willi?"

He looked up, dragging himself from the technical paper he had disappeared into once he'd settled Lili.

"Please, would you come with us to Ravensbrück? There's a rededication of the memorial and a new museum. They have invited Mutti to attend."

Willi's eyes moved between us, shining with his deep love for both of us. "Of course."

Over the rest of the weekend, somewhat mysteriously, my return to Ravensbrück became a thing, despite my never actually agreeing to it.

And their news?

Col had decided how to use Aunt Anastasia's money. This had increased significantly from inspired investment decisions Col and Willi made together. Willi had convinced her that the world was heading for serious climate problems; the increasing amount of carbon dioxide dumped in the atmosphere from burning fossil fuels would warm the climate. Col was creating a foundation to support renewable energy. It would invest in companies with promising renewable technologies. Willi would provide the needed science oversight.

· · · ·

WE WALKED TO RAVENSBRÜCK from the village, Lili sometimes pattering along, holding tight to Willi, Col or me. Mostly, she rode in her pusher, looking around, smiling and chattering about everything she saw. She remained oblivious to the infectious silence that spread from me to Col and on to Willi. At the gates, grasping memories locked my feet to the ground ... until Lili's bright voice freed them. I presented my letter of invitation and they gave me a name badge. We walked into the camp, the summer sun glinting off the nearby lake, mocking my grim memories.

Throughout the brief ceremony of rededication, Col and Willi stood close on either side of me, each providing strength through the clasp of my hands. At three-years-old, Lili sensed her grandmother's deep emotion and the solemnity of the occasion, if she could not yet understand the reason. With the speeches finished, she saw the tears on my face and hugged my legs. Willi reached down and picked her up, settling her on his hip and the four of us melted into one, sharing our breath and love in this place of evil.

Lili stared at me from Willi's arms. "Why are you crying?"

I brushed her cheek with a finger. "I'm crying because this place has many sad memories."

Lili's eyes moved between the three of us. "Why did we come to a sad place?"

My smile was watery. "Even sad places are important, Lili."

Lili remained silent, unconvinced.

With the formalities at an end, Col turned to me. "Please, take us where you need to go."

I knew my mother, like everyone else who died here, had no grave. With my family, I tried to find the place where our barracks had stood – but much had changed during the Soviet occupation and I was uncertain of its exact location. Disappointed and drawn inexorably towards its evil, I turned towards the *Kommandantur*. It held the cells I had slopped-out for over a year; the place where Vogel had pinned me to the wall minutes after he had executed my English friend Colette.

The hatred I had been fighting for years welled up, closing my throat.

Col heard me struggling to breathe and pulled me to her. "We can go as soon as you want to, Mutti. Don't punish yourself."

I swallowed. My throat relaxed enough for a shuddering breath. Others followed.

Unable to speak, I set off towards the brooding structure. Inside, my feet knew the way, turning me down the corridor until I stood before Colette's cell. The cell from which they took my English friend to her execution that November morning some thirty years ago. The door was closed and I sank to my knees, trying to open the hatch through which we had talked. But my fingers scrabbled without success.

"Please, don't try to open that."

I looked up to see a museum guide.

She saw the badge that identified me as a former inmate. Embarrassment and confusion stopped her for a moment. "I'm sorry, but we have not yet had time to prepare any of the cells for public viewing." Her eyes widened. "Were you imprisoned in this cell?"

My forehead pressed against the cell door. "No, not me ... an English girl started teaching me English through this meal hatch ... before they took her through the door down there one morning for execution." I gestured without looking towards the door at the end of the corridor.

Willi leant down, offering a hand to help me up, speaking German. "This was Colette's cell?"

I blinked, stifling the tears and the jagged, ripping memories of that morning.

"Excuse me ... did you mention ... Colette?" An English voice came from the small group that had coalesced near us.

I turned, scanning the faces. "Who asked about Colette?" I asked in English, with a touch of possession.

She is my Colette.

A tall, grey-haired man blinked in surprise at my switch from German to English. "Umm ... that was me. Did you know Colette – an English Special Operations Executive girl?"

I was unsure how to handle this, jealous of my memories of Colette. "Please forgive me, but who are you to be asking about Colette?"

The woman on the man's arm drew herself up. "We are Colette Roberts' parents." She returned my suspicious look. "Who are you?"

She had a French accent. "I am Frida Schmidt." I answered in French, touching my badge. "They imprisoned me here. The Nazis had me working in these cells for the final year of the war." I pushed up the sleeve on my left arm, showing them my blue prisoner number. "Colette started teaching me English." I stopped, unsure if I should say more.

The couple glanced at one another before the woman turned to me. "There's more, isn't there?" It was soft, pleading.

I thought for a moment and turned to the museum guide. She had a confused look on her face, having lost the thread when we switched to French. "Do you speak English?" I asked, in German.

"Yes, but not well," she answered in English.

I switched to English. "Are we permitted to go through that door at the end of the corridor?"

She looked around the group and at the door, unsure of what was happening. "That door? I'm not sure ..."

"Please – could you ask whoever is in charge for permission?"

Her eyes flicked from my forearm to my badge, then she walked off down the corridor.

I turned to Colette's parents, guiding Col towards them. "Please allow me to introduce my daughter, Colette, named to honour your courageous daughter."

Mrs Roberts ignored my daughter and leant into me, eyes brimming with forlorn hope. "Do you know what happened to our Colette?"

I released a gentle breath, an almost sigh. "What had happened to her before she came here, I can't say." I stopped, unwilling to revisit these memories that ripped and tore my psyche. But I was compelled by her parents' need. "It was early in September 1944 that she arrived here." My Colette's hand found mine. She knew what I was not saying – at least not yet.

Mr Roberts glanced at his wife. "She worked as a radio operator for the Special Operations Executive. We know they dropped her into the Vosges area of France in late May 1944. The Nazis captured her there in August. We think they sent ...," he stopped, swallowing before he could continue. "Sent her here after her interrogation. They stamped her file with what looks like 'NN' and there is no record of her being here." His wife's hand was white knuckled on his arm. "We recently found an unnamed mention of a transfer to Ravensbrück at the right time, which is why we are here ..." He limped to a stop.

The museum guide appeared and caught my eye.

I gave the Roberts an apologetic look and spoke to the guide in German. "Are we allowed through the door?"

"Yes."

"Thank you. Could you wait a moment, please?"

She gave me a brief nod.

Willi and Col shared a meaningful glance and Willi walked off, pushing Lili in her stroller. They didn't want Lili to hear what I was going to say – though she would probably not understand it.

I turned to the Roberts, fighting to keep my voice even. "It was 'NN'. It's short for *Nacht und Nebel* – night and fog. They stamped this on the files of people who were to disappear without a trace. It was part of the Nazi's terror tactics." There was no gentle way of dealing with this. I took their hands, hoping to soften my words. "You know Colette is dead and there is no grave?"

After a moment, a single tear appeared in the corner of Mrs Roberts' eye.

My heart was thudding with deep sorrow ... for the Roberts, for Colette ... for myself and everyone sent to this hateful place. I tried to slow its beating with a long inhalation. "My daily morning task was slopping out the cells. When I arrived that morning, Colette's cell door – this door – was open with no guard outside." I saw the understanding in their eyes. "I knew what that meant."

Mrs Roberts glanced at her husband and squeezed my hand. "Please, go on."

I looked sideways at my Col, her face a gentle, supportive encouragement. "A few minutes after I arrived, an SS officer came through that door." I gestured with my head towards the end of the corridor. "He saw me standing in tears here at Colette's cell door. He mocked me for mourning a spy, pinning me by the throat against the wall with a hand that stank from the gunshot."

I took several gulping breaths, trying to corral my emotions.

"The SS officer was *Hauptstürmfuhrer* Vogel." My eyes closed, the memory of him in his immaculate black SS uniform morphing into his picture in the Australian newspaper. "Somehow, he escaped the attentions of the Allies at the end of the war. He turned up in Australia where I recognised his photo in a newspaper."

Be careful ... you can never reveal your part ...

"He ... disappeared after that and is presumed to have died."

Mr Roberts curled his arm around his wife's shoulder, but gave me a searching look.

I turned towards the cell door, worried he had seen in my face something more than I should reveal. "This was Colette's cell – and if you wish, we can go to the yard where ..." I swallowed the saliva flooding my mouth. "That man ended your courageous daughter's life."

And I survived.

The guilt and shame caught my throat, tears threatening to spill down my face. The Roberts shared a glance before Mr Roberts gestured towards the door.

I failed to suppress a shudder, but turned to the museum guide.

Breathe, Frida ...

"Please, open the door."

The lock was stiff, but it turned and the guide opened the door, revealing a small yard with concrete walls and an earth floor. Opposite was another door that opened onto a path to the crematorium.

As our small group entered the yard, the hatred, anger and guilt I had struggled to shed erupted inside me. I screamed without sound at the blue-domed sky and fell to my knees. My silent wail ending in anguished sobs for their daughter, my mother, myself.

Hands and arms surrounded me and, after some unknown time, I felt them. Col and Mrs Roberts were kneeling with me, holding my face so close we shared our breath – and tears.

After a while, a hand gently wiped my cheeks with a tissue. "My dear, what you've been through," Mrs Roberts murmured.

I squeezed my eyes closed, embarrassed at the scene I was making in front of a mother who had lost her daughter in this yard.

The tissue disappeared. A hand caressed my cheek, lifting my eyes to Mrs Roberts'.

"Thank you for being our daughter's friend." She swallowed, controlling her emotions. "Thank you for sharing with us your part in her story."

Mr Roberts took her hand and helped her to her feet. Col helped me to mine. Deep concern written on her face.

I squeezed her hand in reassurance and scrabbled a tissue out of my handbag to blow my nose. I turned to the Roberts. "It was your daughter who started teaching me English." I let my eyes move between them. "These girls all knew their fate and yet they never showed me their fear." I took several breaths before continuing. "A bond developed with your daughter. I sat outside her cell, talking through the meal hatch each day until the guards moved me on ..." I dribbled to a stop, silenced by the memories clustering about me.

"And you named your daughter in her memory." Mr Roberts' hand clasped mine. "Thank you."

"She deserves so much more ..."

Mrs Roberts squeezed my hand, her gaze on an unseen past. "That's true for all the thousands herded into this place." Her eyes were bright with pride and tears. "And our daughter played her part in bringing this horror to an end."

Col's arm crept around my shoulders, her eyes full of love and care. "Are you all right, Mutti?"

"Yes, Liebling," I took a deep breath, letting it out slowly. "Yes." I felt drained – but that dangerous cyst of hate within me was gone. "Yes ... I think I am, for the first time since they imprisoned me here."

"Are you finished?" It was the museum guide, wanting to move us out.

I glanced at Mrs Roberts and then turned to the guide. "Yes, thank you for your help."

We returned to the cell corridor. I walked to Colette's cell and leant my forehead against it. I could find no words for her, but dripped my silent farewell in tears onto the pitted steel.

"Let's go find Willi and your granddaughter." Col's hand was on my shoulder.

I breathed several times and turned. Col handed me another tissue.

The Roberts murmured together before Mr Roberts pulled a card out of his pocket. "This has our addresses in England and Paris." He handed me the card. "Please, stay in touch." His voice a touch embarrassed at the emotion. "Thank you for being there for our Colette."

Mrs Roberts drew me into a hug and kissed both my cheeks. "Merci." She took her husband's hand and they walked off down the corridor. We stood in silence, watching them.

"Where next, Mutti?"

I gave her a wavering smile. "Let's find Willi and Lili."

They were sitting in the sun, chatting happily about the birds swimming in the lake. Willi picked up Lili and drew all of us into a hug.

We shared several breaths, basking in the love of my beautiful family before I broke free.

I turned away from Ravensbrück and we started walking back to the village.

Afterword

Once again – *beware* – this section contains *spoilers* for the other three books in this universe.

There are four stories in this 'universe' and they all share a common timeline – albeit one that is not 'ours': at some point, the world that Col and Willi inhabit diverges.

Colette starts with the commencement of the Second World War (September 1939) and, excluding the epilogue, ends in November 1944. Whilst imprisoned and awaiting execution in Ravensbrück concentration camp, Colette meets a fourteen-year-old German prisoner, Frida, and starts teaching her English. Frida survives and eventually gives birth to Colette (Col), named in honour of her friend in Ravensbrück.

Mrs Henderson's Limp starts with Elise Henderson parachuting into occupied France in May 1944 and ends in December 1945. Her experience witnessing the June 1944 Tulle massacre by SS troops affects her deeply and she tries to banish emotion from her being. She becomes a person of influence in MI6 and oversees the interrogation of Col and her mother when they defect to the west in September 1962.

At the start of *Through my Eyes. Again.* Will Johnstone's seventy-year-old consciousness appears in his twelve-year-old body in October 1962. The book tracks his new life through to August 1970. Along the way, it becomes clear that he is not living in the world of his first life – JFK is shot but not killed and the Soviet Bloc collapses in 1968 when the Soviets try, but fail, to suppress the Prague Spring.

In May 1964, Col and her mother disappear without trace. Will fears that somehow he betrayed them during his visit to east Germany. He carries that guilt through school and university.

Through different Eyes tells Col's and her mother's story following their disappearance. The epilogue links back to *Colette* where Col's mother attends a rededication in August 1975 of the Ravensbrück memorial and meets Colette's parents, Mr & Mrs Roberts. The epilogue of *Colette* tells of the same event, but from Mrs Roberts' point of view.

. . . .

THE STORIES WERE NOT written in chronological order. I wrote *TMEA* first and then wrote *MHL* as a give-away to build interest in the release of *TMEA*. Mrs Henderson isn't mentioned by name in *TMEA* but she does appear (anonymously) when Will visits MI6 in London, trying to find out what has happened to Col and her mother, Mutti Frida.

When *TMEA* was released, readers wanted to know what happened to Col and her mother – and thus *TDE* was born. About halfway through the first draft, I needed Col's mother to recount her experience in Ravensbrück Concentration camp the day Vogel executed Colette. In order to set the scene, I wrote the first draft of the opening of **Colette** and continued writing *TDE*.

But that Colette (for whom Mutti Frida named her daughter), would not leave me alone. She stood at my shoulder demanding I tell her story. For a while, I was writing both *TDE* and **Colette**.

Colette's story is a novella and I finished the first draft before I had completed *TDE*. It went out to my beta readers without its epilogue. I received feedback that the story needed some tidying up of loose ends – and I wrote the epilogue, from Mutti Frida's point of view.

Colette went out to my beta readers also without its epilogue – but once again my readers told me that the story needed more – and I wrote the epilogue for **Colette** from her mother's perspective.

Although Mrs Henderson remains a largely unexplored character, I have no intention of writing more in this universe. It has occupied my writing life more than three years (I have a day job as well) and it's time to move on.

Look out for my next project – you can keep abreast of its progress by subscribing to my Newsletter at

https://preview.mailerlite.io/preview/66622/sites/76863099932509909/e2Es6r

I look forward to seeing you there,

Robert Hart

Brisbane, Australia

March, 2023

Also by Robert Hart

Through my Eyes. Again.
Mrs Henderson's Limp
Colette
Through different Eyes

www.ingramcontent.com/pod-product-compliance
Lightning Source LLC
Chambersburg PA
CBHW020828030726
47496CB00001B/139